TIDE OF FORTUNE

Nineteen-year-old Kerenza Vyvyan's estranged family has been missing for a year on a trading voyage to the Mediterranean. When her father returns to raise the ransom needed to free his wife and elder daughter held hostage in Tangier, he demands Kerenza sail back with him on the packet, *Kestrel*, but *Kestrel*'s commander is Nicholas Penrose, the man who broke Kerenza's heart. Following attack by a French privateer *Kestrel* eventually reaches Tangier. Tentatively reconciled, Kerenza and Nick draw strength from each other, until tragic events force Kerenza to make a promise she fears will part them forever...

TIDE OF FORTUNE

TIDE OF FORTUNE

by

Jane Jackson

Magna Large Print Books
Long Preston, North Yorkshire,
BD23 4ND, England.

British Library Cataloguing in Publication Data.

Jackson, Jane
    Tide of fortune.

    A catalogue record of this book is
    available from the British Library

    ISBN   0-7505-2441-3

First published in Great Britain 2004 by Robert Hale Limited

Copyright © Jane Jackson 2004

Cover illustration © Barbara Walton by arrangement with
Robert Hale Ltd.

Published in Large Print 2005 by arrangement with
Robert Hale Ltd.

Magna Large Print is an imprint of Library Magna Books Ltd.

Printed and bound in Great Britain by
T.J. (International) Ltd., Cornwall, PL28 8RW

To Emma: daughter and friend

Acknowledgements:

My very special thanks to Thor Kuniholm, Director of the American Legation Museum in Tangier, without whose interest, generosity and encouragement this book could not have been written.

I'd also like to thank Djamal Merabet for his assistance with the Tamasirght language, Dianne Webster and Bob for seafaring advice and charts, and the three Janets for keeping me sane.

And to Mike, love as always.

Chapter One

'*Must* we go?' The words were out before Kerenza could, stop them. It was too soon. She needed more time. *But how long would it take?* She had not seen him since– While her mind shied away from the still-raw memory, her skin burned with relived mortification.

He would be back any day now. The Lisbon run rarely took longer than four weeks even in winter. And when *Kestrel* returned, her respite would end. For with village life and society centred on the packet service, it was inevitable that they would meet again.

'Indeed, we must.' Aurelia Danby's nod was decisive. 'Maude Tregenna is a dear friend. And though Harry is now a senior captain, I've known him since we were children.'

Kerenza shivered. To snub her like that, and in public, Nicholas Penrose could have offered her no greater insult. And she still did not understand *why*. What had prompted the sudden switch from attentions that promised far more than friendship, to cold withdrawal? Sensing her grandmother's concern she tried to concentrate, forcing herself to respond.

'I saw the *Lady Anne* when they were bringing her in alongside the quay. She's suffered dreadful damage. Half her main mast shot away, hatch covers and skylights all smashed, and her jollyboat beyond repair.'

'But no one killed,' her grandmother reminded. And as their eyes met the words hung unspoken between them. *This time.*

Sometimes she woke, swollen-eyed, *hating* him for what he'd done. Yet despite the shock, the hurt, and an ocean of tears, she loved him still. It was a tiny flame. Barely a glimmer in the darkness that filled her soul. And though she mocked herself for a fool, it burned on bravely, refusing to die.

Aurelia's handsome features stiffened in disgust. 'Why can that appalling little Corsican not confine himself to attacking naval vessels? At least they are well armed and able to defend themselves. What possible honour can there be in besieging packet ships?'

'None at all, Nana.' An involuntary smile twitched Kerenza's mouth at her grandmother's indignation. 'But honour is not their object. What Napoleon's privateers want is the ship to sell as a prize, and the cargo of course. Being on the Jamaica route *Lady Anne* was carrying bullion as well as rum and tobacco.'

Aurelia's expression held grim satisfaction. 'Well, this time they got nothing. Harry saw them off and brought the *Lady Anne* and all her crew home.' Her tone softened. 'Kerenza, Maude has Harry back safe. If she wants to hold a dress-ball to celebrate, how can we refuse to share her relief and delight?'

Shame prickled, and Kerenza felt herself flush. Her grandfather had been a packet captain. It was seven years since he had died: killed during attack by an American privateer soon after

12

leaving New York. If her grandmother possessed enough generosity of spirit to be happy that her friend's husband continued to return home safely when her own had not...

'I'm sorry, Nana. Of course we must go. Only–' she hesitated.

'My love, I'm aware it's not easy for you to be in company at the moment. And I know *Kestrel* is due back any time now–'

'It's not that, Nana.' Honesty compelled Kerenza to add, 'Well, not *just* that.'

'What, then? Though I imagine I can guess.'

Kerenza drew the paisley shawl tighter across her slim body. Her high-waisted apple-green muslin gown had long sleeves and was double-layered. But this past month she had felt constantly cold. 'Attending balls and parties when–' She shrugged helplessly. 'It just feels wrong to be going out and enjoying myself.'

'Ha! So at least you admit that you do enjoy yourself?'

Kerenza nodded guiltily. 'Sometimes. Quite often, in fact. Though I know I shouldn't.'

'Why, for heavens' sake?' her grandmother demanded, visibly exasperated. 'What possible purpose can it serve for you to cut yourself off from society? Surely you have more sense than to believe that remaining at home, brooding and miserable, will somehow bring your parents back sooner.'

'Nana, we don't even know if they are still alive.'

'We have heard nothing to suggest they are not,' Aurelia countered.

13

'No,' Kerenza had to agree. 'But it's been almost a year since they disappeared.'

'All the more reason for continuing to hope. My dear, I know Mr Penrose has caused you great unhappiness.' Kerenza flinched but appearing not to notice, her grandmother continued, 'Until then you were handling the whole wretched matter so well.'

She wasn't really. She lurched between hope and despair, between love because they were after all her family, and loathing for the way they had blamed her for something beyond her control. But if her grandmother could face the world, or at least the village, with calm self-possession, how could she do less?

'Nana, sometimes when I try to picture them, I can't see their faces clearly.'

'My dear child, after all this time it would be very strange if their images had not blurred a little.'

'Yes, but it seems so – disloyal.'

Aurelia snorted. 'And what reason have you to feel loyalty towards any of your family?' Her tone changed, betraying for the first time a hint of anxiety. 'Kerenza, if – *when* – they return, will you want to go home again?'

'No!' Kerenza's response was swift and vehement. 'Nana, you must know I've been happier here with you than I ever was there. It's just–' She shrugged helplessly, not sure herself what she meant or what she felt.

'Listen to me, child. We know the ship was sighted in Leghorn six months ago, so it cannot have sunk in a storm. And if it was sufficiently

14

seaworthy to reach the Italian coast, then presumably it had first delivered your parents and sister safely to Tangier. Clearly something has prevented them getting word back to us. But I think we should assume that wherever they are, they are together.' She sniffed. 'For all the comfort *that* will be.'

'Nana!'

'Forgive me, my dear. I should not have spoken so. They are your family, and indeed mine. Although' – her tone hardened – 'they never valued you as they should, and certainly not as I do. But enough of that.' She dismissed the subject with a brief flick of bony fingers. 'Kerenza, regarding ... this other matter.'

Wincing, but grateful for her grandmother's tact, she lowered her lashes and blinked stinging eyes.

'Pleading a head cold excused you from two supper-dances and Mrs Edwards's card party, but if you continue to decline invitations you will inevitably provoke speculation and gossip. You cannot want that.'

'No. No, I don't.' Kerenza shivered again. Knowing how quickly gossip spread in the village, inevitably embellished as it passed from one mouth to another, she had managed, in public at least, to maintain a brave face. The effort had cost her dearly, the flesh melting from her bones. Minnie, the housemaid who doubled as her dresser, was spending an hour every afternoon taking in gowns that had fitted perfectly two months ago. But through pride and sheer effort of will she had succeeded in convincing all who

15

knew her that Nicholas Penrose was of no particular importance or interest. He had simply been one of the many young packet and naval officers in whose honour parties and dances were held most nights of the week.

'Neither would I. Nor,' Aurelia added gently, 'would it be wise to permit young Mr Penrose, or any man for that matter, the conceit of believing himself your only source of happiness.'

But he is. And always will be. Furious and helpless at the tyranny of her heart, Kerenza swallowed. 'I know you're right.' Perhaps if she said it often enough she could make herself believe it. 'Don't worry Nana. I won't let you down.'

Aurelia rose quickly from her chair and grasped Kerenza's shoulders.

'My dearest girl, of course you won't.' Her strong features softened in a loving smile. 'You have more strength and courage than you realize.'

Biting her lip, Kerenza glanced out of the window. A sky the colour of bluebells hinted at spring. But in the harbour, visible across the roof of the old cellars, the water looked dark and cold. Small boats pitched on choppy foam-filled waves and the larger ships stirred and tugged at their moorings. A gun boomed, making her start as it signalled the arrival of another packet ship bearing letters, dispatches, and news from abroad. But hope had been blunted by too many disappointments.

Drawing her away, her grandmother guided her towards the door. 'Come, my dear. Let's go upstairs and decide which of our gowns we shall wear. We must look our best. Maude will want to make this a very *special* occasion.'

16

Nicholas Penrose stood at the starboard side of the quarterdeck, watching the crew move faster and with greater purpose than at any time during the voyage. The echoes of the signal gun were lost beneath the squeal and rattle of blocks and the bosun's bellow as the two huge gaffs were lowered and their canvas swiftly roped to the booms.

'Ready the cutter!' he shouted, watching two seamen run to obey.

In the four weeks he'd been away not an hour had passed that he hadn't thought of her. Her face haunted him. He saw her as he had seen her at the parties and dances: her eyes sparkling like sunlight on the sea, her cheeks flushed.

'Load the mailbags, sir?'

He nodded, indicating the portmanteaux, weighted with cannon balls and shrouded in tarpaulin, standing against the companionway hatch.

Thank God he'd found out in time. The ache in his chest felt like a kick from a horse. But at least he had not made a complete fool of himself. To think he had been planning to propose marriage. *Christ, it hurt.*

Glimpsing movement he turned to see the second mate emerge from the companionway, his sea-going gear exchanged for the regulation dark-blue coat, blue breeches, white stockings and black buckled shoes. Nick raised his brows in silent question, and felt his heart sink as Maggot shook his head.

'You let him go alone, he fall overboard and drown.'

Nick bit back a curse. 'Take over.' He glanced

17

down at his faded salt stained coat, wool trousers and boots. 'I'd better change.' He turned toward the aft companionway.

Hurled along by a south-westerly gale *Kestrel* had taken only seven days to cover the distance between Lisbon and Falmouth. But the fast passage had been paid for in damage to canvas, spars and rigging. And though Maggot had shared the watches, Nick had slept little. His eyes were sore and gritty and every muscle ached from combined tension and exhaustion. And he still hadn't decided what to do.

'You go quick,' Maggot growled, looking over Nick's shoulder. 'Customs boat coming.'

'Did you–?'

'Is all safe,' the second mate reassured him. Pulling a leather drawstring purse from inside his jacket he held it up. 'He come, he go. No questions, no trouble.'

Nick ducked through the hatch and clattered down the brass stairs. Catching sight of her in the crowded street his heart had soared with pleasure at the unexpected meeting. Then memory had kicked in, his head resounding with the warning that had destroyed his hopes and dreams, his vision of the future.

As the colour drained from her face, he had glared into her eyes; torturing himself by seeking the guilt he knew would be there. Not seeing it, he had experienced an instant's lacerating doubt. But by then he was past. She was behind him. Forever. He had done the only thing possible. But his fury at being made a fool of was overwhelmed by a wrenching grief. *He had loved her.*

At the bottom of the stairs he turned aft towards the captain's quarters. With only a token knock he opened the door.

An oblong table bolted to the cabin sole filled the space between the arms of a padded leather bench that formed a shallow U shape at the rear of the day cabin. The table's surface was a clutter of books, charts, an inkstand, ruler and octant.

Samuel Penrose was seated on one end of the bench, his head bowed over a steaming mug clasped between hands that shook uncontrollably. Beneath the fragrance of strong coffee Nick detected other, less pleasant smells.

Toy emerged from the tiny sleeping cabin carrying a covered bucket and a bundle of linen. Shooting a brief glance at the captain, he hurried across to Nick.

'I done my best, sir,' he whispered.

'I don't doubt it,' Nick kept his own voice low. 'How did you manage to shave him and get him into his uniform?'

'"Tisn't no trouble when you knows how, sir. Been with him fifteen years I have. Be some poor job if I couldn't do the necessary when he's a bit under the hatches.' Loyalty made Toy's tone slightly defensive. 'But you can't let'n go up to the packet office by hisself.'

'I can see that.' As Nick smothered a yawn, Toy shook his head.

'Post office should never have sent'n back to sea. 'Twas bleddy obvious he wasn't fit. How could he be after what he been through?'

Nick gazed at his uncle, anger warring with compassion. After Nick's father died when he was

19

ten, Sam Penrose had assumed responsibility for him, his mother and his two sisters. It was Sam who had paid for his schooling and his apprenticeship. It was thanks to Sam that at twenty-four he had twelve years' seagoing experience, his mate's ticket, and a driving ambition to one day own and command his own packet ship. He owed Samuel Penrose.

But this, Sam's first voyage since his escape from prison in France, had been spent below deck either raving drunk or sprawled unconscious on his bunk.

Nick's nails dug into his palms. Without Maggot...

Toy cleared his throat. 'Sorry, Mr Penrose.'

'It's not your fault, Toy.' He ran his fingers through salt-matted hair, craving a hot bath, a decent meal, and at least ten hours' uninterrupted sleep. But they would have to wait. There was still much to be done. 'The Customs boat's on its way.'

Toy sniffed. 'That'll be Jim Petherick. Greedy sod, he is. Anyhow, don't you worry Mr Penrose. 'Tis all took care of. Bosun made sure both watches got everything stowed while we was passing the Lizard. And he done the collection. Maggot have got the purse.'

'Yes, he showed me.' Had Maggot paid his share as well? He must remember to ask, and if so to reimburse him.

'Jim won't hang around, not if he know what's good for'n. I reckon by the time you're ready he'll be gone again. There's hot water in your cabin. I told the boy to fetch it down when he brung the captain's.'

20

Half an hour later, after the briefest of inspections, the Customs Officer had departed, the heavy purse nestling inside his coat.

Clean and tidy in his best uniform, Nick sat in the cutter's bow. His uncle, as *Kestrel*'s commanding officer, sat at the stern with the two leather portmanteaux containing the mails and dispatches at his feet.

A captain's first job on returning to port was to hand over the mails to the packet agent. Some captains waited for one of the clerks to come out to them. But Sam Penrose had always preferred to take the bags ashore himself to hand over to the packet agent in person. And if Nick could keep him upright long enough, the usual procedures would be observed. But what about the next trip?

The voyage home had been a waking nightmare that allowed little time for rest. But Nick had spent his few quiet moments wrestling with an insoluble problem. Did he remain aboard *Kestrel* knowing that, though Sam was the ranking officer his mental condition coupled with his drinking made him incapable of command? That responsibility for the ship, the mails and any passengers would fall instead on *his* shoulders?

The alternative, if he considered this voyage repayment of his debt to his uncle, was to apply for a mate's berth on a packet bound for Jamaica where opportunities for private trading would greatly increase his savings. But if he left *Kestrel*, so would Maggot. Saving Maggot's life had bound the Tanjawi to him with an oath of gratitude and loyalty stronger than chains of iron. How would Sam manage? Who else would care enough to cover for him?

At least the struggle to reach a decision had given him something to focus on, to take his mind off Kerenza Vyvyan. Nick rubbed his face. *He was so tired.*

Back on board the packet, Maggot was supervizing the departure of passengers and their luggage. The carpenter and sailmaker, both trusted hands, had already organized their gangs. Tomorrow morning both jollyboat and cutter would be sent to pick up ropes, spars and canvas. And with luck, by tomorrow evening most of the repairs would be complete. Only then would the crew be allowed ashore. With the money made from their ventures and goods to sell they would be intent on a good time. Many of the ordinary seamen – criminals, men escaping the press, harbour dregs hired each voyage – would simply disappear. New men would have to be hired to replace them.

But that was next week's problem. And if he decided to leave, it wouldn't be his. Right now he had enough to worry about.

As the cutter's crew bent and strained at the oars, Nick angled himself so he could look toward Falmouth. Sam had told him years ago that a mate could not learn to be a captain. Only when he had the responsibility of command would he discover whether he was up to it.

Nick knew he had what it took, though he had found out through necessity rather than choice. He wished there were someone he could tell. There was his mother, of course. She would be proud, but she would worry. His gaze was drawn past the hunched figure of his uncle, through the forest of masts, to the village of Flushing on the far side of the river. The light was fading. But the final rays of a rose and turquoise sunset were reflected in the upper windows of elegant Queen Anne houses that lined the street above the quay. Here and there pinpricks of yellow light showed that lamps were being lit.

Kerenza would have understood what it meant to him. *How could he know that?* Her eyes had told him. He looked away, clenching his teeth so hard that pain shot up through his jaw into his temple. Her eyes had said so much. *But to how many others besides him?*

Chapter Two

After handing her pelisse to a waiting maid, Kerenza followed her grandmother across the hall towards the ballroom where the warm air was fragrant with the scent of flowers and perfume.

Light from three huge chandeliers sparkled on jewels at ladies' throats and wrists, and gleamed on gold braid adorning the officers' blue coats. Dancing had already begun; the music supplied by a quartet seated on a small raised platform in the far corner.

Looking around, Kerenza saw that every girl her age, and many of the older women, were wearing white, declared by the London magazines to be the latest all-seasons fashion. But her grandmother had stood firm.

23

'No, Kerenza, with your colouring it would be most unwise. White will make you appear sallow. Let the rest of them resemble a bunch of candles if that is what they wish. You must wear pastel shades; pale green, apricot or peach; yellow perhaps, though not lemon; and definitely not blue or pink.'

For this evening Kerenza had chosen a gown of primrose muslin gathered behind, with scalloped sleeves and a muslin ruff edged with lace. Pearl drops in her ears matched the single strand at her throat. Minnie had brushed her hair thoroughly. Then, after stroking it with a silk handkerchief until it gleamed like a polished chestnut, had arranged it to fall in loose curls down her back.

Walking with her grandmother through the double doors, Kerenza was immediately aware of glances and whispered exchanges behind swiftly raised fans, and felt heat rush to her face.

'Courage, my love,' Aurelia murmured beside her. 'You are without doubt the prettiest girl here. Was I not right about the colour?' She clicked her tongue. 'How pale and insipid they all look. Do you hear that noise? It's the sound of a dozen mamas grinding their teeth.'

'Nana!' Kerenza raised a gloved hand to her mouth to hide her smile, feeling better at once. Her grandmother was right. It was her gown they were talking about. After all, Nicholas' attentions had not persisted long enough for anyone to suspect a particular attachment.

He was – *had been* – her first love, and the pain of his rejection had almost destroyed her. She knew she should forget him, learn from the

24

experience, and move on. God knew she had tried. Was still trying. After what he'd done, after the humiliation and anguish she'd suffered, it should be easy. But it wasn't. How stupid was that?

'Aurelia, at last. You had me worried.' Standing inside the doors to receive her guests, Maude Tregenna greeted them with genuine pleasure. Resplendent in a gown of purple and lace, her tortuous arrangement of ringlets was crowned with a purple turban and three white ostrich plumes.

'For shame, Maude, as if I would miss this.' Aurelia leaned forward to kiss the air beside her friend's pink cheek. 'When you give a ball it's the talk of the village for weeks.'

'Well, you are here now, and I am delighted to see you. Harry, look, here is Aurelia come to welcome you home. And Kerenza: my dear, what a pretty dress. I swear you are a very vision of spring, isn't she, Harry?' Taking one of Kerenza's hands and patting it, she confided with an arch smile. 'There is one gentleman who will be particularly pleased to see you. I swear he has been watching for your arrival this past half-hour.' Rolling her eyes to indicate where Kerenza should look, Maude squeezed her hand then let it go and turned to greet more late arrivals.

Hope and dread coiled in Kerenza's stomach. But it was John Carthew who inclined his head in smiling acknowledgement. Returning the widower's bow with a curtsy, Kerenza released the breath she hadn't realized she was holding and followed her grandmother toward the chairs and sofas where those not dancing could watch and chat. She felt shaky and confused, unsure if she was relieved or disappointed. She yearned to see Nick again. But at the same time the prospect dried her mouth and raised gooseflesh on her skin.

After that terrible moment in Market Street, it had cost her every ounce of courage to attend Captain and Mrs James's rout. But she knew Nick had accepted an invitation. And she needed to know why he had cut her. He owed her that.

But while she chatted with forced gaiety to acquaintances of both sexes, he arrived late, preoccupied and unsmiling. He had not danced. Nor had he once looked in her direction.

As Mary Blamey approached with bright inquisitive eyes, Kerenza braced herself.

Mary raised her fan to shield her mouth. 'Whatever's wrong with Nick Penrose?'

Kerenza shrugged lightly. 'Nothing that I'm aware of. He looks perfectly well. Though I did hear his uncle is not in good health, so–'

'That's not what I mean, and you know it.'

'Then what do you mean, Mary?' Kerenza was proud that her voice emerged calm and level from a throat as dry as ashes.

'Oh, come, Kerenza. These past weeks the rest of us might as well have stayed at home for all the attention he's paid us. You were the only one he had eyes for. Yet tonight he hasn't been near you. Have you quarrelled?'

'No.' It was the truth. A quarrel required words. He had said nothing. He had not spoken to her on that terrible day, or since.

'So why is he avoiding you?' Mary demanded, avid and relentless.

'Mary, really. You exaggerate. N-Nick has many friends and I certainly would not have him neglect them on my account.' Kerenza's skin burned with humiliation, but she refused to acknowledge her body's betrayal. She would sooner die than give Mary Blamey the opportunity to crow. 'You do him an injustice to believe him so rag-mannered.'

Mary tossed her fair curls. 'Well, it seems very odd to me–'

The band struck up again, drowning the rest of her words, and on the floor new sets were forming. Three young officers approached, each pleading for Kerenza to partner him. Pairing one with the dimpling and eager Mary, she pressed a gloved hand to her bosom and begged the other two to excuse her for the moment.

Promising to come back and ask her again they departed to find other partners. But as she turned, Nick was nowhere to be seen. A few minutes later she overheard someone say he had left early because he was sailing at dawn. That had been almost four weeks ago.

Surveying the room, Aurelia murmured softly, 'Courage, my love. Send the gossips elsewhere for their sport.' Without waiting for a reply, she settled herself comfortably on one of the sofas and adjusted the folds of her dove-grey silk. 'Kerenza, John Carthew is a good man, with a thriving business. And his two girls think the world of you. Could you not consider...?'

'Nana, he's...' *not Nick* 'old.' Kerenza whispered.

'Old?' Aurelia's brows climbed. 'My dear child,

he's not yet forty.'

'But that's still twice my age.'

Aurelia sighed. 'Oh well, it was just a thought.' She patted Kerenza's hand. 'All I want is your happiness. You know that, don't you?'

'Yes, Nana.'

'Ah, he's on his way over. Smile my love. We are here to celebrate. Allow Maude the pleasure of seeing you enjoy dancing.'

'Good evening, Mrs Danby.'

'Mr Carthew.'

'And Miss Vyvyan. It is indeed a joy to see you here tonight. You have been much missed.'

'You are kind to say so, sir.'

'Nothing kind about it. I deal in facts, Miss Vyvyan. And I have missed you. I swear no other young woman in this village is as light on her feet as you are.'

Recalling how much she owed her grand-mother, and glimpsing the love and relief on Maude Tregenna's beaming face as she looked up at her husband who, had things gone differently, might have come home in a wooden box, Kerenza made a huge effort. Widening her mouth in a smile she shook her head.

'You flatter me, sir. And I must advise you to keep such remarks to yourself, or risk finding yourself very short of partners.'

'I could bear it, Miss Vyvyan. Your absence from the Eversons' dance meant that as well as severe disappointment, I also suffered badly bruised toes.'

Kerenza felt her smile become easier, more natural.

28

'I can only conclude,' he added in a low voice, 'that certain young ladies–'

'No names, Mr Carthew,' Kerenza warned. 'For you surely cannot expect agreement from me if you criticize my friends.'

'My pain and injuries were so great that I have *quite* forgotten who they were. Only that they defied all natural law. For while *appearing* light and graceful, they were cursed with two left feet and iron-toed slippers.'

'Mr Carthew!' In spite of herself, Kerenza giggled. 'Have you not heard the old saying that a bad workman always blames his tools? Perhaps it was not after all *they* who were at fault?'

'Indeed, you may be right. Perhaps the truth of the matter is that I dance atrociously, and it is your skill that allows me to appear proficient.'

'Now you are teasing.'

'Me? How could you think it?' He leaned forward slightly. 'Your arrival has been noted by some of the young packet officers. So before I am thrust aside and trampled in the rush, will you do me the honour of standing up with me for this dance?'

Kerenza hesitated.

'Please, Miss Vyvyan? How else can I appear to best advantage? Besides, I should so much enjoy being envied.'

His gentle flattery was balm to Kerenza's battered self-esteem. While they moved through the familiar steps he related amusing snippets of village gossip. Even as she laughed she was aware of aching loss. But for the first time it was accompanied by anger. Anger as bright and sharp as a blade. How could Nicholas Penrose treat her so? She had done nothing to warrant such hurtful or offensive behaviour.

Watching Sam Penrose stumble from the boat onto the granite steps and feel the solidity of the stone quay beneath his feet was, Nick thought, like watching a man wake from a nightmare. Taking his first unsteady steps, Sam had clung to Nick's arm.

'Do you want to rest for a minute?' Nick had indicated a flat-topped iron bollard ready, if his uncle looked like falling, to drop the heavy portmanteaux, the captain's log and the passenger list, to catch him.

'No,' Sam rasped. 'Let's get it over with.'

Nick had kept the pace deliberately slow as they made their way along the quay, pity battling with frustration and impatience as he watched his uncle's painful efforts to pull sick body and broken spirit together.

Now, seated in the packet office, still whey-faced and red-eyed, Sam's words were firm even if his voice was not.

'Can't do it. It's not possible, not in three days.'

The packet agent leaned forward in his leather chair. From the top of one of the piles of paper covering the surface of the vast desk, he picked up a thick package wrapped in oiled cloth and fastened with wax seals. Edgar Tierney's upper lip lifted in a smile that did not reach his small eyes. There was no warmth or welcome in them, only mild impatience.

'Captain Penrose, these are urgent dispatches

30

from the Admiralty in London. They have to be delivered with all possible speed to Admiral Hotham who is presently commanding the navy's Mediterranean squadron. *Kestrel* is the only packet available.'

'I tell you, we can't do it. It's too soon. We need more time.'

Hearing the underlying note of fear – returning to sea would always come too soon for Sam Penrose – Nick addressed his uncle. 'With your permission, sir?' As Sam conceded with a shaking hand, Nick turned to the packet agent.

'Mr Tierney, *Kestrel* is back in Falmouth four days early due to a severe gale. The ship has suffered damage. It will take time to put that right.'

'Then I suggest you get about it, Mr Penrose. I should not need to remind you that we are at war.'

Anger lanced through Nick. Pompous and portly, the packet agent had never ventured outside Falmouth harbour.

'No, you don't, Mr Tierney.' With an effort Nick kept his voice even and his face impassive. He was only *Kestrel*'s mate, not her commander. To make an enemy of Edgar Tierney was unwise. The packet agent carried considerable influence with both packet-ship owners and the post office. This power enabled him to make life easy or difficult for packet commanders.

But Nick could not sit silent while this pompous buffoon pontificated about realities of which he had no experience to men who did.

'Captain Penrose knows better than most what

31

the French are capable of.'

'Quite.' Edgar Tierney drew the captain's log forward and tapped fat white fingers on the cover. He didn't open it. There was no need. Tierney had known before *Kestrel* sailed that Sam Penrose wasn't fit. He had relied on Nick's loyalty to his uncle to ensure the packet made the trip to Lisbon and back without mishap. Nick recognized Tierney's unspoken threat and felt his blood run cold.

The log fell far short of a full and detailed record of events on board. And the entries had been made not, as the law required by the captain, but by the mate. So it wasn't only Sam's future lying beneath Tierney's hand. It was Nick's too. *He'd had no choice. For much of the trip Sam couldn't even sit up let alone write. And submission of an incomplete log could get a captain dismissed.* Tierney had known that Nick would protect his uncle for as long as he could.

The agent looked up, speaking directly to Nick. 'You will complete your repairs, you will ensure you muster all the crew necessary, and *Kestrel* will leave for Gibraltar in three days' time. This is not a request.' With a brief meaningful flick of his eyes in Sam's direction, he arched one eyebrow. 'I trust I make myself clear?'

Nick felt sweat trickle down his sides. His plans to transfer to a Jamaica packet, to escape for seventeen weeks from constant reminders of Kerenza Vyvyan scattered like dust on the wind.

Nick sensed his uncle's swift, anguished glance. Sam too had recognized the agent's warning. *Kestrel* must sail, and he must be aboard. Refusal would not only cost him his contract and his income, Tierney would see to it that both master and mate faced criminal charges.

Nick gave a terse nod. There had never really been a choice. 'Perfectly clear.'

Edgar Tierney rubbed his hands together. As he beamed, his eyes narrowed to cold glittering slits in his fleshy face. 'Well, that's settled. I trust it was a successful voyage?'

Nick knew he was not referring to the speed of their crossing, or the fact that they managed to avoid attack by French warships and privateers. Clenching his teeth, carefully expressionless, he reached inside his uniform jacket and withdrew another kid purse fastened with a leather drawstring. It clinked as he laid it on the desk.

The agent scooped it into one of the desk drawers with practised speed. Then, radiating satisfaction, he relaxed against the glossy button-backed leather.

'Thank you, gentlemen. Don't let me keep you. You will have much to do to be ready in time.'

Nick turned to his uncle. Staring blankly at the floor, Sam seemed to have shrunk. Nick helped him to his feet, aware of the agent's dispassionate gaze.

'Oh, by the way,' Tierney added, as they reached the door, 'you'll be carrying passengers.' His lip lifted again, revealing small uneven teeth. 'And as they're willing to pay for cabins, additional food and the services of a steward, you stand to make a handsome profit.'

Nick was damned if he would thank the man. Tierney would have already taken his commission for booking the passengers' berths aboard *Kestrel*.

'The list?'

Tierney gestured vaguely. 'One of the clerks has it. Ask in the office. There were three names yesterday. But I've no doubt all the berths will be taken by the time you sail.'

As Nick led his uncle out, the agent's warning followed them. 'Three days, Mr Penrose.'

Supper was over. Refreshed and fortified, everyone had returned to the ballroom where rising levels of conversation and laughter ensured that Maude Tregenna's spring ball would be remembered as a resounding success.

Seeing Maude hurrying through the crush towards them, Kerenza touched her grandmother's sleeve to attract her attention.

'My dears,' Maude smiled brightly, 'you simply must come and see the pretty gift Harry brought back for me.'

As Aurelia's brows rose in surprise, Maude made a small urgent gesture with her fan towards the open double-doors. Kerenza glimpsed the greatcoated figure of her grandmother's butler in the hall before he quickly stepped back out of sight.

When they reached the hall, Maude ushered them into the drawing-room where Rapson was waiting.

'I'm sorry to interrupt your evening, madam. But there is a matter requiring your attention at home.'

It seemed to Kerenza that a look weighted with meaning flashed between servant and mistress. But his voice was calm and his manner as stolid as always. So, Kerenza reasoned, whatever had brought him here, though obviously important, couldn't be desperate. She opened her mouth to ask, but her grandmother laid a warning hand on her arm and she closed it again.

'Thank you, Rapson. We'll come at once.' Aurelia turned to her friend. 'I'm so sorry, Maude.'

'Nonsense, my dear. Rapson wouldn't have come without good reason.' A maid brought their wraps.

'Please convey our apologies to Harry.'

Maude cut her short. 'Harry will understand. I hope it's nothing serious. But if there is anything we can do, you know where we are. Off you go now.'

As soon as the Tregennas' front door closed behind them Kerenza expected her grandmother to ask Rapson what had happened. But she didn't. Nor did he volunteer any details. Forbidden by good manners to enquire into matters that might be none of her concern, Kerenza began to shiver as curiosity solidified into apprehension.

They hurried home through chilly moonlit streets thronged with weaving sailors and giggling girls. As they passed the open doors of inns and alehouses, sounds of laughter and singing mingled with the smells of roast meat, fried onions, beer and tobacco smoke.

A few minutes later, she followed her grandmother up the steps and in through the front door.

'Your sitting-room, madam,' Rapson murmured. Without waiting to remove her long cloak,

35

Aurelia walked swiftly down the hall.

Uncertain whether she should follow or wait, Kerenza slipped off her pelisse. Dropping it onto a chair she saw her grandmother open the door, and pause, utterly still. As she disappeared inside, her startled voice floated back down the hall.

'William. What a wonderful surprise.'

Kerenza froze. *William?* Could it be–? Running down the hall she whirled in through the doorway and stopped, staring at the haggard emaciated man struggling to his feet from an armchair.

'Papa?' Her choked whisper betrayed her shock.

'Kerenza.' As he held out a shaking hand, tears gathered on his red-rimmed eyelids and trickled over crumpled grey-white skin furrowed with suffering. 'My dear girl. I feared I might never see you again.'

For a split second all the misery she had endured at home held her rooted to the spot. Then, overwhelmed by a combination of guilt and relief that the awful waiting, not knowing, was over at last, she rushed forward. 'Oh Papa. Thank God you are safe. It's been so long and we were so dreadfully worried.'

As she hugged him the smell stopped her breath. He reeked of tar and bilge water, of old cooking, stale sweat, and alcohol. As he patted her shoulder clumsily she drew back revolted, instantly ashamed of her reaction, yet craving fresh air. Clasping her hands tightly, she forced a smile, struggling for emotional balance in a world turned suddenly upside down.

'How are mama and Dulcie? When did you arrive back? No doubt they wanted to go straight home. Are they both well?'

'Patience, child,' Aurelia chided. 'Give your father a chance to answer.'

William Vyvyan collapsed back into the chair and passed a trembling hand across his face.

'They did not return with me. I must pay a ransom before they will be freed.'

'*Ransom?*' Kerenza repeated, bewildered.

'Who is holding them, William?' Aurelia asked. 'And where?'

'Tangier. They are in Tangier, at the governor's palace.'

'But–' Kerenza began.

'No,' William interrupted, his voice cracking. 'No more questions, not now. I'm too tired and have too much to do. I have come straight from the packet office. There's a ship leaving for Gibraltar in three days. I have to raise the ransom money in time to be aboard her. Kerenza, you must come back with me to Tangier. Your mother and sister – I wasn't permitted to speak to them, though from what I could see they seemed well enough. But after all they have been through they will need someone to care for them on the voyage home. Someone they know, someone who may be relied upon not to–Well, you know,' he gestured vaguely.

No, she didn't know. Not to *what?* Ask questions? Kerenza's gaze sought her grandmother's. What should she do? She didn't want to leave the only security and happiness she had ever known. *You must come back with me to Tangier.* She didn't want to go with her father. She didn't want to be responsible for the wellbeing of two people who had made her life utterly miserable. Yet how could

37

she refuse? They were her family. Her reluctance was echoed in her grandmother's eyes.

Aurelia's mouth trembled briefly, then she tilted her chin. Her features tightened and holding Kerenza's gaze she gave a decisive nod.

Kerenza swallowed. 'Of course, Papa. But will you be able to raise the money in so short a time?' A tiny treacherous part of her hoped that he might not. Then she wouldn't have to go. Immediately a scalding wave of shame washed over her.

'I must,' William said simply, rubbing his face as if that might erase his exhaustion. 'The next Gibraltar packet doesn't sail for three weeks. I can't wait that long. I dare not. If I don't get back within a certain time–' His voice broke.

'Come, William,' Aurelia rose to her feet. 'You are exhausted. Rapson will prepare a bath and I'll have a tray of supper sent up to you.'

He pinched the bridge of his nose, swaying. 'I ought to–'

'You can do no more tonight.' Aurelia said. 'What you need now is food and sleep. You can return to Falmouth first thing in the morning.'

Beyond arguing, William shrugged. Grey with fatigue, he turned to Kerenza. 'I won't have time to come over again before we sail. I'll join the ship from Falmouth. You must arrange for one of the village boys to row you out from here. I'll see you on board.' He shuffled toward the door: thin, round-shouldered, looking a lifetime older.

Kerenza gazed after him, too confused and jangled to know what she felt. It was too much to take in all at once. What had happened to him?

He was a shadow of the prosperous merchant she remembered. And what of her mother and sister? What would they look like now? The room was warm, but she felt chilled. She rubbed her arms as unease crept over her skin and seeped into her bones.

'Papa?' she called quickly, as he reached the threshold. 'Which packet are we sailing on?'

His forehead puckered. He appeared to be on the verge of collapse. 'What?'

'The ship's name, William,' Aurelia prompted. 'So Kerenza may be sure she boards the right one?'

'Oh. It's *Kestrel*. She arrived back from Lisbon early this evening.'

Chapter Three

'I don't know how you're ever going to get it all in, miss.' Minnie shook her head. 'Not with the bedding and all.' Her plump face was pink with exertion. Wisps of fair hair had escaped from beneath her frilled cap and clung to her damp forehead and neck. She picked a thread from the white apron covering her blue calico dress, shrugging helplessly as she surveyed the mound of dresses, shawls, undergarments, stockings, kerchiefs and nightwear strewn across the coverlet.

'I can't,' Kerenza said simply. 'There won't be room.' She threw back the lid of the trunk releasing the sweet scent of the cedar wood balls lying in the bottom to keep moths away. Riffling through the pile of clothing she began selecting items and passing them to Minnie, who folded them expertly then carefully laid them on the carpet.

'Best if I don't put 'em in until you're sure.'

Kerenza nodded. 'The trouble is, though it's still winter here it will probably be much hotter in Tangier.'

'Yes, well, you got to get there first,' Minnie reminded her. 'There won't be no fire to keep you warm on that there boat. And I seen more meat on a butcher's apron than you got on your bones just now.'

Kerenza sighed. 'Don't start that again, Minnie. I'm perfectly well.'

The maid gave a muffled snort. 'If you say so, miss. But I know what I see, and I can't help worrying.'

'Well, I wish you wouldn't. It doesn't help. I have to go and that's all there is to it. Now, which do you think?' She held up two round gowns: one of plain muslin, the other spotted. 'The apple-green or the lilac?'

'The green. Look handsome with your hair, it do.' Taking the dress, she shook it out then laid it on the carpet and folded it to minimize creasing. 'You shouldn't be going by yourself. 'Tis never right, a young lady travelling alone.'

'Minnie, you know perfectly well I shan't be alone. I'm travelling with my father.'

'Oh, yes? No disrespect, miss, but I can't see him being much use when it comes to looking after your clothes, or dressing your hair, or–'

40

'No, you're absolutely right. Somehow I will have to manage all by myself. Honestly, Minnie,' Kerenza chided, 'to hear you talk, anyone would think I was helpless or stupid.'

'Now you know that wasn't what I meant, miss. And you can mock all you like, but 'tis never right nor proper. I should be going with you, and that's the truth.'

I wish you were. Kerenza managed to bite back the words. Minnie's concern was making this difficult enough already. 'I know, but it's just not possible. Rapson tells me that *Kestrel* only has three passenger cabins, and all are booked. As it is I shall be sharing with another lady. It will be nice to have company. I hope she's pleasant.'

Minnie sniffed, her frown deepening, but before she could reply the door opened.

'Ah.' Aurelia's gaze swept from the chaos on the counterpane to the neat pile on the carpet. 'I see you are coming along.' Catching Kerenza's eye and instantly reading the silent plea she turned with a smile. 'Minnie, after all this activity I think my granddaughter would benefit from a cup of hot chocolate. Would you be so kind?'

The maid straightened, nodding in approval. 'Just what I was thinking meself. Bring one for you as well, shall I, madam?'

'Yes, do.' As the door closed, Aurelia seated herself on the padded velvet stool that stood in front of the dressing-table. 'Was Minnie fussing?'

'I know she means well, but–' Shaking her head, Kerenza made a space amid the remaining garments and sank down on the bed. Then,

41

seeing anxiety cross her grandmother's face, she forced a smile. 'Being limited to one trunk has made it really difficult to choose what I should take.' She indicated the double stack of neatly folded garments. 'I thought I would travel in my riding dress. It's warm, and will leave more room in the trunk for … everything else.'

'A most sensible idea,' Aurelia agreed. 'Now.' She looked from the trunk to the dressing-table. 'Have you packed creams to protect your face and hands from cold wind and salt spray?'

'It's in the little pots beside the soap.' She hesitated. 'Nana? You will let me come back, won't you? You won't decide I ought to stay with mama and Dulcie?'

Aurelia reached across and took Kerenza's hand. 'Of course not. This is your home for as long as you want. And while you're away you will be very much missed.' Though her manner was calm and reassuring, strain was visible in the lines around her eyes. 'But instead of dwelling on our separation, we must look forward instead to your return. And in the meantime we will both have plenty to keep us busy.' After a brief pause she leaned forward. 'I've been wondering about your mother and sister's response to all that has befallen them. I have to say that rather than hold them and demand a ransom, I would have expected their captors to pay your father to take them away.'

Startled that her grandmother should actually voice sentiments she had felt guilty even thinking, Kerenza giggled. 'Nana!'

'Can you picture them doing anything other

42

than moan and whine and be a burden to all concerned?'

Kerenza tried. 'No, but–'

'Exactly. Once they are back in Falmouth your task will end and you can return here. In the meantime, however–'

'I will do all I can to make them comfortable,' Kerenza promised.

'Of course you will. But that wasn't–' Aurelia rose from the stool and began to pace. Anxiety flared in Kerenza at her grandmother's uncharacteristic hesitancy. *What now?* 'Kerenza, this trip would not be easy for you under any circumstances. But the fact that you must undertake it aboard *Kestrel* makes it even more difficult. I have not forgotten that for three weeks Nicholas Penrose paid you a degree of attention that encouraged you to believe his affections were seriously engaged and that he would shortly declare himself.'

Startled, Kerenza looked up, heat flooding her face.

'I may be old,' her grandmother's tone was dry, 'but there is nothing wrong with my eyesight, or my memory. However, I do not believe in prying. I felt sure that if anything occurred about which I should be informed, then you would tell me.'

'Oh, Nana. Why does it have to be *this* ship?'

'As to that, you heard what your father said. He must return to Tangier within a certain time. And as it will be at least two weeks before another packet leaves for the Mediterranean, he has no choice in the matter. Though it does seem curious that *Kestrel* is to sail again only three days after

43

returning from Lisbon. Such a fast turnaround is most unusual. But no doubt there are excellent reasons. As for Mr Penrose' – her features hardened – 'that he could cut you in public without reason or explanation convinces me he is not and never will be worthy of you.'

Rising, Kerenza gripped her grandmother's hands. Whether she was giving or seeking reassurance she could not have said. 'You're right, Nana. But knowing that doesn't stop it hurting.' Her chin quivered.

'Oh, my dear.' Aurelia's grasp tightened convulsively. 'Believe me, if I could bear the pain for you I would. It will lessen, I promise. The important thing is not to let it show. Do not be tempted to question him, Kerenza. If you wish to maintain your dignity you must remain aloof. Only *after* he has apologized, and assuming you are convinced his apology is sincere, should you allow him to explain the reason for his appalling behaviour.' Her grip tightened again. 'My dearest girl, in all honesty, I do not anticipate it. So you must be strong. Easier said than done, I know, but pride and self-respect will assist you.'

So will anger, Kerenza realized. But she would not betray that either. God knew she'd had years of practice at hiding her emotions. Only since coming to live here had she felt secure enough in her grandmother's love to occasionally drop her guard and reveal how deeply her feelings ran.

But while she was aboard *Kestrel* she would not permit anyone, least of all Nicholas Penrose, to glimpse the passions that simmered behind the mask: the hurt, the betrayal, and worst – *most shaming* – of all, the yearning for him she had not yet been able to banish.

'Don't worry, Nana. I'll be all right. It was very hard at first. But I'm growing stronger every day.' She forced herself to smile. 'I shall be gone only a few weeks. And when I return and am boring you to death with tales of my travels, you will wish me away again.'

The next two days flew by in a blur of activity. Word had spread that William Vyvyan was back, looking terrible; but there was neither sight nor sign of his wife or elder daughter. With rumours growing more outlandish by the day, Kerenza faced a barrage of questions every time she ventured outside the front door.

Eventually, though it offended every sensibility, Aurelia reluctantly acknowledged there was only one way to halt the speculation. Rapson was sent to three carefully selected shops where, during the course of making his purchases, he allowed sympathetic enquiries to break down his legendary discretion.

On his return home, he assured his mistress that unless he was very much mistaken, by nightfall everyone in the village would have been told the facts of the matter. And so it proved.

Aware now that Kerenza was sailing with her father to bring her mother and sister home, the villagers wished her well. But their hopes for her safe return were inevitably followed by suggestions of remedies they swore by as preventives or cures for seasickness. As it hadn't occurred to Kerenza that she might suffer this malady, their insistent advice increased the weight of her anxiety. For despite her brave assurances to her grandmother, she was far less confident than anyone could have guessed, both about the voyage and what would be expected of her in Tangier.

But as she packed a small wooden box with dried and powdered ginger root, arnica ointment for bruises, dried camomile flowers as a sedative and digestive; and a bottle of paregoric, she felt she must surely be prepared for most eventualities. Then Minnie hurried in carrying a jar of thick honey.

'You mustn't go without this, miss. My brothers swear by it. Out on the boats they're always getting cut and scratched. And seawater is terrible for turning cuts bad. But honey do heal them up in no time. Wonderful stuff it is, miss. My gran do take a spoonful in boiling water for a sore throat. Soothes it lovely, she says. And there isn't nothing like it for settling your stomach. I was just thinking, you got some long way to go, and 'tis bound to get rough—'

'Yes.' Kerenza forced a smile. 'Thank you, Minnie. By all means put it in, if you can find space.'

An hour later, Rapson tapped on the door and pressed a small flask of brandy into her hands. 'I hope you will have no need of it, miss, but it would be foolish indeed to embark on a sea voyage without such an excellent remedy by you. I understand a few drops in water taken with a hard biscuit swiftly settles a queasy stomach.'

Even as she swallowed hysterical giggles – why was everyone determined to assume she would be a poor sailor? – Kerenza's eyes prickled at his kindness. 'Thank you, Rapson. How very thoughtful.'

She was about to close the lid when her grandmother entered. She held out a small dark bottle bearing a label on which the word *warning* loomed larger and blacker than the dosage instructions.

'I obtained this from the apothecary, Kerenza. It's a mixture of camphor julep, ether, laudanum and magnesia.'

Kerenza's brows shot up. 'That sounds awfully strong, Nana. I really don't think–'

'No, my dear, you misunderstand. I did not intend it for you. I see no reason why you should suffer any physical discomfort whatever while at sea. However, I cannot feel the same confidence in your mother and sister. As you will be required to look after both of them on the voyage home, possessing the means to relieve their suffering with a draught that encourages sleep will allow you to get some rest.'

Clutching the bottle tightly, Kerenza hugged her grandmother with heartfelt gratitude. 'Thank you, Nana.'

Then, after rising at dawn and some last-minute bustle, it was time to go.

With a final look around her bedroom, Kerenza turned to the cheval mirror to check her appearance. Her holly-green riding habit, made of fine wool cloth, was light but warm. The skirt had been cut without a train for easier walking. This, she suspected, would prove a huge advantage during the next few weeks. A primrose muslin kerchief filled the gap between the lapels of the fitted jacket. Her feet were snug in woollen stockings and leather ankle boots. Minnie had

47

braided her hair into a coil over which she wore a helmet cap of pleated green velvet. Her black beaver hat with the jaunty feather would have been more stylish but difficult to keep on in any wind above a light breeze.

'You *are* strong. You *will* survive,' she assured the pale image staring back at her. Then, turning away, she picked up the leather travelling bag that had belonged to her grandfather. Scarred and salt-stained, the brass corners tarnished, it was still sound. In it, Kerenza had packed her writing case, pens and ink, two books, a tinderbox, candles and a holder, and a waterproof bag of oiled silk containing soap and face cloth, toothbrush and powder, and the jars of face and hand cream.

Descending the staircase to the wide hall, she saw her trunk standing near the front door. As well as her clothes, the box of medicines, and a bundle of soft rags plus old newspaper and string in which to wrap them for burning, Minnie had managed to cram in three towels, a pillow, two sheets, two blankets and two pillowcases.

Aurelia was waiting for her, a dark bundle in her arms. 'Now, are you sure you have everything? Rapson will take your trunk down to the quay and see you safely aboard the boat that will take you out to the packet.'

'Nana, you're fussing.' Kerenza forced a teasing note past the lump in her throat as she smoothed York tan gloves over icy fingers.

'Oh dear, am I? And I can't abide people who fuss.' She raised her arms and the dark bundle tumbled into loose folds of navy serge. 'Come here and let me put this on you.'

48

Kerenza switched her gaze from the standing collar, the loop and button fastening, to her grandmother. 'But that's–'

'Your grandfather's boat cloak. I cannot think of a better use for it. It will be cold at sea,' she went on, before Kerenza could speak. 'You'll need more than that riding dress to keep you warm.' She settled the cloak around Kerenza's shoulders. 'And as Zenobia and Dulcie will no doubt appropriate your blankets for the return voyage, you will be very glad of this.'

'Oh, Nana.' Enfolded by the thick material that reached to her ankles, she felt immensely comforted by its heavy warmth. 'Thank you so much.'

'Yes, yes. Now, give me a kiss, then you must go.' Aurelia's eyes were suspiciously bright. 'Your father will be anxious to see you safely aboard.'

Surprised and moved by the strength of her grandmother's hug, Kerenza clung for a moment, drawing the familiar fragrance of lavender-scented soap deep into her lungs. She squeezed her eyes tight shut to dispel treacherous tears then opened them wide and, gathering her resolve, stepped back.

'You take care of yourself, Nana. And don't worry about me. I'll be fine. You know the old saying: what doesn't kill you makes you stronger? Well–' mentally she crossed her fingers – 'it didn't, and I am.'

'My dearest girl, I'm so proud of you.'

Giving her grandmother a final kiss, Kerenza walked briskly through the open front door. Outside, Rapson had loaded her trunk on to a trolley made of thick wooden slats attached to

49

small iron wheels and was already trundling it along the street. Not daring to look back, she raised a hand in farewell, and followed Rapson's receding figure down to the quay.

The morning was chilly and damp. Mist hung in a fine veil over the water, softening the outlines of the ships. Sound carried on the still air. She could hear the splash of oars and orders being shouted. Anchor chains rumbled, capstans creaked, blocks rattled. Snatches of rhythmic chanting as seamen hauled on ropes was accompanied by the flap and crack of canvas as sails were loosed from their yards or hoisted on huge gaffs up tall masts.

Kerenza felt a quickening inside. She took a deep breath and inhaled the tang of burning wood, frying bacon, and the sweet fragrance of freshly baked bread. This was home. This was where she belonged. She knew nothing about the place she was going to, or what she would find when she got there. Terror closed her throat, and her footsteps faltered.

She could see Rapson at the edge of the quay, talking to a strapping youth clad in loose trousers and a blue checked shirt covered by a stained and faded jacket. A red kerchief was knotted around his thick neck, and a grubby cap with the brim pulled down kept the pearly sun, still low in the sky, out of his eyes.

The young man raised a finger to his cap. 'Morning, miss. You got a nice day for it.'

Rapson turned. 'This is Joe Laity, Miss Vyvyan. He will see you and your trunk safely aboard the packet.'

As Kerenza smiled her thanks, the two men were

already carrying her trunk down the granite steps to a sturdy boat. After setting her leather bag near the stern, Joe extended a large calloused hand.

'Ready, miss?'

She glanced at the butler, who gave her an encouraging nod.

'Get along now, miss. The sooner you're gone, the sooner you'll be back with us again. God speed.'

Not trusting her voice she nodded. Then, putting her hand into Joe's, she stepped on to the rocking boat and quickly sat, drawing the leather bag against her feet and gathering the folds of the cloak closely about her.

Joe flicked the mooring rope from the iron ring, slid out the long oars, and with slow powerful strokes pulled the boat across the crowded harbour.

It was still early, but already the water was busy. Pilot gigs were racing from the harbour into the Carrick Roads, competing to reach the incoming merchant and packet ships. Oyster boats were heading out for a day's dredging. Chandlers' boats were ferrying out supplies. Jollyboats and cutters carried seamen and passengers to and from other packet ships.

'Not far now, miss,' Joe said, hauling on the oars.

Kerenza simply nodded, looking past him to the ship they were approaching. The packet looked battered and dingy. Scarred black paint had been dulled by the constant lash of salt seas and was streaked with rust from the iron fastenings securing the mast stays to her side. Then Kerenza caught her breath as she saw that behind the shabby appearance *Kestrel's* flared bow, tapered lines and chiselled stern were those of a thoroughbred built for speed. And the swifter the voyage, the sooner she would be home again.

Shipping one oar, Joe half-turned and cupped a hand to his mouth.

'Yo! *Kestrel!* Passenger to board!'

Kerenza didn't recognize the face that peered down at her topped by greying hair tied back in a short pigtail.

'This 'ere's Miss Vyvyan,' Joe yelled. 'Come to join her father she is.'

Above them the head nodded. 'Mr Vyvyan's already aboard. Throw up a line.' He disappeared.

After a few unpleasant moments on the rope and wood ladder, Kerenza arrived on deck just in time to see her bag and trunk being carried by two sailors towards the open doors of the aft companionway.

'I'm the passenger's steward, miss,' announced the pigtailed man. 'Name of Broad. I'll take you down to your cabin.'

As she followed the wiry, bow-legged figure, Kerenza glimpsed cannons lashed to the ship's side. Her skin tightened and she tried to swallow surging anxiety. Men swarmed about the deck. Some appeared reasonably clean and tidy, but others were unkempt and filthy, their jackets and trousers little more than rags. All were busy at different tasks: loosing sails, coiling ropes, shifting sacks of fresh vegetables and barrels of salted meat, slotting wooden staves into capstans and windlass, urged on by the bosun who slapped a short thick piece of rope against his grimy palm as he bellowed orders.

Kerenza's eyes widened at the size of the huge wheel attached by a stout wooden column to the deck with the binnacle and a raised skylight in front. Behind it was a thick wooden grating for the helmsman to stand on and an odd-looking structure with a flat front, a curved back, and a door in the side.

On the far side of the deck, apparently oblivious to the chilly morning, a man wearing a leather apron over his check shirt and loose canvas trousers stood with brawny arms folded and head tipped back gazing towards the upper reaches of the massive mainmast. As the seamen carrying her trunk disappeared down the companionway, Kerenza saw an officer's uniform topped by black curly hair. But even as her heart gave an uncomfortable thud, she knew it wasn't Nick. *Nick was taller.* The man half-turned, gesturing and pointing skyward.

Startled, Kerenza whispered to the steward, 'Who is that?'

Broad looked round. 'The second mate, miss. Not Cornish o'course. But he's some fine seaman for all that. Now, you watch your head when you go through the hatch.'

Following him down the curving brass stairs, Kerenza's nostrils quivered at the thick miasma of lamp oil, wet wool, tarred timber and old cooking. At the bottom of the stairs she waited with the steward to let the two seamen who had carried her trunk pass by and climb the stairs, trying to ignore the stench of stale sweat lingering in the narrow passage.

'There you are, miss. You was the last. Lady Russell is already inside. Up ahead is the saloon where your meals will be served. Breakfast is at eight, dinner at midday, tea at five, and a cup of hot chocolate about nine, before you settle down. The boy will bring you hot water morning and evening, unless we get a bad blow. The galley fires is doused then, for safety. Billy will knock to empty the slop bucket an hour after he brung the water. Anything else you want, you just ask me. All right?'

'Yes, thank you.'

'Right, if you'll excuse me, miss–'

'Just one more thing. Which is my father's cabin?'

'There, miss.' Broad indicated. 'Second on the left. But I b'lieve he's in with the captain.'

'Where–?'

'The door behind the stairs. But – no offence, miss – 'tis best not to go knocking unless you've been invited. You get settled in. We'll be sailing the minute Mr Penrose get back with the mail.'

Kerenza moistened her lips. 'I see. Thank you.' No doubt the captain had some kind of strongbox, and her father would be arranging safekeeping for the ransom money until the ship reached Tangier.

As Broad nodded and scurried up the stairs again, Kerenza walked along the passage. Behind her, light from the open hatch spilled down the companionway stairs. Ahead of her sunshine filtered into the saloon through the skylight's thick glass. But most of the passage

54

was in semi-darkness.

To her left, voices drifted out through the six-inch gap between the top of the closed door.

'Betsy, I wish you wouldn't–'

'I know my duty, Donald Woodrow, even if you have forgotten yours.'

'Please, my dear, there's no call to–'

'Oh yes there is. And I don't take kindly to your manner. After all, it wasn't *me* who–'

A clattering on the deck above made Kerenza jump. Then the man spoke again, pleading, placatory, but too softly now for her to catch the actual words. Not that she wanted to. She loathed arguments. And though the raised voices had nothing to do with her, just hearing them knotted her stomach. Reminded of the past, anxious about the future, she pressed her hand against the grinding ache in her midriff, silently praying that she could like the woman with whom she would be sharing for the next few weeks. Then, drawing a deep breath, she tapped lightly on the door and opened it.

Chapter Four

Kerenza's heart dropped as she saw how small the cabin was. Beyond the two trunks currently occupying most of the floor space, there was just enough room for two cots set one above the other, and a nightstand with a cupboard underneath. There were no portholes or skylights, only

55

an oil lamp suspended from the deck-head.

The light, falling across the face of the woman seated on the lower bunk directly opposite the door, illuminated the planes and hollows of her face. Still swathed in a fur-lined pelisse of burgundy velvet and matching hat, she looked strained and tired, and her expression was not welcoming.

Dread opened like a void in Kerenza. Swallowing, she bobbed a curtsy. 'L–Lady Russell? I'm Kerenza Vyvyan. We – it is my understanding that we are to share?' She waited, not breathing, as she was scrutinized.

Lady Russell's face relaxed. 'Oh, thank goodness.' Her voice was pitched so that Kerenza could hear, but not loud enough to carry beyond the cabin. 'I'm sure you will understand when I confess that I was ... anxious. No doubt you were as well?'

Limp with relief, Kerenza nodded.

'I really could not have borne–' Gesturing towards the passage, Lady Russell grimaced at the muffled but still audible sounds of complaint.

'Nor I, ma'am,' Kerenza said fervently.

'Now I need worry no longer.' Concern puckered her forehead. 'I hope that you will also be comfortable with the arrangement?'

'Oh, yes, ma'am. Indeed I am. It's just–' Kerenza hesitated. 'Forgive me, your ladyship, but–'

'Please, no more *ladyships*. The title belongs to my husband. He is Colonel Sir George Russell. I am really quite ordinary.' Her smile was both wry and impish. 'Considering the enforced intimacy of our circumstances it would be quite ridiculous to stand on ceremony. Besides, I can see we are going to get along famously. You must call me Judith, and I shall call you Kerenza. But I interrupted you. You were about to say?'

'Only that – and I do not mean to be impertinent, ma'am – it's just … I am astonished that you should be travelling alone.'

'It was not intended. However, my companion had the misfortune to slip on an icy path and break her leg. She cannot travel until it is mended, and it was impossible for me to remain with her.'

Wondering why, and realizing the reason was none of her business, Kerenza turned away and started to unfasten the button at the neck of her heavy cloak.

'No, don't take it off,' Judith said. 'Let us leave our unpacking until later and go up on deck. It's a beautiful morning. We should enjoy the fresh air and sunshine while we can.' She held out her hand. 'Would you mind helping me up?'

Surprised, Kerenza grasped it. As Judith lurched awkwardly to her feet, her pelisse fell open.

'Oh,' Kerenza blurted and immediately flushed. 'Do forgive me. I didn't mean – it's – I didn't expect– Oh dear, I do beg your pardon.'

'You needn't apologize. I understand perfectly.' Judith laid one hand protectively on the heavy swelling beneath the high waistline of her gown. 'Now you see why I could not delay my return.'

Kerenza tried to ignore a flutter of panic. 'How soon?'

'Not for another month at least, according to the doctor I consulted last week. And if you think it strange I should be travelling in my present

57

condition, I must tell you that you are not alone. My husband did not want me to make the journey to Cornwall. And I could have wished it otherwise. But my grandmother was asking for me. She raised me after my parents died, so how could I refuse her? I'm so glad I made the effort. We had four wonderful days together before–' She stopped abruptly and looked away, covering her quivering mouth with her fingers.

Thinking of how much she loved and owed her own grandmother, Kerenza touched Judith's arm in an instinctive gesture of sympathy. 'I'm so very sorry.'

Clearing her throat, Judith shook her head with a wry watery smile. 'You must forgive me, Kerenza. I am not usually so rag-mannered as to burden a new acquaintance with my private concerns.'

'But I understand. You see, I, too, live with my grandmother,' Kerenza said, surprising them both.

Judith looked up from pulling on her gloves. 'But – are you not travelling with your father?'

What else had she heard? 'I am. It's a long story.'

'Then it will keep for another time.' Taking Kerenza's proffered hand for support, she stepped carefully between the trunks and out into the passage.

'You go first,' Judith urged at the bottom of the brass stairs. 'I need time.'

So do I. Thinking of what lay ahead, and wanting to delay for as long as possible the moment she must face Nick Penrose, Kerenza shook her head. 'No, you will be safer if I'm behind you, in

58

case you should miss your footing.'

One hand on the rail, Judith glanced back over her shoulder. 'My dear, pray it doesn't happen. Were I to fall, I'd squash you flat.' Reaching the top of the stairs, Kerenza stepped through the hatch. Hearing Nick's voice, blood rushed to her face and drummed in her ears. For a moment she was shielded. Then Judith moved aside and there he was, broad shoulders filling his gold-braided blue coat, blue breeches clinging to muscular thighs. She fixed her gaze on the two leather portmanteaux at his feet. But was startled into looking up as Judith addressed the officer beside Nick in a strange, guttural language. The second mate's teeth flashed white against his olive skin, and his delight was evident as he replied in the same tongue. Catching sight of Kerenza, he bowed.

Turning, Judith drew her forward. 'Kerenza, allow me to present the ship's officers. Mr Penrose, this is Miss Vyvyan.'

Bowing briefly in Kerenza's direction, he addressed Judith. 'I beg you will excuse me, ma'am. I must speak to the captain.' Without waiting for a reply, he strode past and disappeared down the companionway.

Kerenza's face burned. He had acted as though they were strangers unknown to one another. *No.* He would have shown greater courtesy had they really been meeting for the first time. Judith's presence and attempted introductions had made it impossible for him to ignore her. That he still did not wish to speak to her was only too plain. Struggling to mask her humiliation, she heard the second mate's harsh voice.

'Is very busy time–'

'Of course,' Judith said. 'I should have realized.' She turned. 'Kerenza, I'd like to present the second mate, Magrahi Murabet.'

Kerenza dropped a curtsy. 'Mr M – M–' she felt her blush deepen as she stumbled over the unfamiliar sounds.

'Maggot.' He bowed. 'Everyone call me Maggot.' His teeth flashed in a grin. 'More easy to say, no? You stay on deck? To be safe you stand back there.' He indicated the left-hand stern quarter. Then with a nod he left them and went forward, pausing to speak briefly to a seaman who fingered his forehead then scurried away. On the fore and main-masts the gaffs were being hoisted, drawing the huge fore-and-aft sails up with them. With the sun climbing higher, the gentle breeze was freshening. It caught the canvas and Kerenza felt the deck move beneath her feet.

'Are you all right?' she asked quickly, as Judith gripped her arm.

'I will be when I have rediscovered my sea legs. Meanwhile I need something to hold on to.' They crossed to the stern quarter and Kerenza inhaled the oily smell of linseed and turpentine that her grandfather had told her was rubbed into the wooden rail daily to stop it turning black. She heard bleating, glanced towards the bow, and saw the nanny goat that would provide their fresh milk penned in a large wooden cage just behind the foremast.

'You know,' Judith confided, 'I find it very odd that a man as attractive as Mr Penrose should be so devoid of charm. His manner toward you was

60

positively rude.' She frowned. 'In fact, the more I think about it, the less acceptable it becomes. And so I shall tell him. No doubt he will eat with us in the saloon–'

'No,' Kerenza begged, her voice low and intense. 'Please don't say anything.'

Judith's brows rose in astonishment. 'But, my dear, you surely cannot condone–'

'No, I don't. But–' Kerenza thought frantically. How could she dissuade Judith from confronting him without disclosing information she was desperate to keep secret? 'It is my understanding that the captain has not been well. He was a prisoner in France,' she added in a whisper.

'Oh, the poor man.'

'Indeed. And this has placed an additional burden of responsibility on Mr Penrose. In such circumstances he will have little time or inclination to chat to passengers. I think we should just forget it.' She bit her lip. *He had virtually snubbed her again, yet to protect herself she was forced to defend him.* Lowering her lashes, afraid of what Judith might see, she was acutely aware of her new friend's assessing gaze.

'I cannot like it. But if it is what you prefer....'

'Yes, it is. Truly.'

'In that case I shall say nothing.'

Standing beside Judith, Kerenza watched the houses and quays of Falmouth and Flushing recede as the schooner headed out of the Carrick Roads. Gazing towards the house that she now thought of as home, she pictured her grandmother and Minnie and Rapson. But a yearning to be back safe with them brought a choking lump to her throat. Quickly she turned her face towards the wooded slopes and gorse-studded moorland running from St Just in Roseland to St Anthony Head. Better to look forward. Except her eyes were so clouded by tears all she could see were bright shards of colour like a fragmented rainbow.

Footsteps behind her were followed by the second mate's harsh voice as he murmured a few incomprehensible words in a tone of enquiry. Was he addressing her? She blinked quickly to dispel the tears. But as she glanced over her shoulder Judith answered him in his own language. With a nod and a brief bow, he returned to his position near the wheel.

'Is everything all right?' Kerenza asked.

'That was Maggot's question,' Judith smiled.

'Do you know him, then?'

'We have met before. He has relatives in Gibraltar.'

'I expect that's why he's concerned about you.'

Judith laughed, then brought her head close to Kerenza's. 'My dear, I am not the subject of his concern: you are.'

Kerenza felt her eyes widen. 'Me? Why?'

'According to Maggot, when Mr Penrose received the final passenger list he became unusually short-tempered and uncommunicative. It appears his mood has not improved.'

Kerenza swallowed. 'Wh-why should you think that has anything to do with me?'

'My dear, I have no right to ask, and you are certainly not obliged to satisfy my reprehensible curiosity, but it occurs to me that there might be an alternative explanation for Mr Penrose's appalling discourtesy. You will note I said *explanation*, not *excuse*. And it is that you and Mr Penrose are not, as I assumed, strangers to one another.'

Kerenza turned her face to the cold breeze. 'You are correct. We are – were – acquainted. I once thought that we were friends. I was mistaken.'

Judith's fingers closed on hers. 'Oh, my dear. I'm so sorry.'

'Please.' Kerenza cleared her throat of the tears fogging her voice. 'It is past, and of no importance. Let us talk of other things.' She turned to look out over the rail. 'Where is Maggot from?'

'Tangier. His father was what we would call Berber. But I believe his mother had some English in her background.'

'Was that Berber you were both speaking just now?'

Judith nodded. 'One of the dialects. Some of our servants in Gibraltar are from Tangier, so I thought it a good idea to learn the language. And though I'm sure my accent leaves much to be desired, it appears my efforts are appreciated as we seem to have far fewer problems than previous governors did.'

Kerenza turned a startled gaze on her companion. 'Your husband is governor of Gibraltar?'

'Oh no,' Judith corrected with a smile. 'But he is on the governor's permanent staff. He's a superb administrator. But he still misses India. We couldn't have stayed though. That second bout of fever nearly killed him.' She sighed. 'It's all been very unsettled here. Gibraltar has had three governors in the past two years. The most recent appointee is Sir Henry Clinton. But he's

63

currently in Jamaica. Or he might possibly have returned to Cornwall. He had a house there, you know. Anyway, until he arrives to take up the post, General Rainsford is the acting governor. But in truth it's George who keeps everything running smoothly. My husband is a most remarkable man.' Her expression, as she spoke of him, revealed her pride and happiness. 'I was – I *am* – very fortunate.'

This poignant echo of her own recent feelings sent Kerenza's thoughts back to the night she and Nicholas Penrose had been formally introduced: the night of the Antrims' party.

Looking into his eyes, inexplicably deserted by her hard-won poise, she saw his polite smile fade. She took his proffered hand and, as his fingers closed over hers, experienced for the first time in her nineteen years the quaking thrill of sexual attraction. During that first dance she talked too much while he said almost nothing. When it ended she was terrified he would walk away and not return. But he did, regularly throughout the evening, as if drawn by a magnet. With other partners she smiled and responded just as she should to their remarks, but could not resist scanning the crowd for his broad shoulders and dark head.

She talked lightly of commonplace matters as befitted a public occasion. But each time their eyes met a far more complex exchange was taking place. And the deepening intensity of his stare made words superfluous. The crowd, music and laughter receded into the distance. Held fast in his gaze, trembling on the brink of the unknown, a moment's fear was vanquished by heart-racing anticipation.

Then someone called his name and he was forced to turn away. The abrupt return to reality had left her shaken and disoriented, but she had glimpsed, tasted, *lived* emotions she had not known existed.

That night he had filled her dreams. Next morning, when Minnie brought her hot chocolate, also on the tray was a small bunch of winter pansies. The accompanying card thanked her for an *unforgettable* evening, and was signed simply, *Nick*.

During the next three weeks they saw each other almost every evening at balls, parties, suppers and dances. Never in her life had she known such happiness. Walking along Market Street the day after a Royal Navy frigate arrived in Falmouth with dispatches from the Mediterranean, she saw Nick coming towards her. Heart leaping, smiling her delight, she quickened her pace. *And he had walked straight past.*

Flinching at the relived pain, she slammed a mental door on shattered hopes that had proved so hollow. 'Your husband will be relieved to have you back.'

Judith nodded. 'And I will be glad to get home.' A brief spasm of anxiety crossed her features as she rested a gloved hand on the curve of her belly, barely visible beneath the folds of her velvet pelisse.

Kerenza touched her arm. 'It won't take long, perhaps two weeks. Maybe less, if the wind remains westerly.'

In the meantime, Nick had made it clear he had no wish to speak to her. That being the case she was free to ignore him. *Only it wasn't that simple.* Already Judith and Maggot had noted the air of strain. How long before her father and the other passengers noticed it too? What then?

Her head aching with questions to which she had no answers, Kerenza stared at choppy water that sparkled like sapphires in the sunshine as the packet passed the lead-covered elm pole marking the dangerous Black Rock, and headed out of Falmouth Bay.

Later, after they had returned to the cabin and unpacked their bedding, Kerenza offered to make up both cots.

Judith shook her head. 'It's kind of you, Kerenza, but I do not expect you to take on the duties of a maid.'

'I know that, ma'am – Judith,' she amended hurriedly, as her companion frowned. 'But this cabin is rather cramped. And – well – with the greatest respect, your present condition does mean you take up more space than I do, as well as being less agile. So would it not be more comfortable if you were to rest for a moment on one of the trunks and let me make up both our beds?'

Judith burst out laughing. 'How can I argue with such tact, or such common sense?'

Later, just before dinnertime, Kerenza left Judith tidying her hair and went to knock on the door of her father's cabin. There was no response, and no sound from within. Glancing towards the closed door leading to the captain's quarters she recalled Broad's warning not to knock unless invited, and debated what to do next. She had not seen her father since his unexpected arrival at her

66

grandmother's. Were it not for the fact that the steward had confirmed it, she would have begun to wonder if he were actually on board. Suddenly the captain's door opened and Nick emerged.

Kerenza flinched. After an instant's frozen silence both spoke at once.

'What–?'

'I was–'

The frown lines creasing his forehead and bracketing his stern mouth deepened as he gestured abruptly for her to continue.

She took a quick breath and folded her hands so he should not see their tremor. 'I was looking for my father.'

'He is dining with the captain.' He was clearly angry, and containing it with difficulty. But whether the cause was her father, the captain, or the fact that he had been forced to speak to her, she had no way of knowing. Questions clamoured but she held them back. If she did not ask, she would not face the ignominy of him denying her answers.

'I see. Thank you.' Turning, she started down the passage and after an instant, heard the clang of his boots on the brass stairs. Heart pounding, she was forced to stop as Judith emerged just in front of her.

'Did you see him?'

Kerenza was grateful for the dimness in the passage. 'Yes–' *Her father. Judith meant her father.* 'No, I didn't. I'm informed he's dining with the captain.'

Accepting this with a nod, Judith walked ahead. Kerenza followed, tension cramping her stomach.

The savoury smell of cooking was strong, but she had no appetite. Yet somehow she must eat. Just to survive this voyage would demand every ounce of strength she possessed.

On the right of the narrow saloon were two closed doors. At the far end the passage continued through another door currently fastened back. To her left a long table was surrounded on three sides by benches with backs and seats of brown padded leather. Tucked under the open side of the table was a single chair. A middle-aged man and woman were already seated on the long bench. The man struggled to his feet, swaying with the schooner's dip and rise.

The dark broadcloth of his frock coat, waistcoat and breeches proclaimed sober respectability.

Judith extended her hand. 'Good afternoon, Mr–?'

'Woodrow, ma'am. May I present my wife?' He turned to the stout woman. 'Betsy, my dear–'

'Lady Russell,' Betsy Woodrow gushed, smiling widely. 'We never expected to find ourselves in such august company.'

'Do not let it alarm you, Mrs Woodrow. I daresay we shall all survive the encounter.' A diplomatic smile softened the slight briskness in Judith's tone.

Uncertainty shadowed Betsy Woodrow's expression for a moment then she threw up her hands and twittered, 'Oh, Lady Russell, how droll.' Her gaze shifted. 'And you' – she looked Kerenza up and down – 'must be Miss Vyvyan.'

'Mrs Woodrow, Mr Woodrow.' Kerenza bobbed a curtsy then, quickly cupping Judith's elbow as

68

the ship plunged, guided her to the seat at the top of the table.

'You're travelling with your father, I believe?' Betsy's eyes were bright and hard, reminding Kerenza of jet beads.

'I am,' Kerenza replied, and returned to the remaining seat.

'We have not yet had the pleasure of making his acquaintance. No doubt he will be along directly.'

'No, ma'am. He's dining with the captain.'

Betsy frowned. 'Surely the captain will be joining us here?'

'Not today.'

Nick's voice behind her made Kerenza's heart lurch painfully.

'Good afternoon. My name is Penrose.' He made a brief bow. 'My apologies for not welcoming you aboard personally.'

'Surely it is the captain's duty–' Betsy Woodrow began.

'No, ma'am.' Nick didn't let her finish. 'The captain's first responsibility is to the ship, not the passengers.' As Betsy's eyebrows disappeared into the frizzy curls adorning her forehead, he addressed her husband.

'Mr Woodrow? I understand you are a man of the cloth, sir?'

Kerenza saw Donald Woodrow's hunched shoulders relax. 'I am, sir. May I present my wife? Betsy, my dear, Mr Penrose is–' He hesitated, glancing apologetically at Nick. 'I beg your pardon, but not being acquainted with shipboard terminology I find myself at a disadvantage. How should I describe you?'

69

'I am the senior deck officer.'

'My, my,' Betsy Woodrow simpered, a hand fluttering to the pillowy swell of a bosom swathed in frills and folds of snowy muslin over a dark grey gown that emphasized her high colour. 'What an important position for one so young.' Her shiny face dimpled but the smile did not reach her eyes.

'Age is no measure of experience, ma'am. But between us, *Kestrel*'s officers may claim over seventy years' sea time.'

'There you are, my dear,' Donald Woodrow reassured his wife. 'Did I not tell you there was nothing to worry about.'

Ignoring him, Betsy leaned towards Nick. 'When we came aboard, there was another' – distaste puckered her mouth – 'person on the deck. What is his position?'

Glancing involuntarily at Nick, Kerenza saw his grip on the chair back tighten sufficiently to turn his knuckles white. But he remained calm, if mildly impatient. 'Mrs Woodrow, prior to sailing there would be upward of *twenty* men–'

'I don't mean the crew,' she cut in. 'I was referring to the foreign person, whose uniform, I confess myself astonished to see, is similar to your own.'

'Ah. That is the second mate, my deputy.'

'Your deputy?' Betsy's expression mirrored shock and disapproval. 'But he is–'

'Older than me? Indeed he is, though by a few years only.' Nick's tone remained light, but the underlying note of warning sent a chill down Kerenza's spine. Betsy either did not hear, or chose to ignore it.

'I was going to say he's not English.'

'Indeed, ma'am. As you so rightly observe, he is not English, though I understand he has English blood in his ancestry. Of greater importance to me is his gift for reading winds, tides and currents. He is the finest sailor I've ever met, and I consider myself exceptionally fortunate to have his knowledge at my disposal.'

'If he's that good,' Betsy Woodrow remarked waspishly, 'I cannot help but wonder why he is not commanding a ship of his own.'

'He was. Until it was shot to pieces by the French and sank under him,' Nick replied. Then as Betsy Woodrow's mouth pursed, he turned to address Judith. 'Lady Russell, I trust you are as comfortable as circumstances permit? No doubt you would have preferred a single cabin–'

She waved his concern aside. 'With none available the matter is academic.' Glancing at Kerenza, she smiled warmly. 'Nor can I regret it, for Miss Vyvyan has proved to be delightful company.'

'Then you are fortunate, ma'am.' His undertone of bitterness stopped Kerenza's breath like a blow. As he pulled out the chair and sat down, heat rushed to her cheeks. She bent her head, feverishly hoping her flush would be attributed to shyness. Was this a foretaste of what she might expect for the next six weeks? *How would she cope?*

'These little brass rails around the edge of the table are very inconvenient,' Betsy complained.

'On the contrary,' Judith said, 'I can safely promise that in a few days you will be very glad of them. Speaking for myself, I prefer my food on my plate and my plate on the table rather than in

71

my lap.'

'You speak for all of us, I'm sure, Lady Russell.' Donald Woodrow's smile was anxious.

'Ah, Broad.' Nick greeted the passengers' steward as he staggered in bearing a tray containing a platter of sliced ham, separate dishes of boiled potatoes, carrots and cabbage, and a small bowl of mustard.

'What's this?' Betsy Woodrow demanded. 'I expected a hot dinner.'

'The veg is hot, madam,' Broad replied, unloading the dishes.

'But that meat is cold. So what is that savoury smell?'

'That's the crew's dinner, madam. Boiled salt pork and split peas. 'Course, if you was to prefer that to this 'ere cold ham–'

'No, the ham will do.'

'Right, madam.'

'Thank you, Broad. We will manage now.' Nick said.

'As you wish, Mr Penrose.' Taking the empty tray, the steward withdrew.

'These vegetables don't look very hot to me,' Betsy huffed. 'Lady Russell, may I pass you the–'

'No, please,' Judith said hastily. 'Do help yourself, Mrs Woodrow.'

'Well, if you're sure,' Betsy simpered, and spooned a lavish helping from every dish on to her plate. Shuddering, her husband looked away quickly.

'Is your journey for business or pleasure, sir?' Nick enquired.

'Some family business requires our attention,'

Betsy answered before her husband could respond. Mesmerized, Kerenza watched as she took thick slices of pink ham liberally marbled with fat then topped them with a large dollop of mustard. 'My husband is a dedicated man, Mr Penrose. Too much so for his own wellbeing.'

'Please, my dear,' Donald Woodrow's smile grew more nervous. His wife ignored him.

'The drawback to a generous nature is that people tend to take advantage. Sometimes they want more than he is free to give. Isn't that so, Donald?'

His smile was a grimace of shame and desperation. 'I don't think–'

'That is part of your trouble, Donald,' Betsy chided, with syrupy sweetness. 'You don't think. And you are far too willing to believe the best of people.'

He looked at her for a moment, and Kerenza glimpsed the light of battle raging in his tired eyes. But the spark died. 'As a minister,' he said quietly, 'how can I do otherwise?'

'Do you have children, Mrs Woodrow?' Judith enquired with a deftness that filled Kerenza with relief and admiration.

A martyred smile twisted Betsy's mouth. 'Unfortunately we have not been blessed. I can only conclude that God had a purpose in denying me the joys of motherhood. And that was to ensure I would be free to help my husband in his work.'

Kerenza shot a glance at Donald Woodrow. Round-shouldered, wretchedly miserable, he stared at his empty plate.

'People have no idea how much organization is

73

required for a parish to function as it should.' Glancing from Nick to Kerenza, as if daring them to argue, she focused her gaze and her attention on Judith. 'Naturally, Lady Russell, you will understand that I refer to a properly run parish. Of course there are plenty of the other kind. Far too many.' She sighed, 'But I suppose one must be charitable.'

'Indeed, one must,' Judith agreed gravely. 'For your vision of an ordered world is one to which few would aspire.'

As Donald Woodrow glanced up, visibly startled, and Nick raised his hand to mask a sudden bout of coughing, Kerenza saw Betsy's grease-slicked lips purse in a smirk of pride and satisfaction. *She thought the remark a compliment.*

The meal continued. While Betsy chewed noisily and Judith drew the minister into conversation, Kerenza cut a sliver of ham and a small portion of vegetables into tiny pieces. The man she hated for the pain he had caused her, who had been the first to touch her heart, was sitting barely an arm's length away eating with swift efficiency. And though her throat felt so stiff and tight she was terrified she might choke she knew she must do the same.

Quickly clearing his plate, Nick excused himself to return topside. His departure allowed Kerenza to relax and as her shoulders dropped she realized she was aching all over from accumulated tension.

'Would you mind terribly if I had a little nap?' Judith said, when they returned to the cabin. 'Though my condition has brought me great joy,

I do find the constant movement of the ship very tiring.'

'Of course you must rest,' Kerenza said quickly. 'I shall go to the saloon and write to my grandmother.'

'You would do far better to go up on deck and enjoy the fresh air.'

'Later, perhaps. The watch is changing, and I certainly would not want to get in the way.' Nor, for the moment, could she face another encounter with Nick.

'My dear girl, you cannot spend the next two weeks down here. You need company, conversation. If Maggot is free, ask him to tell you about Tangier.' She dropped her voice. 'Then you need have no concerns about being cornered by Mrs Woodrow.' Easing herself down onto the pillow she sighed. 'Poor Mr Woodrow. I hope it was worth the punishment.'

'What do you mean?' Kerenza covered her with a blanket.

Beckoning her closer, Judith whispered, 'I suspect Mr Woodrow is being hauled off to visit family in Gibraltar to distance him from one of his lady parishioners.'

Kerenza gasped. 'But – but he's a minister.'

'He is first a man, Kerenza,' Judith reminded softly. 'A good man who is constantly required to offer comfort to others yet clearly receives little himself. I do not think for one moment that he has done anything to discredit his calling. But though his lapse is probably minor, I fear he will spend the rest of his life paying for it.'

Kerenza was awed by Judith's perception, and

by her compassion. 'Do you really think so?'

'I am sure of it. I have met other women of Betsy Woodrow's type. Women of narrow mind and strong will who seek to impose their values on all around them. Utterly convinced that they alone are right, they have no conception of the damage they do or the hurt they inflict. Such women spend their lives avidly seeking sin, and finding it in the most innocent exchange.'

Kerenza shivered. The situation between her and Nick was already difficult. The very thought of Betsy Woodrow watching, asking questions or jumping to conclusions, demanding denial or explanation – no, it would be insupportable.

'Then perhaps it would be better if I do not talk to Maggot. I am quite used to my own company–'

'No, that will not do!' Judith pushed herself up on one elbow.

'I told you only so that you may be on your guard. Surely you will want to learn something of Tangier? Who better than Maggot to answer your questions.' She patted Kerenza's hand. 'Go along. I shall enjoy a little sleep and see you later.'

Chapter Five

Sliding on to the nearest seat, Kerenza opened the small box that had once belonged to her grandfather. She took out the pen shaft and fitted a nib, then unscrewed the top of the squat inkbottle. Opening the leather case she dipped the pen and after heading the sheet *Packet ship Kestrel*, and the date, and wrote *Dearest Nana*.

The clatter of boots on the brass stairs then brisk footsteps in the passage brought her head up with a jerk and her heart leaping into her throat. Shutting the writing case she dropped the pen, which promptly rolled under the fiddle rails at the edge of the table and fell to the floor as Maggot walked in.

Picking it up he handed it to her with a smile. 'Where is Lady Russell?'

'She's resting.'

He pulled a wry face. 'Not good time for sleep. Will be much noise.' The door to the galley and fo'c'sle opened and Broad peered in.

'Ready for your dinner, sir?'

'Yes. Very quick, please. Mr Penrose fire guns soon.'

Rolling his eyes, Broad disappeared.

'Guns?' Kerenza gulped. 'Are we being attacked?'

Pulling out the chair, Maggot sat down. 'No, no. Is nothing to worry.'

Kerenza released a shaky breath. 'Then why–'

'New men in crew. They must learn.'

Broad reappeared with a tray and set it down in front of the second mate.

Kerenza gathered up her things. 'I'll leave you to your meal.'

'No. Please, you stay. Is business for your father in Tangier?' Picking up his knife and fork he began to eat.

'In a way,' Kerenza answered carefully. It was business that had taken her father, mother and sister to the Mediterranean a year earlier. Her father had wanted to ensure his trading agreements with Tangier would be maintained, despite the disruptive effects of the war with France. She turned the pen in her fingers. 'What is the city like?'

Swallowing his mouthful, Maggot grinned. 'Many things same like Falmouth. Lot of churches, and a castle, very big, on top of hill. But is also very different. Tangier has wall all around.' He shrugged. 'Is very broken now. Some people building houses on it and make gardens. Much of castle fall down. There is small market-place inside city and big market-place outside. People from mountain tribes come to the big market with camels and mules.'

Kerenza tried to picture the scene. 'What do they buy and sell?'

Maggot shrugged. 'Many things. Meat, fish, soap, sugar, also sandals, bowls, pots for cooking, cloth, silver. Women sell fruit. They sit in middle and all around are melons, tangerines, dates and raisins.' He grinned again. 'The women look very strange to you.'

'Why?'

'They wear hats made from straw.'

'What is so strange about a straw hat? I often wear one in summer.'

'Not like this. This one is very big.'

'How big?' Kerenza was fascinated.

'*Very* big. Bigger than this.' He stretched his arms wide. 'Hat is turned down at edge so no one see woman's face. And because hat is so big, is also making shade for the fruit.'

Kerenza smiled. 'What a very sensible idea.'

Sounds of suppressed argument were swiftly followed by a rattle and bang as the door was flung open. Betsy Woodrow stumbled in and clutched the frame for support. Maggot immediately rose to his feet and made a brief bow. Betsy ignored him.

'Ah, Miss Vyvyan, I thought I heard your voice. I am astonished to find you here alone.'

'But I am not alone,' Kerenza pointed out.

Shooting a glare of disapproval at Maggot, who had resumed his seat and was forking up the last of his meal, Betsy turned again to Kerenza.

'I mean, as I am sure you must be aware, that you are without female company.'

'I came in to write some letters,' Kerenza replied, indicating her writing case.

'And Lady Russell?'

'She is resting. Her condition–'

'Yes,' Betsy interrupted, raising a hand. 'I'm sure there is no need to elaborate, especially in front of–' She flapped a hand, disdaining even to glance in his direction.

'Maggot,' the second mate said helpfully. Standing up again he pushed his chair under the table. 'I go now. Miss Vyvyan, please you tell Lady Russell about the guns? Is not good for her to have shock–'

'*Guns?*' Betsy gasped. 'What guns?'

As she caught Maggot's eye and saw the gleam of mischief, Kerenza quickly bit her lip, for to smile would only increase Betsy's irritation and provoke further questions. 'It's nothing to worry about,' she reassured her, as Maggot departed.

79

'Apparently there are a number of new men in the crew, so Mr Penrose–' Just saying his name kindled a rush of warmth. *Please let it not reach her face.* 'Mr Penrose has ordered a practice firing of the guns.' Rising to her feet, she picked up her writing materials. 'I must go and warn Lady Russell.'

Sitting around the table a short time later, the Woodrows, Judith and Kerenza listened to the pounding of feet above their heads, the rumble of the wooden truck wheels, bellowed orders, and then the deafening thunder of cannons.

After more noise and shouts the ship began to change direction. Blocks squealed as ropes were loosed and others hauled in. There was a brief sensation of weightlessness as *Kestrel*'s head came up into the wind, then with a jerk her canvas filled and she surged forward on the opposite tack.

As the ship tilted over at an even greater angle the clang and clatter of pans falling in the galley was followed by a stream of curses. Betsy shrieked and clutched the edge of the table. Her husband cleared his throat before telling them all he was sure everything was just as it should be. Judith and Kerenza remained silent but clasped each other's hand as the guns roared again, not in unison but in a rolling cannonade that seemed to go on forever. When eventually it stopped no one moved. In the ear-ringing silence Kerenza waited. Above her head the sounds altered, losing their urgency. There was another brief hiatus as the ship returned to her original course.

She released her breath. 'I think they've finished.'

'So I should hope,' Betsy gasped, flapping a handkerchief in front of her face. 'Donald, fetch me my vinaigrette. I have such palpitations as you would not believe. It is quite intolerable that we should–'

'There is a war on, Mrs Woodrow,' Judith reminded her drily. 'For myself, I can only applaud Mr Penrose's foresight in preparing the crew for an eventuality I'm sure all of us hope will not occur. And now, I think I should welcome a little fresh air. Kerenza, would you be so kind as to accompany me?'

The following morning as the bright beady eyes swivelled toward her, Kerenza braced herself. Betsy's smile was a mere widening of the mouth, devoid of goodwill or humour.

'Are you not concerned, Miss Vyvyan?' she enquired with spurious concern, 'that we have been at sea four days now, and your father has not joined us for a single meal?'

'Not really, Mrs Woodrow.' Kerenza was finding the barbs easier to deflect. For each morning before they left the cabin Judith whispered bracing encouragement in terms that, could he hear them, would surely horrify her diplomat husband. 'My father has not been well. Just at present he finds being in company something of a strain.'

'Is that so?' Betsy's tone was waspish. 'Yet he is able to spend much of each day with the captain to no ill effect.' She snorted her disapproval. 'And that's another thing: no one else has even *seen* the captain let alone spoken to him. It seems a very odd way to run a ship. A captain should be *visible*. How else is he to retain the respect and control of his crew?'

'I would imagine a successful and far-sighted captain employs officers in whom he may place total trust,' Judith replied, carefully lowering herself on to the bench closest to the door. The Woodrows were in their usual place, their backs to the ship's side, so Kerenza moved to the far end of the table facing the stern.

'Well, I still think–' Betsy began, then stopped, her attention diverted by the sound of footsteps in the passage.

As Nick entered the saloon his gaze caught Kerenza's, but instantly he looked away. She saw his fist clench and felt her own heart contract. *She had to stop reacting like this.*

'Ah, Mr Penrose–' Betsy began.

'Good morning.' His tone and manner were abrupt, preoccupied. The smart uniform he had been wearing the day they sailed had been replaced by an old blue jacket bleached across the shoulders by strong sun, scuffed unpolished boots, and dark breeches that were snagged and salt stained. Windblown hair fell across a frowning forehead, there were shadows like purple thumb-prints below his eyes, and his weathered tan was blotched with the pallor of exhaustion. But he had shaved and the faint fragrance of his soap, borne on the draught from the passage, wrenched Kerenza's heart. As she fought crowding memories, he closed the door.

'Broad will be bringing your breakfast, so I'll be brief.'

'Will you not be joining us?' Judith inquired pleasantly.

'No, ma'am.'

'Really, Mr Penrose, this is too–' Betsy turned crossly to her husband as he touched her arm. 'What *is* it, Donald?'

Ignoring her, Nick continued, 'I thought you would wish to be warned. The weather is changing, and that will mean rough seas.'

Kerenza had been vaguely aware of subtle alterations in the ship's motion. Her sleep had been disturbed by an increase in the number and volume of creaks and groans from the timbers. Now, she understood the reason for the additional activity on deck during the night.

Anxiety flitted across Judith's face as she caught Kerenza's eye. But her calm demeanor gave no hint of concern as she looked up at Nick. 'How long is it likely to last?'

He shrugged. 'I'm sorry, it's not possible to be specific. Maggot thinks a couple of days. But it could be longer.' As Kerenza and Judith exchanged a wry glance he continued, addressing the table at large, 'You may go top-side until dinnertime. But after that, for safety's sake, I must ask you to remain below. One more thing: anyone who does decide to venture on deck this morning does so at his or her own risk, and is to remain well aft of the mainmast so as not to get in the way of the crew.'

Kerenza guessed this was aimed at her, since she spent more time up there than any of the others did.

'You should prepare yourselves for some discomfort.' He turned to leave, but paused in the doorway. 'With respect, Mr Woodrow, I'd appreciate it if you would stay out of the fo'c'sle.'

Donald Woodrow's ears turned red, and Kerenza saw his throat work. 'Of course, Mr Penrose. Please accept my apol—'

'Mr Penrose,' Betsy censured Nick, ignoring her husband, 'even the lowliest of men has a right to the comfort of God's Word.'

Kerenza had assumed the minister's visits to the fo'c'sle were his own idea, a brief escape. But he had obviously been bullied into it.

'True,' Nick snapped. 'But only at a time deemed appropriate by the captain or myself.' He turned again to the minister. 'Mr Woodrow, would you be willing to conduct a short service on Sunday morning, perhaps an hour before dinner? I'm sure the men would appreciate it. Some of them, anyway.'

Donald Woodrow's visible strain dissolved in a smile of pleasure. 'Indeed, sir, I should be delighted.'

With an abrupt nod, Nick spun on his heel, apparently oblivious to Betsy's muttered condemnation of his manners and appearance. As he disappeared towards the companionway, the door at the forward end of the saloon opened. Accompanied by the smell of hot fat, Broad entered carrying a large tray from which he unloaded a heaped platter of fried pork strips coated in breadcrumbs, a dish of boiled eggs, a plate of bread and butter, a large pot of coffee, and a smaller one of tea.

The faint clang of Nick's boots on the

companionway was followed a few moments later by the bosun shouting orders and the thump of running feet.

Avid and greedy, Betsy Woodrow began piling fried pork on to her plate. Kerenza looked away. Taking a boiled egg she saw Judith grimace slightly then reach for a slice of bread and butter.

An hour later they were back in the cabin, Judith sitting on the edge of the lower cot while Kerenza knelt in front of her trunk refolding and tidying the contents. The motion of the ship had become far more pronounced, and the cabin sole was tilted at an angle that meant to reach the door required a walk uphill.

'It's no good,' Judith said. 'It is probably very weak and self-indulgent of me, but I shall have to lie down.'

Kerenza looked round. 'Are you feeling ill?'

'Not exactly,' Judith sounded unsure. 'But the way the ship is pitching – it's so difficult to be comfortable.'

'Then of course you should lie down. You must not risk a fall. Here, let me help you.' Removing Judith's shoes she straightened up, holding on to the wooden frame. Seizing her own pillow from the upper cot she bent and tucked it behind Judith's back. 'Is that better?'

'Oh, indeed it is. Thank you so much.' She lowered her voice. 'How Mrs Woodrow could eat all that fat–' She broke off with a shudder. 'I am so grateful to you for asking about Gibraltar. At least our conversation spared us having to watch.'

'But when someone makes so much noise,' Kerenza whispered, pulling down her blanket

85

and covering Judith with it, 'it is very difficult to remain unaware. In fact, it was so *awful* I was afraid–' She stopped.

'Of what?'

'I'm ashamed to admit it.'

'An attack of giggles?'

Kerenza nodded. 'Isn't that terrible?'

'Indeed, it is.' Judith scolded. 'Quite appalling.' Then she patted Kerenza's hand. 'And I should know for my tongue is bitten almost in half. However, we may be justly proud that despite intense provocation we did not succumb.' Her sigh ended in a tiny moan. 'Do you think Broad might have anything to dispel a slight queasiness?'

Kerenza reached into her leather bag. 'We need not trouble Broad. I have something here that will help. Actually, I have an astonishing number of things.' Opening the wooden box she drew out the package of ginger-root. 'Everyone in the village was very generous. In fact so many people pressed their favourite remedies for seasickness upon me that I'm sure I could set up a shop. Anyway, it's good that you managed to eat the bread and butter because ginger is more effective if you have something in your stomach.' She stood up. 'I'm just going to fetch some hot water.'

While Judith was drinking the prepared infusion, there was a knock on the cabin door. Kerenza opened it to find Billy, the ship's boy, with the slop bucket. Telling him to wait outside, and shushing Judith's protests, she quickly emptied the chamber pot, rinsed her hands, added the washing water from the basin, then passed the bucket back to him.

'Oh, that's better,' Judith breathed, handing over the empty cup and lying down again. 'Very soothing. My dear, I feel so guilty.'

'Please, don't,' Kerenza begged. 'When I imagine what this voyage would have been like for me if I'd had to share with someone like Mrs Woodrow.'

'Heaven forbid!' Judith made a fending-off gesture. 'It doesn't bear thinking about.'

'Indeed. So please don't apologize. Truly, there's no need. Try to sleep a little. And if you can't, well, think about your husband and the welcome you will receive. He'll be so happy to have you home.'

Judith smiled up at her. 'You are a very special young woman.'

Kerenza shook her head; glad the lamp behind her kept her face in shadow. *Not special enough.* 'I shall leave you to rest now.' Pulling on her hat, she picked up her grandfather's heavy cloak and slipped out, closing the door quietly. She paused to fasten the cloak, staggering as the schooner rose and plunged. The air in the passage was colder but less stuffy, and the sounds of the ship were louder.

At the bottom of the brass stairs, drawn towards the daylight after the cabin's gloom, she hesitated, glancing towards her father's cabin. He must know she was on board. Surely he would realize she had tried to see him? The fact that he had made no attempt to seek her out could only mean he did not wish to. So what would be the point of knocking?

He was her father. Yet she had hardly recognized

87

him the night he had arrived so unexpectedly at her grandmother's house. He had said he needed her. But it seemed that until they reached Tangier he had no desire to see her and preferred to spend his time with Captain Penrose. Though considering their similar experiences, it was hardly to be wondered at if the two men derived comfort from each other's company. For who else could appreciate or truly understand what they had suffered?

To feel slighted was foolish. It was just that she had hoped the voyage would provide an opportunity to get to know her father again, to overcome their estrangement. She knew only a fraction of what he had been through – was *still* going through. For not until her mother and sister had been rescued would his nightmare end. So instead of condemning his behaviour, she should try to make allowances. But in order to do that she needed to see him, talk to him.

As she lifted her hand, anxiety gripped her. *Was this such a good idea?* Dismissing her doubts, she tapped on the door. She waited a moment then tapped again. This time she was sure. More a growl than recognizable words, at least it proved he was there. She reached for the handle and realized her heart was galloping and her throat paper-dry. Why was she so nervous? He was her father.

Turning the handle she opened the door, recoiling from the gust of fetid air pungent with brandy fumes and the sour-apple smell of the chamber pot. The cot filled half of the narrow cabin. At the far end Kerenza saw a shaking hand emerge and push aside the greatcoat flung across as an additional blanket. William Vyvyan's face appeared, pallid and creased. 'Wha'?' he mumbled, puffy eyes narrowed against the light

'It's me, Papa, Kerenza.'

He groaned, withdrawing his head like a tortoise.

She stood frozen. Was he unwell? The smell of brandy told its own story. But was it more than that? Should she offer help? But to do what? She swallowed. 'Papa?'

'Go away. Get *out!*'

The rebuff was as brutal and shocking as a slap. Quickly she pulled the door shut and stood, trembling, her heart hammering against her ribs. She could not return to the cabin without disturbing Judith. And should Betsy discover her in the saloon without a book, writing materials, or even some sewing, the questions would amount to an inquisition. She could not face it.

Grasping the rail with one hand and the skirts of her cloak in the other, she ran quickly up the brass stairs to the deck. Above her, low grey cloud with a strange apricot tint raced across the sky obscuring the few remaining patches of blue.

As she stepped out of the companionway the biting wind snatched her breath. But it cooled her burning face, tasting clean and sweet after the foulness below. Holding on to the hatch she glanced around. Two men in the ratlines high above the deck were trying to free a tangle of wood and canvas, all that remained of the main topsail, while others put reefs in the two huge fore and aft sails. Nick's warning not to get in the crew's way echoed in her head. A seaman at the huge wheel nodded briefly, then switched his gaze to the compass in front of him.

A door opened on the lower side of the curve-backed structure behind him and Maggot emerged. Seeing her, his swarthy face creased in a grin and he came forward, sure-footed as a cat despite the packet's leap and plunge.

'You want fresh air, yes? Sun gone, but no rain yet.'

Not trusting her voice she simply nodded, and took his proffered arm. Passing the low skylight behind the binnacle housing the compass, a movement below caught her eye. She was looking down into the captain's cabin. But her heart tripped on a beat at the sight of Nick bent over a chart-strewn table trying to rub the tension from the back of his neck.

As she stepped into the lee of the oddly shaped hut, the roar lessened and the sensation of being pushed by a giant hand suddenly ceased. The wind in *Kestrel*'s sails had tilted the schooner so that the heaving foam-streaked water looked awfully close. But this small space offered greater protection than any other part of the deck.

'Is safe here,' Maggot said. Studying her, he frowned. 'You sick?'

'No.' Kerenza shook her head and quickly wiped an errant tear from her cheek. 'It's just the wind. I'm fine. Thank you.' To distract him she indicated the oddly shaped hut. 'What *is* this?'

'It protect man at wheel. One side is store for paint, lamps and oil. In other side is' – his glance slid away for a moment as he struggled –'is jakes

90

... muzpot ... for men.'

Realization dawned. 'Of course,' Kerenza said quickly, feeling herself blush. She recalled over-hearing her grandfather complain about having to organize a *bucket and chuck it* latrine shelter for officers and crew on deck in order to avoid offending the sensibilities of female passengers. She sought hurriedly for another question. 'Why is the back curved like that?'

'Sometimes waves very big, very strong. If back straight like front,' Maggot shrugged, 'sea would smash, and wash away.' He glanced along the deck then back to her. 'I go now. Come back short time. Yes? You wait.' It was a warning. As she nodded, he bowed and left.

But relief at being able to stop pretending all was well was swiftly followed by despair. She felt so dreadfully *alone*.

Judith Russell's appreciation made performing small tasks for her a pleasure not a hardship. So resisting the urge to confide was becoming ever more difficult. Yet resist she must, for Judith was already burdened with recent bereavement plus the anxiety and discomfort of making this voyage so close to her confinement.

But on top of Nick's implacable coldness and Betsy Woodrow's constant sniping, her father's rejection was almost too much to bear. Kerenza held on to the rail, swaying with the movement of the ship as scalding tears slid down her cheeks. Sobs convulsed her. Biting hard on her lower lip she choked them down. She must not let go. Then she heard her grandmother's voice.

Come now, Kerenza. That's enough. The words

were brisk and crystal clear. But behind the sternness Kerenza divined the love that for the past four years had been helping to rebuild her shattered self-esteem. *This is not an easy situation. But you surely did not expect it to be. For occasional relief from over-stretched nerves a little weep is an excellent remedy, but to become a watering pot will swiftly inspire scorn rather than sympathy.*

'Miss Vyvyan?'

Startled, for she had not heard anyone approach, she jerked round. Nick stood frowning down at her, blocking both her view of the deck and her escape.

Chapter Six

Fizzing shock tightened every nerve. She felt briefly faint as blood drained from her face then rushed back engulfing her in heat. Turning her head away, she raised the gloved hand furthest from him, swiftly wiped her wet face, swallowed hard, then faced him again.

'Mr Penrose?'

'If you are unwell, it would be wiser–'

'I am perfectly well, thank you.'

His glance lingered on her tear-stained cheeks. His expression was set and hard, giving nothing away, but a muscle jumped at the side of his jaw. 'Then may I suggest you spend some time with your father? Were you to do so, he might feel less need to seek the captain's company.'

The implication that she was neglectful brought Kerenza's chin up. 'If the captain does not desire my father's company, surely he is capable of saying so?'

'You *know* the captain is not a well man.' The rage and pain in his piercing gaze unnerved her, for it was far greater than his accusation warranted.

'Indeed, I am sorry for it. But if you, the senior officer and his nephew, are unable to influence the captain's behaviour, why do you assume I have any chance whatsoever of influencing my father?'

He avoided answering and instead threw another accusation. 'You are, of course, aware that your father brought a considerable amount of brandy aboard?'

She stiffened. 'I was not. Nor am I responsible for my father's actions. Mr Penrose, I should tell you that my first meeting with my father since this ship left Falmouth took place less than half an hour ago.'

Grim-faced, he stared at her. 'Why so long? Did you not–?'

'I have tried every day. But my father was never in his cabin; he was with the captain. And as I was warned by the steward not to knock on the captain's door, what was I supposed to do?'

His face tightened. 'You say you talked with your father a short time ago?'

'To say we talked would be an exaggeration. When I knocked on his door he – he asked to be left alone.'

'And you obeyed? Did it not occur to you that he might be in need of–'

'Whatever my father currently has need of,' Kerenza cried, 'it is certainly not me. He made that abundantly clear.' The injustice of being blamed for something that she could not have prevented even had she been aware broke down what remained of her self-possession. 'You may believe me, Mr Penrose,' she said bitterly, 'when I tell you that I have no more wish to be aboard this ship than you have to see me here.'

The skin around his nostrils whitened. 'In that case, why did you come?'

'Because my father asked – no – *demanded* that I accompany him. He made it impossible for me to refuse. He needs me to take care of my mother and sister on the voyage home.'

'Where are they now?'

'I understand they are at the governor's palace in Tangier.'

'They are guests of the governor?'

'No, they are his prisoners.'

He stared at her. 'I beg your pardon?'

'My mother and sister are being held for ransom,' Kerenza said wearily. 'Surely you knew?'

'No, I did not. Why should I? With only three days in which to arrange repairs and get the ship ready for sea again, I had little time ashore, and none to listen to gossip.' He stopped, as if jabbed by an unwelcome thought, then continued, 'My sole interest in the passengers was to learn how many would be aboard, and to ensure adequate provisions for them as well as the crew. I had no idea of names or identities until I collected the final list with the mail just before we sailed.'

When you became unusually short-tempered and

94

uncommunicative. Kerenza bit her tongue. She had said too much already.

His frown deepened. 'I don't understand. The British Government is on friendly terms with Morocco. The sultan, Mulai Suleiman, and the Dey of Algiers have both agreed treaties that allow British naval and merchant ships sailing to the Mediterranean to purchase a pass guaranteeing protection from attack by pirates or privateers. So why is the governor holding your mother and sister?'

'I don't know,' Kerenza cried helplessly. 'I know only what my grandmother pieced together from what little my father told her the night he arrived back in Cornwall. Perhaps you have forgotten,' *or choose not to remember.* Betraying heat climbed her throat and flooded her cheeks but she forced herself to carry on. 'My parents and sister left Falmouth for Tangier a year ago. My father had chartered a ship to carry a cargo of wool and cotton goods to trade for a return cargo of fruit, wine, hides and olive oil.'

'There is nothing wrong with my memory.' It seemed from his grim expression that he remembered far more than he wished to.

Nor mine. She looked away, too bruised to risk further hurt. 'On the outward voyage the ship was captured by an Algerian privateer. My mother collapsed with a fever, and my father persuaded the Algerian captain that she might have smallpox. The captain put my father ashore in Algiers and he was imprisoned there. Then the wound he had sustained during the attack became infected. I understand that when he recovered, my father

95

struck some kind of bargain with the Algerian captain. When eventually he arrived back in Tangier he was told that my mother and sister were guests of the governor, who would be pleased to return them to him on payment of a substantial gift, the size of which would increase the longer they remained in the palace. I don't know how he got back to England, only that he arrived in Falmouth the same day that you returned from Lisbon.' She paused for breath. 'He went directly from the ship to the packet office and learned from the agent that the next Gibraltar packet was not due to leave for another two weeks. But *Kestrel* would sail for Gibraltar within three days. My father had no choice, and nor did I.'

She gripped the rail, staring through clouds of fine spray at the heaving masses of dark water marbled with foam.

'Miss Vyvyan.' Nick's voice was hoarse with strain. 'I need – there is something I would – I believe you are acquainted with my cousin, Lieutenant Jeremy Ashworth?'

She turned her head, gazing at him blankly. 'I beg your pardon?' *What had that to do with anything?* His question brought back memories long-since buried beneath far more important events.

Alone among her group of friends and acquaintances attending the supper-dance that evening, she had not been instantly impressed by the tall blond 3rd lieutenant. Beside her, Sophie almost swooned as he entered the room. 'Kerenza, look! It's Lieutenant Ashworth. His father is captain of the *Hercules*, you know. Is he not wonderfully handsome?'

Perhaps because her heart belonged totally and irrevocably to Nick, Kerenza was able to observe the newcomer with greater objectivity. 'To be sure, he has regular features.'

'Regular? Oh, Kerenza!' Sophie stamped her foot in intense irritation. 'Is that all you can say? I swear he is the handsomest man I have ever seen. See how his hair gleams?' Sophie sighed dreamily. 'Like gold sovereigns. And that smile!'

'Indeed,' Kerenza murmured. 'He is all charm.' *And self-importance.* Though of similar height, he lacked Nick's breadth of shoulder. He was air and quicksilver to Nick's earth and iron. She sighed, wishing Nick had been able to come. He had planned to. But in a hastily written note delivered to her that afternoon he apologized that an urgent family matter made his attendance impossible. *His uncle, or his mother?* However he hoped to see her very soon.

She had read the note several times, sensing behind the careful phrasing all his frustration and disappointment. The childhood loss of his father and consequent early responsibility had enhanced Nick's natural reserve. But his inability to frame flowery compliments did not indicate lack of feeling. On the contrary, often when their eyes met what she read in his gaze made words not merely inadequate but unnecessary.

She would have willingly remained at home herself. But having accepted the invitation, good manners demanded she attend.

'Oh, Kerenza, he's looking this way.' Raising her fan so it masked the lower half of her face, Sophie fluttered it provocatively. 'I wish I had worn my

97

gown with the pearl rosettes. It is far prettier than this old rag. Oh,' she squeaked, 'he's coming over. Do you think he'll ask me to dance?' Kerenza had remained silent, wary without knowing why, yet not wanting to dash her friend's hopes.

Lieutenant Ashworth had bowed to them both. After dropping a curtsy Kerenza started to turn away as if to speak to another acquaintance, politely indicating to the lieutenant her lack of interest and expectation. But to Sophie's devastation it was Kerenza he asked to dance.

Caught by surprise, she had no time to think of an acceptable excuse. And before she could demur, he was leading her into the set where she felt her smile grow fixed as he boasted at length about the actions in which his ship had been involved. He cajoled her grandmother – who either did not notice or completely misinterpreted Kerenza's pleading glances – into allowing him to accompany them in to supper.

Though she knew herself the object of envious glances, Kerenza was not flattered. Her discomfort increased when, having introduced Nick's name into the conversation by informing her that Nick's mother and his own were sisters which made Nick his cousin, he then spent an astonishing amount of time comparing Nick's seagoing career unfavourably with his own.

Eventually she shook him off by appealing to his vanity: reminding him that he owed it to all the other young ladies present to spread his addresses more evenly. She returned to her grandmother, only to learn that he, had announced his intention to request permission to call on her.

'No, Nana, absolutely not. He is the most insufferable, conceited, odious–'

'I thought so too,' her grandmother agreed, stopping Kerenza in mid-rant. 'But had you liked him, I would have made an effort to be pleasant. Ah well.' She sighed. 'You may be easy, Kerenza. I shall ensure he pays his respects elsewhere.'

'Am I correct?' Nick's voice jolted her back to the present. 'You are acquainted with Lieutenant Ashworth?'

Kerenza thought fast. Good manners, and the family relationship existing between the two men, demanded she say nothing detrimental – even though Lieutenant Ashworth had dearly felt no such constraints. 'We have met,' she answered carefully.

'That's all? You *met?*'

'Yes. At the Roseworths' supper-dance.'

'As you and I met, at the Antrims' party' It was his first acknowledgement of what they had shared, but his tone chilled her with its bitterness.

Swallowing the lump in her throat, Kerenza shook her head. 'Oh no. You are mistaken. The two events could not have been more different.'

He stared hard at her, as if trying to see into her heart, read her thoughts, and she could feel tension emanating from him. 'Would you call him a friend?' As she started to shake her head, his eyes narrowed. 'Something more, perhaps?'

'No!' Her denial was immediate and she realized both her tone and expression betrayed her distaste. It could not be helped. 'We were introduced. He favoured me with his attention' – recalling his snide criticism rekindled her indignation – 'until persuaded he should not neglect the other young ladies. He indicated a wish to call on me. However, I preferred him not to do so.'

Nick's face was as grey and hard as granite. 'Indeed? Others remember it differently.'

Kerenza stared at him, bewildered. 'What others? I don't understand.'

'No?' His scepticism stung.

'No! Perhaps if you were to explain–'

'What point would it serve? Your recall of events is so different from my cousin's.'

He didn't believe her. She had yearned, ached, for a chance to talk to him, to find out what had happened, why he had changed. What had Lieutenant Ashworth to do with it? Unless – it was clear that the two cousins had talked and her name had been mentioned. But what had Lieutenant Ashworth said? And why would he so distort the truth? What did it matter now? Having nothing to hide, she had answered Nick's questions with total honesty. *He didn't believe her.*

She could scarcely breathe for the pain. Her eyes filled, but she tossed her head, blinking furiously. She would *not* break down in front of him. Dignity was all she had left. She met his gaze directly. 'I have no idea why your cousin should lie to you, Mr Penrose, but as you have chosen to believe him,' *and not me,* 'you are right: we have nothing more to say to one another.' She looked past him and saw the second mate. Having caught sight of Nick he was turning away. 'Maggot!' she cried desperately. 'Please – I want to go below.'

'Wait.' Nick reached out to steady her. 'I will escort–'

'No!' Kerenza recoiled. 'You have done enough.'

By nightfall the wind had risen to a full gale, whipping up high waves whose rolling tumbling crests filled the air with icy spray. It screamed through the rigging and buffeted the crew as they slid and staggered along the steeply angled deck.

Sending Maggot to the wheel with an able-seaman to help him, for it would take the strength of two to hold the packet to her course, Nick ordered both watches topside. Eventually his voice cracked from trying to shout above the deafening noise, and Nick had to use Billy to convey his orders to the bosun.

'Hold fast,' he warned, gripping the boy's bony shoulder. 'One hand for the ship and one for yourself.' And he had watched, tight-lipped, as the boy raced away trying to dodge the seas crashing in over the lee rail and swirling knee-deep along the deck.

He had brought down the fore-topsail immediately the main blew out. The gaffs on the fore and mainmasts had followed soon after. Now the schooner tore along under foresail and headsail, climbing steep, foam-veined mountains, careening down into the trough on the other side, only to face the slow, shuddering climb once more. It was exhausting and uncomfortable, but the ship was in no immediate danger.

A mocking cheer eased the tension when, after being confined for two hours in the cramped paint store preparing all the lamps, Ned Burley had eventually staggered out, splattered with oil and cursing angrily.

Handing over command to Maggot, who remained at the wheel, Nick went below. Hunger gnawed at his stomach and his eyes were sore from the salt spray. His first task after eating would be to write up the log. At the bottom of the companionway he struggled out of his tarpaulin coat and hung it on the hook, rubbing head and face with the towel Toy had left for him. He paused, glancing up. The sudden drumming indicated another torrential downpour.

Looping the towel round his neck, he started along the passage. Passing William Vyvyan's cabin, he saw again the expression on Kerenza's face as she told him her father had refused to see her despite insisting she come. Bewilderment he could understand, or surprise, even irritation. But she had been hurt, deeply hurt. Why? She had not lived with her parents for several years.

According to Kerenza, it was to manage the Danby house during her grandmother's illness that she had moved from Falmouth to Flushing. But once well again, her grandmother, having grown accustomed to her presence, had asked her to stay on. And because of the great affection that existed between them she had been happy to do so.

Though it struck him as a little unusual, he had accepted the explanation and thought no more about it. Until the evening Jeremy, his ship on a brief visit to deliver dispatches and pick up supplies, had paid a duty call on his aunt who had been unable to contain her delight at the increased number of invitations her normally shy son was accepting. Instantly divining the cause,

Jeremy had pressed Nick for a name. When told, he had said nothing, and changed the subject to talk of events in the Mediterranean. But later, when they were alone, Jeremy had sadly mocked Nick's gullibility.

Pressed by Nick, he had, with a great show of reluctance, revealed the *real* reason Kerenza Vyvyan lived with her grandmother. The truth was she had been banished from the family home. What some generously termed *an excess of high spirits*, and others less charitable called *unsuitably forward behaviour*, was fast blackening the family's good name, not to mention wrecking any hope of her elder sister achieving a good match.

Nick refused to believe it. But even as he denounced Jeremy's sources as at best misinformed and at worst gossipmongers, Jeremy reminded him that by his own admission he had not known her long, nor did he know her well.

'Perhaps she is improved. But in the past– Of course, being so much away at sea, you cannot be expected to have heard about her flirtations. Some were beginning to call her *fast*. As for her dancing–' Jeremy shook his head. 'I will not deny she is light on her feet and a pretty mover. But my mother would never permit either of my sisters to behave with such lack of decorum. But when control is left to a doting grandmother, what can one expect?'

Nick thought back to the Antrims' party. He had looked into her eyes as they were introduced. They were strangers, and yet the shock of recognition had been profound. His own reaction was mirrored in her widening gaze as he took her hand. Never easy making light conversation, he had been unable to think of anything to say.

She had filled the silence with inconsequential chatter, and he had been grateful. Understanding as he never had before that his sisters' prattle before an important occasion was rooted in nervousness. Her soft, slightly husky voice and breathless laugh were so different from most girls' nerve-rasping squeaks and giggles, he would have been content to listen to her all evening.

'Think about it, Nicholas,' Jeremy had urged softly. 'Kerenza Vyvyan goes almost every night to parties and dances. Can you imagine her content to remain quietly at home while you're away at sea for weeks or months at a time? Having been indulged by a wealthy grandmother, can you see her willing to forego a new wardrobe every season and the freedom to buy any trinket that takes her fancy just so that you may save to buy your packet ship? Her manner toward me at the Roseworths' convinces me otherwise. But I will say no more.'

Nor had he. And though Nick burned to ask for explanations, for details, he could not. Because asking would betray his interest; asking would reveal how much he cared; asking would expose his emotions and leave him vulnerable. And asking would give credence to Jeremy's insinuations.

But like a slow infection, his doubts grew and multiplied, gradually poisoning his memories. Though Nick had not recognized the Kerenza he knew as the girl Jeremy described, certain facts could not be denied. They had been acquainted less than a month. Work and family pressures had filled his days, limiting time in her company to

104

evenings at social gatherings where opportunities for quiet conversation were few and brief. Of her past he knew only what she had told him. Why would she lie? But then again why should Jeremy lie? He was family. They had known each other since childhood.

Yet despite everything Jeremy had said, and despite his own fears, Nick knew he loved her. And if he loved her, because he loved her, how could he ask her to give up a life of security and comfort when it would be years before he could offer anything remotely similar? How could he put her in the position of having to make such a choice? *How would he bear it when she turned him down?*

Better to end it now: free himself with one swift cut. After two sleepless nights, meeting her unexpectedly in the street had nearly undone him. *One swift cut.* He had kept on walking.

Brief dizziness made him stumble against the bulkhead. Inside the cabin Kerenza shared with Lady Russell the murmur of voices stopped. Swiftly pushing himself off, he overheard the familiar sounds of argument from the Woodrows' cabin. If that was marriage, he was better off without it.

As he entered the saloon, Broad teetered towards him with a tray of hot chocolate. 'Give me a minute, Mr Penrose. I got a nice pan of stew keeping hot.'

Nick slid behind the table. 'See to the passengers first. I've waited three hours. Another five minutes won't kill me.'

He was halfway through his stew, eating it with hunks of thickly buttered bread, when the door from the passage was flung back and Betsy Woodrow lurched in.

'Ah, Mr Penrose.' Closing the door she squeezed into the padded seat. 'I need to speak to the captain on a matter of some delicacy. So if you would be so good—'

'The captain is fully occupied running the ship, Mrs Woodrow—'

'Indeed,' she cut in. 'His ability to do so without ever leaving his cabin is an astonishment to us all.'

'And as I told you the day we left Falmouth,' Nick continued, as though she had not spoken, 'he has delegated care of the passengers to me.'

'With respect, Mr Penrose, you are far too young for me to—'

'In that case, ma'am, I must ask you to excuse me.' Nick bent his head once more to his supper, willing her to leave.

'Well, really!' She blew down her nose, making clear her irritation and disgust. 'Then it appears I have no choice.'

'There is always a choice, ma'am.'

'Not when it is a matter of duty and conscience. Now I would not wish you to think I found this anything but painful—'

'Mrs Woodrow.' Revulsion hardened Nick's voice. 'I must shortly return to my duties. What is it you want to tell me?'

Betsy thrust out her chest and drew back her chin, reminding Nick of a pigeon. 'The amount of time Miss Vyvyan and that per— your deputy spend talking together is altogether inappropriate.'

106

Anger coursed through Nick, swelling to a fury that caught him by surprise. But though Betsy Woodrow's spiteful meddling disgusted him, it was not the sole cause of the turmoil inside him. *He was jealous.* He had watched Kerenza and Maggot at the rail; had seen the interest in her expression as she listened. Her brief smile had twisted his heart. And had made him realize how rarely she smiled now. Yet during those few weeks they had been – close – her smile had been constant, radiant, lighting her face from within so she had appeared to glow.

Wrenching free of memories that haunted him day and night, making him question his worth, his judgement, his decision, hurling him from remembered pride and delight into an abyss of despair, disillusion and shame, he raised his head.

As he met her self-righteous gaze, he saw Betsy Woodrow flinch.

'Miss Vyvyan's father is the person to whom you should address your concern.'

She snorted. 'Mr Vyvyan may as well not be aboard for all the care he shows for his daughter's reputation. And Lady Russell's condition makes it impossible for her to be aware of all that is going on.'

'What, in your opinion, *is* going on?'

'I dread to imagine. But a young woman without suitable guardian or chaperon is prey to all kinds of dangerous and improper influences.'

Stifling his anger and disgust, Nick enquired, 'Who, exactly, are you accusing of improper behaviour? Surely not Miss Vyvyan?' Even as he spoke he was struck by the bitter irony of his question. Had he not done exactly that? Only he had not voiced any accusations. He had said nothing. He had listened, and allowed doubt to persuade him. And the fear – that he was right? Or that he was wrong and had made a dreadful mistake? – had been eating away at him ever since.

Something in his face made Betsy's pugnacious gaze falter, and she raised a hand to her cap. 'No,' she admitted. 'Not yet. However, considering the lack of supervision aboard this ship, a situation that permits persons unlikely to be familiar with the rules and customs of English society to consort with a young woman clearly unaware of the unfortunate impression this may give rise to–'

Nick cut her short. 'You refer, I assume, to the second mate. Allow me to reassure you, Mrs Woodrow. Miss Vyvyan could not be in safer or more respectful company. As for her reputation, if her father has no objection to her choice of companion, I see no reason for you to concern yourself. Now, if you will excuse me.' He stood up, and waited pointedly, leaving Betsy with no alternative but to follow suit.

She clung grimly to the door. 'I only hope you don't live to regret this, Mr Penrose.'

'Goodnight, Mrs Woodrow.' Shutting the door firmly on her departing figure, Nick returned to his chair. Pushing aside the congealing remains of his supper, he rested his head against his clenched fists and closed stinging eyes. Regrets? Where did he start?

Chapter Seven

Leaving the saloon, Nick went to the captain's cabin. The pungent smell of brandy was stronger than usual as he opened the door. He closed it quickly behind him. He knew the passengers were curious, even suspicious. But none had actually seen the captain distraught and incapable through drink. Nor must they.

Neither Samuel Penrose nor William Vyvyan appeared to have noticed his arrival. Slumped in the corner of the padded seat, William continued talking, his glass clutched in shaking hands against his chest. His speech was slurred, his tone a mixture of anguish and justification. 'I should have stopped it. But how? There was never a moment's peace. Anyway, what could I have done? All too late.'

Nick had heard those same words every day. Did William Vyvyan think that by repeating them he might somehow change the outcome, do whatever it was he should have done? What was he seeking: punishment or forgiveness?

Sam was sprawled forward across the table, his face resting on an outstretched arm. His skin looked grey, his eyes were half-closed, and a silver thread of saliva hung from the corner of his slack mouth. One hand clasped the brandy bottle. Beneath the other, a glass lay on its side and runnels of spilled brandy glistened on the chart.

Nick's fingers curled into fists and a roar of

frustration swelled in his chest. *Damn him. Damn both of them to hell and back.* He dived forward, scrabbling among the debris littering the table for the captain's log. Finding it, he extracted it carefully, and breathed a sigh of relief. It was dry and unmarked. Edgar Tierney might be prepared to accept log entries made in a hand other than the captain's, but Nick would not be able to afford a bribe large enough to persuade him to ignore a logbook stained and smelling of brandy.

Placing the log on the cluttered shelf out of the way, and with nothing else to hand, Nick quickly wiped the chart dry with the sleeve of his coat. He'd have to think up some excuse to explain the smell, but right now that was the least of his worries.

As his uncle twitched, mumbling unintelligibly, Nick was submerged by a wave of anger and loathing, but it receded just as quickly. Powerful emotions demanded energy, and he was simply too tired. Reclaiming the log, he also lifted down the polished wood block that held inkbottles and pens, and sat down on one end of the padded bench. Rubbing the back of his neck, feeling the tendons bar-taut, he opened the book, picked up a pen, and stared at the blank page.

'I should have stopped them,' William started again. Jerking round, Nick glared at him. William was oblivious, staring blank-eyed into the past, trapped in his guilt. 'I shouldn't have let it go on. It wasn't right, the way they both picked on her.'

Nick froze. This was new.

'Why did they do it? The look on her face ... I couldn't bear it. But what could I do? She tried;

I'll give her that. She even apologized, goddamn it. Not her fault she wasn't a boy. Pretty little thing. Prettier than Dulcie. That made it worse. I didn't know what to do. They wouldn't listen anyway. In the end she ran away. Fled from her own home. They were better then. Dulcie had her mother to herself, and Zenobia could forget her disappointment in her failure to have a son. Aurelia don't think much of me. Don't blame her. Can't face K'renza.' He shuddered. 'The shame – my fault, you see.'

Nick listened intently, taut as a mast stay.

'They warned me but I didn't listen,' William muttered, tears trickling down his haggard face. 'Should never have ... not an *Italian* ship.' His face contorted. 'How d'you live with the guilt?'

Sam roused himself. 'Not enough guns,' he said thickly. 'Packet ship's a target for any bastard privateer. Post office don't give a damn. Lose a ship, hire another.'

William blinked, frowning at him. 'Wasn't a packet. I chartered an Italian brigantine. Cheaper, see? But I bought a pass. Didn' forget that. Sure we'd be safe.' He gave a bark of laughter. 'Did you know the Algerian pirates target Italian ships?'

Sam moved his head on his sleeve. 'Religious war. Catholics and Muslims.'

'Without that pass, they'd have sold me for a slave!'

Indignation swiftly died. 'It was my fault. All of it. I can't face her,' he moaned, and Nick realized William's ramblings had come full circle to Kerenza again. 'Not like this. But I can't – I need – without the brandy I–' He shuddered, his face

111

a mask of self-loathing.

Nick felt no pity, only disgust. For while his younger daughter's life was being made wretchedly miserable by her own mother and sister this man had stood by and done nothing to stop it. Small wonder Kerenza had run away. Yet in claiming her move to Flushing was to keep house for her sick grandmother she had protected the very people who had ill-used and betrayed her. That she had done so was understandable, for she was protecting her name as well as theirs. But why had Jeremy told him such a different story?

Setting down the pen, Nick buried his face in his hands. Already haunted by her expression of bewilderment the day he cut her, now every time he closed his eyes he saw the devastation on her face as she recoiled from him and shouted for Maggot's assistance. *What had he done?*

While the weather remained bad, Nick kept Maggot at the wheel. He was the best helmsman aboard, and the regular crew swore the ship ran drier under his handling. But this meant standing Maggot's watch as well as his own.

Snatching rest when he could, Nick collapsed on to his cot and into oblivion, only to wake with a start after two or three hours unable to settle again for his mind's tormented churning.

After forty-eight hours of howling wind and vicious seas, the gale moderated to a spanking breeze. The thick blanket of cloud rolled away and sun rose in a sky the colour of cornflowers. Maggot relinquished the wheel to Collins, the most experienced able seaman, and stumbled bleary-eyed down the companionway to wash before having his breakfast.

Continuing to drive himself relentlessly, Nick oversaw sail changes, organized teams under the sailmaker and carpenter to repair canvas and spars, and sent another gang to replace frayed or broken rigging.

Having worked since before dawn, he told Broad to bring his breakfast to the captain's day cabin. If the steward wondered at Mr Penrose's recent habit of taking his meals elsewhere than the saloon he had the good sense not to mention it.

The snores from behind William Vyvyan's door were echoed in the sounds behind the heavy curtain that separated Sam Penrose's sleeping quarters from the day cabin. Wrinkling his nose at the stench, Nick jammed a wedge under the door to stop it closing, then opened the skylight. A cold draught instantly freshened the air.

He made the night's entries in both logs while eating his breakfast. Then after gulping down a second cup of coffee he went to his cabin to wash and shave, and returned to the deck.

Moving to the port side he raised the glass. Warm sunshine was burning off the morning fog but the Portuguese coastline was still hazy. Not that there was much to see, for this part was low and sandy with few prominent features.

Footsteps on the brass stairs drew his gaze sideways. But it was Betsy Woodrow who emerged from the companionway, blinking in the bright sunlight. Wrapped in a brown kerseymere cloak, she wore a plain brown bonnet over her cap with the ribbons tied beneath her double chin in a

113

drooping bow. Her husband followed her out, one hand clapped to his round shallow-crowned hat. A bow of greeting was accompanied by his usual anxious smile.

Not wishing to be drawn into conversation, Nick merely nodded and raised the glass again.

'Deck ho!' bellowed the lookout from the foretop. 'Sail on the port beam.'

Nick swung round with the glass, but could see nothing. Cupping one hand to his mouth he shouted back, 'What is she?'

'Lugger, sir. She's a big 'un. Two, no, three masts.' The men on deck exchanged glances. 'Bleddy 'ell!' The lookout's voice rose. 'She's a Frenchie, sir!'

As Maggot appeared beside him, Nick's gaze flew to the sails. As well as fore, main, staysail and jib, *Kestrel* was already wearing her square topsails and flying jib.

'We put up topgallants?'

After an instant's hesitation Nick shook his head. 'It would shift the force of the wind too far from the hull.' He kept his voice low. 'In these seas she could lose her topmasts.' They both glanced at the dark blue lumpy ocean filled here and there with curls of foam. 'But we'll never outrun her in open water.'

'How far to Cabo Carvoeiro?'

Catching the gleam in Maggot's dark eyes Nick knew at once what he had in mind. His own thoughts raced. 'The tidal stream runs south on the ebb. Instead of taking the channel off the cape, we lead him between Farilhoes and Berlenga.'

114

'Current sets on to Berlenga,' Maggot whispered.

'It's dangerous,' Nick warned.

'You no trust me?' Maggot grinned.

'I beg your pardon, Mr Penrose,' Donald Woodrow began apologetically, but was interrupted by the lookout.

'Deck ho! That lugger, sir. I see 'er before. Privateer, she is. Sails out of Brest.'

Betsy shrieked and reeled back, colliding with her husband who staggered against the freshwater barrels. 'A privateer? Oh dear God. We'll all be killed, or kidnapped and held for ransom.' She turned on her husband. 'This is all your fault. We wouldn't be here but for you. Oh, where are my smelling salts? I feel quite faint. I'm going to swoon, I know it.'

'Now, now, my dear, I'm sure–' Donald Woodrow looked up, startled, as Nick caught his arm.

'I believe your wife would be more comfortable if you took her below.'

Recognizing an order when he heard it, the minister nodded quickly. 'Yes, of course, right away. Come, my dear–'

'Well, really,' Betsy began.

'Not now, dear.' Flashing his anxious, placatory smile, he hustled his complaining wife towards the companionway from where Kerenza had just emerged.

'Miss Vyvyan, you must come below at once,' Betsy ordered. 'A French privateer is chasing us. God knows what will happen. Where is the captain? Why is he not in command? To leave our fate in the hands of–'

115

'Please,' Kerenza interrupted. 'You go ahead. I will follow you down.' As Betsy disappeared, trailing loud complaints, Kerenza turned to Nick.

His heart contracted at the physical changes wrought by strain. Her cheekbones were sharply defined, her pallor accentuated by bruise-coloured shadows beneath her eyes. Yet she was perfectly calm, almost detached. He had the distinct impression that no matter what dangers the coming hours brought, they would touch her little, because for her the worst had already happened. *He was responsible for that: he, her father, and his cousin Jeremy. What reason did she have to trust a man? How could he even begin to earn her forgiveness?*

She met his gaze directly. He saw no anger, no hate: though God knew he deserved both. Whatever her feelings, they were hidden behind an impenetrable barrier. Once he had been able to look into her soul. Now all he could see was his own reflection, and it shamed him.

'Is there going to be a fight, Mr Penrose?'

'I hope not, Miss Vyvyan. But–'

She did not let him finish. 'I am not seeking reassurance, merely information. If there is a fight, it is likely there will be casualties. If you will tell me where you keep the dressings and bandages?' Intercepting the glance that passed between Nick and Maggot, she simply said, 'Ah. Then with your permission, I have a sheet that will serve.' Without waiting for his response she turned towards the companionway.

'Thank you,' Nick called after her. But she did not look back.

'Deck ho! She's coming up fast!'

'What is time?' Maggot demanded.

Nick took out the watch that had once belonged to his father. 'Just after ten.'

'Is full moon. Low water half-hour ago. Tide rising now.'

Nick thought fast. Timing was crucial. They had to stay out of range of the lugger's guns. But if they reached the channel too soon, he would rip out *Kestrel*'s bottom. 'You take the wheel.' Nodding, Maggot moved away and Nick yelled to the bosun. 'Mr Laity, have the stern chaser run out and the fire buckets filled.' His heart pounded against his ribs. He would trust Maggot with his life. But it wasn't only his life he was risking. It was the lives of everyone on board. *Kerenza and her father, Lady Russell and her unborn baby, the Woodrows, his uncle, Toy, Broad...* He shook his head. He could not afford doubts or distractions.

'Billy!' he shouted, beckoning to the boy. 'Come with me.' He dived down the companionway, feet clanging on the brass stairs. Telling the boy to wait, he hurried into the day cabin, went to the small cupboard above the stern shelf and took out the keys to the magazine.

Toy came out of the sleeping cabin, carrying a basin with a cloth over it.

Glancing from the basin to the steward's face, Nick stopped. 'What? What's happened?'

'He's bleeding.'

'How? Did he fall? Has he cut himself?'

Toy looked away, his mouth unsteady. 'From inside.'

Christ. Closing his eyes in despair, Nick sucked

117

in a ragged breath. 'Tell him–' What words of comfort could he offer that his uncle would believe? There were none. He shook his head. 'I'll come down again as soon as I can. But it might be a while. There's a French privateer on our tail.'

Toy's face contorted with fury. 'Sink the bleddy bastards, sir!'

'I'll do my best. But you know the rules as well as I do. We have to run. Only when we are cornered may we fight.' But if it came to a fight, it would mean the end for *Kestrel* and everyone on board. 'Take care of him, Toy.'

Unlocking the magazine, Nick placed the cloth bags packed tight with gunpowder carefully in a wooden bucket and handed it to the waiting boy. *Kestrel*'s carronades and brass sternchaser had limited range and were fit only for close fighting. And though each of the squat cannons needed only two men to operate it, they could not match the four-pounders the lugger was most likely carrying.

The post office had stripped the packets of heavy guns to reinforce its order to flee rather than fight, and thus ensure fast delivery of the mails. The limited protection of the carronades gave a packet captain just enough time before being captured to sink the mails and despatches. At least, that was the theory.

'Walk, Billy,' Nick warned. 'I don't want you tripping over.'

The boy nodded, his teeth chattering with nervous excitement.

The privateer was slowly shortening the distance between them. Through his glass, Nick could see

118

scores of man crowding her deck. They were cramming on more sail and running out the guns. How long before they tried a ranging shot?

He glanced at Maggot who had braced himself, legs apart, his hands light on the spokes as *Kestrel* hurtled towards the dark dot of land on the starboard bow. Plunging through broken foaming crests, her sharp bow sent spray flying skyward in glistening rainbow-hued veils.

The rising tide was both ally and enemy. It might, if luck was on their side, rid them of their pursuer. But the sea was growing increasingly turbulent as a battle developed between wind, tide and current. Nick looked back at the lugger. Lying hard over, she was throwing up clouds of spray as she crashed through the short steep seas.

Minutes ticked by. As the bell was struck marking the half-hour, the Frenchman fired a ranging shot. The crack and boom thundered across the water. His muscles tensed against the lacerating impact of flying metal, Nick raised the glass, and was relieved to see it fall short and wide. The sound of a ragged cheer made him look round.

Dressed in his best uniform, Samuel Penrose emerged from the companionway and stood, pale as death, gripping the hatch to steady himself. He looked forward at the watching crew, then up at the sails, then started aft.

Nick's protest died unspoken as he saw the burning glitter in his uncle's eyes. Had it taken this, the threat of attack, to rouse him from the paralysis of fear and rekindle his pride, his spirit? He opened his mouth, but Sam spoke first.

'You are heading in the wrong direction. Put

119

her about. At once, if you please.'

Time stopped as Nick stared at his uncle in disbelief. Sam Penrose had never *officially* relinquished command. If Nick disobeyed a direct order from the captain he would be guilty of gross insubordination: an act that would have to be entered in the log, and would destroy his treasured hopes of one day commanding his own packet ship. Yet to do what his uncle demanded would condemn the schooner and all on board to certain death.

'Jump to it,' Samuel Penrose snapped. 'You're wasting valuable time.'

'Captain,' Nick strode forward. 'A word if you please?' Standing close he lowered his voice. 'Sir, you – we can't–'

'*Can't?*' Sam glowered. 'Have a care, boy. *Morwenna* is under *my* command, and don't you forget it. Mr Laity!' he roared past Nick. 'Stand by to wear ship!'

Morwenna? Nausea flooded Nick's mouth with saliva, and he swallowed hard. *Morwenna* was the ship Sam had lost.

'Wear ship it is, sir!' Laity yelled back after an instant's hesitation.

'Captain, please–'

'Not now, boy,' Sam rapped. 'Get about your business.'

Both watches leapt to the halyards. *Kestrel* began to turn away, her stern to the wind, pitching and rolling in the buffeting waves as her speed fell off.

Samuel Penrose ground the knuckles of one trembling hand into the palm of the other. 'I've been waiting for this. Run from Javert and his murdering crew? Let them escape after what they did? Never! I'm going to blast their evil hides.'

Blocks squealed as the two huge booms swung across. The yards were braced, the sails filled and were sheeted home, and *Kestrel* surged forward on her new course, plunging into the spume-streaked waves.

Appalled, realizing the glitter in his uncle's eyes was the delirium of fever, Nick gripped Sam's arm. 'Listen to me. That's not *Hirondelle*.'

Sam shook him off, backing towards the starboard rail. 'Don't try to fox me, damn your eyes! Of course it's *Hirondelle*. Javert must have heard of my escape. But he's not going to get me this time. I'll see him in hell first.'

'Look at her!' Gripping his uncle's arm again, Nick pointed towards the lugger, fighting the urge to shout. 'Look at her hull, her sails. That's no schooner. It's not *Hirondelle*.'

Sam stared at him. 'What's wrong, boy? Afraid?' Turning his back on their pursuer he pulled Nick close, his eyes betraying torment as he dropped his voice to a hoarse whisper. 'Better to die than be afraid, boy. Fear eats away your soul.'

Hearing the crew's shouts of raucous challenge, Nick recognized the brave, hopeless defiance of men staring death in the face. He glanced forward. As Nick glimpsed the puff of smoke from the lugger's bow chaser, Maggot spun the wheel. It was a courageous desperate move.

The *boom* was still reverberating across the water when the ball, at the limit of its range, ploughed along *Kestrel*'s starboard rail then fell into the sea. Stiffening, Sam Penrose jerked

121

forward against his nephew, his eyes widening in surprise. With a guttural sound that was half groan, half whimper, he crumpled and started to fall, one leg of his breeches already crimson.

Nick grabbed him, yelling for the bosun. 'Laity! Two men to carry the captain below! And ask Miss Vyvyan for bandages.' He looked down at the closed eyes and lips that were blue-white and compressed against pain. As the men carried their unconscious burden towards the companionway, Nick tore his eyes from the bloody trail. The ship must come first. That was the price of command.

Surprised by *Kestrel*'s abrupt turn-about, the Frenchman had also altered course, using his bow-chaser to try and turn *Kestrel* off, intending to rake her with a broadside. But Nick had no intention of obliging.

'Stand by to come about again, Mr Laity.' This was a risky manoeuvre given the state of wind and sea. But Nick knew it would convince the lugger's captain he had the packet on the run and within his grasp.

Men sprang to the halyards with even greater alacrity this time. Maggot put the helm down, and *Kestrel* turned, her canvas flapping and snapping for an instant before the sails filled once more. The schooner leapt forward. Nick looked back at their pursuer. The lugger was gaining on them, but she was carrying so much canvas that the wind had laid her right over and her windward guns pointed skyward.

Nick watched as they left the island of Farilhoes to starboard, and Maggot guided *Kestrel* diagonally across the channel towards Berlenga. He knew Maggot would be feeling both tide and current through the pressure of the schooner's rudder and her response to his demands. They were committed now. With the lugger behind and invisible death lying in wait ahead, their survival depended on the Tanjawi's exceptional knowledge of the coastline. Of his nerve Nick had no doubt.

He swallowed at a sudden vivid image of razor-edged rocks like sharp black teeth lying just below the surface of the dimpled blue water, ready to rip open the ship and devour everyone on board. *Kerenza*. Thrusting fear away, he looked over his shoulder at the lugger, closer now, rearing and diving, throwing up clouds of spray as it shouldered the seas aside with brute force.

Another *boom* reverberated and, just ahead, the water erupted. Now the Frenchman had their range he would be loading grape and chain-shot, aiming for the masts and rigging, preferring to disable rather than sink. He wanted money and any cargo. A sunk ship offered no pickings.

Despite the freshness of the breeze, beneath his coat Nick's shirt was clinging to his back and he felt a bead of sweat tickle as it slid down his temple. He wiped his forehead on his sleeve, smelled the brandy, and wrenched his thoughts from distractions he could not afford. Looking sternward he saw the French captain piling on more canvas, intent on his prize, oblivious to the danger.

A long harsh grating sound from deep in the ship stopped Nick's heart and his breath. But *Kestrel* flew on. Licking dry lips, he looked back and began silently counting. *It was taking too long.*

123

Maggot had misjudged the line.

Then, with a tremendous grinding and tearing, the lugger stopped dead in the water, shivering like a mirage from the force of the jolt. Deafening cracks like gunfire were followed by shrieking groans as the three masts toppled forward, ripping the heavy canvas as if it were paper, snapping stays and halyards like strands of cotton. They smashed on to the deck, crushing everything in their path. The weight and force of the triple blow burst the lugger apart like a squashed fruit. Wild water rushed in through the splintered planking and quickly finished what the clawing rocks had begun. Within moments the privateer and her crew were pulped wreckage, strewn over the tossing waves.

Chapter Eight

Seated at the table in the saloon with her back to the door, Kerenza had ripped her spare bed sheet into four pieces and begun tearing one of them into long strips. Also on the table, alongside the pile of soft white linen was her box of remedies. Opposite her Judith swayed with the motion of the ship, head bent over the baby shirt she was embroidering.

Her gaze drawn to the tiny garment, Kerenza thought of all the joy, love and hope it signified, and looked away quickly. She had few fond memories of her own family. Only since living with her grandmother had she felt secure in someone's affection. Meeting Nick, having him seek her out, reading in his eyes the admiration, warmth, and stronger emotions that had made her quiver inside she had begun to believe herself worthy of love, deserving of happiness. She had even dared to dream of a shared future: of marriage and children: children who would be loved as she had never been. Blinking to clear her blurred vision she tore off another length. The ripping sound resonated inside her.

'Well, I'm appalled,' Betsy said, from her usual place against the ship's side. Kerenza smothered a sigh as she made another small cut in the sheet's top edge. 'It was my understanding that in time of war packet ships, as well as naval vessels, are supposed to carry a doctor. I suppose I should not be surprised that this ship carries no doctor. It is, after all, under the command of an invisible captain. But to learn there is not even a bottle of paregoric aboard.' She rolled her eyes in disapproval. 'It is as well I had the foresight to bring my own. As for being expected to give up one's bed linen for bandages, well.'

'No one expects such sacrifice from you, Mrs Woodrow,' Judith soothed, glancing up.

'No, indeed,' Kerenza added quickly. 'I'm sure there is more than enough here. Hopefully it will not be needed.'

'Then you will have destroyed an excellent sheet to no good purpose,' Betsy retorted. 'Where are you going, Donald?' she demanded, as her husband stood up and began edging between the seat and the table towards Kerenza.

'It will soon be dinnertime.' He flashed his anxious smile at Kerenza. 'I thought I might try to persuade Mr Vyvyan to join us today.'

Betsy snorted. And recalling her father's response when she had attempted to see him, Kerenza grew tense. 'Oh, I don't think–'

'You mentioned that your father had been ill, Miss Vyvyan,' Donald said. 'I daresay in his weakened state even the smallest task requires great effort. While he would not wish *you*, or indeed any of the ladies aboard, to see him at a disadvantage, he may be more willing to consider an offer of aid from me. After all, are we not, to coin an apt phrase, in the same boat?'

Forcing a smile to show she appreciated his attempted humour, Kerenza sought desperately for words to dissuade him. She did not want to offend. But nor did she want to reveal the real reason for her father's absence.

'We paid extra for the services of a steward,' Betsy reminded him severely. 'Surely such tasks are his job? I see no reason for *you* to–'

'Mr Broad is preparing our dinner, my dear. I will not be away long. Indeed, if Mr Vyvyan–'

The rolling boom of a cannon made them all jump. Kerenza caught Judith's eye as they both looked up. Shadows flitted to and fro across the skylight. Above the ever-present creak of the ship's timbers and rush of water past the hull, they heard shouts and running feet.

As Donald staggered out into the passage the ship suddenly changed direction again. Kerenza braced herself against the seat with one hand, holding the table edge with the other, and saw

126

Judith drop her needlework to do the same. Betsy was thrown forward against the edge of the table, grunting as the air was forced out of her lungs. She fell back, red-faced and gasping for breath, angrily adjusting her cap and her kerchief. Reminded of a thoroughly ruffled chicken, Kerenza bit her lip. Laughter bubbled in her chest as nervous tension sought escape. She did not dare look at Judith.

'What are they doing up there?' Betsy demanded 'Why can they not settle upon a direction? All this turning about is extremely uncomfortable.' She looked past Kerenza. 'Back already? Did Mr Vyvyan not welcome your offer? I suppose we must assume–'

'I did not see him.' Something in Donald Woodrow's voice made Kerenza look round. He clung to the doorframe, pale-faced and clearly shaken. 'The captain–' He swallowed. 'Two seamen were carrying him into his cabin. Miss Vyvyan, Mr Penrose told them to ask you for bandages. I said I would convey the request. There was a great deal of blood. I fear the wound may be serious.'

Kerenza's stomach turned over. Meeting Judith's glance she stood up quickly gathered a bundle of strips, two of the large pieces and her scissors.

'I will come with you,' Judith said, trying to lever herself out from behind the table.

'No.' Kerenza shook her head even though she would have derived great comfort from Judith's calm presence and common sense. 'You must not, please. Your condition – it would not be good for you. Besides, the captain's servant will be there.

127

I'm sure he'll know what to do.' Hoping she was right, she scooped up the wooden box. Though if the captain's wound really was serious, of what possible use would a selection of remedies for seasickness be? Then she recalled the sedatives. They might help if nothing else was available.

'Well, I cannot like it,' Betsy announced. 'it is neither seemly nor, in my opinion, necessary. Lady Russell, surely you cannot condone a young unmarried woman–'

'Extraordinary situations call for extraordinary measures, Mrs Woodrow. Were it not for my circumstances' – Judith laid a hand over her swollen belly – 'I would go in her place.'

'A noble sentiment, Lady Russell.' Betsy gushed.

'Nonsense.'

'I would not wish you to think me lacking in charity.' Betsy adjusted a fold of her kerchief. 'Naturally, had I any knowledge of medical matters I would offer to go myself. But I fear my limited experience would render me of little use.'

Kerenza stared at her. What experience of battle injuries did the minister's wife imagine *she* had?

'Rest assured, Mrs Woodrow,' Judith said, 'my opinion of you is in no way altered.' Turning her head she smiled warmly at Kerenza. 'I have every confidence that Miss Vyvyan will prove equal to whatever is required of her.'

Though relieved to be spared Betsy Woodrow's critical company, and touched by Judith's compliment, Kerenza's apprehension increased. Hurrying along the passage she saw two sailors emerge from the captain's cabin. They were

128

sombre-faced, their bare legs and feet splattered with blood that still dripped through the brass stair-treads and left a glistening trail of garnet splashes.

Moistening dry lips, trying to prepare for what lay inside, she suddenly remembered Lizzie Gendall who had learned her skills as a herbalist and midwife from her mother and grandmother. It was Lizzie who delivered the village's babies and laid out those who had passed on. And when Aurelia Danby had fallen ill she had ignored suggestions that she call the doctor and had sent for Lizzie instead. Short and plump, Lizzie's brusque manner hid a kind heart. Kerenza over-heard her grandmother telling Maude Tregenna it was as well that Lizzie kept a close tongue considering the secrets she must know. Kerenza had asked Lizzie once which remedy she found most effective.

'Clean water: hot to wash, cold to drink. Keep clean inside and out, and let nature do the healing.'

Kerenza had wondered if the reply was a gentle tease. But the fact remained that most of the people Lizzie Gendall treated got better. Which was why everyone trusted her.

Kerenza took a breath. 'Has Mr Toy asked for water?'

The men looked at one another. 'No, miss.'

'Then would you ask Billy to bring two jugs, one of boiling water and one of cold, as quickly as possible?'

The seaman tugged his forelock, clearly relieved to be given an order. 'Yes, miss.' Both disappeared

129

up the stairs.

As a courtesy and to warn of her arrival, Kerenza rapped on the door and entered, closing it behind her. She paused for an instant to get her bearings. Sunshine poured in through the barred skylight in the deckhead. A lamp for the night hours hung from a nail in one thick crossbeam. Wood panelling lined the cabin with recessed finger-holds that indicated sliding doors. A railed shelf crammed with sea junk was set back above a padded bench seat that followed the curve of the stern and enclosed a table hidden beneath a clutter of charts, books and instruments.

She had looked down through that skylight, seen Nick bent over a chart unaware he was observed, and felt yearning pierce the agony and bewilderment of his rejection. Once she had been so sure that he loved her. *And she, fool, loved him still.* But those few minutes with him on deck, his questions, his disbelief, proved she had been wrong.

Shaking her head to dislodge memories too painful to revisit, she moved past a squat stove standing on an iron plate towards what appeared to be another small cabin. The grubby canvas curtain that normally screened the doorway had been fastened back with a short piece of even grubbier rope. She heard groans, harsh breathing and glimpsed movement. 'Mr Toy?'

The captain's servant appeared clutching a blood-soaked towel. His hands were scarlet, the edges of his coat-sleeves wet and dark. Shock and fear were vivid on his furrowed face. Spotting the bundle of linen in her arms he beckoned her forward.

'Quick, miss. He's bleeding some bad.'

Fighting a surge of nausea, Kerenza hurried across the cabin. The sickly smell of fresh blood was overpowering in the small space. Heavy and cloying, it overlay other fouler smells. She breathed through her mouth, shallow inhalations, willing herself not to retch as she dumped her armful onto the flat top of the trunk at the foot of the cot. 'I've asked for hot water to be brought.'

Urgently dabbing and wiping with one hand, Toy held up what looked like a canvas belt with a small brass plate threaded on to it. 'This should stop the bleeding, but–'

'Can I help?' Kerenza asked, swiftly winding strips of torn sheet into a thick wad. 'If I hold the pad you could–'

'No, 'tisn't that. I can't put it on because there's something in his leg.' The steward probed carefully. 'But I can't see–' His breath caught on a gasp as Sam Penrose, cried out, flinching violently. Toy jerked back.

'What? What is it?'

'A knife.' He glanced round, frantic. 'I need a knife, his breeches is in the way.'

'Here,' Kerenza snatched up the scissors and offered them with trembling fingers. But after a moment's fumbling, Toy groaned with frustration and thrust them back at her.

'You do it. You'll have to.' His voice rose, insistent, as she recoiled. 'My fingers is too big. Hurry we got to stop him bleeding. Here, I'll hold that, you cut – there, down from the rip.'

Kerenza worked the scissors; her hands growing wet and slippery as Toy dropped one saturated

131

wad of cotton and snatched up another, frantically trying to stem the relentless welling. The material was thick, the scissors small and within seconds her fingers were cramped, the ache in them agonizing. Clenching her teeth she kept cutting. Beside her, Toy talked softly and continuously to his captain.

'Come on now, Cap'n, you hang on. We been through bad times before, but we survived. And we come home safe and sound. Come on, Cap'n, sir. They bleddy Frenchies won't get the better of us. You just hang on.'

Almost crying from pain, Kerenza shook the scissors off and pulled the material aside. Her gorge rose as she saw the ragged sliver of wood, as thick as her forefinger, sticking out of the captain's inner thigh. Swallowing the bitter taste of bile, she looked in panic at Toy.

'Oh, Jesus,' he whispered. 'Oh sweet Jesus. What should us do?'

'I don't – I can't–' She shook her head. If they left it, they could not apply the tourniquet. But if they tried to remove it – she couldn't make the decision. She didn't have the right. *Nor did she want the responsibility*. Clumsy, because her hands were trembling so badly, she tried to fashion another pad.

From somewhere deep in the ship came a strange grating sound. A vibration shivered through her feet right up her spine and into her skull. She and Toy looked at each other. Suddenly the captain convulsed with a brief, hoarse cry. As blood spouted from the wound Kerenza screamed and shied backwards.

'I'm sorry, I'm sorry,' she whispered, ashamed of her reaction. 'I didn't mean to–'

'Oh, my God! Quick, give me more rags. Hurry!'

But as Kerenza stuffed them into Toy's hand and he pleaded desperately with his captain not to give up, promising all would be well, Samuel Penrose released a slow, rattling breath. Even in the dim light she could see the change in his face. Grooves dug by stress and agony were smoothing out. Relief that he was no longer in pain was swiftly followed by fear. Samuel Penrose was not fighting death he was embracing it, welcoming escape from a life that had become unbearable.

'No!' Toy's raging plea tore at her heart, and tears spilled down her cheeks, scalding, unstoppable. 'Come on, Cap'n, fight, dammit. You can't let the bastards win.'

Glancing from Sam's oddly waxen face to the wound, Kerenza saw that the pulsing had stopped.

'Captain,' Toy begged.

Kerenza lay her bloody hand gently on his. 'It's over. He's gone.' She had to force the words from a stiff aching throat. 'I'm so sorry.'

'No,' Toy whispered, and Kerenza knew it was not denial, but unwillingness to face dreadful loss. She had never witnessed death before. A few weeks ago she had wanted to die. But she had not understood the terrible finality. She knew now that despite the pain she had suffered, and felt still, life was a gift. Its very fragility made it infinitely precious.

A rapping on the door made her jump. 'I'll go.' She pressed Toy's shoulder and felt it shaking beneath her fingers. 'You will want a few minutes alone–' Unable to go on, she straightened up. Pausing only to grab a scrap of linen to wipe her eyes and nose, she walked stiffly across the day cabin.

Billy held out two enamel jugs, one steaming. As she took them his eyes widened at the blood on her hands.

'Please, miss, how's–?'

'Thank you, Billy.' She cut him short. 'Close the door will you?' He scuttled out.

While the weeping steward covered his captain's body with a blanket, Kerenza gathered up all the sodden pads and set them aside to be burnt. Then, with gooseflesh erupting over her entire body at the sensation of blood drying like tight gloves over her knuckles and fingers, she poured water from both jugs into the basin on the nightstand. Soaping her hands, she rubbed them hard, palm and back, as if by removing the blood she could also wash away the nightmare images that still filled her head.

Drying her hands on a piece of clean sheet she emptied the red sudsy water into the chamber pot and refilled the basin for the steward. Out in the day cabin, she crouched by the little stove and was about to open the door when the clang of boots on the brass stairs made her heart buck. She straightened up, moving towards the door as it opened and Nick burst in. Seeing her he checked, startled, and for an instant his expression, usually so guarded, betrayed far more than anxiety.

Knowing what his uncle had meant to him, a wave of sympathy submerged her own hurt, grief and anger. 'Nick, I'm so sorry. I–'

'No.' Shock and shame raced like storm clouds across his features. The self-reproach in his eyes stopped her breath as he took a step towards her.

'The fault is entirely mine.' His voice was low and intense. 'It is I who must ask *your* pardon, though God knows you have little reason to grant it, or to forgive me.'

'No.' She reared back. 'Stop. You– I didn't – you misunderstand.' But even as she silenced him, fearing he would be embarrassed or even angry at his error, the physical weight of her grief was suddenly lighter. 'I was not– What I mean–' She bit her lip hard and gestured helplessly.

His gaze fell on the pile of bloody rags, then flicked to the sleeping area. In the silence she heard Toy heave a deep shaky sigh and blow his nose.

'I'm sorry,' she whispered, watching the colour leave Nick's face as he realized his mistake: realized what she had really been trying to tell him. He swayed slightly and she saw his recognition of all that the loss of his uncle, *Kestrel*'s captain, would mean. His throat worked as he swallowed and a muscle started twitching in his jaw as he clamped his teeth together. Then with a brief formal bow he moved past her as Toy emerged, wiping tears from his seamed face.

'We done our best, Mr Penrose, but...' He shook his head, clearing his throat loudly. 'The good Lord knows I shall miss him awful, but the truth is–'

'He was glad to go?' The savagery in Nick's voice startled Kerenza. But though she didn't

135

understand his anger she knew his instinct was correct. Sam Penrose had left this world willingly.

'Not from you, Mr Penrose,' Toy's voice was strong, his reply firm. 'Don't you ever think that. He couldn't have been prouder of you if you was his own son. But you know so well as I do, prison done for him. Not the same man, he wasn't. Nor ever would be. Well, he's out of it now, God rest his soul. What about the Frenchie, sir?'

'Sunk with all hands.' Nick was terse. 'Maggot lured him on to rocks, ripped his keel out.'

'Bleddy good job too, begging your pardon, miss.' Ducking his head respectfully, Toy turned back to Nick. 'Looks peaceful as a sleeping babe, he do, sir.' His voice broke. 'You see for yourself.'

As Toy stood aside so Nick could enter the cramped sleeping cabin, Kerenza picked up the bloodstained bundle and started towards the door.

'This is too much for the small stove. I'll ask Broad—'

'While you're there, miss.' Toy held out one of the jugs. 'Would you ask'n for more hot water? The captain got to be laid out proper.' His voice wobbled and her throat thickened in sympathy.

'Of course.' As she quietly closed the door, her father's opened.

Though dressed, he looked unkempt. His clothes were stained and creased, his puffy eyes bloodshot and greying stubble covered his sagging jaw. Seeing her he flinched, muttered incoherently, and started to retreat. But as he caught sight of the bloodstained bundle he froze. 'Good God, what happened? Are you hurt? How—?'

'It's not mine,' she said quickly. Could he really not have heard the gunfire, nor felt the ship's violent changes of course? 'There was a chase.'

'A chase?'

'A French privateer. It's over now. He was sunk. But a ball hit the rail and the captain was injured.' She shuddered at stark images she could not escape. The gaping wound: the protruding splinter of wood, blood spurting unstoppably from a pierced artery.

'Is it serious? Can I see him?'

Kerenza swallowed, shaking her head. 'He – he died, Papa.'

'Died?' William repeated blankly, then sagged against the bulkhead. 'Sam Penrose is dead?' He seemed unable to believe it.

'I'm sorry Papa. You had become friends, had you not?' Kerenza lifted the jug. 'There are things I must do. But they won't take long, and then–'

William turned blindly, feeling his way back into his cabin.

'Papa, please, don't go.'

'You get on,' he mumbled, waving her away. 'I'm not fit company, least of all for you.'

'That's not true,' she cried desperately. 'You have been much missed. I'll ask Broad to bring you hot water, and some coffee. You should not be alone. And the other passengers are anxious to meet you. Please join us in the saloon. It will soon be time for lunch. Though apparently we must call it dinner while we are on the ship.' Realizing she was starting to babble, Kerenza bit her tongue. But anxiety drove her to add, 'Papa, you need to be well and strong when we reach

Tangier. Mama and Dulcie will depend upon it. And upon you.'

Shaking his head, he closed the cabin door.

Wanting to scream with frustration, Kerenza bit hard on her lower lip and looked up the stairs towards daylight. Blue sky and sunshine mocked the horror of the past hour. Captain Penrose was dead. For everyone else on board, once the ripples faded, life would simply continue as before. But for Nick the change was irrevocable.

She saw his face again, heard the intensity in his voice as he had begged her forgiveness. Then realizing his error he had withdrawn behind formality. Did he regret? *No.* She must wait until she had time alone, time to think.

Drawing fresh clean air deep into her lungs, willing her heartbeat to slow, she started down the passage. At least she had seen her father and spoken to him. And he no longer seemed angry with her.

She entered the saloon, the gory bundle down by her side to conceal it as best she could. 'I'll be back in a moment.' She hurried through the door leading to Broad's cubby-hole and the galley before Betsy, mouth already open, could start asking questions.

The sympathy in Judith's eyes brought a lump to Kerenza's throat as she finished relating a brief – and carefully edited account of what had taken place.

'Oh my dear, how awful for you. And for Mr Penrose as well.'

'The Lord giveth and the Lord taketh away,' Betsy pronounced.

'Just so, my dear,' Donald murmured. 'Miss Vyvyan, you have just come from the captain's cabin. Might I be of help, do you think?'

'I am sure that both M-Mr Penrose and Toy would appreciate your kindness, sir. But both are very busy right now, so perhaps if you were to wait an hour or so?'

Nodding, he sank back onto the padded leather. 'Of course. One wishes to comfort, but not to intrude. Mr Penrose must be particularly grateful to you, Miss Vyvyan.'

Kerenza shook her head. 'He has no reason to be, sir. There was so little we could do.'

'But you tried,' the minister said gently. 'And Captain Penrose was not alone.'

'Well, I would not wish to be thought lacking in all proper feeling,' Betsy broke in. 'But it has to be said that for the captain to pass away so quickly he must have been quite beyond help. So, Miss Vyvyan, having done your duty as you perceived it, you need not blame yourself in any way.'

Kerenza folded her hands tightly in her lap. 'Thank you, Mrs Woodrow. That is a great comfort.'

Betsy nodded, oblivious to Kerenza's bitterness.

Broad had just carried in the tray containing a platter of boiled beef with dishes of boiled potatoes, carrots, cabbage and a jug of gravy, when Kerenza saw Judith look past her.

'Mr Vyvyan,' she smiled. 'You join us at last. We are so glad to see you.'

Swivelling round, Kerenza saw that her father had made an effort. Though his coat and breeches

139

looked as if he had slept in them, he had shaved and found a clean neckcloth. A neat wig with a rigid roll curl each side and a short pigtail covered his lank hair. But his face was the colour of ashes, and sweat glistened on his forehead and upper lip. Realizing he was on the verge of retreat, she scrambled out of her seat quickly. As she slipped her arm through his she could feel him trembling.

'Lady Russell, may I present my father, William Vyvyan.'

'Mr Vyvyan, it is a pleasure to make your acquaintance.' Judith extended her hand, and Kerenza gently drew her father forward so he could take it. 'I am sharing a cabin with your daughter. And I must tell you she is a delightful companion.'

Bowing over her hand, William's voice was rough as he muttered, 'Thank you, ma'am.'

'Mrs Woodrow, Mr Woodrow, my father.'

'Mr Vyvyan,' Betsy inclined her head, her mouth pursed in censure. And Kerenza knew the sharp eyes had noted every stain and wrinkle, the missed patch of stubble, the bead of dried blood, the pouches beneath his eyes and network of fine veins that lay across his nose and cheeks like patches of purple lace.

Awkwardly rising to his feet behind the table, Donald Woodrow, extended his hand. 'Mr Vyvyan. It is a pity that we should meet for the first time on such a sad day. But we are glad to see you, sir. We understood from Miss Vyvyan that you have not been in good health. I hope you are beginning to feel better?'

'A little, thank you.'

'But these things take time, do they not?'

'Do sit down, Mr Vyvyan.' Judith indicated the chair tucked against the table. 'I think it unlikely either of the officers will be joining us.'

As William pulled out the chair and sat down and Kerenza slid into her seat again, Betsy leaned forward and began to help herself from the dishes.

'I do not wish to cause alarm, but I have to say I am not at all convinced of Mr Penrose's suitability for command.'

Kerenza clenched her teeth, staring at her empty plate, not daring to say anything. Of all at the table only she knew that Nick had been in command ever since the ship left Falmouth, and probably during the whole of *Kestrel*'s previous voyage to Lisbon.

'Oh, come now, Mrs Woodrow,' Judith said, taking a small portion from each of the dishes. 'The very fact that we are sitting here about to eat this meal indicates to me that Mr Penrose possesses remarkable courage and tactical skill. It must be a shocking thing to see one's captain struck down. Yet setting aside his personal anxieties he not only evaded capture, he caused the French privateer to sink. No, Mrs Woodrow, I cannot share your doubt.' She turned to William Vyvyan. 'I understand you run a trading business to the Mediterranean, Mr Vyvyan? My husband and I are currently living in Gibraltar and I must say I do not know how we would go on without regular visits from ships bringing in all those things we have come to rely on for our comfort.'

Relieved that she was no longer the focus of

141

attention, and grateful for Judith's ability to redirect conversation from contentious subjects to harmless ones, an apparently effortless ability honed to perfection by the demands of diplomacy, Kerenza turned to her meal. But after forcing down a few mouthfuls, her stomach rebelled and she set down her knife and fork feeling shaky and slightly sick, suddenly overwhelmed by the enormity of the morning's events.

'Please excuse me, I must–' Sliding out of her seat, she slipped out of the saloon and walked quickly along the passage towards the companionway. The open-work brass treads had been wiped clean, and the trail of blood leading into the captain's quarters had gone. She ran up the stairs. Perhaps in the fresh air and sunlight she might escape her tortured thoughts.

Chapter Nine

As she reached the top of the companionway, Kerenza suddenly realized she had forgotten to put on her cloak. She hesitated for a moment then stepped out over the coaming. She would not take cold in the spring-like warmth. As for her lack of a hat, who would even notice? The crew had more important concerns. The only person likely – no, *certain* – to disapprove was Betsy Woodrow. But she was below and hopefully would remain there.

Looking round, Kerenza saw the carpenter and a couple of hands replacing the length of rail splintered by the French privateer's cannonball. The rest of the duty watch was busy with various tasks. The remainder of the crew were down in the fo'c'sle having their dinner. The silence seemed strange. Normally while working on the continuous repair and replacement of rigging the men talked. Sometimes the banter flared into snarling quarrels. But a few well-aimed blows of the short length of thick rope carried by the bosun swiftly ended these.

Maggot was by the mainmast talking to the bosun. Both had their backs to her. As she passed the skylight on her way towards the stern the temptation to look down was too strong to resist.

Seated at the newly tidied table, his jacket discarded, the sleeves of a loose and crumpled white shirt rolled halfway up his forearms, Nick was writing in what appeared to be a journal, his head supported on one hand. Wrenching her gaze away she caught the eye of the able seaman at the wheel and felt her colour rise.

He bobbed his head. 'Aft'noon, miss.'

'G-good afternoon.' They had never spoken before. And she was surprised that he should speak without first being addressed.

'Begging your pardon, miss.'

'Yes?'

'Well, we 'eard what you done this morning. Much appreciated. Just wanted you to know. Hope you don't mind.'

'No, not at all. Thank you.'

With a jerky nod, the seaman checked the compass then raised his gaze to the topsail.

Kerenza continued towards the stern. Usually

143

the crew behaved as though the passengers were invisible. But with this helmsman most often at the wheel when she came topside, deliberately ignoring him seemed ill mannered. So after their second encounter she had started to acknowledge him with a brief nod.

On one of her rare visits to the deck Betsy Woodrow had witnessed the silent exchange. Later, over tea, she took Kerenza to task.

'Miss Vyvyan, I'm sure you intended mere courtesy. But to men such as these your conduct might well be seen as overly *familiar*.'

Stung, Kerenza felt heat rise in her cheeks, but she kept a tight rein on her temper and her tongue. 'I have no reason to think so, ma'am. Nor can I believe it in any way wrong to recognize the presence of men to whom we owe our safety while we are at sea.'

Exasperated, Betsy had turned to Judith. 'Lady Russell, I know you will support me in this. For surely such behaviour is tantamount to making friends of one's servants.'

With a sigh of mock penitence Judith had shaken her head. 'Alas, Mrs Woodrow. I fear I must disappoint you. You see, my husband's job is extremely demanding. It would be almost impossible but for the dedication and loyalty of our staff and servants. Over the years both he and I have discovered that appreciation inspires even greater commitment. And I will confess that among my personal servants are some I do indeed think of as dear and trusted friends.'

As Betsy flushed, her mortification self-inflicted, Judith demonstrated kindness as well as

144

tact by changing the subject to the new season's fashions.

In her corner between the paint-store and the stern, Kerenza rested her forearms on the wooden rail and gazed eastward at the restless glittering ocean. She had deliberately chosen the lee side, even though being closer to the water meant flying spray dampened her face and hair. Running her tongue across her lips she tasted salt.

The upper, or weather, side of the ship was traditionally the captain's domain. Though Nick wasn't on deck now he might come up in a little while. She did not want him to feel obliged to speak to her. In the captain's day cabin he had started to apologize and she had stopped him. If he came up on deck and found her, apparently waiting, might he try again? Did she want him to? The truth was, she wasn't sure. Might it not be less painful to leave things as they were? The relief and surging joy she had felt earlier were being smothered by suspicion.

Why had he apologized? Because he thought she had? That alone was surely not sufficient incentive. Something else must have prompted his change of heart. But what? He had severed their attachment without a word of explanation. Though from the tone and content of his questions, it was clear to her now that his cousin had had something to do with it.

Surely if she had really mattered to him he would have trusted her, believed her? But he hadn't. She had believed their attraction, *their love*, to be mutual. But what if it existed only on

145

her side? Perhaps she had seen what she wanted to see.

No stranger to rejection, she had learned over many years to deal with it. And though not all her strategies had been successful she had survived. Given her previous experience she should have been more wary, less willing to trust. Instead, she had opened her heart to him. And he had almost destroyed her. She could not take that risk again.

The watch bell struck, and with a deep shuddering sigh she turned her head. Maggot and the bosun had both disappeared, and the sail-maker was sitting on the deck by the capstan. With his ditty bag beside him and a piece of coarse sail canvas in his lap, he was setting stitches in a steady rhythm, using a metal palm to force the needle through, then drawing up the thick thread. After a moment he tied a knot and cut the thread with a folding knife. As he lifted the sailcloth she saw its long narrow shape, realized its purpose, and her skin tightened in a shiver.

Donald Woodrow lurched down the deck to the rail, one hand clapped to the shallow crown of his round hat. 'Ah, Miss Vyvyan. Forgive me, I did not mean to intrude upon your privacy. After the very distressing events of the morning I understand very well your desire for a quiet period in which to compose yourself. Though given the nature of our surroundings, space and solitude are not easily found.'

Her resentment of his arrival dissolved. The minister was gentle, well intentioned, and possessed a kind heart. Which was more than could be said of his wife.

She smiled at him. 'I come here every day. To see nothing but ocean all around helps put things in perspective.'

He nodded. 'Miss Vyvyan.' He seemed to be struggling to find the right words. 'May I beg a moment of your time? I wanted – that is – it cannot have escaped your notice that my wife is a woman of definite opinions, which, as you have witnessed, she is wont to express in a forthright manner. Sometimes her wish to offer counsel overrides consideration for the sensibilities of those to whom she is speaking.'

Sometimes? Kerenza longed to point out that Mrs Woodrow never presumed to lecture Lady Russell. But seeing he had not finished, she bit hard on the inside of her lower lip and remained silent.

'I am – painfully – aware that Mrs Woodrow has singled you out for guidance and advice. I beg you will forgive her, Miss Vyvyan. And I hope you will forgive me when I say that I did not expect to see such courage and compassion in one so young. It is because I have observed these gifts in you that I ask you to try and understand.' He smiled sadly. 'I am in part responsible. You see, my wife harboured ambitions for me that were far beyond my capabilities, or indeed, my aspirations. Had we been blessed with a family she would have found an outlet for her energies in supervizing their welfare and upbringing. However, it was not to be.' In the small weary shrug Kerenza read despair. 'Miss Vyvyan, I find nothing in your manner or behaviour deserving of criticism. But to my wife your youth, and your

147

easy friendship with Lady Russell, are a reminder of too many unfulfilled hopes and bitter disappointments. It is a heavy burden for her to bear.'

Kerenza raised her eyes, studying him in wonder. 'You have been very frank, sir. And I hope you will not think me impertinent when I say your loyalty does you great credit. For I cannot help being aware that I am not the only target of Mrs Woodrow's criticism. Yet you have responded only with patience and kindness.'

He met her gaze for a moment, nodding slowly, then turned to leave, saying over his shoulder, 'And that, Miss Vyvyan, is my burden.'

At five o'clock, enveloped in the navy boat cloak and wearing her bonnet, Kerenza helped Judith up the companionway stairs. All hands had mustered on deck dressed in their best shore-going rig. *Kestrel* had been turned into the wind, the huge fore and aft sails were reefed in, and the ship was lying hove-to. Looking round she saw Nick and Maggot at the starboard rail, sombre and formal in their best uniforms as they watched two seamen set one end of a broad plank on the rail and support the other end on a trestle.

Catching sight of her, Maggot indicated the chair placed beside the skylight. Kerenza recognized it as the one from the saloon.

'This for Lady Russell.'

Kerenza met Nick's piercing gaze for an instant and looked away swiftly.

'How very kind,' Judith said. 'Thank you so much.' She leaned heavily on Kerenza's arm as they crossed the deck.

'Are you cold?' Kerenza enquired softly, helping

148

Judith sit, and willing her to say yes. 'Would you like me to fetch a blanket?' The warmth had gone from the day, but she could feel her entire body flushing under Nick's scrutiny. Since leaving Cornwall almost a week ago he had ignored her. Why was he watching her now?

Drawing the folds of fur-lined burgundy velvet across her knees, Judith glanced up and patted Kerenza's hand. 'No, I'm perfectly comfortable.' Her brows lifted a fraction. 'Would you be easier on my other side? I think you would be out of the breeze.'

And angled away from Nick. Moving to stand behind Judith's shoulder, Kerenza saw her father emerge from the hatchway looking drawn and ill. She offered him a tentative smile. But he seemed not to notice. Instead of joining Judith and herself he chose a spot between the companionway and the water barrels. Staring into space, deep in his own thoughts, he defied approach.

Then Betsy Woodrow arrived, her face puce from the effort of climbing the steep stairs. She too stood apart, raising her hand to the hat tied on over her frilled cap, then fussing with the ties of her grey cloak. Her husband came last. Bareheaded and carrying a Bible, he stood beside the companionway as the captain's body, sewn into the sailcloth shroud with cannonballs at his feet, was carried up from below by two seamen and laid gently on the plank.

The sight of the canvas-wrapped body rekindled horrific images and Kerenza quickly averted her gaze, her heart pounding as she fought a resurgent sense of helplessness and guilt. Could she

149

have done more? Toy had asked her what they should do. Should she have tried to remove the splinter? Might it have made a difference? *Stop*. It was too late now.

The sinking sun tinted the clouds pink and beamed golden rays on to the dark restless sea as Donald Woodrow began the service with a prayer.

She had seen Sam Penrose welcome death, and had watched Nick try to absorb the loss of his uncle and mentor, and his captain. Though the personal loss was deeply sad, the death of *Kestrel*'s captain meant that as the senior officer, Nick was now solely responsible for the safety of the ship, the mail, and the passengers.

Her father, distant and unreachable, had found in Sam Penrose a kindred spirit. Her vision blurred. As she blinked away tears she heard Nick clear his throat, and saw the book tremble in his hands as he began to read the twenty-third psalm. His voice steadied and grew stronger with each line. When he had finished he looked up, straight into her eyes. As shock coursed through her, he turned his head to scan the crew's weathered faces.

'Many of you sailed with Sam Penrose on other ships. You knew him well. It's fitting that one of *you* should say a few words.' His gaze moved to the bosun. 'Mr Laity?'

Snatching off his hat, the bosun gripped the rim, turning it in his scarred hands. 'Thirty years I knew him. He was hard, but he was fair. Looked after his men, he did. God rest his soul.' As his words were echoed and heads nodded,

Laity jammed his hat back on. Nick gestured for the minister to continue.

While Donald Woodrow intoned the words of committal, Kerenza swallowed repeatedly as Nick and Maggot gripped the plank near the trestle and raised it high, sending Sam Penrose's mortal remains to their final rest in the Atlantic Ocean.

A few minutes later, Nick gave the order to get underway. And as the crew quickly dispersed, Kerenza saw her father disappear down the companionway and guessed she would see no more of him that evening. He would seek solace in a bottle of brandy. Betsy Woodrow followed him down, calling her husband to assist her and voicing her hope that tea would not be long.

The ship's tilt as the wind filled her sails and her gathering speed caused Judith to stumble as she rose to her feet. Kerenza caught her and offered a supportive arm.

'I'll go down first,' she said, as they reached the companionway. 'Then I can steady you.'

'What about the chair?'

'I bring chair,' Maggot said.

'You are all so good to me.' Judith shook her head.

Kerenza waited at the bottom of the stairs looking up as Judith descended.

Three-quarters of the way down, she smiled. 'You see? All is well.' As the final syllable left her lips, the ship suddenly plunged then rose sharply. Losing her grip on the rail, Judith gave a sharp cry as she tipped forward.

Reaching out, Kerenza caught her and though

151

they both staggered, neither fell. 'Are you all right?'

Judith nodded quickly. 'Yes. I'm fine. It jolted me a little.' Pressing a hand to her bosom she blew out another laughing breath. 'Thank goodness it was only three steps. Had I fallen on top of you' – she shook her head – 'you would have suffered far worse than me.' She slipped her arm through Kerenza's. 'Let us take off our hats and cloaks and have some tea.'

'Would you like to lie down?' Kerenza suggested, her own heart still beating uncomfortably fast as she tried to block the repeating image of Judith falling. Everything was all right. She had landed on her feet. She was safe: the baby was safe. But it must have been a nasty shock. 'I could bring your tea to you in the cabin.'

Judith squeezed Kerenza's arm. 'That is very sweet of you. If we had more space and some natural light, I would enjoy it very much. Not because I feel at all ill,' she added, squeezing Kerenza's arm in reassurance. 'But respite from Mrs Woodrow's opinions would be welcome.' She sighed. 'However, now we are underway again, I think it will be easier to sit at the table. At least in the saloon we have fiddle rails to stop our plates and cups from sliding to the floor.' Releasing Kerenza's arm she opened the cabin door. 'I *do* hope Maggot joins us.'

'So do I.' Not only was the second mate informative and entertaining, his presence ensured Betsy Woodrow did not linger.

But as the meal progressed it was clear neither Maggot nor Nick would be coming down.

Kerenza's relief far outweighed any disappointment.

'Where is your father, Miss Vyvyan?' Betsy demanded. 'Should you not try to persuade him to join us?'

'I think not, Mrs Woodrow. I'm sure he will return to the table tomorrow. But tonight he prefers to be alone.' Kerenza glanced up at the skylight then focused on her plate, aware of Judith talking to the minister, and longing for the moment they could leave.

She heard shouts as the log was hove and the course and speed noted. Then four bells signalled the end of the first dog-watch when helmsman and lookouts were changed; and bosun, carpenter and sailmaker left the deck, their day's work finished. As *Kestrel* sailed on in the approaching darkness, on deck a seaman would be lighting the binnacle candles and side-lamps.

Later that night, Kerenza lay, staring up into the darkness, the deckhead less that two feet from her face. It astonished her how quickly she had adjusted to the continuous noise of the ship: creaking timbers, the thump and hiss of the sea against the hull, the regular clang of the watch bell, shouts from the lookout, and the additional racket of sail changes.

She was already awake when Billy brought the hot water, and while Judith remained in her cot, Kerenza quickly washed and dressed. She picked up her riding dress. *Too many memories.* Folding it neatly she placed it on the rumpled blanket, opened her trunk, and lifted out a long-sleeved round gown of pale-green muslin. After brushing her hair and twisting it into a chignon secured on top of her head with pins, she put the riding dress in her trunk and closed the lid. Then, emptying the basin, she refilled it with hot water and picked up her cloak. 'I'll go and see what the weather is like.' She left the cabin, closing the door behind her.

Twice she had offered assistance, but Judith had declined, citing the lack of space and her own bulk. Interpreting the refusal as a desire for privacy, Kerenza had not offered again.

Nodding to the helmsman, she crossed to her favourite spot, inhaling deeply. The air was cool, crisp and sweet. A stiff breeze filled the sails, driving *Kestrel* through the sapphire swell at a spanking pace.

Today was Sunday, and once the necessary ship's business was complete all crew, except those performing essential tasks, would have the day off. This was their one chance in the week to shave and bathe, then oil and replait each other's hair.

When the watch bell struck the half-hour and the glass was turned, Kerenza went below again. Seeing the hot water jug still full outside her father's door, Kerenza hesitated, then went on down the passage. The smell of frying bacon and coffee made her stomach contract, and she realized she was hungry. Seeing the cabin empty she hung her cloak on the hook behind the door. Passing the Woodrows' cabin she heard the familiar sounds of sniping and placation. Sympathy for the minister was pushed aside by hope that she might finish her breakfast before Betsy emerged.

Judith was alone except for the steward who was setting the tea and coffee pots on the table. She smiled a welcome.

'How is it up there?'

'Beautiful.' Kerenza turned. 'Mr Broad, could I ask a favour?'

'You can, miss. What do 'e want?'

'My father...' She tugged her earlobe. 'I'm concerned that he... I had hoped he would...'

'You sit yourself down, miss, and I'll go and see if Mr Vyvyan might be wishful of some help.'

Kerenza smiled through a surge of relief. 'That's very kind of you.'

'Nothing of the sort, miss. 'Tis what I'm here for.' He stumped out of the saloon and down the passage.

By unspoken agreement they ate quickly, and Kerenza was helping Judith to her feet when the Woodrows entered the saloon. Her arm through Kerenza's, Judith exchanged greetings on the threshold but kept walking.

Back in the cabin, she caught her breath and sat heavily on her cot, pressing a hand to her lower back.

Kerenza felt a flutter of anxiety. That was the second time this morning. 'Are you in pain?'

'It's nothing.' Judith waved aside her concern. 'The merest twinge. I must have jarred something yesterday when I came so heavily off the stairs. I should have been more careful. But truly, I'm fine. Though I must admit, considering the angle of the ship, I'm a little nervous about climbing the companionway stairs this morning. In fact, I think I'll give the service a miss and stay

155

down here.'

Kerenza nodded. 'Would you like me to stay with you?'

'There's really no need. I'm perfectly all right. And I know how much you enjoy the fresh air.'

'I can enjoy it later. The thing is' – she looked pleadingly at Judith – 'if you felt you had need of me, I wouldn't have to spend the next hour with Mrs Woodrow.'

'Ah.' Judith blinked. 'Do you know, it has just occurred to me that my hair is in desperate need of washing. And if everyone is topside for the service it offers the perfect opportunity. We could be private and comfortable in the saloon without inconvenience to anyone. Would you be so very kind as to help me?'

Kerenza beamed. 'It would be my pleasure.'

As soon as she heard the minister and his wife pass by the door, then Betsy Woodrow's heavy tread on the companionway stairs, Kerenza helped Judith along to the saloon and made sure she was comfortable, this time on the chair.

'For it will be easier if I can stand behind you.'

Then hurrying back to the cabin she collected towels, both sets of brushes and combs, flannel squares, and from each trunk a bottle of hair wash and one of sweet oil.

Leaving the cabin she heard voices: her father irritable and reluctant, Broad calm and persuasive. Releasing her relief in a soft sigh she turned towards the saloon.

'Miss Vyvyan?'

She froze. Behind her a door clicked shut and Nick's swift footsteps approached.

'I hope that after yesterday – that your night's rest was not too much disturbed.'

She had watched his uncle die. Good manners forbade she ignore him. Half turning she kept her gaze fixed on the bundle in her arms. 'No more than yours, I imagine.'

'Then you will not have slept at all.'

His quiet intensity brought her head up and she realized that once again they were at cross-purposes. She shook her head quickly. 'No–'

He raised one hand, palm facing her. 'Forgive me, I should not have – now is not the time.' He took a breath. 'Will you be attending the service?'

Looking away, she shook her head. 'Lady Russell's accident has left her a little shaken and–'

'What accident? And why was I not told?'

'Because–' *Because you already had too much to concern you. And because I dare not be in your company. For when I am with you I cannot trust my heart or my head.* She swallowed. 'Because it was not serious. The ship's plunging threw her from a lower stair. But she kept her feet and did not fall. It startled her, but no more than that.'

'How do you know?'

'I was with her, and was able to catch her.'

'You're sure she is all right?'

Kerenza recalled Judith's brief grimaces of pain, and her insistence that all was well. Perhaps such pangs were normal in late pregnancy. And if they were not, what would be achieved by adding her concern to the weight of responsibilities already on his shoulders?

'She says she is perfectly well. But preferring not to climb the stairs this morning she asked me to stay with her.'

'She could not have better company.' With a brief bow he turned towards the stairs.

A few moments later, knowing her chaotic emotions were visible in her heightened colour and unable to do anything about it, Kerenza entered the saloon. Judith looked up and smiled.

'There you are. For a moment I feared that Mrs Woodrow had returned. Then it occurred to me that you were having difficulty finding the bottles. I fear my trunk is sadly untidy.'

'No. I found them right away.' Kerenza set down her armful, and concentrated on placing things neatly so she could keep her head averted. 'As I left the cabin, Mr Penrose enquired if we would be attending the service and when I said no, wanted reassurance that you were quite well.'

'I hope you told him that I am?'

'I did. Do you prefer to use your own wash? I have a bottle of rosemary water mixed with borax which gives excellent results.'

'I should like to try that.'

Draping a towel round Judith's shoulders, Kerenza quickly unpinned her hair and brushed it out. Then after shaking the bottle she opened it, tipped it against one of the flannel squares, and starting at Judith's hairline stroked the cloth over her scalp.

Judith sighed. 'That is so relaxing.'

'I heard Maggot say that if the wind remains westerly we are less than two days from Gibraltar.' Kerenza was anxious to deflect attention from herself. 'What are you most looking forward to when you leave the ship?'

'Seeing my husband. Then, I think a hot bath.'
'Oh yes,' Kerenza sighed. 'And a proper bed.'
'A floor that doesn't tilt.'
'Being able to spread my arms without hitting anything.'
'Fresh clothes every day. And privacy.' Reaching up, she patted Kerenza's hand. 'I was not looking forward to sharing a cabin. But in fact I have enjoyed it. Though I fear I have put you to a lot of trouble. And don't think I am not sensible of your tact in removing yourself from the cabin each morning.'
'No, not at all,' Kerenza demurred. 'What little I have done, I have done with pleasure. I have far more reason than you for gratitude. Without you to deflect Mrs Woodrow's attention my journey would have been miserable.' Judith's head was now thoroughly wet. Kerenza recorked the bottle and drew the comb through to spread the wash from root to tip.
'You are very good at this. How did you become so skilled?'
'Well, I have always done my own. Then, when my grandmother was ill, I started doing hers as well. She found it soothing.'
'I hope she is fully recovered?'
'Oh yes, this was some time ago. She enjoys excellent health now. Which is as well, for every day she receives invitations to balls and parties and suppers.' Remembering Judith's rank and position Kerenza suddenly felt shy. 'I expect you do a great deal of entertaining.' She saw Judith's shoulders lift as she sighed.
'It is a necessary part of my husband's job. In

159

Gibraltar, our most frequent guests are senior naval officers from the Mediterranean Squadron. In fact, you may be acquainted with one of our recent guests, Captain Ashworth? I remember him saying his home was in Falmouth.'

Setting down the comb, Kerenza picked up a towel and began gently to rub Judith's scalp. 'I do not know Captain Ashworth. And though I have met his son I could wish I had not.'

Judith swung round her eyes alight. '*My* dear, do tell. What did you dislike in him?'

'Apart from his arrogance and vanity?' Anger bubbled up as Kerenza remembered that evening. 'He spoke at great length about his adventures and his importance, and I think he took it amiss when I was not sufficiently impressed. But what really made me take him in dislike were his slighting remarks about ... about someone known to both of us. If his father is similar, then I shall not be sorry if I never meet him.' Gathering Judith's long tresses in the towel, she rubbed them hard.

'Admiral Hotham appears to think well of Captain Ashworth as a commander,' Judith said. Though he hinted that the captain is perhaps over demanding of his officers and crew. Personally, I found Captain Ashworth proud to the point of arrogance, and very much on his dignity. He spoke several times of his son, and clearly expects great things of him. One can only hope, for the young man's sake, he is equal to the task.'

Dropping the towel, Kerenza picked up Judith's silver-backed brush and swept it through the long tresses, lifting them over her arm to allow air through. 'Well, I cannot think well of him. In fact, I suspect–' She caught herself. 'Still, as *he* holds himself in the highest esteem, I doubt he cares in the least for anyone else's good opinion.'

'I fear you may be mistaken in that,' Judith's voice held a note of warning. 'I have met many such men, young and old. And too often the opposite is true. But, tell me, of what do you suspect him? And though it should not be necessary – for you must know that in our conversations I have been most dreadfully indiscreet – I give you my word that anything you tell me will be treated as a confidence.'

Kerenza had never imagined confiding her fears or her shame to anyone. But Judith's gentle encouragement and the intimacy of the moment made the need too powerful to resist and suddenly all her suspicions, confusion and terrible hurt came tumbling out.

Chapter Ten

When it had all spilled out Kerenza sank down on to the bench facing Judith, exhausted and trembling from emotions that had swept her up like surf boiling over a reef, then thrown her back on to the rocky shore of the present.

'So you believe it is Lieutenant Ashworth who is responsible for the rift between you and Mr Penrose?' Judith pressed.

Kerenza turned the silver brush between her fingers. 'I believe he may have said something about me. I can think of no other explanation for … what happened. But as for responsibility' – she raised a stricken face – 'that lies with Mr Penrose.'

'My dear.' Leaning forward, Judith laid a hand over Kerenza's. 'It is as well that the Woodrows and your father have had other matters on their minds, because it is only too clear to me that this quarrel is causing both you and Mr Penrose a great deal of unhappiness. You say Mr Penrose has attempted to apologize. Could you not find it in your heart to forgive him? By your own account when this misunderstanding occurred you and he had been closely acquainted for only a short time.'

Setting the brush on the table, Kerenza reached for the second bottle. She poured a little into her cupped palm, inhaling the familiar fragrance of lavender essence that perfumed the sweet olive oil. 'I could forgive him for listening to what his cousin told him; I could even forgive him for giving some credence to whatever he was told. After all, why should he doubt the word of a naval officer who is also a member of his own family? And, as you say, we had not been … had not known each other very long. But what I cannot forgive–' Her voice wavered and she had to swallow before she could continue. 'What hurts so much is that he did not ask *me*.'

They were six at table for dinner. As expected, Betsy enquired the reason for Kerenza's absence

162

from the service.

'You must hold me responsible, Mrs Woodrow,' Judith intervened. 'I did not think it wise to attempt the companionway stairs twice in one day. And, as I wish to spend an hour or so on deck this afternoon, I prevailed upon Miss Vyvyan to remain with me this morning to keep me company and she was kind enough to oblige.'

Betsy's sharp eyes flicked to Judith's glossy hair now pinned up in a smooth coil, but she made no comment. Kerenza shifted her gaze to her father, marvelling at his appearance. He was sober, his jaw freshly shaved, his clothes brushed, and his neckcloth neatly tied about a clean collar. She wondered how Broad had achieved the miracle. Maggot joined them and, within minutes, to her husband's obvious embarrassment, Betsy was enquiring pointedly into his background.

'You want to know about my family?' Bitter-chocolate eyes gleamed above high cheekbones. 'My father's father was pirate. Have much hair on his chest.'

As Betsy spluttered, Judith smiled round the table. 'It's an old Moorish saying, signifying a man of action, a very brave man.'

Maggot nodded, then his brows gathered, and for an awful moment Kerenza feared he was going to claim the literal as well as allegorical truth of his statement. 'He was Tamazirght, from Rif mountains.'

'Tamazirght is what the people we call Berber call themselves,' Judith said, as everyone looked to her for explanation.

'He take his ship from Salé to England, to

163

Cornwall. He see girl in village, very beautiful, very sad. So he put her on ship and bring her to his house.'

Betsy's eyes bulged with shock and her florid face reflected horror. 'He *kidnapped* her? That's terrible! It's wicked! It's–'

'No, no, is very good,' Maggot was earnest. 'She happy. They have many children.'

'Your grandmother was a Cornishwoman?' Kerenza said, fascinated, while Betsy muttered under her breath.

Maggot nodded. 'My father is second son. He no like the sea.' Shrugging his incomprehension of such an attitude, Maggot continued, 'He become *tagir*, merchant, in Tangier. He trade with Spain, Gibraltar, Italy. Build good business. Make lot of money. He marry girl from Gibraltar.' He shot a sly grin at Betsy. 'Her father was English sailor.' He sighed. 'My mother very beautiful. But she die of fever.'

'How old were you?' Kerenza asked.

He held up both hands, palms out, fingers spread. 'Then my father marry again. She is Tanjawi. Her husband die. She no have children. Is very kind to me. They are very happy. But three years ago my father is on ship to Livorno. Is attacked by French warship and he is killed.'

'What about your stepmother?' Kerenza asked.

'She no with him on the ship. Was at home running business. Now she run small hotel.'

'That reminds me.' Judith turned to Kerenza's father. 'Mr Vyvyan, please don't think me impertinent, but before you left Tangier did you make arrangements for somewhere to stay on

164

your return?'

William shook his head. 'To be honest, ma'am, my thoughts were only of my wife and daughter.' Kerenza tried to ignore the pang inflicted by this reminder of her own unimportance, remaining carefully expressionless as he continued, 'I was concerned with getting to England to raise the money, then finding a ship to return me as quickly as possible to Tangier. Perhaps the British consul—'

Judith and Maggot both shook their heads. 'He may not even be in Tangier when you arrive,' Judith explained. 'The sultan has a habit of summoning various consuls then keeping them waiting for days or even weeks before granting an audience. It's not unheard of for them to be sent back without ever seeing the sultan. The British consul is not alone in receiving such treatment. Other consuls are also forced to make similar fruitless journeys.'

'You stay at hotel of my father's wife,' Maggot announced with the air of a magician completing an amazing trick.

Kerenza caught her father's eye, saw his hesitation, glimpsed Betsy Woodrow's bosom swelling as she drew breath to add her own opinion to a matter that in no way concerned her, and spoke quickly.

'That sounds like an excellent idea, Papa. You will surely have enough to do when we arrive without the additional worry of finding somewhere for us to stay.'

After another hesitation, William Vyvyan inclined his head towards the Tanjawi. 'Much

165

obliged to you,' he said gruffly.

After dinner, they all went up on deck, and passed the afternoon in the sunshine. The crew sprawled in groups at the forward end of the ship. Some washed clothes in a wooden bucket while others worked at fancy knots or small wood-carvings. One or two whittled clothes-pins that were much sought after.

Sitting with Judith when Nick came on deck, Kerenza kept her eyes averted. She mulled over what Judith had said about forgiveness, but could not forget that he had preferred to cut her. And even when he had found her on deck, and questioned her, he had chosen to take his cousin's side. She had not meant enough to him then. Why should it be different now? And what of the future? Would his instinct always be to believe anyone else before her? How could she trust someone who had so little faith in her?

She gazed out over the port rail and listened as the minister talked of reaching Gibraltar within a day or two. She would miss Judith. As the sun dipped, the afternoon grew cool and the passengers returned to the saloon for tea.

During the night, woken by the squeal of blocks and rattle of rings as the big gaff sails were reefed in, Kerenza was tipped from one side of her cot to the other as the ship changed direction. The tilt and plunge increased and her heart sank as she realized that the wind must have shifted and the sea was becoming rougher.

Venturing on deck the next morning, the difference was instantly visible, and the contrast shocking. The previous day had been one of blue skies, sunshine, and sparkling sapphire water. Now the sea was a froth of white caps, and the sky the colour of curdled milk. Through the haze she could just make out a brown smudge on the horizon which she knew must be the coast of Spain.

The rest of the day brought them no closer. A strong east wind funnelling through the straits made it impossible for *Kestrel* to approach. Hour after hour passed, and the packet could only beat to and fro, making no progress.

Lookouts were doubled and tension made the crew surly for, held back by wind and sea, the packet was increasingly vulnerable to attack by French warships or privateers. The weather dominated conversation at every meal. When might the wind change or drop sufficiently to allow them to enter the straits?

'It's so frustrating,' Judith cried, in a rare display of annoyance, as they left the cabin to go to the saloon for tea. 'I'm only a few hours from home. If only this horrible wind would ease.' As the ship rose and fell, she steadied herself against the bulkhead with one hand, pressing the other to her lower back and bending her head as she sucked in a sharp breath.

Kerenza's sympathy was tinged with concern. 'I wish there was something I could do.'

Straightening, Judith's smile reflected her tiredness. 'And I must stop grumbling. You have been so kind and so patient. This delay is surely just as frustrating for you.' She slipped her arm through Kerenza's, pressing it gently.

As they entered the saloon, Kerenza was forced

to acknowledge that her feelings about reaching Tangier were not as clear or straightforward as Judith imagined. Of course, she hoped her mother and sister were well and unharmed. But as for seeing them again, and having to care for them on the voyage home, she wasn't looking forward to that at all, which made her feel guilty and ashamed.

With Betsy Woodrow engrossed in her food and the minister deep in conversation with her father, Kerenza was free to follow her own thoughts. But these were in such a tangle she found little comfort in silence. Neither Nick nor Maggot joined them. Even Judith, normally so skilled at raising topics to which all might contribute was unusually quiet.

They went early to bed, everyone admitting weariness from the uncomfortable contortions of the ship. As she turned out the lamp and climbed up into her cot, Kerenza hoped for Judith's sake that the wind might drop during the hours of darkness and allow them in the morning to begin their approach to Gibraltar harbour.

She fell asleep quickly, physically and emotionally worn out. Waking with a start, she wondered what the time was. It must still be night, for there was no glimmer of light visible in the gap above the door. Nor, she realized with a sigh, had the weather changed. So what had wakened her?

Hearing the faint clang of the watch-bell and footsteps on the deck, she closed her heavy eyelids. They flew open again an instant later, her heart racing at the sound of a soft groan. She knew now it was this that had roused her from the depths of sleep. Propped on one elbow she leaned over the edge of her cot.

'Judith? Is something wrong?'

'I don't – I'm not sure. I do feel cold.'

The note of uncertainty sent a spear of unease through Kerenza's stomach. 'Are you in pain?'

'Not exactly.' But the silence had lasted a fraction too long. 'It's just – my back aches so badly.'

Trying to ignore the painful thumping against her ribs and dreading the answer, Kerenza forced herself to ask. 'Do you think the baby is coming?'

'I don't know. But I'm afraid it might be. And it's too soon.'

The fear in Judith's whisper smothered Kerenza's panic as she swung her legs over the side of her cot and dropped to the cabin floor.

'Lie still while I light the lamp.' Her hands were shaking so badly it took several attempts before the wick burned steadily and had ceased to smoke. Shivering in her nightdress, as much from apprehension as from the night's chill, Kerenza pulled the blanket from her cot and crouched to place it over Judith who was lying on her side.

'I'll go and find the steward. We need hot bottles for your feet and your back.'

Judith's eyes were huge, and the lamplight revealed both pain and anxiety. She gripped Kerenza's fingers where they rested on the edge of the cot. 'Please don't be long.'

'I won't, I promise. I don't think I'd better go like this, though.' She indicated the thin white cotton. 'Can you imagine what would happen if Mrs Woodrow were to see me? She'd wake the entire ship with a fit of hysterics.'

169

'I'd prefer she didn't know,' Judith said. 'About this, about me.'

'No doubt she is fast asleep and will remain so,' Kerenza soothed, hoping fervently that this was indeed the case. Quickly shedding the white cotton, she pulled on her shift and over it her green muslin gown. Stuffing her bare feet into cold shoes, her hair falling in a long loose braid over one shoulder, she picked up the woollen shawl she had been wearing as a bed jacket, crossed the ends over her bosom and tied them at the back. Leaving her hands and arms free it was warm but far less bulky than her cloak.

'I'll be as quick as I can,' she promised, and opened the door quietly, her heart giving an unpleasant lurch when Judith tucked her head to her chest as a groan was wrenched from her.

Creeping past the Woodrows' cabin, Kerenza heard two sets of snores. Their rhythm did not alter as she closed the saloon door carefully behind her. At the far end, the door leading to the galley passage was fastened back. Seeing a faint glow she felt a rush of relief. Someone was still awake. Hearing low-pitched voices talking quietly, she knocked softly on the bulkhead to warn of her arrival. Looking in she saw Broad and Toy sitting on stools either side of the galley stove, a half-empty bottle of rum on the stained floor between them.

'I'm so sorry to intrude,' she said quickly, as they looked up, startled. 'But Lady Russell is – unwell.'

Exchanging a glance, the two men rose to their feet, Toy catching up the rum bottle. 'Babby on

170

the way, is it?' Broad asked.

Kerenza shrugged helplessly, twisting her fingers. 'I'm not sure. She fears so. She has severe back pains. She's been having them for nearly two days. And she's complaining of cold.'

Toy looked at Broad. 'What do 'e think? You've seen babbies born aboard before.'

Kerenza peered at the steward, her emotions swinging between shock and hope. 'Have you, Mr Broad?'

'Two, over the years. But we had a doctor aboard, and both ladies had a maid with 'em. I never had no personal experience like.'

Kerenza tried to hide her disappointment. 'Do you know if there are any hot bottles aboard?'

'I think there's an old tin one in my cupboard,' he said. 'I'll go and see.'

'And I'll put the kettle on,' Toy volunteered. 'Like a cup of tea, would she?'

'Oh, how kind. That would be marvellous.'

Toy sighed. 'As one soul depart, another do get born.' His voice faltered, and after sniffing hard he squared his shoulders. 'Put a cup on for you as well, shall I?'

'I'd appreciate that, thank you.'

'Dear life.' He shook his head in sympathy. 'All due respect, miss, but you're having some time of it.'

'Told Mr Penrose yet, have you?' Broad asked, trying to unscrew the top off a dented oblong tin, another tucked under his arm.

'Not yet.' Kerenza had been trying not to think about that. But clearly he would have to be told. And courtesy, as well as necessity, demanded she be the one to tell him. Part of her dreaded seeing him again because of all the turmoil it would stir up, but the other part, the deeper, yearning, treacherous part, was already reasoning that the cause was legitimate, not merely an excuse.

'I think I had better do it now. Mr Toy, do you know if the captain has – had – any medical books?'

'What do you want they for?' Toy asked, bewildered.

Broad rolled his eyes in exasperation. 'Why d'you think?'

Kerenza explained, 'I'm hoping that one might have a chapter about – that would be helpful in – in the current situation.'

'Doctor prob'ly had some books,' Broad said thoughtfully. 'Bound to have done. He left a great pile of stuff when he jumped ship in Jamaica.' He lowered his voice, shooting Kerenza a meaningful look. 'Bit too partial to the rum, he was. I mean, we all like a drop now and then to keep out the cold, but,' – an indrawn breath hissed between his teeth as he shook his head – 'used to get the shakes something awful, he did. Like a leaf in a gale. I wouldn't trust him to sew on a button, let alone sewing up–'

'Miss Vyvyan don't want to hear none of that,' Toy interrupted, glaring at the steward before turning back to Kerenza. 'If I remember right, the captain, God rest his soul, dumped all the doctor's stuff in one of the sea berths. You ask Mr Penrose, miss. He'll know.'

'Bring anything to wrap these in, did you?' Broad held up the two tins. 'They'll be too hot to carry like they are.'

Kerenza raised empty hands. 'I'm sorry, I didn't think.'

'Don't you worry, I'll find something in the slop chest, a strip of old blanket or something. 'Tis all clean,' he assured her quickly. 'Cap'n always made certain we carried spare clothes and a blanket or two. Some of the men we take on haven't got a rag to their back, poor bugg– poor souls,' he amended hastily.

Kerenza was thinking hard, trying to recall all the relevant snippets of information overheard in conversations in the village shops, and between her grandmother and Lizzie Gendall.

'I don't suppose the chest might contain any sheets or towels?'

Broad looked doubtful. 'No call for anything fancy like that in the fo'c'sle, miss.'

'Oh well, never mind. Anything soft and clean will do. Old shirts would be fine, especially if they are linen or cotton. I will need to tear them up. But I'll make sure they are replaced,' she promised quickly.

'Don't you go fretting about that just now, miss,' Broad said. 'You got more'n enough on your mind.'

Far too much. Kerenza forced a smile. 'I must get back. I promised I wouldn't be long.'

'You go and tell Mr Penrose, then, miss,' Toy said. 'I'll bring a tray to your cabin soon as the kettle have boiled again.'

At the door Kerenza hesitated. 'You will try to be quiet, won't you?' she begged. 'Lady Russell doesn't – she's anxious that none of the other

173

passengers are disturbed.'

'Yes, and we all know who she mean by that,' Broad muttered darkly. 'Can't say as I blame her neither. One partic'lar person – naming no names – have done nothing but complain since coming aboard. I seen her kind before. Wouldn't give you the time of day if she could charge for it. And about as much use as a ripped sail. Well, we all seen that the other day. But you can forget her, miss; she won't wake.'

Kerenza fought the overwhelming temptation to ask how he could be so sure. She felt guilty already that she had not stopped him; asking him to explain was completely out of the question. But it seemed Broad was determined she should know why.

'Doses herself she do, from a great bottle of paregoric. Billy seen it when he collected the slops. 'Twas full when she come aboard, but 'tis near enough empty now.' He nodded confidently. 'She won't wake, miss.'

Kerenza tried not to show her shock. If Betsy Woodrow had consumed a full bottle of camphorated tincture of opium in ten days she must have the constitution of an ox. *Or be accustomed to it.* She turned to go, swept by a wave of sympathy for the minister.

Opening the saloon door into the passage, and greeted once again by the loud saw-like snores, Kerenza released the breath she had been holding. Back inside the cabin she crouched beside Judith.

'Broad found two tin bottles and is filling them. He'll bring them along as soon as he finds something to wrap them in. And Toy is making some tea. How are you?'

About to answer, Judith screwed her eyes shut, her face contorting as another pain gripped her, clearly longer and stronger than earlier ones.

Kerenza watched, feeling wretchedly helpless. Then, acting on instinct, she abandoned diffidence and caution and slipped her hand into Judith's.

Judith gripped her fingers tightly. As the pain passed, her face relaxed and, opening her eyes, she smiled tiredly. 'You are such a comfort. A cup of tea sounds wonderful.'

'I have to leave you again.'

'Must you?'

'Only for a few minutes. The doctor may have left some medical books behind. And as this is the first time for both of us I want to be sure I do everything properly.'

Judith moved her head uneasily on the pillow. 'Please don't be long. I know it's foolish of me but when I am alone I start to feel afraid.'

'No, you are not to worry.' Kerenza projected into her voice all the confidence and reassurance she could muster. 'Everything is going to be fine. Just try to rest. Between us we will cope admirably.'

A groove appeared between Judith's brows. 'This is not at all suitable, you know.'

Glancing round the cabin, Kerenza shrugged. 'Well, no, it's not,' she agreed. 'These are not the surroundings anyone would have *chosen*, but–'

'No,' Judith broke in. 'I mean it's not suitable that you, given your age and unmarried status,

175

should have to–'

'Now you sound just like Mrs Woodrow.'

Though weak and a little breathless, Judith's laugh was genuine. 'God forbid.'

'I promise you, I have a good idea of what will happen. It's one of the many benefits of living in a village. One overhears all kinds of useful things in shops and at tea parties when married ladies are talking.' Squeezing Judith's hand she stood up. 'I'll be back before you have time to miss me.'

Outside in the dark passage she leaned against the bulkhead, trembling slightly from reaction and shocked at the ease and fluency with which she had embroidered the truth, *no, lied.* Yet what else could she have done? Judith's labour had begun and all the wishes in the world would not halt it now. Of *course* it would be better, safer, and more suitable, if among the passengers there were a married woman who had borne children of her own. Such a person would be of far greater use to Judith than herself. But there was only her. One thing she was sure of, and it was plain common sense: the mother-to-be needed to be kept calm and as free of worry as possible.

Circumstances could hardly be worse. If bluff, even lies, would help Judith through her ordeal, then she would supply them. Judith had befriended and protected her. The hours ahead offered an opportunity to repay that kindness.

Her father's cabin was dark as she passed. Leaning close she heard the slow reverberation of deep sleep. But a strip of light beneath the captain's door indicated that Nick was still awake, even at this hour.

Her pulse quickened and she was suddenly acutely aware of the loose braid hanging over her right shoulder, the old shawl tied across her gown, and her bare legs. She shut her mind to such concerns. This was not about her. Right now, except to Judith, she was of no importance: it was Judith who mattered. She raised a hand and tapped softly.

'Yes?' He sounded preoccupied and very tired.

Bracing herself she opened the door, stepped inside, and closed it again, all in one swift movement.

'Ker– Miss Vyvyan?' he corrected himself. Dropping the pen with which he had been writing he rose quickly to his feet and slid out from behind the table.

Jacket discarded, sleeves rolled up exposing his forearms, shirt loose at the neck where threads of dark hair curled at the base of his throat, the intimacy of his dishevelled appearance made her once more aware of her own. A wave of heat engulfed her. She was glad to be outside the circle of light cast by the lamp.

Anxious that he should not misconstrue the secrecy of her visit, or her reasons for coming, she launched quickly into explanation.

'I'm so sorry to disturb you. But both Toy and Broad thought you should be informed at once. I would have told you anyway, though perhaps not quite yet–'

He raised a hand to stop her. 'Told me what?'

He looked so tired. 'It's Lady Russell. She's not – that is, she's–' Kerenza faltered.

'Is she unwell? She must be, otherwise you

177

would not be here. What's wrong? I thought – did you not tell me she was unharmed by her accident?'

Alert for accusation, Kerenza heard only an effort to wrench his thoughts from whatever had occupied them before her arrival and focus on this new development.

'I did, and she was. She's not ill exactly.' She gave up. There was no time to dress the matter in tactful phrases. She moistened her lips. 'The pains she was having are not, after all, the result of a pulled muscle. I think the baby is coming.'

Nick stiffened. 'Are you sure?'

Lifting her palms Kerenza blurted, 'I'm not sure of anything. But she believes it to be the case. Anyway, the reason I'm here – Toy says the doctor might have left some medical textbooks behind. If he did I'm hoping one of them will have a chapter on – on how to manage a confinement. He thought they might have been stored in one of the sea berths?'

Nick shook his head. 'No, they are definitely not there. But it's possible–' Turning, he wrenched up the seat on which he'd been sitting and looked into the space beneath. As he dropped it again, Kerenza's heart fell with it and she clasped her hands together, trying to contain her anxiety. Moving to the other side and propping the seat against the back, he reached in, raked around, and lifted out two battered volumes, their leather covers scratched and fraying at the corners. Replacing the seat, he opened the top one.

'*Observations on the Diseases Incident to Seamen,*' he read off the title page. 'I hardly think you are

178

likely to find any help here.'

Holding her breath in desperate hope, she watched him run his index finger down the list of contents. 'May I have the other one? If we both look–'

Glancing up he passed her the second book. 'Have you considered asking Mrs Woodrow–?'

'No.' She didn't wait for him to finish. 'Mrs Woodrow is not a mother. Besides, Ju– Lady Russell asked me not to wake her. In fact, she forbade it. She – she was kind enough to say that she prefers my company.' She heard the note of defiance, but it was too late. She could not take it back now. Let him make of it what he would.

'Who could blame her?' he said softly, returning his gaze to the page. 'Mrs Woodrow may have some excellent qualities, but if compassion and kindness are among them, they remain well-hidden, whereas you.' Kerenza's breath caught and her heart gave a great leap. 'According to Toy, who has good reason to know, you possess both in quantity.'

Hot, confused, she bent her head over the book, angling it towards the light and turning the pages with trembling fingers.

Nick cleared his throat. 'Please believe I intend no offence, but have you any experience of – in these matters?'

She shook her head. She'd had no experience of battle wounds either. And while she had watched, helpless, the captain had died. She closed her eyes, willing the terror away. Suddenly a spark of hope flared and she looked up at him.

'Have you?'

His eyes grew wide, and had the situation not been so fraught she might have laughed at his expression. 'No!'

She shrugged, trying to hide disappointment and the stirring of fear. 'I just thought perhaps – Broad mentioned two previous occasions.'

'Both were managed by the doctor. And the lady had a companion with her to assist.'

'I must get back.' She turned to leave, clutching the book like a talisman. She had not, at first glance, found what she sought, but it might yet be there. 'I promised I would not be long.'

He followed her. 'I will tell Toy to move your trunk into my cabin.' Shock jerked her head round and she saw his startled frown as he shook his head, indicating a sliding door in the bulkhead above the seat. 'I'm sleeping in one of the sea berths.' The sudden tightening round his mouth told her he had not been able yet to move into his uncle's sleeping cabin. Remembering the smells, the blood-soaked rags and sodden blanket she shuddered, and understood. That was how he had known the doctor's books were not where Toy had suggested. 'Surely it would be easier for you and Lady Russell if you had more space?'

Of course it would. Hot with embarrassment, she strove for dignity. 'Thank you.' Leaving the day cabin, acutely aware of him behind her, *so close, yet on opposite sides of a chasm of hurt and misunderstanding*, she glimpsed two blacker shadows silhouetted in the saloon doorway.

Chapter Eleven

'Got the bottles here, miss. All right, Mr Penrose?' Broad murmured.

Tucking the book under her arm Kerenza took them. Now wrapped in strips of blanket, their warmth was instantly comforting. 'Thank you,' she whispered.

'Tea's here, miss,' Toy added.

'I'll be back in a moment.' She left Nick conferring with the two men and went into the cabin. Tossing the book onto her cot she placed one bottle by Judith's feet, then leaned in to put the other at her back.

'How often are the pains coming?'

Releasing a shuddering breath, Judith drew another and let it out more easily. 'That was the first since you left.'

How long had she been with Nick? Ten minutes? Less?

'Toy is waiting outside with the tea. And to afford us more space, Mr Penrose has suggested taking my trunk to his cabin now that he has moved into the captain's. May I allow them in to remove it?'

'Yes.'

Kerenza heard the uncertainty and guessed Judith felt keenly the indignity of her situation. 'It will only take a moment, then we will be private again.'

'They won't disturb Mrs Woodrow, will they?'

'According to Broad,' Kerenza confided, as she helped Judith lever herself up against the pillows, 'even cannon fire would not disturb Mrs Woodrow tonight. Apparently she is a firm believer in the sedative powers of paregoric.'

Judith blew a sigh of relief. 'Thank God. But I doubt Mr Woodrow is. And I would be happier if he were not woken.'

As Kerenza opened the door, Toy thrust two cups into her hands.

'No use bringing a tray, miss,' he hissed. ''Twould have slid about all over the place. I thought cups would be easier.'

Passing one cup to Judith, Kerenza stood in front of the cot, a human shield, while the two men lifted her trunk and manoeuvred it out into the passage. She gulped down the tea. Hot and strong, it revived and steadied her. As she followed Broad and Toy to close the door Nick was waiting.

'Is there anything else you need?'

Kerenza thought hard. 'Broad said I might have two shirts from the slop chest, for clean rags? A spare blanket would be useful. An old one,' she added quickly, 'in case – there could – it might get–'

'Yes, I understand,' he interrupted much to her relief.

'And a bucket, again an old one, and hot water.'

'Would you like another lamp?'

'Oh, yes, that would be marvellous.'

'Shall I take that?' He indicated her empty cup.

'Thank you.' As she handed it to him she was

182

overwhelmed by a confusion of yearning and uncertainty. It would be foolish to read too much into his willingness to help. No doubt his gratitude was genuine. But she must never forget that Judith was an important passenger and his responsibility. It was natural – indeed only to be expected – that he would do everything possible to secure the comfort and safety of the wife of an important member of the governor's staff. But until the packet reached the Rock it was in her desperately nervous and inexperienced hands that the wellbeing of both Judith and her baby lay.

'I'll bring everything as soon as I–'

'You need not come yourself,' Kerenza blurted. 'One of the stewards can–'

His expression hardened and she sensed his withdrawal. 'As you wish.' Abruptly he turned away.

Angry with herself, and with him, for there was no time now to explain – even had he been willing to listen – her awareness that even at this hour he had still been working and that in coming to his cabin she had interrupted him. She closed the door. Drawing a deep breath she hoped would calm the turbulence inside and refocus her attention, she fixed a smile to her mouth as she turned to Judith.

'Are you warmer now?'

'I am, thank you. And the tea has eased my thirst. Did you find a book?'

'Yes.' Lifting it from her cot, Kerenza carried it closer to the lamp.

'Can you see to read?'

'Yes.' She checked the chapter list again. 'Mr

Penrose has kindly offered another lamp. It should be here shortly. Ah, I think I've found what we need.'

'Good.' The strain in Judith's voice brought Kerenza's head up. Dropping the book, she knelt and held Judith's hand as her breathing quickened and her lips peeled back from her teeth in a grimace of agony. Drawing her legs up, Judith writhed as the contraction gathered strength, peaked, and slowly subsided. Breathing heavily she sagged against the pillows and passed her hand across her face.

Sensing this was no time for soothing platitudes, that comfort and reassurance required confident actions, Kerenza snatched up the book again and read swiftly. She turned the page, and turned it back in disbelief. That was *all*? Wanting to scream with frustration, instead she clamped her jaws together. Why should there be more? After all, it was not doctors who attended and supervised confinements, but midwives. And midwives learned by apprenticeship and practice not from books. She would just have to manage on the little information there was. She read it again to imprint it on her memory. Then a soft tap on the door announced the arrival of Broad with a blanket, three clean but badly frayed shirts, and a wooden bucket. Behind him stood Toy with a lantern and a large jug of steaming water.

Putting blanket and shirts on the top cot, standing the jug in the bucket then wedging it in a corner to ensure it wouldn't topple or spill, Kerenza lit the lantern. The additional light was welcome. Being able to see more clearly would

184

make everything, if not easier, at least a little less difficult. Hanging it from a hook on the bulkhead, Kerenza knelt beside Judith.

'May I get a sheet and towel from your trunk?'

'My dear girl,' Judith smiled weakly, 'you don't need to ask. Take whatever you want. I have some clean shifts in there somewhere. Cut them up if you need to. They will provide a soft wrapping for the baby.'

Lifting the lid, Kerenza took out what she needed, plus a clean nightdress and the little nightshirt Judith had been embroidering. It was not quite finished. She glanced over her shoulder as she heard the tell-tale change in Judith's breathing. Crossing the small space she crouched, holding one of Judith's hands in hers while with the other she smoothed back the hair from Judith's sweat-dampened forehead.

'You are so good and attentive,' Judith gasped when she could speak again. 'But I fear that if you leave what you're doing each time I have a pain, then nothing will be ready.'

She wasn't alone in that fear. Kerenza could tell the pains were coming faster. 'All right, but the moment you want me to stop and be with you just say so.'

Folding the old blanket into a thick pad about two and a half feet square, she covered it with the remains of her torn sheet, then lay the oldest and most ragged of the shirts on top. Next she found her scissors and began to cut up the remaining shirts into napkins and pads. She was still apprehensive. But having things to do made it easier to set her nervousness aside. Lastly she cut

185

up two cambric shifts, taking narrow strips from one as binders for the baby's cord.

Minutes ticked into hours, and the strength and frequency of the contractions increased. But, growing visibly more exhausted, Judith sank into apathy. She no longer made any attempt to talk or even to respond during the brief respite between pains.

Anxiety coiled in Kerenza's stomach, forming a tight knot. Was this what marriage and motherhood were about? When she had over-heard whispers, seen eyes rolled heavenward, she had suspected exaggeration in order to win admiration or sympathy. No longer was she surprised that married women never spoke of such things in detail. For surely if girls were told the truth of what they might expect, the reality rather than the nebulous rosy dream, how many would opt to remain single? One would need to love very deeply to be willing to bear such pain. Yet what other life was there for a woman when her status depended upon marriage? Perhaps if one were loved enough, or ambitious enough, then all this agony was a price worth paying. But how many knew when they walked down the aisle, that this would be the result? And how many, even if they were told, would truly believe it?

Eventually, after once again wiping Judith's face and throat with a damp cloth, she made a decision. 'I'm going to fetch my box from the trunk.' Surely there was something in it that might afford a little relief?

Her chest heaving, Judith didn't respond.

Kerenza wondered if she had even heard. Plum-coloured shadows had developed beneath her eyes.

Climbing stiffly to her feet, Kerenza wiped her hands on her dress and quietly opened the door. As she emerged, blinking, she was astonished to see the grey light of dawn filtering down the companionway. The night over, it was a new day. From the Woodrows' cabin the snores continued unabated. Hearing a sound, she turned to see Broad appear in the saloon doorway, rubbing his face. 'Any news, miss?'

She shook her head. 'Not yet.'

'Can I get you anything?' He staggered towards her down the angled passage.

'Have you been there all night?'

'Seemed best, miss. In case you was to want something.'

That is kind. Some more hot water, please. I'll fetch the jug.'

'Be long will it, d'you think?'

She spread her hands, worried, helpless. 'I hope not, for Lady Russell's sake.' Ducking into the cabin she returned with the jug and the half-full bucket.

'You'll have 'em both back in two shakes,' he promised. 'I kept the fire in all night.'

As he disappeared into the saloon again, Kerenza started towards the companionway. Nick's former cabin was on the right at the bottom, opposite her father's. The light was briefly blocked and, as she heard footsteps on the brass stairs, her heart gave its now familiar semi-painful leap. But it was Maggot who turned towards her.

187

'Baby is here?'

Kerenza shook her head. 'I wish it were. I don't know how long – she's so terribly tired,' she blurted. 'And the pains are so severe–'

'She need *kif*,' Maggot announced.

'What's that?'

'Is from a plant. You can smoke or chew. But for Lady Russell I make a drink. Is very good, take pain away for short time.'

It sounded wonderful. But Kerenza was wary. 'I'm not sure if–'

Maggot stepped very close, his gaze level with her own, and suddenly as hard as Cornish granite. 'You think I harm her?' he demanded softly.

'No.' Kerenza felt her tension lift, knowing it was the truth. 'Thank you. Please bring it as soon as you can.' Turning she went back into the cabin.

Judith was able to swallow only a few mouthfuls of the brown liquid, and shuddered violently at the taste. But its effect was swift, softening and smoothing out the creases of agony. The contractions were almost continuous, separated only by a few seconds. Kerenza took a last look at the book then knelt beside the cot.

'I think it's time to get you ready.'

Nodding briefly, Judith clasped Kerenza's arm and leaned forward so the pillows could be propped up. Then she tried to help by raising her body so Kerenza could slide the thick pad beneath her.

Pouring fresh hot water into the basin, Kerenza bathed Judith's lower body, briefly shy at performing such an intimate task, yet deeply moved by Judith's trust and acceptance. As she wiped her dry with a rag, saving the towel for the baby, Kerenza was startled by the board-like rigidity of Judith's abdomen as the contraction took hold. Replacing the sheet and blanket over Judith's hips, she emptied the water into the chamber pot – she had another use for the bucket – poured a little more into the basin and, with Lizzie Gendall's advice echoing in her ears, carefully washed the scissors.

Faster and harder the contractions came. Judith's lips were beginning to crack and the lamplight gleamed on the perspiration that dewed her face and darkened the hair at her temples.

'Kerenza,' she gasped suddenly, 'it's – I have to–' She curved forward, straining, panting, then straining some more.

Throwing back the sheet, Kerenza saw a gush of fluid, a bulge, and then the baby's head appeared.

'Wait! Wait!' she cried in terrified urgency, using her little finger to clear the baby's mouth.

'I can't–' Judith gasped, grunting with effort as the next contraction pushed out first one shoulder, then the other. Then, in a slippery rush, the rest of the baby slithered out into Kerenza's waiting hands, still tethered to Judith's body by a spiralled silver-blue cord.

'Oh Judith.' Choked with awe and elation, Kerenza could barely speak.

Judith heaved herself up on her elbows, her voice cracking. 'What–?'

'A little girl.' Tears were streaming down Kerenza's cheeks and she had to force the words

189

past a lump in her throat so big it threatened to choke her. 'You have a beautiful baby girl. She's perfect, absolutely perfect.' Now she understood. This moment, this wonderful incredible moment was worth all the hours of effort and pain. But her delight was briefly eclipsed by the memory of Nick's face as he had walked past her in Falmouth's main street. The sense of loss was crippling.

With infinite care, she lifted the tiny, twitching body, marvelling at its warmth, its *aliveness*, and laid it on Judith's stomach so she could see and touch and be reassured. The baby gave a thin *wa-aa-aa* and waved her arms.

'Listen to her,' Judith laughed, 'she sounds like an angry kitten. And why not, my darling,' she crooned, stroking her daughter. Then she gave a sharp cry as another contraction wrenched her.

Kerenza tore her gaze from the baby as the dark mass of the afterbirth appeared. She must concentrate for, though the worst was now over, there was still much to do.

While Judith talked softly to her daughter, her exhaustion banished by euphoria, Kerenza tied the cord a hand-span from the baby's body, and again a further inch beyond. Then, swallowing, fearful it must surely cause pain, she picked up the scissors and, gritting her teeth, cut it. The baby seemed oblivious.

Pouring more clean water into the basin, she set it on the tilted floor beside the cot so Judith could see. 'As soon as she is washed and swaddled you will be able to hold her properly.'

'She is beautiful, isn't she?' Judith lay back, her

head turned sideways on the pillows, watching with tired hungry eyes as Kerenza lifted the flailing baby and lowered her into the water.

'She is utterly gorgeous.' Kerenza had never felt anything like the emotion that gripped her now. The weight of that little head against the inside of her forearm filled her with an overpowering need to protect this tiny scrap of humanity from anything that might harm her. 'She's so strong,' she marvelled, washing the little body and kicking legs with Judith's soap, relieved that the lilac hue of the baby's skin was beginning to turn deep rosy pink. 'Have you thought of a name for her?'

'I'd like to call her Georgiana, for my husband, and her second name will be Kerenza, for you,' Judith replied through chattering teeth.

Kerenza looked up quickly. 'Your husband might have other ideas.'

'Perhaps, but he will quickly adapt them,' Judith said. 'Especially once he learns how much we both owe you.'

Lifting the baby out and laying her on a clean piece of soft shirt, Kerenza dried her with Judith's towel. Then after binding her abdomen with a strip of cambric, she wound a clean piece of shirt around her for a napkin, dressed her in the tiny nightshirt that was too big, and wrapped her in pieces of Judith's shifts. Finally, she untied the shawl from her shoulders refolded it, and lay the baby on its soft warmth.

'I shall put her in my cot just for a moment while I make you comfortable.'

'I'd give anything for a cup of sweet tea,' Judith murmured, racked by violent shivers.

'And you'll have one, I promise,' Kerenza smiled. Quickly bundling up the afterbirth in the rag on which it lay, she dropped it in the bucket. Then she washed Judith, placed a wad of soft rags between her legs, removed the soaked blanket, and helped her into the clean nightdress. As she drew up the covers, Judith caught her hand.

'I'll never be able to thank you enough. Never. If you hadn't been here–'

'It was my privilege,' Kerenza said with simple truth, grasping Judith's hand in return. 'It was the most amazing, wonderful, moving–' Her throat closed and she shook her head, then followed Judith's gaze as she looked up.

Running feet thudded overhead, then came the familiar sound of the blocks as ropes were loosed and hauled in. Kerenza grabbed the cot edge as the angle of the deck altered then levelled out. Looking at each other they spoke simultaneously.

'The wind's changed!'

'We may reach Gibraltar before nightfall,' Judith said.

'It will certainly be a very special homecoming for you.' Kerenza tried to smile, aware suddenly of how much she would miss Judith's warmth, humour and common sense.

'One my husband will certainly not forget in a hurry. And in the meantime, I think I should try to feed my daughter.' Judith held out her arms as Kerenza placed the still-crying baby in them. 'Before she wakes the entire ship.'

'I'll go and fetch that cup of tea.' Kerenza doubted Judith had even heard.

She opened the door and looked towards the

companionway. It was full daylight. The smells of frying pork and hot coffee told her breakfast was being prepared. It had been a long night. And despite all that might have gone wrong, nothing had. Mother and baby were fine. So why did she feel so deflated, so bereft? She was tired, that was all. As she knocked on the captain's door it was wrenched open and she jumped.

'It's over? Is everything all right?' Freshly shaved, his thick hair still wet and bearing the furrows of a comb, Nick was wearing his best uniform.

Kerenza nodded, suddenly aware of her own dishevelled appearance. 'Lady Russell gave birth to a beautiful daughter about an hour ago. Mother and baby are both well. I'm about to fetch her a cup of tea, but I thought I should tell you first.'

'Thank you. I'll note it in the log.' His brows gathered. 'You look very tired.'

Shrugging, she crossed her arms in instinctive self-protection. Without the shawl she was cold. 'I'm sure I look a total wreck. But–'

'No!' He was gruff, abrupt. 'I didn't intend– What I should have – what I *meant* was that you have just endured a long and worrying night, and that on top of a time of great strain.'

She wished he hadn't explained. The tenderness in his voice was more than she could handle. Helpless to stop the sudden scalding tears, she covered her face with her hands.

'Kerenza?' His voice was raw, and thick with pent-up emotion.

She lifted her head, inhaling deeply as she wiped her wet face with her fingers. 'I'm sorry. It's – as you say, it's been a long night, and I am indeed very tired. Will you excuse me? I must–'

'Why do you not rest now? Surely Broad, or Toy could–'

'No, not yet. I don't think Lady Russell would wish to see or be seen by anyone just at the moment.'

The corners of his mouth flickered, his expression half shyness, half shame wrapped itself around her heart. 'No, of course not. Please,' he gestured towards the saloon and she had no choice but to lead the way. But she'd only taken two steps when she remembered the honey and stopped so suddenly he cannoned into her, catching her arms to steady her as she stumbled back.

'I'm sorry,' she said, breathless. 'I just – I have to fetch...' Blindly she reached for the door handle.

He waited outside, holding the door open to allow light in while she threw back the lid of her trunk, trying to ignore the smell of his soap, his clothes, *of him*, that permeated the small cabin.

Clutching the jar of honey, her face on fire, Kerenza heard voices as she passed the Woodrows' door and hoped she would be safely back in the cabin with Judith before Betsy emerged.

'Sit down,' Nick said. And, too tired to argue, Kerenza slid into the nearest bench as Broad emerged from the small galley, his expression both anxious and expectant.

'Everything all right, miss?'

'Indeed it is, Broad. Lady Russell has a baby daughter.'

'Well, now,' he beamed. 'That's good news, that is. Both all right, are they?'

194

'They are both fine. Lady Russell would love a cup of tea.'

'Could do with one yourself, I shouldn't wonder. Won't be no more'n a couple of shakes. I've had the kettle on this past two hours.' He turned away then turned back. 'Begging your pardon, miss, but I got to say it: done a bleddy handsome job, you have.'

'Thank you.' Feeling her eyes prickle again, she bent her head, rubbing the back of her neck where all the tendons were as tight as mast stays. Then, to Kerenza's horror, Betsy Woodrow's voice suddenly increased in volume as her cabin door opened. A moment later she sailed into the saloon.

'Good morning, Mr Pen–' As she caught sight of Kerenza, horror replaced her frosty smile. 'Good heavens above, Miss Vyvyan. What on earth has happened to you?'

'Nothing, Mrs Woodrow. I am–'

'Then what on earth has possessed you to appear in public looking like what I can only describe as–'

'Someone who has just passed an exhausting and anxious night helping a fellow passenger to give birth,' Nick interrupted.

'Mr Penrose!' Betsy cried in affront, her hand flying protectively to her bosom. 'Such language.' Then she registered what he had said, and Kerenza watched her face become suddenly shapeless, like melting wax, before she was able to reassert control.

'Lady Russell has had her baby?' the minister said from behind his wife.

'She has, sir,' Nick confirmed. 'Just over an

hour ago. Isn't that right, Miss Vyvyan?'

Kerenza nodded.

Feeling for the table, Betsy sat down. 'But why wasn't I called?'

'For what purpose, Mrs Woodrow?' Nick enquired coolly. 'Was it not your self-confessed lack of experience that prevented you helping when the captain was injured?'

Kerenza looked at him, wondering how he knew, for he had not been present. Then realized immediately that indignation would have ensured either Broad or Toy told him. Betsy bridled, her colour deepening. 'That was different.'

'I think not. In any case, Lady Russell had all the help she could need in the person of Miss Vyvyan.'

'But – but Miss Vyvyan is unmarried. It is quite wrong that she should–'

Kerenza stood up. 'Mrs Woodrow, I'm sure you will be happy to hear that Lady Russell has a beautiful and healthy baby daughter.'

'Has she indeed?' Donald Woodrow sounded genuinely delighted. 'That is truly wonderful news. It must have been an anxious and difficult time for you, Miss Vyvyan.'

'More so for Lady Russell, I think, sir,' Kerenza said gently.

'Indeed, indeed.'

'That is exactly my point,' Betsy snapped in exasperation. 'However, we must give thanks for God's grace. Perhaps after breakfast I will visit Lady Russell and offer my congratulations.'

'No, ma'am.' Kerenza blurted.

'I beg your pardon? What do you mean, *no?*'

Betsy demanded. 'I declare, Miss Vyvyan, you take a lot upon yourself.'

'I mean, ma'am, that Lady Russell is very tired, as I'm sure you must understand. I think it likely that as soon as she has drunk some tea, she will sleep. She is in great need of rest.'

'Well!' Betsy sniffed, clearly furious, but with no grounds on which to argue.

Relieved to see Broad come in, Kerenza went to meet him and set the honey jar on the tray between two steaming cups of tea.

'You go on, miss,' Broad murmured. 'You can open the door. I'll bring the tray.'

Betsy sighed loudly. 'Are we ever to get our breakfast this morning?'

Judith drank her tea sweetened with two spoonfuls of honey. Kerenza did the same. Then, making sure Judith was comfortable with the baby snug in the crook of her arm, Kerenza extinguished the lantern and turned the other lamp down low. Judith's heavy-lidded eyes had closed even before Kerenza crept out carrying the tray and closed the door quietly behind her.

'Take that for you, shall I, miss?' Billy offered. 'I left your water outside the door,' he pointed down the passage.

Ten minutes later, after washing her face, too tired even to think about eating, Kerenza climbed into Nick's cot, buried her face in the pillow, and sobbed herself to sleep.

Chapter Twelve

Kerenza crawled up from the oblivion that had eventually engulfed her after some unpleasant dreams during which she was either fleeing from unidentifiable terrors, or desperately searching for something she couldn't name, something that remained always just out of reach. She was dimly aware of a sound that wasn't the usual creaks, bells, thuds, squeals, footsteps and shouts that went on day and night: a sound that was rhythmic, demanding, and growing louder.

She forced her eyelids open and saw, in the light through the gap above the door, surroundings she didn't recognize. *Where was she?* Then memory flooded back. She was in Nick's cabin, in Nick's cot. But there was no time to dwell on the fact, for what had woken her was an urgent knocking on the door.

'Yes?' Her throat was dry, her voice husky. 'Who is it?'

The door opened a couple of inches. 'It's Broad, miss,' the steward said through the gap. 'I'm some sorry to wake you, but the baby's been crying this past half-hour and Mrs Woodrow says that if someone don't do something, then she'll have to because 'tis never right.'

Kerenza propped herself up on one elbow and rubbed her face to banish sleep and bring herself fully awake. 'Has Lady Russell called for help?'

'No, miss. And I didn't like to take it on myself to go in, but–'

'I'll come at once. How long have I slept?'

''Bout four hours, miss. 'Tis almost dinner-time. I'm some sorry to have woke you, but–'

'No, it's all right. I'll be just a minute or two. Would you ask Billy to bring hot water to Lady Russell's cabin?'

'Billy's doing the slops, miss. I'll bring it myself.' There was a note of relief in the steward's voice as he closed the door.

Kerenza pushed back the blanket and swung her legs over the edge of the cot. Splashing her face with last night's cold water, she put on her green muslin. Quickly unbraiding her hair she brushed it out then pinned it up in a neat coil. Then rummaging in her trunk she found a high-waisted jacket of dark green wool with long, close-fitting sleeves and a standing collar. Blessing Minnie for packing it, she put it on and buttoned it up. The circumstances of the previous night had been exceptional, so had her dishevelled appearance. There would be no excuse today, and no allowance made, especially by Betsy Woodrow. But what really frightened her was that Nick had seen her at her most vulnerable. She could not allow that to happen again. Control over her appearance signalled control over her emotions. If she were neat, tidy, and properly dressed, there would be no hint, no clue to betray the seething turmoil inside.

As she left the small cabin, Billy staggered down the passage carrying the slop bucket.

'All right if I do yours, miss?' he piped, tugging

the hank of fair hair that flopped over his forehead.

'Yes. Then come to Lady Russell's cabin.' Kerenza knocked on Judith's door. 'It's Kerenza,' she said, as she opened it and went in.

'Oh, thank heaven.' Judith sank back on to the pillows, clearly agitated. Her pallor emphasized the purplish-brown shadows beneath her eyes. Lying beside her the baby was red-faced, her eyes shut, mouth open, and chin quivering with each heartfelt wail. 'I have been listening to Mr Woodrow in the passage trying to dissuade his wife from coming to see if there is anything I need. You must stop her, Kerenza. I really could not cope with–'

'You won't have to,' Kerenza said quickly. 'No one can enter this cabin without your permission, not even Mrs Woodrow.'

Judith sucked in a deep breath. 'No, no, she can't, can she. It's just – and I know I'm being foolish, but there is nowhere to hide and she is so very determined.'

'Would you like me to make it known that you are still exhausted and not yet up to receiving any visitors?'

'Would you? I should be so grateful.'

'No one will get past me, I promise. How are you feeling?'

Judith's face crumpled in distress. 'We both slept a little. When Georgiana woke I fed her, but since then she has not stopped crying.'

'Surely that is a good sign?' Kerenza didn't know whether it was or not, but it was certainly not good for the new mother to be so tense. 'She is showing you that despite being so small, she has strong healthy lungs.'

'Yes, but to cry for so long.'

'Perhaps she is uncomfortable.' A brief knock on the door brought their heads up quickly. As Judith shook her head violently, Kerenza called, 'Who is it?'

'Broad, miss. With the hot water.'

Kerenza opened the door to take the jug and, as Broad turned to leave, the Woodrows' door opened and Betsy emerged.

'Ah, so you are there, Miss Vyvyan. Do you have any idea what you are doing?'

About to say *I beg your pardon*, Kerenza swallowed her anger. Instead, aware of Judith's exhaustion and anxiety, she said, 'Yes, thank you, Mrs Woodrow, everything is fine.'

'How can you say so? That child has been crying for at least half an hour. It is most distressing, and must surely be causing Lady Russell great concern.'

Billy staggered up with the slop bucket.

'Will you excuse me?' Kerenza spoke to Betsy over his head. 'One moment, Billy.' As she emptied the chamber pot into the bucket she caught Betsy's gasp of horror – presumably at the fact that she was performing the menial task – smiled at the boy, and closed the door. 'It may be,' she said to Judith, as she crossed to the nightstand and poured half the water into the basin, 'that little Miss Russell needs changing. Would you like me to see?'

'Oh, yes, please. I know you are probably right, and that she needs to exercise her lungs, but to hear her crying so.' Her voice wavered, and Kerenza saw her eyes were brimming. 'I feel so foolish and helpless.'

'You are still very tired.' Fetching clean rags, she lay the baby on the blanket at the foot of the cot, and loosened the wrappings. As she rolled up the nightshirt, the little legs kicked and Kerenza's nostrils twitched.

'Oh, my goodness.'

Glancing sideways Kerenza saw Judith eyeing her daughter in appalled amazement.

'My poor darling,' Judith crooned, leaning forward to stroke the tiny head with its downy thatch. 'No wonder you were crying. And with such a task to perform, I fear Kerenza may quickly join you.'

As the oozing napkin was removed the thin shuddering wails died to occasional hiccups. By the time Kerenza had washed, dried, folded and tucked a new napkin around and between little legs that kept kicking or drawing up like a frog's, her back was aching and her shift clung damply. Leaving the baby beside her mother, she quickly cleared away the debris, wrapping the soiled napkin in another rag. Emptying the basin, she rinsed and refilled it, then set out Judith's soap, towel, and a wad of clean rags on the top of the trunk.

'Would you like my help?' At Judith's hesitation, she continued quickly, 'I promise you, it's no trouble. But if you prefer to have a few minutes alone, would you allow me to take the baby as far as the saloon? A change of air will do her no harm and I know Broad is most anxious to see her. He stayed up all night in case we should need anything.'

There was a hint of relief in Judith's smile, and Kerenza realized that the intimacy of the previous night had been a matter of necessity, and that now Judith wanted to reclaim a small measure of privacy and independence.

'Then of course you must introduce her to them. But don't be away too long.'

Adjusting the shawl, Kerenza nestled the baby, now peacefully asleep, in the crook of her arm and left the cabin. In the passage the savoury smell of stewed meat made her mouth water. She was suddenly hungry. Approaching the saloon, she saw Nick seated at the table. Remembering the unexpected intimacies of the previous evening, of guard dropped, of help offered and gratefully accepted, a shivery weakness stirred deep inside her. *No.* It was too dangerous.

As she reached the door he turned his head and rose quickly to his feet, sending the chair scraping across the floor. It was clear from his expression that he, too, was remembering. She felt her face grow hot, the rising colour a betrayal. The Woodrows were in their usual place, their plates almost empty. Her father, in the seat Judith normally occupied, had barely touched his. He glanced up, his gaze vague, his brow furrowing as if he was trying to place her.

'So, this is our youngest passenger.' Keeping his distance Nick peered at the baby. Usually so decisive he appeared awkward, almost shy. Behind the table, the minister scrambled to his feet and Betsy put her knife and fork together.

'She cried a great deal. I hope nothing is wrong.'

'Nothing at all.' Kerenza smiled down at the baby. 'She simply wanted her napkin changed.'

Betsy's hand flew to her bosom. 'Really, Miss Vyvyan, the dinner-table is hardly the place for such details, especially in mixed company.'

Kerenza's colour deepened. 'You're right, I'm sorry.' She turned to her father. 'Isn't she beautiful, Papa?' Tipping the baby so he could see she longed to ask. *Do you remember me at this age? Did you love me then? Are you proud of me, Papa? I helped her into the world.*

He glanced briefly at the tiny face framed in the white cambric of her mother's cut-up shift and Kerenza's shawl. 'She's well enough.' His gaze didn't linger. 'You were saying, Mr Penrose?'

Her eyes prickling, Kerenza bent her head, adjusting the fine wool.

'We'll talk later, Mr Vyvyan.' Nick held the chair. 'Please, Miss Vyvyan, sit down. Is Lady Russell in good health?'

Kerenza blinked rapidly before looking up. 'You haven't finished.'

'I need to know, Mr Penrose,' her father persisted. 'How long must we remain in Gibraltar, and how long will it take to reach Tangier?'

'Everything will be done with all possible speed, Mr Vyvyan.' Hot embarrassment washed over Kerenza as Nick switched his gaze back to her and she saw his disgust soften to pity. 'I can move across to the bench. Please, take my place.' His tone defied argument and she sat.

'Thank you. Lady Russell is fine. But she is

very tired and certainly not up to visitors, so we are giving her a few minutes alone.'

Broad came in from the galley passage. 'Well, look at that. Isn't she handsome?' Beaming, he straightened, addressing Kerenza. 'Lady Russell ready for some dinner, is she? You just say the word and I'll bring a tray.'

'That's very kind of you. Perhaps in about a quarter of an hour?'

'No trouble at all, miss. Now what about you? I reckon your stomach must think your throat have been cut.'

'Well, really!' Betsy huffed.

'I am hungry,' Kerenza admitted. Hearing Betsy sniff, she glanced up and saw her glaring at the baby. Betsy's expression was angry and hostile, but it only took an instant for Kerenza to realize that the glitter in her small eyes was not caused by anger but by tears.

She recalled the minister's confession, and relived the overwhelming rush of emotion she had experienced as she helped Georgiana enter the world. That moment had changed her, shifting her perspective and deepening her perception. Now with sudden insight she saw how jealousy and rage had warped Betsy Woodrow in the same way that constant harsh winds deform even the strongest tree.

Betsy's ready criticism, her need to control, to demand the highest standards in others' behaviour were driven by grief at her barrenness, and shame at her failure to achieve what for most women was inevitable.

Impulsively, she stood up again. 'Mrs Woodrow,

if you have finished, I wonder if you would be so kind as to hold Georgiana for a few minutes so that I might have my dinner?'

Betsy's eyes rounded and her mouth fell open, but for once not a sound emerged. Quickly she shook her head.

Wincing, Kerenza turned to the minister, trying not to notice the arrested look on Nick's face. She had obeyed her instinct, an instinct that had been right about Judith, yet so wrong about Nick. 'Mr Woodrow? No doubt you have held many babies during services of baptism, would you be so kind?'

'No.' Betsy's voice sharp.

Already tense and bracing herself for yet more criticism, Kerenza turned and saw Betsy hold out her hands.

'I will take her. Give her to me.'

Glimpsing gratitude on Donald Woodrow's face, Kerenza leaned over and laid the sleeping baby gently in Betsy's arms. 'It's very good of you.'

'She's so small.' Betsy's voice held awe, concern, and the inevitable hint of censure. 'Are you sure she's warm enough?'

'I think so, while we are below deck. I expect Lady Russell will carry her beneath her pelisse when she leaves the ship.' Kerenza smiled her thanks as Broad set a steaming plate of stewed beef and vegetables in front of her.

Nick finished and stood up. 'I must ask you to excuse me.' He turned to Kerenza. 'I'd be obliged if you would pass on my felicitations to Lady Russell.'

'Of course.'

'Mr Penrose, shall we reach Gibraltar today, do you think?' Donald Woodrow voiced the question Kerenza had been about to ask.

'If the wind holds, we could arrive during the early evening.'

'And how long must we remain there?' William Vyvyan demanded anxiously.

'No longer than necessary,' Nick replied.

He walked out before anyone could ask further questions. He was still trying to understand what he had felt seeing Kerenza walk in with that tiny bundle in her arms. Babies had rarely figured in his thoughts, except when his sisters' children were born, or if he was invited to join colleagues celebrating the birth of a son. That was women's business. But the effect of seeing Kerenza carrying that baby had been a shock: like an unexpected blow, powerful and disorienting.

Not yet twenty, and without experience of younger brothers and sisters, she had risen to the challenge. It had required great courage and he sensed the experience had changed her in some indefinable way. Yet she had received not a single word of praise from her father. Nick's fingers curled. What he had seen in her face had made him want to grab William Vyvyan and shake him until his teeth rattled. The man did not deserve such a daughter.

Walking into the day cabin he shut the door and leaned against it. *Who was he to criticize? What of his own behaviour? Had he not thrown her love back in her face? Had he not been too blind to see past the superficial gaiety of self-protection to the fear beneath?* Too wary to risk being hurt – or worse, laughed at – he had listened to lies. Worse, he had been willing to believe them.

Why had Jeremy lied to him? He would find out. And when he did... But right now even that did not matter as much as regaining her trust. Words were cheap. Apologizing was not enough. Not, he realized suddenly, that he ever had apologized. He had to show her he was worthy of her love if he was ever to stand a chance of regaining it. And he wanted that. By God, he wanted it.

He pushed himself away from the door. After checking the chart he stood up, lifted the seat, and took out the strong box. Unlocking it he removed the package of dispatches lying on top of the soft leather bag of gold sovereigns that made up the ransom money with which William Vyvyan was buying the freedom of his wife and elder daughter. As he closed and relocked the box he wondered if they were worth it.

Slipping the package into a satchel that he slung into his sea berth, he pulled the door shut and left the cabin. Passing him with a grin and a nod, Maggot went below to have his dinner.

Kestrel flew along under full sail, her taut canvas filled by the fresh north-westerly breeze. The crew went about their business with new purpose. On the port side was Spain, bleak, brown and sandy. Fourteen miles away across the Strait the low green hills of Morocco were visible in the late afternoon sunshine. Ahead across the wide bay was their destination, a long, high promontory rising out of the sea. From a jagged spine steep green slopes fell to tiered plateaux of

208

grey shale and white limestone that formed rugged cliffs.

Nick raised the glass and scanned the water, noting the British navy ships heading into and out of the naval dockyard north of Rosia Bay. Dotted across the Straits were shebecs, dhows, schooners and other merchant vessels. Some would be bringing goods to Gibraltar from Morocco and other Mediterranean countries, others returning to pick up fresh cargoes.

As the sun slipped out of sight behind the Spanish hills, taking with it the day's warmth, Nick went below, retrieved the satchel, and returned with it to the deck.

'Mr Laity, prepare the signal gun, two seamen below to bring up the trunks, then make ready the cutter and the jollyboat.'

'Aye, sir.'

The topsails were lowered, the gaffs on the fore and mainmasts dropped, jibs and headsails taken in, and with just a staysail to keep her under way, *Kestrel* glided into Rosia Bay, turned into the wind and, as she began to drift sternward, the anchor was dropped.

'What you do?' Maggot asked, appearing beside him. Normally Nick would have been first off the ship.

'I'll send the Woodrows ashore in the jollyboat. I'll take the mail and Lady Russell in the cutter.'

The seamen emerged from the companionway, set down the first trunk, and went down for the next.

Putting down the second one they stood aside, exchanging a glance, to allow Betsy Woodrow on to the deck.

'Are you quite certain nothing has been left in the cabin?' she demanded of her husband as he stepped over the coaming. 'I think you should go down again and make sure.'

'My dear, I promise you.'

'Oh no, Donald, no more promises. You have been unable to keep those already made, so I fail to see–'

'Please, my dear,' the minister said wearily, beyond embarrassment. 'Not now.'

'Perhaps, Mr Woodrow,' Nick intervened, 'you will go first? In case your wife should require assistance.'

'Of course.' He gripped Nick's hand hard. 'Thank you, sir, for bringing us here safely. I wish you God speed and a safe arrival on all your future voyages.'

'Do hurry up, Donald,' Betsy sighed. 'You're keeping everyone waiting.'

'Goodbye, Mr Woodrow.' Nick shook his hand, and meeting the minister's sad eyes added softly, 'Good luck.'

As Donald Woodrow clambered down into the jollyboat, his wife offered Nick her hand in a manner that reminded him of a dog holding up an injured paw.

'Well, Mr Penrose, I suppose I too should thank you for getting us here safely. It has certainly been a most unusual voyage. I have to say, much of it was not at all as I expected.'

After the briefest contact courtesy permitted, Nick dropped her hand. 'Indeed, ma'am,' he agreed without expression. 'Travelling in wartime must always be dangerous and unpredictable. But I hope you may find one pleasant memory to take with you?'

She blinked, startled, and was about to speak when Kerenza appeared at the hatchway.

'Please forgive me for interrupting, Mrs Woodrow. Mr Penrose, Lady Russell wishes to know if she should come up.'

'Not for a few minutes,' Nick said. 'I'll send word.'

'I hope,' Betsy spoke severely to Kerenza, 'you will take care to see that baby is properly protected. The evening air has a distinct chill.'

'Indeed I shall,' Kerenza smiled. 'Thank you for your concern. She will remain below until the last possible moment.'

With a noncommittal grunt, Betsy turned away. Her complaints about the lack of space on the jollyboat floated back to the deck, gradually diminishing as the distance widened.

Nick watched as the cutter was lowered and the four oarsmen took their places. Ordering Lady Russell's trunk stowed up for'ard, he nodded to Maggot who ducked down the companionway. A few minutes later Kerenza appeared carrying the baby who was closely wrapped in her shawl. Nick reached the hatch in two strides, leaning down to cup her elbow before she released her grip on the guardrail. As she murmured her thanks without looking up, the swift rosy flush on her cheek kindled in him a surge of hope. She was not as indifferent as she would have him believe.

Behind her, Lady Russell emerged, looking drawn and tired. She smiled as she took his proffered hand and stepped over the coaming. 'Thank you, Mr Penrose.' But already she was turning, seeking Kerenza who had crossed to the rail and now stood forward of a portion that had been removed to form a gateway.

Nick felt her lean heavily on his arm as he led her across the deck. Having stayed behind her on the stairs in case she was overcome by weakness, Maggot now sprinted ahead and swung himself down into the cutter bobbing gently on the blue water.

Nick watched Kerenza kneel, touch her lips lightly to the baby's forehead and pass her down to Maggot. When she straightened up, her face was pink and her eyes suspiciously bright. The distress she was trying so hard to hide, moved him in ways he had not experienced before. As well as not understanding her attachment to a child who wasn't hers, he did not understand why he felt angry, *and jealous*.

Releasing his arm, Lady Russell seized both Kerenza's hands and said, 'I will never be able to thank you enough. I shall miss your company.' A faint wail rose from the cutter and he saw them exchange a smile. 'If by chance the ship has to call before returning to Falmouth, please, if it is possible, come and see me, if only for a few minutes.' She turned to Nick. 'Will you escort her, Mr Penrose?'

He saw Kerenza stiffen and wince, saw the rosy flush climb her throat, and realized she was afraid he might feel the request an imposition. 'It would be my pleasure, Lady Russell.' From Kerenza's shy startled glance and the lift of Lady

Russell's eyebrows, he knew his tone had convinced both that he meant every word.

Leaning forward, Lady Russell kissed Kerenza's glowing cheek. 'Goodbye for now, my dear. Take care of yourself. And try to get some rest. I have been a very demanding companion.'

'I would not have missed a moment.' Her voice faltered and Nick wanted to put his arm around her in protection and reassurance. He saw her swallow then she widened her mouth in a smile. 'You must go. Your daughter is waiting and already you have been standing too long.' She moved aside.

Nick helped Lady Russell down into the cutter. He watched Maggot place the baby in her arms then swing himself up on to *Kestrel*'s deck.

'I don't know how long I'll be,' Nick warned.

Maggot shrugged. 'No matter. I here. Is all safe.'

Nick gripped his shoulder briefly then dropped down into the boat. The lines were cast off and the cutter headed shoreward. Unable to stop himself he looked back. But she had gone.

Kerenza shivered as she went down the stairs. She could hear laughter and shouts from the fo'c'sle as the crew who were going ashore got themselves ready. She had learned from Broad that lots had been drawn and as there was only time for one group to go ashore this time, those remaining aboard would automatically be first off next time.

'There'll be some thick heads tomorrow.' He'd clicked his tongue. 'A few bruises too I shouldn't wonder. Well, 'tis only to be expected if navy boys from the warships is daft enough to bait our lads.'

As she reached the bottom of the stairs her father's cabin door opened and he backed out, dragging his trunk.

Chapter Thirteen

'Papa? What are you doing?'

He turned, grimacing as he pressed his fingers to his forehead. 'Go and pack your trunk. We'll leave *Kestrel* as soon as we reach Gibraltar.'

Startled and bewildered, Kerenza stared at him. 'Leave? But – why, Papa? We'll only be staying there a few hours, one night at most. As soon as Mr Penrose delivers the dispatches–'

'And what if something goes wrong?' She recoiled from the reek of stale spirits on his breath, but he was too anxious to notice. 'What if Mr Penrose is told he cannot leave them to be collected, but must take them on to Admiral Hotham himself? It could be another week before we reach Tangier. No. No, I can't take that chance. As soon as we arrive I shall go to the Waterport Wharf. There's bound to be a merchantman or a fishing boat willing to take us across. If we leave tonight we'll be in Tangier before dawn. Now go and pack while I retrieve my money from Mr Penrose.'

'No, Papa, you–'

'No? Don't you argue with me, girl. Remember why you're here and do as you're bid. Go on!' He waved her away.

Kerenza flinched but remained where she was.

'Papa, we are already at Gibraltar.'

He stared at her. 'We can't be.'

'Perhaps,' she suggested carefully, wary of triggering yet more anger, 'you have been asleep?'

'So? A nap, that's all, after dinner.'

A nap that had lasted six hours. She had not gone to the saloon at teatime. Busy packing for Judith and caring for the baby she had accepted Broad's offer to bring a tray to the cabin instead. And because her father's attendance at meals had always been erratic, no one had mentioned his absence to her.

He glared wildly around. 'What time is it?'

'I'm not sure, but I think it's after seven.' She watched him try to take it in, and felt dismay, pity and shame that her father, once a proud and successful man, should have fallen so low. He rubbed his forehead again, frowning hard.

'Right, well, that's all to the good. We will leave at once. I'm not going to just sit here and wait, not with my wife and daughter only a few miles away. I have to get over there now, tonight.'

'Papa, listen. We can't leave because we can't get off the ship.'

'For God's sake, Kerenza.' Anger sparked in his bloodshot eyes and at the corners of his mouth spittle was gathering. 'Will you stop being so difficult. The packet carries two boats. They're kept on the deck.'

'Yes, but they are not on deck any longer. Both are at this moment on their way to shore.'

'What? They can't be.' He shook his head, then clutched it in both hands, his face contorting in pain.

'I saw them leave. Mr and Mrs Woodrow and their trunks are in the jollyboat. Mr Penrose has taken Lady Russell, her baby, and her luggage in the cutter.'

'No!' he howled, pushing past her and lunging for the companionway. But Maggot was already halfway down.

Kerenza didn't see exactly what happened. But suddenly her father hunched over, stumbling backward off the stairs and crashing backwards against the bulkhead. Agile as a cat, Maggot followed and gripped her father's arm to prevent him falling. William Vyvyan's eyes were wide and unseeing, his mouth open as he strained to heave air into his lungs.

'You are all right, miss?' Maggot demanded over his shoulder. 'I hear shouting.'

'My father is a little confused and upset.'

Maggot nodded. 'Is good he sleep some more. I give him something. You ask Broad to come, yes?'

Kerenza fetched the steward. Maggot met him at the door of her father's cabin where they conferred in low voices. As Broad, giving her a reassuring nod, walked briskly down the passage, Maggot closed the door and gently drew her away.

'You no worry. Your father is all right. Broad will see. Tonight is good you write letter to your grandmother, yes? You have many things to tell. Tomorrow we reach Tangier. Then you are very busy, have no time.'

She had been wondering what to do: how to fill the empty hours now she no longer had Judith to talk to or the baby to look after. Earlier she had

216

considered doing some washing, but abandoned the idea for how would she dry it? Repacking her trunk would take only minutes. It was far too early to go to bed. Despite her physical tiredness, she knew her clamouring thoughts and the tension in her body would never let her sleep.

'I suppose I could.' The more she thought about it, the more sensible the suggestion seemed.

He grinned. 'In saloon there is table, and more light.' He waited while she collected her writing case. As she slid on to one of the short benches, Broad emerged from the galley carrying a steaming jug and a bucket.

'Don't you worry, miss. Mr Vyvyan will be good as new after I finish with him.'

Kerenza thought his smile had an oddly grim edge to it. But as he hurried away down the passage Maggot spoke to her again and she dismissed the notion as a trick of the light.

'I have duties. But I am back soon. You stay here, please, yes?'

He didn't actually say it was important she did so, or that it was safer, but his tone implied both. Grateful to him and to Broad, Kerenza nodded.

He left, closing the saloon door. As she opened her writing case she heard his footsteps in the passage and faintly on the stairs. As she began to write she realized how much there was to tell. So much in fact, that she was able to keep her references to Nick minimal and brief; it was impossible to avoid mentioning him altogether. If his name did not appear at all her grandmother would surely think it strange. After all, everyone in Flushing was aware that though the post office

217

had Sam Penrose's name listed as *Kestrel*'s captain, it was Nick who commanded her. And had it not been for his daring and Maggot's skill she might not be sitting here.

A shiver tightened her skin and she turned the pen between her fingers, staring blindly at the bulkhead as images flashed across her mind and once again she was reliving the bloody horror of the captain's death.

A choking shout followed by sounds of violent retching jerked her back to reality and she looked round, her heart thumping, not sure if the sound was real or part of the memory. A thud against the ship's side marked the return of one of the boats. Shouts from the topside were answered with whoops and jeers. Shoes drummed on the fo'c'sle ladder then crossed the deck. The stomach-heaving sound was not repeated and soon all was quiet again. Kerenza returned to her letter.

A little while later, Broad opened the door from the passage. 'All right, miss? Like a cup of hot chocolate would you?'

She smiled at him. 'Thank you, I'd love it.'

'Be ready in two shakes it will.'

As he crossed the saloon with the bucket and jug, both clearly empty, he trailed an unpleasant smell behind him and Kerenza's nose wrinkled. She recalled the sound she thought she had heard.

'Is my father–?'

'Much better now, miss. Should sleep right through.'

'You're very kind.'

'Just doing my job, miss.'

'We both know it's far more than that.'

'Yes, well, I aren't the only one. Lady Russell would've been in some bad way if it hadn't been for you. Now you finish your letter and I'll get your chocolate.'

She caught her lip between her teeth to hide her smile. His chivvying, always tempered with respect, reminded her so much of Minnie, the housemaid at her grandmother's house. As well as acting as her lady's maid whenever necessary, Minnie had assumed personal responsibility for her welfare. But telling Broad this might offend him, and after all his kindness and willing help that was the last thing she wished to do.

She had added her signature to the final page and was re-reading the four closely written sheets, when she heard the ship hailed and the answering call from the lookout. She listened for the thump against the ship's side. After a few moments, she heard familiar footsteps on the companionway. Nick was back. Her heartbeat quickened and her fingers, as she replaced the top on the inkbottle, were a little unsteady.

More footsteps meant Maggot was coming down as well. She folded the letter and had closed it inside the case when the saloon door opened to reveal Nick. Something in his smile made Kerenza feel as if a dozen butterflies were trapped inside her.

'Miss Vyvyan, I am glad to find you here. I have with me someone most anxious to meet you.'

As he stood aside, Kerenza slid out of her seat, puzzled. She didn't know anyone here. Suddenly apprehension tightened her throat. But Nick had said anxious, so it could not possibly be Lieutenant Ashworth. Apart from it being extremely unlikely he would wish to renew his very brief acquaintance with her, surely Nick would not invite his cousin aboard *Kestrel?* Not after she had made clear her dislike of him? But perhaps in trying to remain polite she had not made it clear enough. In which case this would be the perfect opportunity. Moistening her lips and trying to quell her tumbling thoughts she smoothed palms damp with nervousness down her sadly creased green muslin.

The man who entered was tall and slim and dressed in the gold-braided red jacket, white waistcoat, white breeches and polished black boots of an officer in the Guards. A black military hat edged with gold braid was tucked under one arm. Though he appeared to be only in his mid to late thirties his short wavy hair was streaked with silver at the temples. A sallow complexion betrayed past illness, as did the lines radiating from the corners of his eyes and bracketing his mouth.

'Miss Vyvyan, may I present Colonel Sir George Russell.'

But Kerenza had already guessed his identity, and relief weakened her knees. As she made her curtsy a battle raged inside her between shame at thinking Nick capable of such lack of consideration and vivid, pain-filled memories of the way he had severed his connection with her.

Sir George dropped the large bag he was carrying and made a deep bow. His stern countenance softened in a smile of great sweetness, and she saw immediately why Judith had claimed such good fortune in her husband.

'Miss Vyvyan, I owe you a debt of gratitude I will never be able to repay.'

'With the greatest respect, sir, you owe me nothing. Lady Russell was very kind to me. That I was able to be of help to her was my privilege.' She could have said so much more. She could have told him how – even though it had been terrifying – the experience had moved her beyond words and changed her irrevocably. But afraid he might think her impertinent she held her tongue.

'We will not argue. However, I must tell you that my wife's wish to name our daughter Georgiana Kerenza has my wholehearted support. As soon as she is old enough Georgiana will be told the circumstances of her birth. And I hope that one day you and she will renew your acquaintance. We would be delighted to welcome you back. Next time I hope you may stay longer.' His look was direct, his smile sincere.

Filled with pride and pleasure, Kerenza could feel her cheeks glowing. 'You are very kind, sir.' As she curtsied again, he picked up the big bag he had brought in with him and set it on the table.

'My wife asked me to give you this. The bag itself of no account, but I am instructed to tell you that you may find the contents of use. And now I'm sure you will forgive me if I take my leave. I am anxious to return to my family.' He bowed.

'Thank you again, sir,' Kerenza managed. 'It was good of you to come. Please convey my thanks to Lady Russell, and my very best wishes.'

With a nod and a smile he left. Nick followed him and as their voices retreated down the passage, Kerenza opened the bag. On top was a folded shawl, but it was not hers. As she lifted it out, the folds slipped and she gasped. Of finest cashmere, it was four feet wide, over twice as long, and edged with a fringe. A design of pinecone shapes in deep green, yellow, dark turquoise and scarlet surrounded a pure white centre.

Gathering it up she closed her eyes and burying her face in its softness inhaled the faint fragrance of sandalwood. But even greater than its beauty was its significance. Every time she saw it she would remember how and why it had come into her possession.

Refolding it carefully, she laid it on the table. Then reaching once more into the bag she took out two clean white shirts with cuffs showing only the slightest hint of wear, and two blankets. These, clearly, were intended as replacements for the slop chest. Lastly, there were six crisp linen sheets, three pillowcases, and three towels. One set for her, and one set each for her mother and sister.

'That's some pretty,' Broad said, nodding towards the shawl as he set down her hot chocolate.

'Lady Russell sent it to replace mine, though it's far more beautiful.'

'That's as maybe. But yours was here when that dear baby needed something to keep her warm,' he reminded her.

'Look, she's sent shirts and blankets for the slop chest, and linen so my mother and sister will be comfortable on the journey home. Isn't that kind?' She picked up the cup and drank. Thick, hot and sweet, the chocolate was delicious.

'With respect, miss, 'tis no more than you deserve.'

'What is?' Nick enquired, coming in and closing the saloon door behind him.

Shyly, her confusion increased by his presence, Kerenza set down her cup and indicated the items on the table. 'These were in the bag Sir George brought. Ju– Lady Russell has been very generous.' Returning the bed linen and the shawl to the bag, she pushed the shirts and blankets towards him. 'She sent these for the slop chest.'

'Very good of her,' Nick agreed.

'Bring you some hot chocolate, Mr Penrose?' the steward enquired.

'Thank you.'

The steward left and Kerenza remained standing. Now she and Nick were alone she felt uncertain.

'I hope Sir George's arrival was not inconvenient?'

'No, not at all,' she said hastily. 'It was very good of him to take the trouble.'

'Only – well, for a moment you appeared uneasy, almost anxious. And I wondered why–'

She waved his concern aside. 'No, it was just – when you said – I could not imagine who–' She stopped, afraid she had already said too much.

'Ah,' he nodded slowly. And she knew he had guessed. He gazed at his feet for a moment, then looked up, his weatherbeaten features flushed and frowning. 'You have little reason to trust me. But

223

please believe that I am deeply sorry for the pain I must have caused you. I see many things differently now. As for Sir George, there was simply no time to give you notice. When Lady Russell told him of your part in events, he insisted on returning with me to thank you in person.' She saw his glance move from the cup to her writing case. 'I fear we interrupted you.'

'No, not at all. I was writing to my grandmother, but I had finished.'

'May I?' He indicated the benches.

'O–of course.'

As he slid into the bench seat furthest away she felt the knots in her stomach and shoulders loosen slightly and resumed her own seat. 'Maggot suggested it. To keep me occupied.'

His wry smile echoed her own. But though he caught her gaze for a moment, he did not try to hold it, and looked instead at the shawl. 'There is certainly much you could tell her.'

'There is indeed. But though my grandmother is both open-minded and resilient, I think if she were to read about some of the events that have occurred during our voyage without me there to explain the various circumstances, she would be greatly concerned. To cause her such disquiet would be most unkind of me. So I have written in general terms rather than in detail.'

Broad returned, setting a steaming cup in front of Nick. 'Beg pardon, Mr Penrose, but have you seen Mr Maggot since you come back?'

'I have, Broad. Thank you.'

'Right, sir. I'll be in the galley if you're wanting anything.' As he disappeared, Nick picked up his cup, took a mouthful, then set the cup down again.

'I understand your father wished to leave the ship?'

Though he raised his eyes to hers while he was speaking, he did not try to maintain the contact and it suddenly occurred to Kerenza that this was deliberate, so she should not feel pressured or intimidated. The realization released a little more of her tension and drawing her cup forward she cradled it in her hands.

'I suppose Maggot told you.'

'He had no choice. It is his duty to inform me of anything that might affect the wellbeing of the ship or the passengers. Why did your father want to leave?'

'He was afraid you might be delayed here, or that you might have to take the dispatches to Admiral Hotham yourself.'

He shook his head. 'They will go with a Royal Navy sloop leaving the dockyard in the morning. So what was his plan?'

'To find a fishing boat or something similar to take us across to Tangier overnight.'

Nick shook his head again. 'The Straits are a hunting ground for Tunisian and Algerian pirates as well as French privateers and occasional warships. It's most unlikely he'd have found anyone willing to take the risk. Besides, without the ransom money, how did he expect–?'

'He was not in his right mind.' She bit her lip, wanting to confess her anxiety about her father's drinking and her fears about how it might affect their dealings with the governor, yet prevented by

225

the habit of loyalty even though she knew it had always been one-sided.

'Morocco is a Muslim country, and Muslims are not allowed alcohol.' Her head came up. It was as if he had seen into her mind and read her thoughts. 'So he will find it far harder to obtain.'

'I'm sure you mean to offer comfort. But the truth is that Tangier is a free port with a mixed population. I'm afraid, if he is determined, it might be all too easy.'

'Your father's reason for going to Tangier is to obtain the release of your mother and sister. It's possible his drinking is due – at least in part – to anxiety and frustration. I'm sure that once we arrive things will be different.'

Kerenza wanted so much to believe him. But as she looked up, searching his eyes, she couldn't, for she sensed he didn't believe it himself. She raised the cup to her lips once more, and felt it rattle against her teeth as she emptied it. Clearing her throat she asked the first question that came into her head.

'Where do Sir George and Lady Russell live?'

'In officers' quarters in the town, I imagine. But fortunately he was still in the Convent when I arrived.'

'What was he doing in a convent?' Kerenza asked in bewilderment. 'And why would you go there?'

'No, not a convent, *the* Convent.' His features softened. 'I should have explained: it's the name of the Governor's residence. It was built in the 1500s as a monastery for Franciscan Friars. When it was taken over early this century to be

226

the residence of the senior British officer it kept the name everyone knew and recognized.' He raised his cup, and Kerenza knew he was allowing her to choose whether or not conversation continued.

She had finished her drink. There was no reason to remain in the saloon. Except ... except that this was the first time since she had boarded the packet that she and Nick had had a normal conversation. Yes, they had spoken, but only to request or convey information. And those occasions had been fraught with tension. But this was different, now was different.

He had said he was sorry for the pain he had caused her. That had not been easy for him. Not because he didn't mean it: clearly he did, and every time she thought about it she shivered with pleasure. What had made the apology so difficult was his obvious lack of practice. She wondered if he had ever apologized before in his life. She could have shown him how it was done. Having spent most of her life apologizing for faults real and imagined, she was an expert.

But he had none of Jeremy Ashworth's arrogance or insufferable conceit. She sensed his attitude to mistakes was swift acceptance. The past could not be changed. So look forward not back, and move on.

Since leaving Falmouth they had endured storms, faced death at the hands of a French privateer, he had lost his uncle, she had assisted at a birth. They were both exhausted. And though he had fulfilled his contract by delivering the dispatches, her hardest trial – caring for two

227

people who had made her life miserable – still lay ahead. She didn't want to think about it. Tonight, this moment, was a respite from what had been and what was yet to come. She looked up.

'What is the Convent like?'

Seeing his shoulders drop slightly, she was comforted and reassured. The small easing of strain confirmed that he too was nervous. And that meant her good opinion was important to him.

Leaning forward he smiled, rested both elbows on the table, and toyed with his cup. 'It's built round an internal courtyard full of orange trees and bougainvillea. The front has a magnificent colonnade opening on to Main Street. At the back there's a walled garden. This is a rare luxury in Gibraltar because there is so very little spare land. The grounds extend down to the water and it has its own private landing. As soon as we reached the jetty I sent one of the oarsmen to fetch servants with a chair to carry Lady Russell and her baby up to the house.' He grinned. 'The news spread like a gorse fire.'

She smiled back. 'I can imagine.'

'Sir George came out of the door at a dead run. His face when he saw his wife and baby...' He looked away. 'Seamen are far too sentimental.' His tone was rough and self-mocking. 'I doubt there was a dry eye in that garden.' He leaned back. 'I handed over the dispatches and was asked to wait. Eventually Sir George joined me and insisted on coming to the ship to thank you in person.'

'It was very good of him, but not necessary.'

'He knows, as I do, that but for you the outcome might have been very different.'

Shuddering, Kerenza shook her head. It didn't bear thinking about. She sought urgently for something to steer her thoughts from terrors that still haunted her. 'Did I hear you tell Mrs Woodrow that Maggot once owned his own ship?'

'He did; a mistico. It's a bit like a shebec in that it has three lateen sails, but it's much smaller, rarely above eighty tons.'

'Those ships we passed when we were crossing the bay, the ones with the overhanging bow and stern were they shebecs?'

He nodded. 'They're ideal for the Mediterranean. Their shallow draught allows them to get really close inshore.'

'Was Maggot a trader, then?'

Nick's grin made him look suddenly years younger. 'In a manner of speaking. Actually, he was a privateer.'

Kerenza stared at him. 'You're teasing me.'

He shook his head. 'I'm not. And considering his grandfather and uncle were pirates, the temptation – and the pressure – to join them must have been strong.'

'Is there a difference then, between pirates and privateers?'

'There is indeed. Privateers have a legal commission from the state to capture the ships of any country their ruler is at war with. They have to carry letters of marque to prove their legitimacy.'

'What happens to the ships they capture?'

'Once the state has condemned them as prizes, the ships and their cargoes are sold, and the proceeds divided up between the privateer's crew.'

'Didn't you say Maggot's ship was sunk by the French?'

Nick's face hardened in disgust. 'A privateer three times the size of his mistico. Maggot was the only survivor. He was in the water for twenty-four hours, clinging to some wreckage before our lookout spotted him and we picked him up.'

Kerenza's imagination supplied a vivid picture: Maggot, floating among the dead and disfigured bodies of his crew who must surely have been his friends; amid the wreckage not just of his boat but of his livelihood. How slowly the time would have passed, especially the hours of darkness. She recalled instances of Maggot's kindness, his quick cold anger at her suspicion that he would harm Judith, the mischief in his eyes as he deflected Betsy Woodrow's wrath, his competence in dealing with her father, and his total loyalty to Nick.

'It must have been so lonely for him.' She swallowed the stiffness in her throat. 'How long ago did it happen?'

'Three years. He's been with me ever since.'

'Did he not wish to return to Tangier?'

Nick shook his head. 'Because I had saved his life I owned it.' His mouth twisted wryly. 'That felt very strange. Anyway, he refused to leave me. The old hands were suspicious at first, but within a day he had learned his way around the rigging and within a week he had proved his skill as a helmsman and navigator. When we lost the second mate to fever it made more sense to promote Maggot than take on a new man.'

'Yet I cannot recall seeing him with you in

230

Flushing when you attended the balls and parties.'

He raised his brows. 'Would you have expected to?' She felt her colour rise. 'Exactly,' he said. 'He knew he would be an embarrassment. As it happened he didn't want to come anyway. He couldn't think of the word for *bored*, but he mimed it well enough, rolling his eyes and snoring.'

Kerenza compressed her lips on a smile. 'I can imagine. So what does he do when you are in port?'

'The same as any seamen who has no home or family to go home to. He spends his time on the ship or in waterfront bars. He says the Muslim part of him doesn't drink, but the English bit allows him some ale. Speaking several languages he quickly makes new friends and picks up all kinds of gossip.'

'About the war?' She glanced up as the watch-bell clanged overhead.

He nodded. 'Among other things. He'll be an ideal go-between while we are in Tangier. Though the locals tolerate foreigners because of the trade they bring, they are suspicious of the English.'

'Why?'

'They haven't forgotten the occupation and how the English destroyed the city when they left.' With obvious reluctance he stood up. Quickly, Kerenza rose, carefully replacing the shawl in the bag.

He hesitated. 'Now Lady Russell has gone, would you like to move back into the double cabin?'

She looked up quickly. 'I hadn't really thought. But if you wish to return to yours then of course.'

'No. It's not – I just thought – being so close to the companionway is very noisy. You may find your sleep less disturbed if you are further away.'

She didn't dare meet his gaze. No matter where she lay her head her sleep would be disturbed by dreams of him, dreams from which she woke with tears still wet on her face; dreams that had shamed her, because to yearn for someone who had treated her so badly was surely perverse and unnatural. But tonight he had apologized. Tonight they had talked, tentatively reaching out to each other across the distance created by hurt and anger. He was trying so hard to make her more comfortable.

'Thank you,' she smiled up at him. 'If it is no trouble.'

'None at all,' he said quickly. 'I'll fetch Broad, and we'll move your trunk at once.' As he started toward the galley door, Kerenza was overcome by giggles. He looked back, smiling. 'What?'

She shook her head, covering her mouth with her fingertips. She felt light-headed with relief and happiness and hope. But she couldn't tell him that, not yet.

'My trunk,' she spluttered. 'It is being moved so often, I think Broad will wish it had wheels.'

Chapter Fourteen

Kerenza was woken next morning by the sounds of the ship getting under way. She yawned and stretched, feeling calmer and more rested than at any time since leaving Falmouth. The previous night after transferring her bed linen to the upper cot she had climbed in. Half-expecting to toss and turn she had fallen asleep almost at once. Stirring when the crew returned she drifted off again with a smile on her lips at the amount of noise they made falling over things, *sshhh*ing each other, warning of dire consequences should they disturb her.

Billy rapped on the door. 'Water, miss.'

'Thank you, Billy.' She pushed back the blankets and lit the lamp.

An hour later, much refreshed, her hair brushed, coiled and pinned up high, she rolled up her green gown and stowed it in the trunk. Shaking out the peach muslin, her only clean garment, she put it on, buttoned her dark green wool jacket over it, and left the cabin. In the saloon Maggot stood, both hands on the chair back, talking quietly to the steward who frowned as he listened intently. Looking up as she entered, they immediately stopped talking and both bowed.

'Good morning,' she smiled.

'Morning, miss,' Broad said. 'How about a boiled egg and some fresh bread and butter?'

'That would be lovely. Have you seen my father this morning?'

Broad shook his head as he left. 'Not yet, miss.'

'Your father no wake yet,' Maggot said. 'Is better he sleep as long as possible.'

'I'm sure you're right.' Once awake he would only fret.

'You no worry,' Maggot ordered. 'Eat, yes? Is a very busy day for you.' Then he too left.

Kerenza enjoyed her breakfast. After making sure she had everything she needed Broad retreated into the galley. Toy wished her good morning as he passed through the saloon, returning a few moments later with a cup of coffee she guessed was for Nick. While she ate she listened to the sounds of the ship. Without conscious effort she had become familiar with the daily routine.

By now one watch would have swabbed and holystoned the decks and polished the brasswork. The other watch, roused at 7.30 after turning in at 4 a.m., would be stowing their hammocks and slinging the mess tables, hungry for their boiled oatmeal seasoned with salt, butter and sugar.

She lingered over a second cup of tea, glad of some solitude. A very busy day, Maggot had said. Before nightfall the ship would reach Tangier. Would she see her mother and sister, or was that perhaps too much to expect? Draining the cup she set it down, not at all sure how she felt at the prospect of reunion.

Broad bustled back in and, after thanking him, she went up on deck. Returning the helmsman's greeting with a smile she crossed to her favourite place in the stern. Looking forward along the ship she saw Nick at the mainmast, taking sick call.

A short line of sorry-looking men waited their turn. Two had bruised swollen faces and black eyes, confirming Broad's prediction of a fight. The others stood with the drooping heads and hunched shoulders of men to whom bright light and loud noise were painful. Maggot stood nearby ready to dose them with the only two remedies the ship carried: James's Powder to reduce fever, calomel or castor oil to flush out unbalanced humours. Judging by their appearance, it was the latter that most would receive.

Catching her eye Nick nodded, then turned back to address the seaman in front of him.

Tingling from the top of her head all the way down to her toes, both pleased and self-conscious at his acknowledgement, Kerenza rested her forearms on the rail and looked out over ruffled water that glittered in the morning sun. The wind had backed, and was once again blowing from the south-east. But now, instead of holding them back, making them wait, it was speeding them towards their destination.

Gazing backward over the stern she watched Gibraltar retreat. She thought of Judith and Sir George, and their baby. She recalled the minister standing here beside her, one hand clapped to his round shallow-brimmed hat, his eyes filled with guilt and sadness as he had pleaded for her compassion. Had holding Judith's newborn baby been sufficient to crack the hard shell of envy and resentment that had encased Betsy Woodrow's heart for so long? Kerenza hoped so for both their sakes. But that chapter of her life was over. She turned to look forward. Ahead, hazy in the distance, lay the Moroccan coast.

'Deck ho!' the lookout bellowed from the foretop. 'Sail on the port quarter. Looks like a shebec, sir. Three masts.'

Maggot and the bosun began yelling orders, men swarmed across the deck, and Kerenza immediately turned to Nick who pointed towards the companionway. She nodded and hurried down the stairs and along the passage.

Entering the saloon she stopped. 'Papa!'

Dressed but unshaven, he was seated at the table drinking a cup of coffee. A plate of bread and butter remained untouched. His face was grey and haggard. His eyes little more than slits in pouches of puffy flesh. He tried to speak but his voice was cracked and hoarse as if he had a sore throat. From his brief gesture she assumed the effort was too great. As he lifted the cup it shook so violently he needed both hands to raise it to his lips. Her thoughts raced but she moved with deliberate calm. 'This is a pleasant surprise. I didn't expect to see you up yet.'

He set the cup down, rattling it against the saucer, and with his elbows on the table sank his head in his hands.

Kerenza slid into the seat opposite. She opened her mouth about to offer to fetch him something for the headache from which he was so clearly suffering, but the *boom* of a cannon stopped the words on her tongue and made her start. Her father jumped violently, his gaze jerking, wide and fearful, from skylight to door and back to her.

'What's happening?' he rasped. 'Are we under attack?'

Having no idea, she shook her head. 'I don't know. The lookout warned of a ship approaching, but–'

'I'm going to find out,' he cut across her, struggling to his feet.

'Papa, wait.'

'Get out of my way,' he muttered, pushing past and blundering out into the passage. The door to the captain's day cabin stood open and Kerenza followed her father, unable to stop him as he barged in, slamming the door back against the bulkhead.

'What's happening?' William demanded, hoarse with fear. 'Are we being attacked? Why are our guns not firing?' His tone changed, anxiety turning to suspicion. 'What are you doing?'

Coming in behind him, Kerenza saw Nick glance up, clearly startled by their arrival. She shrugged helplessly.

He had lifted one of the seats and was bent over the open strong box. 'No,' he said. 'We are not under attack. That was just a warning shot to–'

'That's *my* money in there.' William's voice climbed. 'You've no right – *I* need it – my wife and daughter – I won't let you–' He lunged forward and Kerenza grabbed his arm.

'Papa, no, stop.'

He flung her off and she stumbled backward.

Nick straightened, taut with fury. 'That's enough, Mr Vyvyan! Control yourself, sir. I don't want your money; I came for this.' He waved the folded sheet of thick creamy paper, through

237

which Kerenza could see the shadow of a thick wax seal. 'I have no intention of jeopardizing this ship or anyone on it.' His gaze flickered briefly to Kerenza and she felt instantly stronger, safer. He knew what he was doing. 'If I were to order our guns to fire, the Algerian would cripple or sink us in minutes. How then would you rescue your wife and daughter?'

Kerenza watched her trembling father reach blindly for the nearest bench and sink on to it. 'I'm sorry,' she whispered, as Nick closed the strongbox and dropped the seat back into place. 'He didn't mean–'

'*You* have nothing to apologize for.'

Wincing inside, for it was abundantly clear Nick considered her father's behaviour inexcusable, she indicated the paper. 'What is that?'

'Our guarantee of safe passage I hope. It's the pass I paid for back in Falmouth. It should convince the Algerian captain to let us proceed.' He started for the door. 'Mr Vyvyan, kindly return to the saloon, and stay there.' Turning to Kerenza he lowered his voice. 'On no account is he to come topside. If you have any trouble, call Broad and Toy.' Next moment he'd gone, taking the stairs two at a time.

'Come, Papa' she slipped her hand under his elbow, half-expecting him to jerk free. But he rose unsteadily and allowed her to lead him out of the cabin. As she paused to close the door, he looked up the companionway. The light fell across his face and her heart was wrenched by the dread stamped across it. She drew him away along the passage and he shuffled after her, moaning under

238

his breath.

Back in the saloon she guided him into his seat then crossed to the galley door and called for the steward, hurrying back and drawing the chair forward so that her knees almost touched her father's.

'What if the pass doesn't work?' William moaned. He turned to Kerenza with a suddenness that made her jump, seizing her hand, his grip painfully tight. '*Algerian* he said. What if it's the same one? The one who took us captive last year? What if he finds out I'm on board?'

'Papa, please try to calm yourself. There is no reason to think it is the same man. And even if it is, Mr Penrose has the pass. The Algerian cannot know you are aboard. Nor will he if we remain down here.'

'You wanted me, miss?'

Kerenza swung round as Broad bustled in wiping his hands on a grubby cloth. 'Oh yes, please. I was wondering if Maggot – would you be so good as to ask him if he could spare a moment?'

Broad sucked in a breath through pursed lips. 'I'll try, miss. But this isn't the best time.'

'I know.' She tried to convey with her eyes what she could not say aloud. 'But my father is *extremely* anxious.'

'Ah.' She could almost see him recalling what he'd heard about her father's past, working out possible reactions, and weighing their consequences. 'Right. Back in two shakes, miss.' He hurried out and along the passage.

'What if they refuse to recognize the pass?' William demanded. 'The Algerians think any Chris-

239

tian vessel, no matter what nation it belongs to, is a lawful prize. If they find my money–?' He stopped, shuddering with dread at the visions thrown up by his imagination. He gripped her hand more tightly. 'We should never have stopped. Penrose is too young, too inexperienced. He doesn't–'

'No, Papa. That's not true.'

Tossing her hand away, he glared at her through swollen and crusted eyelids. 'What do you know? You're just a girl. You've been nowhere. You've seen nothing. How dare you! Telling me what's true and what isn't. Who do you think you are?'

Clammy with shock at his aggression, her heart hammering painfully, Kerenza clasped her hands on her lap and held herself very straight. 'I'm your *other* daughter. I did not ask to come; I'm here because you insisted upon it. You said you needed me.'

'And I do, I do.' He sagged as all the fight and anger was replaced once again by anxiety. 'Forgive me. I didn't mean – I should not have said – but you have no idea.' Slumping forward with his elbows on the table, he clasped his head in his hands, shaking it.

Hearing footsteps on the stairs then, and in the passage, she looked up as Broad came in, hope subsumed by anxiety as he shook his head.

'I'm sorry, miss. Mr Maggot can't come now. He's doing the talking for Mr Penrose with that there Algerian.'

'You see?' William cried, glaring from one to the other. 'Didn't I warn you? He won't accept the pass. I'll be taken prisoner again. What will

240

become of my family then?'

'Now, now, Mr Vyvyan. That's enough of that.' Broad was firm. 'Mr Penrose knows what he's doing. I'll fetch you a nice cup of tea.'

'Tea?' William blazed. 'Are you mad? Any moment those murdering cut-throats could overrun the ship and come bursting in here. You want to make tea? Go on, then. Go and do it. Pretend none of this is happening. Pretend everything is just fine. Go on, get out. You're no use here.' He covered his face with his hands, racked with violent shudders.

Visibly angry, his lips tight with indignation, the steward looked at Kerenza.

Hot with shame, she cleared her throat. 'If you are making tea, Mr Broad, I'd really appreciate a cup.' She tried to smile. 'I daresay Mr Penrose and Maggot will welcome one too the minute this business is settled.'

He gave a brief nod, 'You aren't wrong there, miss. Be all right, will you?' His glance flicked to her father and back.

She nodded and Broad stumped out. Kerenza turned to her father who was totally immersed in his own fears. It was like looking at a stranger. He was her father but she no longer knew him. Then, reminding herself of what he had been through, she tried hard to make allowances.

But his behaviour was hard to forgive and impossible to condone. He was not alone on the ship. Whatever happened would involve everyone aboard, not just him. She might have felt more compassion had he indeed been a stranger, because then she would have had no expectations.

She would not have been hoping that after years of disappointment and betrayed trust he might have wanted to make amends.

Tears pricked. Afraid they might fall and betray feelings he would never understand, afraid any sign of weakness in her would only reignite his own terror, unable to sit still any longer, she stood up quickly and walked out of the saloon. But there was nowhere she could go, not even to the privacy of her cabin. She was trapped by the need to ensure her father remained where he was.

She leaned against the bulkhead. Then increased noise from the deck and a subtle shift underfoot told her the packet was getting under way again. A figure ducked through the hatchway blocking the light and Nick came down the stairs. Seeing her he came forward.

'Now that's settled there should be no more delays.'

'That's good.' She forced herself to smile. In the dark passage he wouldn't be able to see, but she hoped it might mask her distress.

'I heard shouting.'

Afraid of making a fool of herself she simply shook her head.

'Your father?'

'He's very anxious.'

'I think you should go topside. You've been down here long enough.'

'But–'

'Go on,' he urged. 'Enjoy the fresh air. There are certain matters I need to settle with your father.' He passed her and she heard the saloon door click firmly shut.

'You all right?' Maggot frowned, as she stepped over the coaming.

Ignoring his question she asked, 'Do you have any more *kif*.'

His frown deepened. 'Why you want that?'

'It's not for me,' she explained. 'My father – he was so afraid of being recaptured. It made him – he's not rational. What worries me is that in his present state he could so easily say or do something that will offend the governor, or indeed, anyone whose goodwill we may need. And if that were to happen–' She clasped her arms across her body, not daring even to complete the thought, let alone voice her dread.

Maggot nodded. 'You no worry. I go see.'

A few minutes later, Toy brought her a cup of tea. 'I'll give you a call when dinner's ready, miss.'

Interpreting that as an instruction from Nick to stay on deck, she nodded. 'Thank you.'

When Billy came to call her, and she returned to the saloon, her father was sitting where she had left him. But now he was clean-shaven and though his hands still trembled he was visibly calmer. He did not look up or speak. His gaze remained fixed on his plate as he ate slowly and with effort.

She was halfway through her meal when Nick joined them. Though she was delighted that he had come, her embarrassment at her father's earlier outbursts was being overtaken by a far deeper fear. For even though it seemed that she and Nick had tentatively begun to rebuild their friendship, what future could it have?

Nick had never made any secret of his ambition

to one day command a packet ship as owner-skipper. Since boyhood his life had been one of hard work and danger as he pursued his dream. He had served his apprenticeship, learned his trade, and gained the necessary qualifications. He had proved himself and his ability beyond doubt. Why then would he, who had so much to offer and deserved so much in return, ally himself to such a family as hers?

She bent her head, pretending to chew. But in reality it was not food but the solid lump of grief in her throat that she found hard to swallow.

Addressing himself to his piled plate and ignoring her father, Nick related an amusing incident that had occurred in Jamaica, only occasionally glancing in her direction. When he finished the story she looked at him. Wanting to convey her gratitude for the way he had dealt with a situation that was beyond her, unable to speak out because of her father's presence, she smiled instead, hoping he would understand. His gaze held hers and for an instant she couldn't breathe.

It was as if those long terrible weeks apart had never happened. But because they had, and because she knew now that he too had suffered, she was still experiencing ripples of hopelessness and yearning long after he had returned to the deck.

Three hours later, she stood at the port quarter, gazing at the walled city of Tangier lying like a tilted cup between two hills. Her father stood further forward, deliberately apart, as he had been since the packet left Falmouth.

Behind her she heard Nick's voice. A moment

later he was at her side.

'As Maggot grew up here, he's the best man to bring us in.'

Amid whitewashed houses with flat roofs piled in terraces against the hillside like a child's toy bricks, were several European-style buildings. Two looked like churches, another like a large and rather grand house.

But it was to the castle on the right-hand side that Kerenza's gaze was drawn. Sprawling over the top of the hill its brooding presence dominated the town.

She leaned towards Nick, her voice low. 'Is that–?'

He nodded. 'The governor's palace.'

Unease slid like a drop of icy water down her spine. She told herself not to be foolish. The worst was over. They had arrived safely. Once the formalities had been completed and the money handed over, her mother and sister would be released and *Kestrel* would return to Falmouth. Would it really be that easy? And if it were, what then?

Kerenza clasped her upper arms, trying to rub away the gooseflesh that tightened her skin. As the ship sailed shoreward she saw to the right of the crescent-shaped beach a long stretch of huge jumbled stones running in a straight line out into the bay. Rollers driven by the stiff breeze broke over it, tossing up clouds of spray as they crashed in a welter of white foam.

'What's that?'

To her surprise it was her father who answered. 'What's left of a massive mole the British built as a breakwater and jetty when they occupied the city. They blew it up when they left.'

Wanting to ask *why*, Kerenza bit her tongue. She knew little about politics and no doubt there were very good reasons. But to deliberately destroy something that must have cost huge amounts of money and years of hard work to build seemed to her a terrible waste.

As Maggot guided the packet into the bay, the two big gaff sails were dropped and *Kestrel* glided towards an anchorage at the more sheltered eastern end of the town. Now they were closer, Kerenza could see that the city walls lay mostly in ruins, though several towers, round and square, still stood. Small houses had been built along the tumbled remains of wall above the anchorage. Gardens, orchards, and fields spread over the low hills beyond. There were no guns on the wall facing the sea. But on the northern edge of the cliff below the castle she saw a few cannon mounted on the remains of a fort.

The twin castles of Pendennis and St Mawes guarding the entrance to the Carrick Roads and Falmouth harbour were in far better repair and yet, strangely, seemed less intimidating. She turned to Nick.

'How do we get in?'

'You see that wall sloping up from the beach?' Nick pointed. 'Behind it there's a ramp leading up to the Water Gate, the square tower with battlements. That's the entrance into the town for anyone coming in by sea.'

As the packet turned into the wind and the anchor splashed down, William Vyvyan turned towards Nick and the companionway.

'When are we going ashore?'

'Shortly. First we have to clear Customs.' As William tensed, and Kerenza braced herself for another outburst, Nick turned away, making it clear the matter was not open to argument or discussion. Then, speaking for her ears only, he added, 'And Maggot must go and see his stepmother about your accommodation. But as she doesn't know he's alive, seeing him again will be a shock. Obviously he'll be as quick as he can, but – you do understand?'

She nodded. 'Of course.'

Now they were finally in Tangier she was suddenly very nervous. How it would be when she met her mother and sister again? This would be the first time they had met or spoken in three years. How should she greet them? Should she simply wait and let them make the first move? What would they say? Would their experiences have made them more aware of the importance of family bonds? Would they be anxious to forget the past and make a fresh start? Would it include her? *Did she want it to?*

If she were completely honest, she wasn't sure. She had made a home and a new life at her grandmother's where she had been welcomed and appreciated. Despite her grandmother's undemonstrative manner, Kerenza had for the first time in her life known herself loved unconditionally. But even that soothing balm had not entirely healed her wounded self-esteem. If her own mother and sister did not love her then logic dictated it must be because she was unlovable. Yet if her grandmother loved her, and Nick, then surely – here she faltered.

She had *thought* Nick loved her. But had he? Did he? Was she seeing only what she wanted to see? Or was it indeed real and true and having been tested by misunderstanding strong enough now to withstand whatever trouble the future might hold? Half of her wanted so much for it to be so. The other half – the wary half that remembered all too clearly the wrenching anguish of love offered and rejected – wasn't at all sure.

As for her mother and sister: the child she had once been still yearned for their love and acceptance. But she was no longer a child. She would wait: allow them to make the first move.

The sun was dipping below the hills behind the city when Nick and Maggot returned. During their absence, realizing how inconvenient it would be to take a heavy trunk ashore, Kerenza had packed a bag instead. She used the one Judith had sent, putting in essentials for a couple of days, plus a neat roll of dirty laundry in the hope that Maggot's stepmother would have or know of a washerwoman.

Returning to the deck where her father waited, she suggested he did the same. But, impatient and clearly not interested, he waved her away before she finished speaking. So she asked Broad to pack what he thought her father might need.

Now, at last, after a row between her father and Nick over the ransom money – her father had wanted to bring it with them; Nick believed it was safer to leave it aboard in the strongbox overnight – they were in the cutter heading shoreward. Her father was in the stern next to Maggot who had the tiller. Nick was beside her, her bag between his feet.

Shivery, and with an uncomfortable tightness at the base of her skull, Kerenza drew the folds of her cloak closer.

'Are you cold?' he asked softly.

She shook her head, forcing a smile. 'No, I'm fine.' It wasn't true. She felt exhausted. It had been a stressful day. And it wasn't over yet.

'As soon as we land,' her father announced, aggressive in his determination, 'we must go directly to the governor's palace.'

Nick looked over his shoulder. Kerenza closed her eyes. But it was Maggot who responded.

'No.' It was blunt and final. 'Is no good tonight.'

'Why not?' William demanded. 'Dammit, I caught the first available ship, and I've brought the money. He'll want to see me.'

'No, he won't,' Nick said.

'Not tonight,' Maggot added.

'Why?'

'Because there are formalities to be observed,' Nick said. 'Ignoring them will cause offence. And that won't help your cause one bit. It's the governor who has the power here, not you, not us.'

'But I've brought the money,' William repeated desperately. 'He said that as soon as I got back with it my wife and daughter could leave.'

'Then we must hope he's a man of his word, and that you will soon be reunited. In the meantime,' Nick raised his voice as William opened his mouth to argue, 'our first call must be on the

British Consul. Your request to see the governor will have to be made through him. So he will be able to advise on the best approach.'

Heading for the beach, the cutter passed an old wharf. Kerenza saw two galleys laid up inside it, with sheds and storehouses behind. Breathing in the smells of seaweed, rope, fish, tar and paint she was vividly reminded of Flushing. She wished she was back there, that this was all over. But even as the thought formed she found herself fearful of what return would mean. She hadn't wanted to come. But were it not for this voyage, she and Nick would not be in the process of repairing their rift and regaining each other's trust.

The cutter's keel grated on the bottom and, by the time Nick had helped her ashore, Maggot and her father were already on their way up towards the Water Gate. Two of the oarsmen pushed the cutter off.

'It's better that they return to the ship,' Nick said. 'They'll come back for me later. Maggot will stay overnight at the house with you and your father. I'll join you in the morning to accompany you to the palace.'

'Thank you,' she said gratefully.

The archway in the tower was shadowed and beneath the vaulted stone the wind blew strongly, tugging Kerenza's cloak. She shivered. Then they were inside the town, following Maggot and her father. Kerenza's eyes widened at the tall grandeur of a big church. A little further on they entered a busy market-place.

The noise was deafening as vendors urged people to buy, customers haggled, women

250

gossiped, children chased each other squealing with laughter, men argued, beggars pleaded, all at the tops of their voices in languages that sounded to Kerenza as though they were gargling.

She glimpsed small wooden booths, pyramids of melons and oranges and other fruits she did not recognize. A brightly clad water seller carrying an ornate jug and silver cup wandered by, ringing a small bell. One table still displayed a few round flat loaves, fresh and fragrant, another held clay pots. The smells of roast meat, spices, smoking charcoal, hot oil, rotting vegetables and dust burned in her nose.

Her face grew hot with self-consciousness and she was glad of Nick's silent presence beside her as she intercepted sidelong glances and angry glares, frowns of curiosity and contempt. Most of the women were veiled. But those who were not covered the lower half of their faces with one end of their headscarf, still watching her as they turned to each other, and she knew she was being discussed.

Groups of turbaned Arabs swathed in white with seamed faces the colour of teak and long beards sat watching in the shadows, sipping mint tea from small glasses.

Kerenza breathed a sigh of relief as they left the market-place and followed Maggot into a narrow dirt street that climbed steeply. Sloe-eyed, bare-legged Arab boys peered at them from alleys. A girl ducked shyly into the low dark doorway of a flat-roofed house. They crossed another street, and another, then Maggot stopped in front of a larger house with deep-set arched windows and tall

251

double doors of dark wood, and turned to Nick.

'Here is Consul's house.' He knocked.

A few moments later one of the doors was opened and they were asked their business. William started forward, but Maggot held him back.

'My name is Nicholas Penrose, commanding the packet ship *Kestrel*. One of my passengers is Mr William Vyvyan whose wife and daughter are currently guests of the governor. We need to see the consul.'

The door closed.

'What?' William began angrily. But Maggot raised a finger to his lips.

'You wait. Is all right.'

'No, it damn well isn't all right!' William exploded.

'Papa, please,' Kerenza begged. 'I'm sure Maggot knows–'

The door swung open and a servant bowed, gesturing for them to enter.

Chapter Fifteen

Tiny blue and white tiles covered the floor of a cool hallway. Archways leading to more rooms broke ornately decorated walls. The servant led them into a spacious salon, gestured for them to sit, and melted silently away.

'What are we supposed to do now?' William demanded, tense and pugnacious.

'We wait,' Maggot replied.

'Please sit down, Mr Vyvyan.'

Kerenza glanced from Nick to her father. Phrased as a polite request, it was nonetheless an order. She held her breath, praying he would not argue any more. The room was furnished with several tables and couches piled with colourful cushions. After a moment's hesitation, William Vyvyan lowered himself on to one of them. Kerenza unfastened her cloak, slipped it from her shoulders, and folded it on to the couch next to her as she took a seat opposite her father and looked around. A massive urn stood at one side of an archway, and two heavy chests of black wood with intricately carved lids rested against the elaborately decorated wall.

Just as she began to wonder how long they might have to wait, she heard the sound of brisk footsteps.

The man who entered wore a brown frock coat over fawn breeches, white stockings and brown shoes with buckles. Brushed straight back, and receding at the temples, his greying hair curved on to his coat collar. Kerenza guessed his age to be about fifty. His smile was pleasant, but the way he rubbed his palms together signalled unease. She wondered why.

'Good evening. My name is Henry Corbett. I'm the vice consul. I'm afraid Mr Matra is currently in Marrakech.' He turned as the same servant appeared silently in another doorway. 'Would you care for some tea? The locals prefer it with mint, but if that is not to your taste we do have goat's milk.'

Fidgeting with impatience, William, waved the

offer aside. 'I haven't come all this way to drink tea. You must know who I am and why I'm here. How soon can I see the governor?'

Blushing for her father's rudeness, Kerenza bit her lip. But the vice consul didn't even blink.

'I will send a request for an interview first thing in the morning. Though I should warn you that it may be several days before you are granted an audience.'

As Nick and Kerenza exchanged a glance William exploded. 'Several days? Why? Why must I wait so long?'

Henry Corbett spread his hands. 'Because I'm afraid that's the way things are done here. The governor does not recognize as urgent any concerns but his own.' His palm-rubbing quickened, and the dry rasping sound grated on Kerenza's nerves.

Her unease grew. He had answered her father without once making eye contact.

'Surely,' William pressed, 'he will be glad to learn that I am returned? I have brought the money. You can tell him I'm grateful for his hospitality. Tell him any damn thing you like, but make it clear I want my wife and daughter released so that they may return home with me at once.'

Henry Corbett's forehead puckered in discomfort and distress. Seeing him brace himself, Kerenza's muscles tightened. *Something was wrong.* She had sensed it the moment the vice consul walked in.

'What?' William demanded. 'It can't be that difficult. The governor wanted money. And though it's nearly bankrupted me I've brought it. So I see no reason why the matter cannot be settled quickly. Tell me' – his tone became eager, anxious – 'have you seen them recently? Are they in good health and spirits?'

'I did indeed see Miss Vyvyan,' Henry Corbett answered carefully. 'Approximately four weeks ago. And though I have not been permitted to visit since, at that time I found her as well as could be expected in the circumstances.'

'What circumstances? For God's sake, man, tell me in plain English how they are. How my wife is. She's never been strong. I hope she's been properly looked after. If she hasn't, there'll be trouble. I shall make it my business to–'

'Mr Vyvyan,' the vice consul interrupted, his expression grave. 'It is with sincere regret that I have to inform you your wife is no longer– I'm afraid she passed away a month ago.' As William stared at him, he continued. 'She contracted lung fever. There was an epidemic in the town, and it's thought one of the servants carried it into the palace. When it was realized how ill your wife was, the governor was anxious no effort should be spared–'

'I bet he was,' Nick muttered.

'And the doctor was sent for – we are fortunate enough to have an English physician residing in Tangier. However,' Henry Corbett continued, visibly relieved now that for him at least the worst was over, the unpleasant news delivered, 'though the doctor did his best, Mrs Vyvyan did not recover.'

'She's dead? My wife is dead?' William repeated blankly.

'On behalf of the consul and myself, I should like to offer our sincere sympathy.' The vice consul turned to Nick. 'Will Mr Vyvyan be returning to the ship?'

'No,' Nick said. 'Miss Vyvyan and her father are taking lodgings at–' he turned to Maggot.

'Riad Zohra, Derb Brahim,' Maggot supplied. 'Is owned by *mart bebar*, the wife of my father.'

As Henry Corbett nodded, Kerenza rose to her feet. Her mouth and throat were dry. Her mother was dead. She had not seen her for three years, and now would never see her again. But it was as if a smothering blanket had descended on her emotions. Perhaps that was best, for now. There would be time enough later to examine how she felt.

'Mr Corbett, would you be kind enough to give me the name of the English doctor? As you can imagine, my father has been under severe strain for many months.' She glanced towards the figure slumped against the cushions slack jawed, blank-eyed, and pale with shock. 'And now to receive such news.'

'Of course, of course. I will send a servant immediately with a message requesting the doctor to attend you at Riad Zohra.'

Nick and Maggot were already helping a dazed William to his feet.

'One more request, if I may, Mr Corbett,' Kerenza added. 'Will you ask the governor if I may be permitted, on compassionate grounds, to see my sister as soon as possible? Even if arrangements regarding the' – about to say *money*, she changed it at the last moment – 'the *gift* in

256

appreciation of his hospitality might take a little longer?' What would happen about that? Would the governor still expect to receive the same amount? *How could she even think about such details at such a time?* Because concentrating on such practicalities allowed her to avoid looking into her heart where she suspected, and was horribly ashamed to admit, that instead of grief she would find only scars.

'I'll do what I can,' Henry Corbett promised, and turned away quickly, still unwilling to meet her gaze. Was he repelled by her lack of emotion? Had he expected tears and hysterics? Yet what would they achieve except to focus attention on her, when it was her father who was most deeply affected. It was he who needed support and comfort. At least her sister was alive and well. She should be – and was – thankful for that. The priority now was to get her father to their lodgings as quickly as possible and hope the doctor would respond with equal speed.

'Mr Corbett? A final question.'

Kerenza was putting on her cloak, but hearing Nick's voice, she turned.

'Mrs Vyvyan's final resting place?'

'Ah, yes, of course. It was a private burial in the grounds of the English church. There is no headstone, you understand. But the plot is marked with a small wooden cross.'

Kerenza nodded her thanks to the vice consul, then bent her head, ashamed that it had not occurred to her to ask. Nick must surely think her heartless. How could he think otherwise when she had never told him the truth about her relationship with her parents and sister, or the real reason she had left Falmouth to live with her grandmother in Flushing.

Daylight was fading to dusk as they left the consulate, Nick and Maggot supporting William between them. Kerenza followed, carrying the two bags. She was surprised and relieved when, only a few minutes later Maggot led them down a short alley and stopped outside a high wall broken by double doors set in an archway with a top shaped like an onion.

'Is here,' he said over his shoulder, and banged on one of the doors.

A bar was lifted, it swung open, and a veiled servant girl led them through into a small central courtyard about twelve feet square with apartments on three sides. Kerenza just had time to notice a staircase rising to an upper storey with a terrace that looked down into the court before following Nick and Maggot into a room furnished in similar style to the one in the consulate. As they gently lowered William on to a couch, a short plump woman entered the room soundlessly in flat slippers that matched her gold-embroidered ankle-length robe of vivid turquoise. A white scarf covered her head, the ends thrown over her shoulders, and the lower half of her face was veiled.

Maggot greeted her, speaking rapidly in the strange harsh tongue Kerenza had heard in the market-place. Her guess that he was relating the bad news was confirmed as her eyes widened and her hands flew to her cheeks. She looked at William and shook her head. Turning to Kerenza she touched her arm lightly in a gesture of

258

compassion echoed in her dark chocolate eyes. Then, seizing Nick's free arm, she looked up into his startled face and spoke with intense passion.

'*Ateikum-saha, ateikum-saha.*'

Nick turned helplessly to Maggot who grinned.

'*Thamtoth m'beva–*' he struggled for the translation, failed, and shook his head. 'My father's wife, she say thank you.' He lifted one shoulder. 'She happy I no d– that I come back,' he corrected quickly, darting an apologetic glance towards William.

After more rapid conversation, his stepmother called over her shoulder.

'We go up,' Maggot said, as the servant girl came in and was given instructions by her mistress. 'Is two rooms. Mr Vyvyan in one, you, miss, in other.'

While the girl ran ahead carrying two oil lamps, Kerenza followed Nick and Maggot as they half carried her father up the stairs and through the folding double doors into his room. She would have gone in after them but Nick barred her way.

'We'll get him into bed. Did you bring his bag?' He smiled his thanks as she handed it to him. 'The doctor should be here soon. You'll be all right alone for a few minutes?'

'Of course.'

He closed the door gently.

Kerenza followed the beckoning maid through the open doors into her room. It was long and narrow. Against the end wall was a large bed with a canopy that touched the low ceiling. A rug with geometric patterns of red, black and white covered what remained of the floor. A chest and a low table on which the lamp stood completed

259

the furniture. She dropped her bag on the floor at the foot of the bed. She supposed she ought to unpack, but she had another, more urgent need.

'Do you speak any English?' she asked the maid more in hope than expectation. The girl shrugged, spreading her hands and shaking her head to show she didn't understand. Cringing with embarrassment, yet unable to think of an alternative, Kerenza went out on to the terrace and knocking on her father's door called softly, 'Maggot?'

He pulled it open, filling the gap, the lamplight behind him so his face was in shadow. 'Miss?'

She moistened her lips and, knowing he would recognize the shipboard term, blurted, 'Where is the ... jakes?'

He slapped his forehead. 'So sorry, miss. Is very bad of me.' He spoke rapidly over her shoulder to the maid who had followed her. Kerenza heard the girl's soft 'ahhh' of understanding.

'You go with Dina.' Maggot said and, as she heard Nick ask what was wrong, he closed the door.

They crossed the court, passed through a short passage between two rooms and out into another small space that was more of a backyard with a small windowless building of whitewashed mud. Dina opened the door, handed Kerenza the lamp, then caught her arm. Her voice was soft but emphatic as she lifted her left hand, touched Kerenza's, and raised her own again. Then stepping back she waved Kerenza in.

The little room contained nothing except a clay pot of water standing next to a round piece of wood set into the earth floor. Setting the lamp down, Kerenza grasped the handle, lifted what was obviously a lid and recoiled at the smell. There could be no doubt she was in the right place.

Greatly relieved and far more comfortable, she scooped water from the clay pot then patted herself dry with her chemise. Then shaking out her skirts she replaced the lid, picked up the lamp and ducked out through the low doorway.

Back upstairs she looked over the terrace wall down into the court. Savoury smells wafted upward and she could hear the clatter of dishes. It was dark now, the night air surprisingly chilly after the warmth of the day, and she was glad of her wool jacket. She looked beyond the dark shapes of houses on the terraces below to the sea where the rising moon cast a silver path across the water. She could see *Kestrel* riding at anchor, her side lamps lit, others at her bow and stern.

Starting at a rapid knock on the outer door, she watched the servant girl dart across the courtyard. Hearing a man's voice, she knocked quickly on her father's door. Nick opened it.

'I think the doctor's arrived. I'll bring him up.'

'No, you stay, I go,' Maggot said.

'I can wait downstairs–' Nick began.

Kerenza shook her head. 'I'd rather you stayed – if you don't mind,' she added quickly. 'It's just – the doctor might ask – and you know more–'

'Of course I'll stay if you want me to.'

She nodded, grateful. After introducing herself and Nick, and explaining the cause of her father's collapse, she retreated to stand near the door while the doctor made his examination. White-haired, stocky and taciturn, wearing the black coat, waistcoat and breeches universal to his profession, he beckoned Nick forward and questioned him in a low voice.

After drawing up the covers, he turned to Kerenza. 'My advice, Miss Vyvyan, is that you remove your father back to England as soon as possible. His physical health is poor, aggravated no doubt by his experiences during the past year. He needs a long period of rest and a mild diet of easily digested foods that will not over stimulate him. Once he begins to show signs of recovery he would benefit from a tonic. But that lies in the future and the hands of his own physician. In the meantime I suggest laudanum to keep him calm and help him sleep.'

'I have a mixture containing camphor Julep, ether and magnesia as well as laudanum,' Kerenza said. 'It was made up by an apothecary in Falmouth. Would that be–?'

'Ideal,' the doctor replied. 'You know the dosage?'

Kerenza nodded. 'Doctor, Mr Corbett said you visited my mother during her illness.'

'I did. A very sad business. It was clear to me that even before she succumbed to the fever Mrs Vyvyan had suffered greatly. Not through any ill-treatment,' he added quickly. 'But enforced confinement in a strange land among people she didn't know had clearly preyed on her mind.' He sighed, shaking his head. 'The negative effects on her physical well-being and emotional balance meant she simply did not possess the stamina, or perhaps even the will, to fight the fever.' He shook

262

his head again. 'Very sad.'

'And my sister? How is she?'

He turned away. 'Fortunately she suffered no such ill-effects.' He spoke without looking up, his head bent over his bag as he searched for something that proved elusive. 'Indeed, when I saw her last she appeared to be in excellent health.' He closed the bag. 'And now I must go.' He glanced toward the bed once more. 'Mr Vyvyan is unlikely to stir before morning. Sleep will afford him both relief from the shock of his loss, and an opportunity for both body and spirit to rest.'

Kerenza offered her hand. 'Thank you so much for coming.'

He bowed over it, released it, and reached the door all in the space of a few moments. 'Miss Vyvyan, complete your business here and return to England as soon as you can.' He hesitated as if about to say more, then gave a brief nod. 'My condolences.'

'I'll see you out,' Nick offered, a flicker of puzzlement telling Kerenza that he too had noted the doctor's weighted words and abrupt departure.

As their footsteps faded, Kerenza crossed to the bedside and looked down at her father. Beneath the brownish purple shadows surrounding his closed eyes and the fine network of crimson veins that covered his nose and patched his cheeks, the rest of his face had the greyish tone of wet chalk. At the sound of a soft cough behind her she turned. Dina beckoned, indicating she should follow.

Back in her room a bowl of water and a towel had been placed on the table. Pointing to it the girl then pointed to the door and mimed eating.

As Kerenza smiled her thanks the girl vanished.

After washing her face and hands and tidying her hair, Kerenza left the room and crossed the courtyard, hesitant yet drawn by delicious smells and the sound of Maggot and Nick's voices.

In the salon two of the low tables had been drawn together in front of one of the low couches. An embroidered cloth was covered with a dozen bowls and dishes. As she breathed in the smells of chicken and spices her stomach cramped and her mouth watered. Guilt-stricken she stopped. How could she even think of food at such a time?

'Ah, is good you come.' Maggot waved her in. 'Please. You sit. Eat now. Need to be strong, yes?'

Still she hesitated, but knew he was right. She would need all her strength. Doubtless the doctor's advice to leave quickly was well meant. But the speed of their departure depended on the governor. If they had to await his pleasure, it would be hard on her father, and therefore difficult for everyone else. She sat down, waiting for them both to join her.

'May I?' Nick asked, indicating the other end of the couch.

Heat burned in her cheeks as she nodded. 'Of course, please.'

Maggot remained standing. 'Enjoy. I go now.' With a bow and a smile, he strode out.

'I expect his stepmother will want to hear about everything that happened to him,' Nick said. He surveyed the table. 'She's gone to a lot of trouble.'

He was sitting on the edge of the couch. And

she realized suddenly that though he was hiding it well, he too was nervous. A little of her tension evaporated. She looked at the spread. 'There's an awful lot,' she whispered uncertainly. 'Surely it can't be all just for us?'

He nodded. 'Maggot says it is.'

'Oh dear.'

'But we're not expected to eat everything.'

'Thank goodness for that.' Kerenza pressed her fingers to her mouth to smother a nervous giggle. 'It would be awful to offend her after she's gone to so much trouble. And though I'm ashamed to admit it I am hungry. But I couldn't possibly–'

'Ashamed? Why?'

She looked up at him, folding her hands tightly in her lap. 'Surely that's obvious?'

'Not to me.'

She made a small diffident gesture. 'The news of my mother's death, my father's collapse.'

'Neither of which you can reverse. And if you were to fall ill through not eating, how would that help?'

'I know. And you're right.' She gazed down at her hands. 'It's just–'

'You should be sitting in a darkened room with a crust of bread and a cup of water?' His harshness jerked her head up. 'Haven't you been made to suffer enough?' Controlling himself cost him visible effort. 'Forgive me. I should not have – I had no right.' He took a breath. 'Anyway, before you came in Maggot was explaining that while we are not expected to clear the table, we should try to taste every dish. That would make his stepmother very happy.'

'There are so many.' Kerenza marvelled. After a moment's hesitation she lowered her voice. 'I recognize the chicken, the rice, and the shredded salad. But do you have any idea what that is?' She pointed to the largest dish.

'Couscous. It's made from a steamed grain mixed with cubes of fried lamb stewed with chick-peas, onions, carrots, aubergine, raisins and spices.'

As her eyebrows rose in astonishment, he grinned shyly and shrugged. 'I asked Maggot. It certainly smells good. Would you like to try it?'

She nodded, and looked for plates, cutlery and serving spoons. 'Er...'

'Ah, that's the other thing he told me. Here, the correct way to eat is with the fingers, taking a little bit from whatever dish you choose.'

She stared at him. 'You're not teasing, are you?'

He shook his head. 'But you must only use your right hand. That's really important.'

Kerenza felt her colour rise as she remembered Dina's instruction outside the privy. Now she understood the reason for the girl's insistence. Here each hand had its own purpose. Her stomach gurgled and another cramping pang reminded her it was many hours since she had last eaten. It might be days before the governor agreed to let Dulcie go. How would she stay well and strong if she didn't eat?

'Will you go first?' she asked shyly.

'Promise you won't laugh?' The exaggerated glare that accompanied this demand sent a ripple of delight down her spine.

'I wouldn't dare.' As his gaze softened, warmed,

266

she flicked her gaze away, and was relieved when he didn't comment. 'Go on then,' she whispered, and watched him lean forward, dip his bunched fingers into the dish of rice and almonds and slivers of chicken, press it lightly into a ball, then lift it to his mouth.

'Mmmm, that's delicious,' he said, swallowing. 'Come on, you try it.'

Feeling acutely self-conscious, Kerenza picked out small pieces of meat and a stick of green bean. She pinched together a ribbon of lettuce glossy with seasoned oil. But as Nick grew more adventurous, dipping into different dishes, enthusing over the tastes, urging her to try this one then that one, she stopped worrying about the strangeness of eating with her fingers or what she must look like and followed his lead. The flavours, some familiar, some completely new, enhanced rather than satisfied her hunger.

After a few minutes spent concentrating entirely on the food, Kerenza had to ask the question that had been nagging at her. 'Did you notice anything odd about Mr Corbett? His manner, I mean.'

Reaching for more couscous, Nick paused. 'Odd in what way?'

Kerenza frowned. 'I'm not sure. I just had the feeling that there was something he wasn't telling us. It was the same with the doctor. He wouldn't meet my eye, and he seemed in a great hurry to leave.'

'Well, the doctor had come at short notice. Perhaps he had another appointment. And you can understand both of them feeling awkward

267

about seeing your father. They must have known that as well as being a shock, the news would come as a terrible blow to him. To have returned as fast as he possibly could only to learn that he's too late...' He shook his head.

'Do you think the governor really will make us wait several days?'

'I wish I knew. It would make things a d–' he corrected himself quickly, 'a lot easier. I'd have thought that after what's happened he'd want to settle everything and send us away as fast as possible. But who knows how a man like him thinks?'

Dipping his fingers in the small bowl of water he carefully wiped them on, the square of cotton beside it. 'I–' He stopped and cleared his throat. Glancing up, Kerenza saw a dull flush of anger darkening his face. 'When we came through the market-place–'

Kerenza shuddered. 'It was horrible. Many of the men looked really angry. They were clicking their tongues as though I had done something wrong. Do you think I have offended in some way?'

He shook his head. 'Not intentionally. But perhaps to them it's enough that you're English. I think for your safety it would be wiser if you returned to the ship with me.'

She was startled that he would even suggest it with her father lying ill in the room above. Meeting his gaze, she felt her heart give an extra beat.

'I – truly I appreciate your concern. But you must know that I can't.' She looked away. 'Maggot's stepmother would feel deeply insulted at the implication that I am not safe under her roof. Nor can I leave my father. Besides, Maggot is staying, is he not?' At Nick's reluctant nod, she spread her hands. 'What more protection could I need?'

'In here, perhaps. But out in the street.' He shook his head.

'I was just thinking, do you think Maggot's stepmother might lend me an over-gown like the other women were wearing, and a scarf for my head? If I look like everyone else, I'll be invisible.'

His smile faded as he looked at her intently. 'You could never be invisible.' Then, clearing his throat, he added quickly, 'But you would be less conspicuous. It's a good idea.' He pushed himself to his feet. 'I must go.'

Kerenza stood up. Wiping her fingers on the tiny towel, she held out her hand. 'Thank you. For … everything. You have been very ki–'

'Don't.' Grasping her fingers he covered them with his other hand. 'We both know I have not been kind. And I am more sorry for it than you will ever know.' Raising her hand he held her gaze as he pressed his lips to her knuckles. 'I will see you tomorrow.' With a brief bow he strode out.

She stared after him, then looked at her knuckles, still feeling the warm pressure of his lips. He had not wished her a good night, or voiced the hope that she would sleep well, not because he had forgotten, or because he lacked good manners. He had not said it because it would have been mean-ingless. Because of the bond between them – never entirely severed and growing stronger each day – the understanding that made words superfluous, he knew sleep would not come easily for either of them.

Chapter Sixteen

'Maggot, how do I say thank you?' Kerenza demanded, as he entered the salon. Dina was busy clearing away the dishes.

'Is no need,' he waved her plea aside. 'Is good you enjoy.' He grinned, gesturing at the dishes. 'Make you strong.'

'No, you don't understand. Your stepmother has shown us such kindness. What is *thank you* in your language?'

He leaned forward, dropping his voice. '*Ateikum-saha.*'

The same words his stepmother had spoken so fervently to Nick. Kerenza repeated them quietly several times, then nodded. 'One more thing. How do I address her?' As the small creases between his brows deepened, and he lifted one shoulder indicating he didn't understand, she tried again. 'What shall I call her? My name is Kerenza Vyvyan. What is hers?'

While she had been talking, their hostess had come in and after a brief word with Dina who nodded and scuttled out, her glance swept over the remains of the meal. Raising her eyes to Kerenza's she smiled, nodded and clapped her palms softly together.

Turning, Maggot spoke quickly to her. Her gaze flicked to Kerenza then back to her stepson as she replied.

Maggot grinned at Kerenza. 'She give her name to this place, Riad Zohra.'

Moistening her lips, hoping her attempt would at least be recognizable, Kerenza spoke hesitantly. '*Ateikum-saha*, Zohra.'

Zohra's hands flew up in delight. Beaming, she clapped them again, and released a torrent of speech, nudging Maggot whose grin widened.

'She say you talk good. And she very happy you stay here.'

Relieved and delighted at this small success, Kerenza bade them both goodnight. Reaching her room, she found a fire burning in the grate and her bag unpacked. Her laundry had gone and so had her nightdress. Lying on the coverlet was a simple gown of fine white cotton lawn with long sleeves and a deep slit in the round neck.

She undressed and pulled it on, inhaling the faint fragrance of jasmine and sandalwood. Then she unpinned her hair. As the heavy coil fell down her back she threaded her fingers through it, left it loose, and climbed beneath the covers. Lying on her back she watched the dancing shadows on the low ceiling. Listening to the low rumble of her father's snores she was glad he was free, if only for a few hours, from the weight of his loss.

What must he have felt, having made such desperate efforts to bring back the money as fast as he could only to hear that he was too late? Kerenza tried to picture her mother but despite her efforts the image remained blurred, indistinct. She remembered a rounded woman whose youthful prettiness had begun to fade, but she could not distinguish any features. But that vague image was preferable to seeing clearly the sick and damaged person the doctor had described.

A hard knot of grief had formed in Kerenza's chest yet her eyes remained dry. Over the years she had shed enough tears to fill a lake. She mourned the fact there would be no reconciliation, no chance to build bridges or make a fresh start. But perhaps she was deluding herself. Those might not have come about even had her mother lived. But now, unless she could persuade Dulcie to tell her, she would never know *why*.

It took her a long time to fall asleep. And she was jerked awake by an eerie undulating cry. She recalled hearing it at different times during the day. She had meant to ask, but was distracted by other things. It lasted only a few minutes, long enough for her to see that the blackness of night had lightened to pre-dawn grey. The familiar shriek of seagulls reminded her of home and she slid once more into unconsciousness.

During a breakfast of stewed fruit, yoghurt, soft, sweet-smelling flat bread, and small cups of strong coffee, she asked Maggot about the sound.

'Is call to prayer. Good Muslim pray five times a day.' His eyes twinkling he gave a lop-sided grin and shook his head. 'I am very bad Muslim.'

A little while later, Nick arrived, his gaze holding hers as he took her hand, the pressure of his fingers warm and firm as he bowed over it.

'I brought Broad with me. He will do everything necessary for your father's comfort, and ensure that when he wakes he sees a familiar face.'

Her breathing had quickened and she knew

from the heat in her cheeks that her colour was high. Acutely conscious of her body's betrayal and of being watched she took refuge in formality. 'You are very good.'

He shook his head in brief denial. But his look told her he knew what she was doing and why, and her gratitude increased as he matched her formality.

'On my way here I called at the consulate. Mr Corbett has already sent his Jewish interpreter with a note to the governor's palace. If Maggot and I go up there now, as envoys for your father, I hope we might at least be able to speak to one of the governor's staff. It's worth a try.'

'I do hope it works.' Behind her, Kerenza could hear Maggot and his stepmother talking in low voices.

'Miss?' Maggot said. 'The wife of my father say she must go to markets. You want go with her?'

Kerenza was unsure. 'My father–'

'Is in good hands,' Nick said softly. 'It's better if he sleeps as much as possible while we try to set up a meeting with the governor. And you need a rest from caring for others. Do you want to go?'

'Very much,' Kerenza replied. 'But not if I will be stared at as I was yesterday.' Turning to her hostess with an expression of apology she grasped a handful of peach muslin and shook her head.

Zohra flapped a hand, talked rapidly to Maggot, pointed to the saffron caftan and white headscarf she was wearing, then nodded, smiling encouragingly at Kerenza.

'She find Amazirght dress for you. Then you go, yes?'

'Yes.' Kerenza nodded, smiling in gratitude at the older woman. *'Ateikum-saha,'* she said carefully, and was rewarded with a beam from her hostess and a grin of approval from Maggot. Nick's expression of astonished admiration lifted her chin and tilted the corners of her mouth with a tiny rush of pride as she followed Zohra out.

Shrouded in an emerald green caftan with matching embroidered slippers on her feet, her hair covered by the folds of a white scarf, and the lower half of her face hidden behind a veil, Kerenza spent two enthralling, exhausting hours in Tangier's market. She stayed close to Zohra, avoiding eye contact even with other women. There was so much to see. She paused to watch copper and silversmiths tapping intricate designs on trays, jugs and lamp holders, while beside them their young sons polished the finished articles to a dazzling shine.

They lingered at a canopied stall selling joints of fresh meat where a small boy stood waving a bunch of palm leaves tied to a stick to keep swarms of flies away. Nearby lidded baskets contained squawking chickens, and another stall displayed freshly caught fish.

In the centre of the market pyramids of oranges and melons, and shallow baskets of fresh dates were guarded by women who squatted beneath enormous straw hats at least six feet across with turned-down edges that concealed the wearer's face, exactly as Maggot had described to her.

There were piles of onions, carrots, glossy purple aubergines and courgettes. Yet more stalls displayed boxes of soap, raisins, small barrels of

274

sugar and tea. A cotton cloth stretched over a wooden frame shaded cone-shaped piles of powdered spices. Their bright colours and the mingled smells of ginger, saffron, cinnamon sticks and mint leaves assaulted her senses.

Zohra bought from several stalls, demanding in her choices, often refusing what was offered and selecting her own preferences. Gradually her baskets filled, but Kerenza's attempt to take one was gently rebuffed and her attention directed to rolls of fabric that ranged from heavy weaves in indigo blue or black and white stripes, to colourful cottons and fine shimmering silks.

Where did it all come from? She wished she knew how to ask.

The market seethed with people: musicians tapping drums and playing rhaitas, beggars, women shopping, as gaudy as butterflies in their vivid caftans and headscarves, children shrieking with laughter as they darted about, and men coming and going. Men with beards and men without, men in white turbans, in brimless caps, or bareheaded. Men in dusty indigo wraps, hooded striped gowns, and layers of white covered by sleeveless blue robes.

She turned and saw Zohra watching her and read amusement in the older woman's dark eyes. Kerenza raised her brows, and lifted one hand, palm out as she indicated the noisy, crowded, smelly, fly-ridden square.

Jerking her head sideways in a gesture Kerenza interpreted as an instruction to follow, Zohra left the market-place but instead of turning towards her house, she led the way up a wider street. It

275

was thronged with men carrying sacks and baskets, bent double under the weight as they staggered down towards the market-place, walking upright as they returned. Ahead Kerenza could see the ruined city wall and a crenellated tower. The huge doors stood open and armed men were stopping and checking the loads of everyone coming in through the tall arched entrance.

Alongside the tower, a flight of stone steps led up on to a wide walkway just below the battlements. Climbing them, Zohra beckoned Kerenza up. Following her pointing finger, Kerenza looked through the gap and caught her breath.

The undulating plain was crowded with men and animals. Over a wide area outside the wall the grass had been worn away to bare earth and rock. Strings of camels padded in, swaying beneath bulky loads slung from their humps. Donkeys tottered by on tiny eggcup hooves, so heavily laden that only their heads were visible. Tethered mules stood with lowered heads, flicking their ears and constantly swishing their tails against marauding flies as their packs were removed. Barelegged boys in ragged tunics and flapping sandals, their only aid and protection a short stick, herded small flocks of sheep and goats. Strange looking cattle with pale coats, wide horns and long faces stood or lay chewing placidly.

Bellowing animals, the *tonkle* of goat bells, squawking chickens, occasional gunshots as new arrivals fired into the air to announce themselves, and hundreds of men arguing, laughing and haggling at the tops of their voices created a deafening noise. The air was thick with dust, sweat, dung and the sweet stench of decay from fallen fruit and vegetables trampled into the dirt. It stung the back of her nose and caught in her throat. Coughing, her eyes smarting, she turned away.

Zohra pointed to the pack animals, then towards the town and the market.

Still coughing, Kerenza nodded that she understood, wiped her streaming eyes and patted her chest. Zohra rolled her eyes in sympathy, flapped a hand towards the noisy crowd of men in a gesture Kerenza knew her grandmother would have recognized instantly, and led the way down the steps.

Just before reaching the alley they stopped in a lane where two men were tending a bed of coals beneath a dozen cone-shaped clay pots. Zohra handed over some money. One of the clay pots was lifted from the coals and put in a small wooden crate with a thong handle. Gesturing for Kerenza to carry it, Zohra led the way home.

After a quick visit to the yard, Kerenza hurried to her room, took off her caftan, headscarf and veil, washed her hands and face and went to see how her father was.

'He've had a wash and shave and a bite to eat, miss,' Broad said. 'But he got a bit fretful then. So I gave him his dose and now he's sleeping peaceful.'

'You must be hungry yourself.'

'Well, I wouldn't say no. Been a long morning, it has.'

'I'll go and see about dinner.' Hearing a noise down in the court she looked over the terrace wall and felt a surge of pleasure as Nick followed

Maggot in and immediately looked up, raising his hand. With a small shy wave she turned back to the steward. 'Maggot and Mr Penrose are back.'

'You get on down then, miss.'

She found Nick and Maggot in the salon. 'What happened? Were you able to speak to anyone?'

Nick shook his head. 'No one of importance. But Maggot says our presence was noted. We might have better luck tomorrow. How is your father?'

'Sleeping at the moment. I promised Broad some dinner.'

'Is coming now,' Maggot said, as Dina entered carrying a huge platter of steaming couscous. Maggot's stepmother followed with the clay pot Kerenza had carried from the lane. Setting it down on the table she removed the lid, and immediately the room was filled with the delicious fragrance of chicken, onions and spices. Dina returned with a bowl and ladle, handed them to Maggot, then followed her mistress out. Maggot ladled couscous into the bowl and topped it with the savoury stew. 'I take this to Broad.'

'Will you join us after?' Kerenza asked, torn between hoping he would and hoping he wouldn't.

Maggot shook his head. 'No. Please, you enjoy.'

'You've had an interesting morning?' Nick asked, as they began to eat.

By the time she had finished telling him, comparing and contrasting all she had seen with the markets in Falmouth and Flushing, little was left on the platter or in the pot. Kerenza suddenly became aware of his intent gaze.

'What?' Quickly wiping her fingers, she raised the tiny napkin to her mouth. 'Have I got sauce on my chin?'

He shook his head. 'No. It's–' he shrugged helplessly. 'You're beautiful.'

She caught her breath, heat rushing to her cheeks, and looked away. 'Please don't,' she whispered. She knew she wasn't beautiful. According to her mother and sister she wasn't even pretty. *Too thin, too dark. Her nose was too straight, her chin too firm, her mouth too wide.*

He caught her hand and held it tightly, his voice low, intense. 'I know I hurt you, and I'll go to my grave regretting it. I can't change the past, but by Christ, I've learned from it. And you *are* beautiful. It's not – I don't mean–' His struggle to express himself, his sincerity and obvious lack of practice blunted the sharp fears his words had stirred.

She'd listened at dances to young men wooing her friends with compliments and flattery, and knew them empty of real meaning. She didn't want that: not from him. *What did she want?* She didn't know. Yes, she did, but dared not acknowledge it even to herself.

'It's in your eyes and your smile,' he blurted. 'You shine.'

Out in the passage Maggot called to his stepmother. Kerenza wondered if he'd done it out of tact, to warn of his approach. Catching Nick's eye, seeing his mouth twist in frustration and wry amusement, she saw the same thought had occurred to him. Releasing her hand, he straight-

279

ened, reluctantly easing away to a proper distance.

'I must go back to the ship. But I'll send Maggot back before dark. Is there anything you want him to bring?'

You. Kerenza shook her head. She could still feel the strength of his fingers and pressed her hand protectively against her body. 'Except—'

'Yes?' he said quickly.

'If we are to be here for several days – perhaps a book, to read to my father if he should become restless. There are two in my trunk, or perhaps in the leather bag. Neither one is locked.'

'I won't forget.' He stood up. 'Well then.' He hesitated, unwilling to leave.

Shyly she offered her hand. The look on his face as he took it and raised it to his lips aroused exquisite sensations that were almost painful.

'Kerenza,' he whispered.

'You must go.' She looked away, not trusting her voice, her legs, or her heart.

Back on board *Kestrel* Nick listened to the bosun's report of another fight in the fo'c'sle.

'Any serious injuries?'

'No, sir,' Laity said. 'Martin got his arm slashed, but Crowle sewed him up good as new. He can move all his fingers so 'twasn't too bad.' He hesitated. 'Begging your pardon, Mr Penrose, but how long we got to stay here? You know what they do say about idle hands.'

'Then make sure you keep them busy,' Nick snapped. 'And from now on I'll send any men caught fighting to the cable locker.'

'Aye, sir.' The bosun tugged his forelock, his

expression grim as he turned away.

'I find out what happen,' Maggot said.

Nick nodded absently, and dived down the companionway. He had tried to reduce the crew's resentment at having to remain aboard by taking back joints of mutton, sacks of fruit and vegetables, and plenty of fresh bread. Men with a bellyful of decent food were less inclined to fight. But though for the most part the ploy worked, the cost of success came out of his pocket. The longer *Kestrel* lay idle, the faster his profit diminished. It had not been high to start with.

Had Edgar Tierney known this might happen? Had his choice of *Kestrel* for this mission been deliberate? Yet even if that were the case, how could he regret it? For had the packet agent chosen differently, he and Kerenza would not have been thrown together again.

Calling to Toy to bring him a lamp, he went along the passage to Kerenza's cabin. As he raised the lid of her trunk he could smell her. He rested his fingers briefly on a folded garment. Guiltily he snatched them away. She had trusted him to fetch a book. What would she think if she knew he had been pawing her clothes?

Moving aside her writing case he lifting out the nearest book and held it close to the lamp. Expecting a novel or perhaps a book of poems he saw it was neither. The title read: *Travels to discover the sources of the Nile 1768–1773*. The author was James Bruce.

He raised his head, blind to his surroundings, aware that yet again he had *assumed* and she had proved him wrong. She had brought this for her own reading pleasure. There were as many layers to her as an onion. And the more he learned the more he realized what a fool he had been, how badly he had misjudged her and how cruelly she had been hurt: first by her family and then, to his everlasting shame, by him.

Sharing dinner with her at Maggot's step-mother's house was a memory he would treasure to the end of his days. She had seemed glad of his company. Though he shouldn't flatter himself too much. Her pleasure might have been simply relief at having someone to talk to, someone familiar who spoke English. It was not the *reason* that mattered, but the fact that they had spent time together.

Treading very carefully he had set out to make her feel comfortable, safe. Leading by example, he had ensured she ate a decent meal. God knew she needed building up. There was hardly any flesh on her. Which was hardly surprising considering all she'd been through.

Watching her eat he had felt a rush of tenderness. It was swiftly crushed by fierce determination to make amends, to shield her from anything that might cause her pain. He owed her that, and more. But wanting to protect her sprang not from a sense of obligation but something far deeper.

For as long as he could remember his life had been shaped by ambition. And his desire to own a packet ship was as strong as it had ever been. But woven into it and equally strong was a wish, a longing, a need so powerful and relentless, that to fight it was impossible. Yet as each day allowed him to glimpse new possibilities of a future enhanced by her presence, it also brought new discomforts.

He hated having to return to the ship and leave her. Maggot's stepmother was clearly a kind decent woman who had made them all very welcome, even fractious, self-centred William Vyvyan. But he wished Kerenza were back on *Kestrel*. He hated even more the thought of Maggot spending time with her when he could not. He would trust Maggot with his life. She needed Maggot to interpret. And while she and her father were staying in the house Maggot's presence offered additional protection. Besides, surely to God Maggot was entitled to spend his evenings with his stepmother who had for three years believed him dead?

He knew his jealousy and resentment were irrational. But that didn't prevent or soften their dagger-like thrusts.

He thought back over all that had happened, what he had lost, and all he had gained. He had learned so much about Kerenza, and about himself. It was ironic to think that but for Tierney's blackmail none of it could have come about. Nick smiled briefly. One day he'd thank Tierney. It would drive the man mad.

Closing the trunk, he turned to the door then halted. Turning back, he set the lamp down, pulled the top blanket from the bunk and held it to his face. He breathed in the faint scent of her soap. Holding it in his lungs he quickly folded the blanket, picked up the book and the lamp, and closed the door. Pausing to toss the blanket on to his own bunk, he went to the day cabin and wrote up the log.

That night he slept wrapped in Kerenza's blanket. And dreamed. And ached for her.

The next two days followed a similar pattern: kicking their heels at the palace in the morning, dinner at the house, then back to the ship. By the third day the strain was beginning to tell on them all.

When he wasn't asleep, William Vyvyan's grief and anxiety exploded in bad temper. Backed up by Broad, a witness to William's surly impatience with Kerenza, Nick wanted to increase the laudanum dosage. But she had refused.

'I really think it would be better not to. As for my father's outbursts, I understand they are the result of our circumstances, so I do not take them to heart.' Her throbbing head and the tension that lay like an iron bar across her shoulders told a different story. But though sorely tempted she dared not agree. 'What if the governor should summon us? What kind of impression would we make if my father were too befuddled to talk sensibly? The governor knows we are here. Even if it is his practice to make people wait before seeing him, surely he will want the matter settled soon?'

Constant efforts to placate and occupy her father cost her enormous effort. Now she was aware of an additional pressure. For though he said nothing to her, she had overheard enough to realize that Nick faced problems of his own. The longer they remained here the higher the personal cost to him. The crew were bored and restless. More fights meant more punishments and increased resentment.

Caught in the middle, her sympathies torn between Nick and her father, Kerenza was also worried about her sister. Having always been close to their mother, particularly so during their year of shared captivity, Dulcie must surely be feeling dreadfully isolated and afraid.

With her own memories of how it felt to be excluded still vivid, Kerenza could imagine all too clearly Dulcie's loneliness since losing her mother. Thinking about closeness and family reminded Kerenza of her grandmother, her acerbic affection, and the warmth of her welcome into the house at Flushing. But the memory, though comforting, seemed to belong to another time, a different life.

As if all that was not enough, the wind had shifted. Maggot called it the *cherqi*.

'Is a bad wind,' he shook his head.

Hot, damp, and oppressive, it rasped raw nerves and frayed tempers already on edge. Kerenza's skin was constantly clammy, her clothes clung, and her eyes were gritty and sore. And there was no escape, no relief.

Her father's moods swung between incoherent rage and jittery apprehension. Nick returned from the palace tight-lipped with fury, and even Maggot was showing signs of strain. Kerenza felt as fragile as glass.

After dinner on the fourth day, as Maggot and Nick prepared to return to the ship, Zohra sent Maggot back to tell Kerenza to put on her caftan, headscarf and veil, and meet her in the court.

'Where are we going?'

Maggot looked tired, but his eyes held a

285

glimmer of mischief. *'Hammam.'*

'Where's that? Is it far?'

He shook his head. 'Not far. No worry. You will like.'

Zohra was waiting in the court carrying what looked like a leather bucket, its contents covered with a folded white cloth, when Kerenza came down from the terrace. A couple of minutes' walk from the house Zohra turned down an alley. Passing an open doorway the smell of freshly baked bread wafted out into the humid air. The door next to it stood open and after handing some money to a woman sitting just inside, Zohra led the way along a short passage.

It opened into a room where several women sat or lay on couches, their faces and heads uncovered. Kerenza saw with a dart of shock that two of the women's faces were patterned with indigo blue: one on her chin, the other in lines down her cheeks.

While some towelled damp hair, others drew combs through long dark tresses as they chatted. All were glowing and exuded a fresh fragrance that made Kerenza acutely aware of her perspiring skin and unwashed hair.

She guessed this must be a public bathhouse, like the one for the seamen in Flushing. As the women exchanged greetings with Zohra, Kerenza sensed their curiosity. Zohra led her through to another room noisy with the talk and laughter of women and children in various stages of undress.

Zohra started removing her clothes and motioned to Kerenza to do the same. Shyness battled with overwhelming desire for a bath, and

286

was swiftly vanquished. Though she was careful not to stare, Kerenza could not avoid noticing that many of the women, especially the older ones, were brown and plump and soft. They were, she thought wryly, fat roast duck to her plucked chicken. One older woman had a complicated orange-brown pattern running the length of her thighs and calves to her ankles. Though they openly studied her, there was none of the condemnation she had seen in the men's glittering eyes. She sensed what intrigued them was the whiteness of her skin.

Gently turning Kerenza around, Zohra unpinned her hair. As it uncoiled two of the women reached out and gathered a handful, nodding and smiling. Kerenza smiled back. Then Zohra took her into a room cloudy with steam, where they sat side by side on two stools in front of a cistern. Using the bucket to pour water over her head and body, Zohra handed it to Kerenza and began to soap herself. After Kerenza had done the same, Zohra half turned on her stool, grasped Kerenza's arm, and began to scrub it gently with a fist-sized piece of light grey stone. She scrubbed Kerenza's arms, back, legs and feet, and when she had finished, rinsed her with buckets of water. With a tentative smile Kerenza held out her hand for the stone and raised her brows. Beaming, Zohra handed it to her and held out her own arm.

They washed each other's hair, and as Zohra gently massaged her scalp, Kerenza closed her eyes. Minnie usually did this for her. Imagining the maid's expression Kerenza smiled.

With their wet hair hanging in thick ropes down

their backs, Kerenza followed Zohra to two marble slabs. Signalling someone across the room, Zohra lay down on one and waved Kerenza on to the other. Wondering what was coming next, Kerenza started as strong fingers slippery with scented oil began to knead her shoulders. It hurt, and she tensed, resisting. A hand slapped her twice, and a voice scolded. Though she couldn't understand the words, the tone made the meaning plain.

About to sit up, push the hand away, she felt Zohra's touch on her arm, coaxing, reassuring. Making a deliberate effort to relax she received a pat of approval. The deft fingers resumed, moving down her back and legs then returning to work more deeply on her neck, arms and shoulders. Kerenza felt painful knots begin to loosen and tight muscles grew soft and flexible. As tension dissolved and evaporated all her anxieties drifted away. She felt boneless, weightless, and blissfully detached.

After one more soaping, another hair-wash to remove any traces of oil, and several rinses, they dried themselves. Twisting towels around their hair they returned to the outer room to dress and relax. Kerenza felt as if every nerve was wrapped in velvet.

Zohra chatted with several women who had put on caftans over a fine cotton garment resembling the one Kerenza had found on her bed in place of her nightdress the night she arrived. Pulling on her chemise, she looked at her peach muslin, grubby and damp with perspiration. Touching Kerenza's arm, Zohra shook her head.

Amazed at her daring, Kerenza rolled up her dress. Instead she allowed the emerald caftan to float down over her chemise, emerging to see Zohra clap her hands, laughing.

They combed out their damp hair and pinned it up. As they were putting on their headscarves and veils, it occurred to Kerenza that she had shared greater intimacy with a woman she had known less than a week, a woman whose language she did not speak, than with her own mother. Even as the sadness struck deep, she found herself able to accept it. She wondered if the odd feeling of detachment was responsible for her reaction, wondered if she might feel differently when it wore off. And decided she wouldn't.

Zohra picked up her bucket containing the soap, stone and hair wash. Handing the wet towels to the waiting attendant, they walked out into the late afternoon.

As they crossed a wide street, Kerenza heard the sound of horses' hooves. Grasping her arm, Zohra drew her back as a party of men came from the direction of the main city gate and turned on to another street. Though she saw them for only a few seconds, the image was imprinted on her brain.

Black-skinned guards in loose white trousers and red leather boots carried long muskets, presumably to protect the richly dressed young man at their head astride a grey horse whose embroidered and tasselled bridle and ornate leather saddle gleaming with gold proclaimed him someone of importance. Behind them, led by three muleteers, six mules trotted laden with baggage.

Kerenza turned to Zohra. 'Who–' The question died on her lips. But Zohra guessed what she wanted to know.

'Mulai Aruj.'

Kerenza repeated the name to herself as they hurried home. Maggot might know who he was. The young man was heading towards the castle. Might his arrival push the governor into action?

Chapter Seventeen

That night Kerenza slept long and deep, not stirring even when the muezzin called the faithful to prayer at three in the morning. It was Dina who woke her, bringing in a jug of water. She felt deliciously rested. Refreshed, she put on a clean chemise and her apple green muslin – returned washed and ironed with the rest of her laundry. As she combed, coiled and pinned up her hair, her stomach fluttered with pleasure at the prospect of seeing Nick. *Was this wise?* Wise or not, to prevent or deny her attraction to him was beyond her strength or will.

Outside on the terrace she paused, filling her lungs as she looked down towards the sea over purple-shadowed alleys and whitewashed houses gilded by the morning sun. *Kestrel* rode at her anchor on water that glittered like diamonds. She shaded her eyes, searching for the cutter. Had it not yet left? Was he still aboard *Kestrel*? Or could she not see it because it was even at this moment pulling into the beach? He might even be on his way up through the streets. Anticipation sped her along the terrace, down the steps and across the court.

'*Azoufl'ouen,*' Zohra greeted her with a beaming smile and ushered her into the salon where a dish of apricots and dates, a bowl of yoghurt and warm fresh bread were waiting. Kerenza ate hungrily and had almost finished when Zohra brought in a pot of coffee and set it down.

'*Ateikum-saha,*' Kerenza said with a tiny thrill of pride at her hostess's visible pleasure.

Zohra asked a question, closing her eyes and resting her tilted head on her hand, clearly miming sleep.

Smiling, Kerenza nodded. 'Oh yes, really well. Thank you.'

Murmuring approval, Zohra bustled out, passing Maggot who was on his way in.

'So,' he grinned, 'you like *hammam?*'

'Oh Maggot, it was marvellous. I've never felt so clean. Last night was the best night's sleep I've had since we left Flushing.'

'Good morning,' Nick strode in.

'Good morning.' Kerenza's heart gave its familiar leap. 'Would you like some coffee?' Without waiting for his reply she filled one of the small cups and offered it to him. 'Zohra took me to a *hammam* yesterday. It's a bath house for women where–'

'Indeed.'

Startled by his brusqueness, her smile faltered. 'Is something wrong?' She caught her breath. 'Has there been news?'

291

Maggot set down his cup. 'Excuse, please.' He walked out, catching Zohra on the threshold and murmuring in her ear as he drew her with him.

'No.' Nick pushed a hand through his hair. 'Nothing's wrong. Except–' He broke off, gazing at the floor as he jarred his booted heel against the rug. He looked up at her from beneath dark brows. 'I don't think you should be talking about such things to Maggot.'

'But I only – he knew Zohra was taking me, and I didn't see him when we got back last evening.'

'You didn't?' He was very still.

She shook her head. 'No. And this morning I woke up late. He came in only a moment before you did, so when he asked if I had enjoyed it–'

'And did you?' His tone was softer, his posture more relaxed.

'It was wonderful. We were there for hours.'

Puzzlement drew his brows together. 'Why so long?'

She hesitated, but his interest seemed genuine. 'Because it wasn't just a bath.' She stopped, wary and confused. 'I'm sorry, but I don't understand. Why is it wrong for me to talk about it to Maggot, even though it's part of his culture, yet acceptable to discuss it with you?' She was astonished to see a blush darken his face.

'Because you're– I'm–' He swallowed. 'I–'

His voice was so quiet, so muffled, she wasn't sure if she had heard correctly. It had sounded like miss you. A pulse drummed in her ears as her thoughts whirled. But what if she was wrong? What if it was just wishful thinking?

He shook his head abruptly. 'How is your father

this morning?' Though still warm, his tone was more guarded.

'S-still asleep.'

'It's perhaps as well.' He made a brief formal bow. 'If you'll excuse me?'

'Of course.' Bewildered, she watched him stride out, radiating tension. An hour later she was sitting in the salon reading while upstairs Broad tended to her father. Zohra had invited her to go to the market, but she had declined. With the *cherqi* still blowing it was cooler in the house. Besides, she wanted a little solitude, and some time to think. But her thoughts just went round in circles, growing ever more tangled.

The outside door slammed and she looked up as swift footsteps crossed the court and entered the house. Nick strode in, followed by Maggot. The strain that had etched lines on their faces had gone, replaced by a mixture of relief and determination.

'At last.' Shrugging out of his jacket, Nick inserted a finger between his neckcloth and throat. Sweat beaded his forehead.

'Good news?' she ventured.

'The best,' Nick grinned. 'The governor will see your father this afternoon.'

Kerenza shut her book. 'Thank goodness. Broad is with him now. I'm sure this will make all the difference.'

'I hope so,' Nick said with a touch of grimness. 'Anyway, let's hope we can settle the business and get on our way. This wind.' He wiped his forehead on his shirt sleeve. 'And there's something going on up at the palace. It seems the sultan's son returned last evening.'

'We saw him,' Kerenza said, 'when we were on our way home. Only a brief glimpse. He had a party of bodyguards with him, and pack-mules. Why has he come?'

'He live there,' Maggot explained. 'Like to hunt in hills. But this time he is coming from his father. The sultan is in Rabat and send for him.'

'Why should his return have caused tension?' Kerenza asked.

Nick shrugged. 'I've no idea. But people are certainly moving faster, and everyone looks a bit nervous.'

'I listen,' Maggot said. 'But I hear only that Mulai Aruj very angry. And this is making governor very nervous. So now he want we go quick.'

'Please take me with you to the palace,' Kerenza said. 'While you and my father are with the governor, I must see my sister. She may not even know we are here.'

After a brief hesitation, Nick nodded. 'I'd be surprised if she didn't. One of the servants is sure to have said something. Still, seeing you will convince her she'll soon be free and on her way home.'

Kerenza's mouth grew dry as remembered instances of Dulcie's spite sprang up to taunt and threaten. She shuddered, then reminded herself. That was all in the past. She was a different person now. Perhaps Dulcie was too. For surely no one could live through what she had experienced during the past year and not be changed by it?

'Are you all right?' he asked softly.

Rubbing her arms, she nodded again and tried to smile.

He stepped closer, his voice low. 'You needn't be worried or afraid. There'll be no more bullying. You were alone then. You didn't have anyone to look out for you, to protect or care for you. But that's not true now.'

Startled, she looked up, grateful for the reminder. The taunting memories shrank and receded. 'No, you're right. My grandmother—'

'Your grandmother likes to play the dragon. But she has a kind heart. And she'll always care about your happiness.' His smile had a bitter edge. 'She made it very clear to me that she would protect you from anyone she considered unworthy.'

Recalling her grandmother's tart dismissal of what she considered Nicholas Penrose's presumption, Kerenza blushed hotly.

'And I respect her for it,' he added, before she could even begin to try and explain. 'But she isn't here now. I am. And while I breathe no one will harm you. Do you understand?' His eyes flashed like blades.

'Do you?' he repeated.

'Yes.' But she wasn't sure she did. What exactly was he telling her? That he would shield her from Dulcie and her father? *But who would protect her all-too-vulnerable heart from him?* Perhaps his words held deeper meaning. But fearful of being wrong, of laying herself open to embarrassment or, even worse, to his pity, she dared not ask.

On his way back from the palace that morning, Nick had called at the consulate and asked

Henry Corbett's advice, determined to avoid any situation the governor might seize upon as an excuse for further delay.

The vice consul had agreed to accompany them, and to bring along the consulate's Jewish interpreter with whom the governor was familiar. Maggot's presence would reassure William Vyvyan and Nick of the interpreter's accuracy. And the larger the party the more impressive it would appear to the governor.

Next came the question of clothes for Maggot. Should he wear Tamazirght dress or his packet uniform? Maggot clung determinedly to his uniform, reminding them that in the governor's eyes he was already set apart by his mixed ancestry and the fact that he sailed with a foreign *infidel*. At the same time, his uniform proclaimed his employment in the packet service and thus a connection, however tenuous, with the British Government. The governor was too shrewd not to take that into account.

Then it was Kerenza's turn. Because the *cherqi* made it too hot for her cloak, she wondered if it might be diplomatic to wear a caftan. But Nick and Maggot both shook their heads.

'From what I've seen,' Nick said, 'diplomacy is like balancing on a rope. You have to show respect for the rules of the country you're in. But you also have to show your strength by remaining true to your own. I think it would be best if you make clear your family relationship with your father and sister by wearing an English gown.' He pushed a hand through his hair, weary and apologetic. 'Though I think it's very unlikely you'll be allowed into the negotiations.'

Kerenza shook her head. 'I didn't expect it.'

Nick continued. 'The vice consul is coming with us so the governor will recognize that this meeting isn't just a private deal between him and your father. Mr Corbett wants to make it clear, without actually saying so, that there could be political repercussions if this business isn't settled soon. The sultan would not like that.'

Henry Corbett arrived soon after two, accompanied by a thin, anxious-looking man with a grey beard and a fizz of grey hair surrounding the black skullcap he wore above his white gown. Introduced as Mordecai, he bowed nervously to each of them, but remained silent.

With its high neck and long sleeves, Kerenza's apple-green muslin was eminently suitable. But to indicate her respect for local custom and sensibility, and to avoid provoking stares and tongue-clicking, she covered her hair with the white scarf and used one end to shield the lower half of her face.

They walked in three pairs through the narrow streets: Henry Corbett and Mordecai led the way; Nick followed with her father. As she walked at the back with Maggot, Kerenza compared similarities and differences between life here and back in Flushing.

In both places it was men who ordered society. But whereas in Flushing men and women mixed freely, here their worlds were totally separate. Here no woman ventured out unless hidden beneath head-scarf, veil and enveloping robe. But dressed thus she was totally safe. She could walk

297

alone or with other women without fear. It was in Flushing that no woman who cared for her good name ventured unescorted on to the streets after dark. Any who did risked insult, or worse, from drunken sailors.

In the *hammam* the women had been curious, but she had sensed no criticism of her presence or her person. The tone of their laughter and gossip had been teasing and affectionate. Those who left the group were not watched, nor were they remarked on behind their backs. New arrivals were welcomed, children taken on to knees with hugs and kisses. Unselfconscious in their nakedness they had washed each other's hair. She had seen one young mother massaging an old woman's arthritic hands while her toddler daughter, beaming placidly, was passed from hand to doting hand.

In England women mixed openly with men; were courted and flattered at balls and parties. And though clubs existed where men gathered and from which their ladies were barred, society would have ceased to exist were it not for all the suppers, dances, routs and similar events organized by women. But entertaining and enjoyable though such events might be, their true purpose was far more serious and one that made rivalry and mistrust inevitable. They served as a market where men might look for a wife, and parents sought husbands for their daughters or viewed potential brides for their sons.

Here, men and women did not appear to mix socially, even within families. Men ate together. Women ate with other women and children. How then, Kerenza wondered, did men and women meet a possible marriage partner?

It took almost twenty minutes to reach the palace. She followed the men towards the towering walls, climbing ever higher, up steps, through an entrance in the outer wall where they were met by guards who escorted them past storehouses and gardens. She smelled orange blossom, and glimpsed olive, fig, apricot and peach trees. They passed beds of strawberries in flower, lettuce, artichokes and melons. As they approached a complex of arched and crenellated buildings her rapid heartbeat was due as much to apprehension as to the effects of the *cherqi* and the steep climb.

Passing one building where steps led up to a tall narrow arched entrance flanked by two keyhole-shaped window openings, they approached the entrance to the palace. A single domed arch led through a hallway into an open courtyard surrounded by a marble colonnade. They were led through into another large courtyard planted with orange trees with a tinkling marble fountain that spilled bright curtains of water into a wide basin below. Crossing the courtyard past more marble columns to the cool shade beyond, they were halted by the guards. A veiled female servant appeared and motioned Kerenza to follow.

Maggot spoke to the woman, questioning. She hastened to reassure him.

'Is all right,' he said to Kerenza. 'She take you to your sister. She is in harem.'

'The words simply means the women's quarters,' Henry Corbett explained as William, Nick and Kerenza all turned in consternation.

Kerenza attempted a smile. 'I'll see you all later, then.' Maggot and the vice consul nodded. Her glance met Nick's, seeking reassurance. 'I hope everything goes well, and–'

'Yes, all right.' William waved her away impatiently. 'Get along with you. I don't want to keep the governor waiting. He might have no manners, but we must show him we are not to be trifled with.'

'I think, Mr Vyvyan,' the vice consul intervened, 'that you should prepare yourself for a considerable wait. Moroccan time is not like English time.'

'But we have an appointment,' William blustered.

'So we see the governor before nightfall,' Maggot shrugged. 'Maybe.'

As Nick motioned her away with a tiny movement of his head, and a reassuring smile, Kerenza followed her guide. As they walked along cool passages rich with decoration, she caught glimpses of bright robes that vanished around corners or through arches with carved doors that closed as she drew level. She heard soft hisses, and the whisper of cloth slippers on the floor tiles.

Finally they arrived at the entrance to a courtyard paved with stone slabs on which large pots glazed in deep blue and dark red overflowed with leafy green shrubs heavy with scented blossoms of white, purple, yellow and deep pink.

Indicating that Kerenza should enter, the servant bowed and turned away, disappearing round a corner.

Moistening her lips, Kerenza stood for a

300

moment beside a marble column. At first glance the courtyard appeared to be empty. Then, in the shadows of an open porch on the far side, she saw propped on cushions on a low couch a bulky figure swathed in voluminous turquoise trimmed with silver braid. The pointed toes of matching slippers peeped out from beneath the hem. A turquoise headscarf obscured her face.

Kerenza hoped the woman might understand enough to tell her where Dulcie was. Drawing a deep breath, she started across the courtyard. In the scented silence, her footsteps sounded loud on the flagstones. The figure stirred and heaved itself up on one elbow.

'What took you so long? Surely you could have come sooner?' The accusing whine was unmistakable.

'*Dulcie?*' Kerenza stared as her sister swung her legs off the couch and pulled her gown straight.

'Well, who else did you expect to see?'

'I'm sorry, it's just – I didn't expect – your clothes.' Kerenza hugged her arms across her body in an automatic gesture of self-protection. Half-formed and hopeful visions of first moments that had included outstretched hands, a warm hug, relief at her arrival, an apology for the past and a plea that they put it behind them – all of which she would gladly have accepted – evaporated. Those had been stupid dreams. This was reality. Dulcie hadn't changed. Except she had put on a lot of weight. She had always been plump, inheriting their mother's rounded figure. Now she was fat. Which meant that at least there had been no shortage of food.

'For heavens' sake, Kerenza. We were brought here with nothing but the clothes we were wearing.'

'Yes, of course, I'm sorry.'

'Besides, this is far more comfortable. These courts can get very hot.'

About to say that she knew, and tell her sister about Zohra, Kerenza stopped herself. This was not the time. 'I'm so sorry about Mother. It must have been terrible for you to lose her. You had always been close.' She was careful to make it a simple statement, avoiding criticism or complaint. 'And to be here with only each other for company.'

'Company?' Dulcie snorted, fiddling with the silver braid that decorated the front of her caftan. 'All she ever talked about was Papa. All day and half the night. On and on and on, about how he would come the next day or the next week and take us home. But he never did.' Her expression was angry and bitter.

'He was a prisoner himself, Dulcie, in Algiers. Then he fell ill, so it was months before–'

'I know how long it was,' Dulcie shouted. 'I was here, waiting, remember? Trying to make Mama eat, trying to keep her clean. I got fed up with it. You needn't look like that. You have no idea what it's been like for me. I did everything for her. But all she ever talked about was Papa. She didn't have a thought for what I was going through.' Her face crumpled.

'Oh, Dulcie.' Looking at her sister, Kerenza was filled with compassion. 'It must have been awful.'

'It was worse.' Dulcie scrubbed the heel of her

302

hand across her eyes then caught her breath, dropping both hands to her belly.

'What's wrong? Are you unwell?' Kerenza's gaze dropped to her sister's hands then focused on the swelling beneath. Dulcie was certainly carrying– As realization hit her, Kerenza's instinctive reaction was denial. *No.* Dulcie couldn't possibly be. She looked up and saw her sister watching her with an odd combination of defiance, pride and fear.

Kerenza bit the inside of her lip so hard she tasted the salty warmth of blood. It was small wonder the vice consul and the doctor had behaved so oddly. This was the governor's promised protection? How was she to tell her father? What would the shock do to him? He would demand revenge: he'd create a political storm, and Dulcie's condition would become public in a scandal that would plaster the Vyvyan name all over the newspapers. The prospect dried Kerenza's throat. She felt sick. *What about Dulcie? How must she be feeling?*

Summoning every ounce of willpower to force aside her fears and her memories of Dulcie's past unkindness, Kerenza stretched out a trembling hand and laid it over her sister's.

'Oh, Dulcie, I'm so sorry. Papa said the governor had promised you and Mama his protection. How could he have let this happen? Was it – were you hurt? Has the person responsible been caught and punished?'

Pushing Kerenza's hand away, Dulcie levered herself up and walked to the junction between cool shade and the sun's heat. 'It wasn't like that.'

Kerenza straightened up, facing her sister, bewildered. 'What do you mean?'

'I mean it wasn't – I wasn't attacked.'

'Not attacked?'

Dulcie flushed, but her manner was defiant. 'Oh, do stop repeating everything. I wasn't violated. This baby is a child of love.' She rested her hands on the swelling, more pronounced now she was standing.

Kerenza stared at her sister, then moistened bone-dry lips. 'Who?'

'He's a prince,' Dulcie said proudly. 'They don't use that word here, but he's one of the sultan's sons so he's definitely a prince. His name is Aruj.'

'I saw him yesterday,' Kerenza blurted. 'On horseback with his bodyguard.'

Dulcie's face lit up. 'He's back?' But her excitement swiftly faded and her face fell into an irritated frown. 'I've hardly seen him since Mama died. But I suppose being a prince means he has all kinds of important duties.' Her expression softened and she sighed dreamily. 'Isn't he hand-some?'

Kerenza swallowed. 'Dulcie–'

'He wants to marry me, you know.'

'What?'

'He does. That's where he's been: to visit his father. He came to see me before he went. He only stayed a few minutes. I don't think he wanted to go. But when your father is the sultan and he commands you, you have to do as you're told. Anyway, now he's back and I expect it's all settled. Aruj will have told his father that he wants to marry me.' She pressed clasped hands to her bosom and sighed happily. 'I shall be a princess. And when I am' – her mouth thinned and her features grew sharp – 'I shall make changes, starting with some of the servants. I see them, laughing and sneering. I can't do anything yet, but once I'm married they'd better watch out. They won't be laughing then. Oh no.'

'Dulcie–' Kerenza began.

'You really should have come sooner. I've been awfully lonely. Especially since Mama– She became horribly difficult, always talking about Papa, and moaning about what was to become of us. She was so unkind about Aruj. She wouldn't make any effort to understand. She said all kinds of really hurtful things. And none of the servants speak English. Well, I daresay they could if they tried, but they won't make the effort. Their language is impossible. I just can't get my tongue around it. So it's a good thing you've come. I've really missed someone to talk to. Aruj speaks a little English. I think he once had a tutor. But I've hardly seen him–' She caught herself and flashed a bright smile. 'An important man like him must have all kinds of demands on his time.'

Kerenza felt as if she had strayed into a dream, or a nightmare. 'Dulcie, you can't stay here.'

Dulcie's chin rose. 'Aruj loves me. He wants to marry me. I shall be a princess. You can stay and be my companion. I shall need someone.'

'No,' Kerenza shook her head. 'No, I can't do that.'

'But I need you,' Dulcie cried. 'You can't leave me here all on my own.'

'Of course not. Nor would I. Dulcie, Papa

305

brought the money the governor asked for. Even now they are negotiating for you to be released. You can't stay here.'

'You can't tell me what to do! Who do you think you are? I don't want to talk to you any more. Go away. Go on, leave me alone.'

'I'll come and see you tomorrow.'

'You needn't bother unless you're going to be nicer to me. After all I've suffered, I expected more kindness.' With a sniff that reminded Kerenza of Betsy Woodrow, Dulcie turned her back and waddled away. A moment later the slam of a heavy wooden door resounded through the court.

After standing for a few moments, not sure what to do, Kerenza heaved a deep shaky sigh and turned away. Across the sunlit space the woman who had guided her through the maze of passages and courts stepped out of the shadows and stood, waiting.

Chapter Eighteen

In an anteroom patterned with diamond-shaped tiles of green, white, red and black, and furnished with couches and low tables, Henry Corbett sat as calm and immobile as a statue. Beside him William Vyvyan fretted and fumed. Every few minutes he took his watch from his pocket, frowned at it, then heaved a loud and irritated sigh as he replaced it. Mordecai stood behind the couch, slightly to one side of the vice consul. While Maggot gazed out of a window, Nick watched the constant tide of people ebb and flow in front of the broad archway that led out into a lofty hall.

There were merchants in Spanish dress, white-robed Arabs with faces like carved teak, fierce-eyed tribesmen wearing belted tunics over loose trousers tucked into soft leather boots. Among them moved the governor's bodyguards, the black Bukhari appointed by the sultan who served at his forts throughout the kingdom, various officials, other supplicants seeking audience, and household staff. The clamour was deafening. A babble of raised voices and different languages all citing need and claiming importance.

An hour passed. A slave brought an ornate silver tray containing a silver pot and several tiny glasses. After pouring mint tea he retreated as silently as he had arrived. Another hour passed.

Suddenly there was a commotion outside. A handsome young man swept in, the loose open robe over his belted tunic, trousers and boots billowing about him.

'About time too,' William huffed, straggling to rise from the couch. 'Do you have any idea how long–'

Imperiously waving him to silence, the young man turned to Nick.

'You.' His voice was harsh. 'Come.' Without waiting for an answer he strode out.

'Wait,' William called. 'What about me? Well, of all the...'

Signalling Maggot, Nick followed. People

307

scattered, bowing low, as the young man crossed the wide hall and entered a half-open door. As Nick and Maggot reached him, he waved Maggot away.

'With respect,' Nick was polite but firm, 'he must stay. I don't speak your language.'

The young man addressed Maggot. Maggot bowed and replied, and after an instant's hesitation, the young man nodded and stood back. Once all three were inside, he dismissed three slaves who had rushed in, prostrating themselves, and closed the door.

'He is Mulai Aruj,' Maggot told Nick. 'One of sultan's sons.'

Nick bowed. 'Tell him who we are and why we are here.'

Maggot obeyed. But before he had finished, Aruj was already nodding and interrupted.

'He know who we are,' Maggot said.

Nick was puzzled. 'So why is he talking to me? Surely it is Mr Vyvyan?'

Again Aruj interrupted. He paced the floor, gesticulating as a torrent of words flowed from his lips. When he'd finished, he glared at Maggot, and gestured for him to translate.

Maggot swallowed. 'He say his father has arranged marriage for him with daughter of tribal chief. We must take Miss Vyvyan away very quick. She in very much danger.'

Nick didn't understand. 'Why? How can she be? She's under the governor's protection.'

As Maggot translated the question, Nick watched the prince's face stiffen and his eyes flash. He spat a response.

'He say you no ask questions, just take her away.'

'Tell him that is why we're here now, and why we've been coming each day. We want to settle things as soon as possible. But the governor is making us wait. Does he know why?' Nick watched the prince as Maggot put the question, saw more irritation and impatience as he replied.

'Pasha Abd-er-Azzak Medja – is governor's name,' Maggot explained quickly. 'He want money first.'

'Mrs Vyvyan died while she was in his care.' Nick was watching the prince. As Mulai Aruj caught his eye and instantly switched his gaze to Maggot, apparently waiting for him to translate, Nick wondered if the prince understood more than he wanted to admit. Pretending to need an interpreter would certainly allow him time to think before he responded. 'Mr Vyvyan will not hand over any money until he has been permitted to see his daughter,' Nick added, and saw the prince's gaze slide away as a shadow crossed his face. *Something wasn't right.* 'Miss Vyvyan is well?'

As Maggot repeated the question, Aruj gave a brief nod and muttered a reply.

'She is well. But Mulai Aruj say better Mr Vyvyan wait on ship for his daughter. You bring money. Miss Vyvyan leave with you.'

Nick frowned. 'What's going on, Maggot? Why doesn't he want Mr Vyvyan to see his daughter?' He waited.

'If Mr Vyvyan see his daughter,' Maggot said, as the prince paced, 'he make trouble for pasha. Pasha no like English. He tell Hassan es

309

Zimmouri, then Miss Vyvyan in great danger. May be killed.'

'Who is Hassan es Zimmouri?'

'Chief of tribe, and father of betrothed of Mulai Aruj.'

Nick's head had begun to ache. 'But why should *he* want to kill Miss Vyvyan?'

The prince replied briefly, visibly irritated. Maggot stared at him, shock slackening his features for an instant. The prince flicked his fingers impatiently, indicating he should translate. Maggot swallowed.

'What is it? Tell me,' Nick kept his voice calm, but he could feel his muscles tightening. Something was very wrong.

Maggot's dark gaze met his. 'She–' He curved his hands in front of his stomach.

'She's fat?' Nick said blankly.

Maggot shook his head, then gripping his forearms he rocked them as if cradling a baby.

'*She's with child?*' As Maggot nodded, Nick felt the room tip for an instant as he tried to absorb all the implications. 'Mulai Aruj is responsible?'

'I think is not good to ask,' Maggot said, giving the briefest of nods.

Nick's brain was racing as the prince spoke again.

'He say you go now,' Maggot said. 'Put Mr Vyvyan on ship. You bring money tomorrow, take Miss Vyvyan.'

With a regal nod, Mulai Aruj swept out. Nick saw the milling throng part, falling to their knees as, joined by two uniformed Bukharis, he strode through them and disappeared.

310

With Maggot at his shoulder, Nick returned to the anteroom.

As he entered he caught Henry's Corbett's eye and saw immediately that the vice consul was already aware of the situation. *Why hadn't he warned them?* Even as the question formed he knew the answer. Already sick and mentally fragile from his own ordeal, William Vyvyan had needed time to come to terms with the devastating news of his wife's death. It would have been too cruel to inform him at the same time that his daughter had been raped and made pregnant while in the governor's care. But surely Corbett could have said something since? *To whom?* The only people with a right to be told were the girl's father and her sister. *Kerenza.* Her sister's condition would reflect badly on her. And inevitably the news and attendant gossip would spread through both Falmouth and Flushing like a fever.

A fleeting image of Jeremy Ashworth hinting at Kerenza's scandalous behaviour was followed by one of packet agent Edgar Tierney sitting behind his desk sucking air through his teeth and shaking his head. *Troubled family: not a good connection for an ambitious young man.* He fought welling anger. He could not – must not – think about that now.

The vice consul knew, as Nick did, that William Vyvyan would have to be informed. But how, when, and where he learned of his daughter's condition, would need to be carefully planned.

Putting his watch away, William glanced up. Seeing Nick his brows rose. 'Well?'

Nick was spared having to answer by Kerenza

311

entering the room, escorted by a veiled female servant who immediately scuttled away. With the lower half of her face covered, all he could see were her eyes, shocked and stricken as they met his for an instant before she dipped her head. Nick started forward, placing himself between her and the couch.

'Your father doesn't know,' he murmured. 'Don't tell him. We'll talk later.' Taking her hand he bowed over it, and spoke so all could hear. 'Miss Kerenza. I'm sure your sister was happy to see you. I hope you found her well?'

He pressed her fingers gently, and to his consternation saw her eyes fill. But she blinked back the tears before they could fall and spoke so everyone could hear. 'Yes, thank you, Mr Penrose. She's as well as – as can be expected.'

Behind her another servant, male this time, entered the room. With his hand at his chest and a great deal of head shaking he made what was clearly a speech of regret. Then, with a final bow he left. Everyone looked at Maggot, who showed no emotion as he translated.

'Pasha Abd-er-Azzak Medja say he very sad, but the *cherqi* have give him headache. Can see no more peoples today. Please come tomorrow.'

William leapt to his feet, crimson with fury. 'This is intolerable. We are here at his invitation. We had an appointment. I've never known such appalling bad manners.'

Nick watched Kerenza force herself forward in an attempt to defuse her father's rage.

'Papa, Mr Corbett did warn us.'

'Oh, be quiet, Kerenza,' he snarled, and she

flinched as if he had struck her. 'I've no time for–'

'Mr Vyvyan,' Nick snapped. 'You forget yourself, sir.'

William swung round, but before he could speak, Henry Corbett rose and took his arm.

'It is indeed most frustrating,' he sympathized. 'At this very moment the consul may himself be experiencing just such a situation. But in our years here we have learned that to show anger and displeasure weakens our position.' Still talking quietly he steered a stiff-backed William towards the door. 'You see, it plays into the governor's hands by confirming his power. I don't think we want that, do we?'

'No,' William grudged. 'But–'

They moved ahead with Mordecai following. Escorted by guards towards a door opening into one of several courts, Nick turned to Kerenza. 'I can't offer you my arm,' he murmured. 'Men and women aren't allowed to touch in public. But may I walk with you?'

Keeping her head down, Kerenza gave a brief nod. He knew Dulcie was pregnant. But did he know by whom, or the circumstances? He could not. For surely the shame Dulcie's behaviour reflected on the Vyvyan family would have shown in his eyes. All she had seen was sympathy. But when she told him, as she must, that far from being brutally violated Dulcie had welcomed the prince's advances, his encouragement would turn to dismay and disgust. She would have to watch it happen. And part of her would die too.

As they walked back through the narrow

streets, Kerenza wondered if she would reach Zohra's house before her legs gave way. Pain skewered into one temple and queasiness churned her stomach.

'Come on, sweetheart,' Nick said softly, and the endearment wrenched her heart. 'You're doing fine. Once we're inside out of this wind and you have something to eat you'll feel better.'

Sweetheart. To call her that now – he would soon wish he had not. Did he really think she'd be able to swallow? That food would make a difference? None of this was his fault. *Nor was it hers, but she would pay just the same.* How was she to tell her father? Was the prince really going to marry her sister? She could not believe it. Dulcie couldn't possibly stay in Tangier alone. *Surely she would not be expected to stay with her?* These and other thoughts zigzagged across her mind like flashes of lightning.

Back at the house Broad was waiting. After brief instructions from Nick, he bore William Vyvyan off upstairs with soothing suggestions of a nice cool drink and an hour's lie-down before his evening meal.

Ten minutes later, after rinsing her face and hands and trying to prepare herself to tell Nick the full and terrible truth, Kerenza returned to the salon. Dina had set out glasses of fruit juice and a tray of mint tea. Maggot and Zohra had disappeared. Nick waited until she had sat down on the couch then, indicating the seat beside her, raised his brows.

'May I sit beside you? I think it's best we keep our voices down. And it'll be easier to talk.'

314

'As you wish.' It emerged as a whisper. He would move away soon enough.

Half turned towards her, forearms resting on his thighs, he cleared his throat, clasping and unclasping his hands. 'Look, I know this is going to be painful for you.'

A sob caught in her throat and her hand flew to her mouth to smother it.

'Kerenza–' he groaned under his breath and, dropping his head he raked both hands through his hair.

Pulling herself together she took a deep breath. 'I'm sorry. It's – I'm all right. Really. I didn't mean to interrupt. But before we – how did you find out about Dulcie? Who told you?' She couldn't meet his gaze. She didn't want him to see her shame, anger, and grief. Instead she stared blindly at her white knuckles.

'While you were with your sister and we were waiting to see the governor, Mulai Aruj took Maggot and me into another room to talk about getting your sister away as soon as possible. But before we can decide how best to do this I need to know what your sister told you. And you have to hear what the prince told me. I'm asking you to trust me.' *Again.* The word hung, unspoken, between them. 'Can you? Will you?'

Did she have a choice? Despite what he had learned, and despite her father's boorish behaviour, he still wanted to help her. And she needed him, for who else was there? She raised her head and looked directly into his eyes.

'Yes. And I'm really grateful–'

He jerked backward. 'I don't want your

gratitude.' His voice was rough and angry. 'I want–' He clamped his lips together, shaking his head, then glanced up again. 'Did your sister tell you what happened? How she came to be – in her condition?'

Kerenza felt a wave of heat course from her chest to her hairline. She moistened her lips. 'I thought – assumed – she had been – attacked. But she denies it. She believes Mulai Aruj wants – intends – to marry her.'

Nick stiffened. '*What?*' He rubbed his forehead, his expression reflecting anger, helplessness and frustration.

Now they had started, and because his reaction had so closely echoed her own, Kerenza found talking about it was not as difficult or as embarrassing as she had feared. She and Nick had already been through so much together on the packet: her father's drinking, Captain Penrose's death, and the birth of Judith's baby.

'She is convinced of it. She believes he went to see his father the sultan to tell him and ask his blessing.' She watched Nick's face grow hard.

'Mulai Aruj is betrothed to the daughter of a local tribal chief,' he said grimly. 'He told me so himself.'

Kerenza's eyes widened as her hand flew to her mouth. 'But what about Dulcie?'

Nick hunched his shoulders. 'Look, I don't want to sound harsh. God knows–'

'It's all right. There's nothing you can say that I haven't already thought for myself. And even though the situation is impossible, I hoped for her sake that he loved her.'

316

'Perhaps he did.'

'It's kind of you to say so. But I doubt it. She isn't–' *lovable*. Breaking off, Kerenza started again. 'I haven't seen Dulcie for over three years. I had hoped that when we met again – especially after all she's been through, losing our mother and everything – that we might – that she might – but she hasn't changed. The truth is, she has become even more–' Kerenza stopped. Though she still smarted from Dulcie's tongue-lashing, it would be wrong to disparage a member of her family to someone else. 'She must have been very lonely and frightened, especially as our mother was so badly affected by captivity and my father's absence. The prince is a very handsome man. If he showed Dulcie kindness–' Kerenza twisted her fingers. 'But if he wants her to leave, then it's clear he thinks she's become an inconvenience.'

Nick shook his head. 'It's far more serious than that. He says she's in grave danger.'

'In danger from whom?'

'Hassan es Zimmouri. The tribal chief whose daughter he's engaged to.' Leaning forward, Nick dropped his voice still further. 'If the sultan arranged this marriage for political reasons, then neither he nor the chief will want any ... complications.' He caught her hand, holding it tightly. 'The child – when is it due?'

'I don't know.' In her mind she saw her sister's ungainly shape, the effort it took her to stand, the way she leaned back for balance. 'But soon, I think.' She looked up. 'What do you mean, complications?'

'Kerenza, if your sister's child is a boy, he'll be the sultan's grandson. Do you think the chief would allow him, or your sister, to live?'

'But surely – I can't believe–'

'You must. Mulai Aruj made it clear that the chief will remove any threat to his daughter's happiness.'

'Dear God,' she gasped. 'You said my father doesn't know?'

Nick shook his head. 'Not yet. And it would be better if we can keep it from him as long as possible.'

'Surely–'

'Think about it,' Nick urged.

And despite the desperate seriousness of the situation, or maybe because of it, she was acutely aware of his hand clasping hers, the warm strength in his fingers. She glanced down and saw that without being aware of it she had turned her hand. Now their hands were palm to palm, her fingers curled over the back of his, holding fast, drawing comfort and reassurance.

'Your mother fell ill and died while under the governor's protection,' Nick reminded her. 'How do you think your father will react when he learns what has happened to your sister? Can you see him being willing to pay the ransom for her release?'

Kerenza shook her head. 'He's more likely to complain to the British Government.'

'Which would create a political storm. That's why both the prince and the governor want your sister out of the country as soon as possible.'

'Then why is the governor refusing to see you?

You've gone to the palace every day since we arrived.'

'I think there's a power struggle going on between the prince and the governor. The governor still wants the money, despite your mother's death and – and what's happened to your sister. The prince has the authority to overrule him. But it's my guess Mulai Aruj is using the money as a bribe so the governor won't tell the sultan what's happened. The governor is keeping the prince – and us – waiting to prove a point.'

Kerenza nodded slowly. 'Do you think the prince cared for Dulcie at all?' *Or was she just a novelty, an amusement?* Even though as a man would know how men thought, she couldn't bring herself to ask. Imagining how Dulcie would feel when she found out that the man of her dreams didn't want her made Kerenza shrivel inside. *She knew how that felt, and wouldn't wish it on her worst enemy.*

Nick shrugged, clearly uncomfortable, an answer in itself. 'He wants your sister out of the country before the chief can harm her.'

That, Kerenza guessed, was as much to protect himself and avoid any trouble with his father as for Dulcie's well-being. But she said nothing. Nick was trying to offer comfort, though they both knew he was clutching at straws.

He sighed deeply, his forehead furrowed in concentration. 'How do I persuade your father to wait on board *Kestrel* while I take the money to the palace?'

'You won't. It's a matter of principle with him.' She hesitated. 'There's only one way you will get

319

him on to the ship and make him stay there.' She found it hard to believe she could even *think* what she was thinking, much less say it aloud. 'He will have to be drugged.'

Nick squeezed her fingers, and she knew he had already reached the same conclusion. 'I'll take Maggot with me to the palace to translate. But you'll have to come as well, to escort your sister.'

'How will I persuade her to come with me? Tell her that Mulai Aruj does not want to marry her?' Kerenza shook her head. 'She won't believe me.' *She'll say I'm jealous. She'll accuse me of wanting to wreck her happiness.* 'Yet to tell her the truth, that he plans to marry someone else, seems so cruel. I know she'll have to be told sometime. But to do it right now – the shock – especially as she's so close to her time. But if I don't tell her she'll never agree to leave.'

Nick cursed softly under his breath.

Kerenza flinched, and tried to withdraw her hand, but he tightened his grip, refusing to let go. 'I'm sorry.' Her voice wobbled. 'I'm not trying to make difficulties, honestly, but–'

'It's not you I'm angry with,' he grated. 'It's your damn family. They've caused nothing but trouble and grief. And I can't see it getting any better. In fact–' He rubbed the back of his neck with his free hand and, with a grunt of disgust, shook his head.

'I'm sorry,' she whispered.

He frowned at her. 'You've done nothing to apologize for.'

No, she hadn't. But that wouldn't protect her

from the gossip, or her father's expectations that she leave her grandmother and return to Falmouth to look after Dulcie. And what was to become of the baby? How would friends and acquaintances of the Vyvyan family react to a child not only born out of wedlock – an appalling stigma on its own – but a child of mixed race? The shame– Closing her eyes she slammed a door on her thoughts. All that lay ahead. But first they had to get Dulcie away. And there was still so much to be worked out.

'Do I have your permission to speak to the doctor?' Nick said.

'Yes, of course. But why?'

'We need to know how much of the sleeping draught can safely be given to your father to get him on to the ship and keep him there. Knowing the circumstances, I'm sure he'll be willing to help.'

Kerenza nodded. 'Why didn't he say anything? He had visited my mother. He must have noticed Dulcie's condition.'

'I wondered about that. I suppose he kept quiet for the same reason the vice consul did. Neither of them would have wanted to add to your father's grief when he had just been told of your mother's death. Can you imagine the effect this additional disaster would have had?'

'No, you're right.'

'Broad will look after your father.'

She sucked in a breath. 'But what are we to do about Dulcie?'

'I've had an idea. You won't have to tell her anything. At least, not until she's safe on board

321

the packet.'

'But how?'

'The prince will persuade her to go.' Nick's features had set as hard as Cornish granite. 'One more lie shouldn't worry him.' Kerenza winced at the bitter anger in his voice. 'He put her – and us – in this mess. He can help get us out of it.'

Her tongue snaked over dry lips. 'Do you think he'll agree?'

Nick's mouth twisted as he nodded. 'He wants all of us away from here before his father finds out what's happened.'

'When we get home–'

'Time enough later to talk about that,' Nick cut her short, releasing her hand and rising to his feet. 'Right now we need to concentrate on getting your father on to the ship and your sister out of the palace.'

Feeling her cheeks flush at the rebuff, she clasped her hands tightly in her lap and stared hard at them. Of course he didn't want to talk about it. Because when *Kestrel* reached Falmouth he would have accomplished everything he was supposed to on this voyage. The Woodrows and Judith had arrived safely in Gibraltar, the dispatches had been delivered to Admiral Hotham, and though her mother had died, at least her father had his elder daughter back.

Nick Penrose would – and deserved – to be confirmed by the post office as commander of the packet *Kestrel*. Then he would go his own way.

'Will you excuse me?' He indicated the doorway. 'I need to speak to Maggot.'

She forced her lips into a smile. 'Of course.' He must have heard something in her voice because he hesitated and the crease between his dark brows deepened. *Please, no explanations or pity. She couldn't bear that.* 'Go ahead. I'm fine. Really. Ah, here's Dina.' She looked past him as the maid poked her head in, clearly wanting to know if she could prepare the table.

When Nick didn't join them, Kerenza and her father ate alone. This evening the food was presented to them in a fashion more familiar to them at home. They were each given a single plate, her father's larger, containing a portion of rice with a golden butter crust, spiced chicken, bean and lentil salad, and mixed vegetables. But there was still no cutlery.

Throughout the meal William complained – about the food, about having to eat with his fingers, the governor's rudeness, the heat and humidity, and the nerve-shredding effects of the wind – until Kerenza wanted to scream.

Her attempts to empathize were brusquely rejected. How dare she suggest she understood? She was far too young to have any idea of suffering such as he had endured. Realizing he was completely immersed in his own feelings and concerns, that no one else mattered at all, she stopped trying and remained silent.

Forcing herself to eat she wondered about Nick's plan. The food stuck in her throat and lay heavy in her tense, aching stomach. But she knew that without it she wouldn't have the strength to face the next twenty-four hours, let alone the voyage back to Cornwall.

When Dina brought in mint tea signalling the end of the meal, Kerenza looked up and thanked her in her own language. The maid's dark eyes narrowed as she bobbed her head, indicating that behind her face veil she was smiling. Glancing at her father, Kerenza saw him stifle a yawn. She realized suddenly that for several minutes she hadn't heard a word he'd said. But as he yawned again it occurred to her that she hadn't heard him because he'd stopped talking and she had been so deep in her own thoughts she hadn't noticed.

'Some mint tea, Papa?' Kerenza held the pot poised over a tiny glass.

'I suppose so,' he grunted, leaning back on the couch, his eyelids heavy and drooping. 'It does settle the stomach.'

As she started to pour, his eyes closed, his mouth fell open, and he began to snore.

She simply stared at him for a moment, then set the pot down with a clatter as the real reason for the two separate plates dawned on her. Her father's food had contained a sleeping draught. Dina came in, her soft slippers soundless, glanced at William, and before Kerenza could utter a word, she hurried out again. A moment later Nick walked in followed by Maggot and Broad.

As Kerenza jumped to her feet, Nick took her arm and drew her to one side while Maggot and the steward heaved William off the couch.

'Maggot has hired two men with a litter to carry your father down to the beach. Once we're safely away, Maggot will come back here. I'll stay aboard *Kestrel* overnight. The ship will be ready to sail the moment your sister is free. Don't worry about your father. Broad will keep an eye on him.'

As Maggot and Broad left, half-carrying William between them, Kerenza and Nick were left alone. She lowered her voice.

'Why didn't you tell me you were going to–'

'It was better you didn't know.'

It stung, but she had to admit he was right. Had she been aware of the plan something in her manner might have aroused her father's suspicions.

'I'll bring the money with me in the morning. Try to sleep. I know it won't be easy but tomorrow will be a long day. You'll need all your strength.'

She wanted to thank him for all he was doing, but bit the words back. *I don't want your gratitude.* He had hurled the words at her like a curse. So she said nothing. Besides, her throat was so thick with tears she dared not trust her voice. Folding her hands she simply dipped her head once, and tried to smile.

For an instant Nick was totally still. Then, with a sound that sounded as if it was torn from deep inside him, he took two strides forward, seized her shoulders, and covered her mouth with his. The kiss was demanding yet achingly tender. After an instant's frozen shock, her body quickened and she responded instinctively, leaning into him, her mouth softening under his. But with another soft groan he wrenched free and, setting her aside, he walked out.

Dazed, swaying and confused, she raised trembling fingers to her lips, still tasting him, still

325

feeling the pressure. *Their first kiss*. But why now? He had made no declaration of his feelings or intentions. Had they been in Flushing his action would have been considered an insult. What made it different here? Everything they had been through. All they still had to face to secure Dulcie's freedom. She wanted so very much to believe it was heartfelt, that he truly cared about her. She knew he had no gift for pretty compliments or small talk. Nor was it easy for him to express his feelings. But was she fooling herself? This was the first time he had kissed her. Given what he now knew about her family and the problems she would face on their return to Cornwall, problems that were not his responsibility, *had it also been the last?*

Chapter Nineteen

After a night punctuated by vivid but elusive dreams interspersed with periods of restlessness when all her fears lined up to taunt, mock and threaten, Kerenza was startled out of sleep by Dina's knock. When the maid had gone downstairs again, she drank her coffee, then threw back the covers and padded out on to the terrace. Shading her eyes from the low morning sun, she looked across the tiered houses to the sea, seeking *Kestrel*. She ran her fingertips lightly across her lips. *Nick had kissed her*. She had not flirted or invited it the way she had seen some girls do. So he must have done it because he wanted to. And that must surely mean he did care for her a little. She yearned to think beyond the next few hours, but resisted. She would need all her strength and her wits if she was to keep Dulcie entertained and unsuspecting.

Washed, dressed, her hair swept up and pinned, she packed all her belongings. After a last look round she carried her bag – Judith's gift – out on to the terrace, down the steps, and across the court.

She breakfasted alone in the salon. Maggot was probably spending these last moments with his stepmother. After three years of believing him dead Zohra would miss him dreadfully. Faintly in the background Kerenza could hear distant voices and clattering dishes. She gazed around the room, imprinting it on her mind to store with her other treasured memories. Once back in Cornwall, she would find it easier to survive the difficult days – and inevitably there would be many – if she could escape by reliving happier moments.

She heard Nick arrive and her heartbeat instantly quickened. Rising to her feet she pressed cold fingers to her burning cheeks, and was smoothing the front of her gown as he walked in and set down the leather case. The money it contained would buy her sister's freedom. *But at what cost to her father and herself?* And the terrible irony was that Dulcie didn't want her freedom.

As Nick bowed over her hand Kerenza inhaled the lemony scent of his soap. She had to fight a powerful urge to smooth back the thick dark hair that curled on his neck and tumbled across his forehead, tousled by the wind during the trip ashore. Freshly shaved, he wore a clean neckcloth and his uniform coat had been brushed.

Straightening up he looked deep into her eyes. 'All right?' It sounded casual, almost careless. But Kerenza knew the question asked far more than was apparent. He needed reassurance that she would be able to do her part. She nodded.

'Did you sleep?'

A wry smile flickered across her lips as she answered honestly.

'More than I expected, but less than I'd have liked.'

He grimaced. 'That makes two of us.'

'How is my father?'

'Fine. He had another dose of laudanum this morning with his breakfast and is sleeping again. With luck we won't have to give him any more. You ready?'

Swallowing, she nodded, and drew a deep breath. 'What shall I do about my bag?'

'Maggot's just telling Dina to take it down to the beach,' Nick said. 'The jollyboat will take it out to the packet.'

Maggot walked in, and bowed to her. '*Azou fl'ouen.*'

As Kerenza blinked he grinned. 'Sorry, I forget. Good morning.'

Kerenza smiled back. 'Good morning.' Picking up her headscarf from the couch she turned to Nick. 'I won't keep you, I just want to say goodbye to Zohra.' She turned to Maggot. 'How do I say goodbye?'

Maggot shook his head. 'Is not easy.'

328

'I know. She has been so kind. I shall miss her.'

'No,' Maggot waved his hands, intimating she had misunderstood. 'Is not easy in Tamasirght. Is *b'hka-alaghair.*'

'Good God!' Nick murmured, pulling a droll face as Maggot coaxed and corrected Kerenza one syllable at a time.

'Right, I think I've got it,' she took a deep breath, repeating the phrase several times under her breath.

'I fetch her,' Maggot said and disappeared.

As Kerenza shook out the scarf, folded it into a triangle and covered her head, she saw Nick was watching her with an odd expression. Instantly self-conscious, she felt her colour rise. 'What?'

'You.' One corner of his mouth lifted in a lop-sided smile, and his gaze held admiration. 'The things you'll try. My mother would call you remarkable.'

Smiling, she dropped her glance, longing to ask what he would he call her. But that would be fishing. And her grandmother had always told her that a compliment sought was not worth having.

Maggot returned with his stepmother. Seeing Zohra's red-rimmed eyes, Kerenza felt a sharp pricking in her own. She walked forward, holding out her hand. *'Ateikum saha,* Zohra. *B'hka-alaghair.'*

Her hand was ignored. Instead, Kerenza found herself seized in a hug, pressed to Zohra's broad soft bosom, and soundly kissed on both cheeks.

Murmuring in her own language, Maggot's stepmother stepped back, dabbing her eyes and

329

waving them away as she bustled out of the salon.

'She sad we go,' Maggot said, his own eyes glistening as he stared after her. He threw a desperate look at Nick.

'It's time,' Nick said, and picked up the leather case.

The two men walked either side of Kerenza, except when the streets were too narrow, then they went ahead and she followed close behind. The hot wind was gusty, whirling dust and litter. The scarf covered Kerenza's nose and mouth. But her unprotected eyes soon felt sore and gritty.

When they reached the palace they were admitted at once.

'What do I tell Dulcie?' Kerenza whispered frantically.

'Nothing,' Nick was firm. 'You don't know anything. You have come to keep her company while negotiations over the ransom are completed. Ask her about her time here. If you can get her talking about herself all you'll have to do is listen.'

He saw her catch her lip as she gave an uncertain nod. He had asked for her trust, and she had given it. But even though she was trying hard to hide it, he could see her anxiety. *Did he know what he was doing?* By God, he hoped so.

The female servant appeared and beckoned Kerenza to follow. He saw her look back and mouth 'good luck' as she was led away.

Then a male servant, dark-skinned and white-robed, wearing a white rimless cap guided him and Maggot to the same anteroom as before, and indicated they should sit.

'Tell him to inform the prince we are here,' Nick instructed Maggot. 'Make it clear the prince asked to be told of our arrival.' The servant bowed and left. After an hour another servant appeared.

'He say we follow,' Maggot explained. 'He take us to Mulai Aruj.'

In the prince's luxuriously furnished apartments they waited another hour. Then without warning, and unaccompanied by his usual retinue, Mulai Aruj appeared. Nick and Maggot stood. The prince seated himself opposite and motioned for them to sit again. Nick explained his plan, pausing frequently to allow Maggot time to translate. When he'd finished he waited, outwardly calm while his heart hammered painfully against his breastbone.

The prince studied him. Nick forced himself to hold the man's gaze. It was a battle of wills. They both knew Mulai Aruj was in difficulty. They both knew he wanted to be rid of Dulcie with as little fuss and inconvenience as possible. And they both knew Nick's plan offered a solution. But Nick was very aware that the prince resented being in a position of weakness. And this made him very dangerous.

When Mulai Aruj gave a terse nod indicating his agreement, Nick was careful to keep his face expressionless. Any hint of relief or triumph could sabotage the whole scheme.

'You have brought money for Pasha Abd-er-Azzak Medja?' Maggot translated.

Nick showed him the bag.

'I will take it to him.' As he relayed the prince's words Maggot's face was as blank as a bare wall, but his eyes conveyed both anxiety and warning.

Nick could feel drops of sweat sliding down his chest and sides soaking into his shirt. Even without translation, the imperious tone had made it clear this was a command.

'It is a gracious offer, Your Excellency. But I regret I must decline. I am not acting for myself, but for Miss Vyvyan's father. The governor requested the money be given directly into his hands. Mr Vyvyan gave his solemn oath to obey. Honour demands I do what Mr Vyvyan would himself have done.'

'Where is Mr Vyvyan?'

'He was taken ill last night, and was carried to my ship.' Nick knew it was likely the prince had spies watching everything that went on in Tangier, particularly anything concerning foreigners. No doubt he had already been informed, and had asked simply to see how Nick would respond.

'So you are ready to sail?'

'We will leave as soon as Miss Vyvyan and her sister are aboard.'

As the prince stood up Nick and Maggot immediately did the same. 'You will see the Pasha shortly.'

Lying on her couch, Dulcie fiddled with the gold braid decorating the neckline and cuffs of her saffron-coloured caftan. 'We weren't allowed to leave the castle grounds, but at least they let us walk in the gardens.' She heaved a sigh. 'I'm so bored.'

'Shall we walk a little?' Kerenza suggested.

Dulcie shook her head. 'No. I hate this wind. I

feel sticky all the time.'

Kerenza had followed Nick's advice and had kept asking questions that encouraged Dulcie to talk about herself. The trouble was that Dulcie had little positive to say about anything. Her answers were brief, her comments invariably critical.

Kerenza tried again. 'Is there a *hammam* in your apartments? Zohra, Maggot's stepmother, took me to one near her house.'

'What sort of a name is Maggot?' Dulcie interrupted, pulling a face.

'Easier to pronounce than his real one,' Kerenza shrugged and smiled. 'I really enjoyed the *hammam* once I got used to it.'

'The bathing was all right,' Dulcie grudged. 'But after the first time I wouldn't let them massage me. It hurt too much. I was afraid I'd have bruises they were so rough and heavy-handed. And then they kept trying to pull my hair out.'

Kerenza sat up. 'What do you mean? The women set upon you?'

'No,' Dulcie was impatient. 'I don't mean handfuls. They just pulled out one hair at a time.'

'Why?' Kerenza asked, bewildered. 'What was their reason?'

'Aruj told me the Moors believe that fair hair has *baraka*. It's some kind of blessing or power that makes you able to heal the sick and protect against the evil eye.'

'But – surely after Mama–' Kerenza began, then quickly closed her mouth.

'Yes, *Mama* died,' Dulcie said with heavy patience. 'But *I* didn't. I didn't even get the fever.

So they thought Mama must have done something to upset the *jinoon*, the evil spirits. Anyway, I let Aruj have some of my hair. He plaited it into a thin braid that he wears on his wrist. He says it makes him invincible.' Her mouth curved briefly in a proud smile. But the corners soon drooped again. 'Invisible, more like. I know he's busy, but I wish he'd come and see me more often. It's so boring having to stay in the palace. And the slaves are rude to me. Not that I can understand a word they say. But I can tell by their eyes.'

'It's bound to feel strange and a bit lonely here,' Kerenza said, intending to comfort. 'But once you're back home–'

'Home?' Startled, Dulcie pushed herself up. 'I'm not going home. As soon as Papa has paid the ransom and I can leave here I shall go away with Aruj. I'm going to be a princess. What do you think of that?' Fortunately for Kerenza, Dulcie didn't wait for an answer. 'There's nothing for me back in Falmouth.' One hand strayed to her pregnant belly, but she didn't look down. 'No, after all I had to put up with taking care of Mama, it's my turn now. Being stuck in here has been really boring. Still, at least I've had time to pamper myself. Back in Falmouth I was always busy doing things for Mama and running errands. Now I have slaves to bathe me and look after my hair and nails. And I only have to clap my hands and a servant will bring me a drink or some fruit.' Her smile was triumphant. 'I've got people running about after me for a change. Why would I want to give that up? I don't know why you bothered coming. You needn't have.'

Kerenza gazed at her hands, fighting hard to hang onto her temper. Looking up, she caught Dulcie's glare. 'I came because Papa insisted. He said you and Mama would need someone to look after you on the voyage home.'

Dulcie laughed. 'Were you angry? I expect you were. You certainly wouldn't have wanted to come. You should have refused. As you can see, you're not needed after all.'

Kerenza swallowed. 'We didn't know that at the time.'

'Well, you do now, so there. I'm happy. And I won't let you spoil it, not again.'

Kerenza stared at her, shaken. 'What do you mean? *Again?* When did I ever spoil your happiness?' As far back as Kerenza could remember it had always been the other way around.

'When? The day you were born,' Dulcie hurled the words at her. 'Until then I'd had Mama and Papa all to myself. They doted on me. They used to call me their little treasure. Then you had to come along. Mama had a terrible time with you. She made the midwife take you away into another room. She couldn't bring herself even to look, let alone hold you.'

Kerenza gazed at her sister, each word a crushing blow. 'But I still don't understand. What has that to do with you and me?'

'You are so stupid, Kerenza. After a few days' rest Mama felt better. Then she was beside herself with guilt. She was terrified in case anything should happen to you. You only had to sneeze and she was afraid you had lung fever. She believed it was God punishing her for her wickedness.'

Kerenza struggled to work out the logic that made her illness her mother's punishment.

'From then on,' Dulcie glowered, 'you were the centre of attention, fussed over and admired, and shown off to all Mama's and Papa's friends. It was all *the baby* this, and *the baby* that.' A sudden flush reddened her face, her eyes watered and her mouth trembled. 'Nobody noticed me any more.' Her face twisted. 'I hated you.'

It wasn't my fault. I didn't ask for all that attention. I didn't even know. It certainly didn't last long, because I can't remember it. And I would have. Even as these thoughts, and anger at being blamed for situations outside her control, raced through Kerenza's mind, she knew there was no point in trying to explain.

'I'm sorry,' she said quietly, shocked and saddened at the reason for her sister's hatred, and appalled at the depth of it.

'Yes, well, I'm important now. And I'm happy. And I'm going to marry a prince.'

'If you're happy, Dulcie, then I'm glad for you,' Kerenza said.

Dulcie peered at her suspiciously. 'You are? Truly?'

Kerenza nodded, biting the inside of her lip as she fought an overwhelming urge to weep at the tragedy of it all.

Dulcie's eyes narrowed. Then she smirked. 'Admit it, you're jealous, aren't you.'

Jealous? Jealous over a man who used you and now can't wait to be rid of you? Do you love him, Dulcie? Are you capable of loving anyone? Kerenza tasted sudden salty warmth. Some questions must

336

never be asked. They were too cruel.

The approaching sound of a male voice made them both look round. The prince crossed the court accompanied by a man dressed in similar fashion to the vice consul's Jewish interpreter. A veiled female slave followed with a white bundle folded over her arms.

'Aruj!' A smile of delight lit Dulcie's moon-like face, banishing her usual expression of fretful discontent. She looked almost pretty. 'Why didn't you come to see me when you got back? I've been waiting. I'm just so tired today, what with the heat and everything. Oh, this is my sister.' She gestured vaguely.

Kerenza immediately rose and dropped a deep curtsy. As the Jew murmured into the prince's ear, Kerenza realized he fulfilled the same function as Mordecai. But if the prince relied on an interpreter, then how had he and Dulcie–? She shut off the thought, ashamed of her curiosity, telling herself it was none of her business. Only that wasn't true. Dulcie's condition made it very much her business. For Dulcie had involved her in a situation that would change all their lives.

With the briefest of nods at Kerenza, the prince lifted Dulcie's hand and held it between his. But he did not raise it to his lips. Dulcie darted her a sidelong glance before tilting her face and arching her swollen body towards her reluctant lover.

Kerenza turned away. She was embarrassed by Dulcie's attempt to elicit a public display of affection, sickened by the prince's duplicity, and anxious neither should glimpse her reactions.

'Now the ransom has been paid' – the prince's voice was deep and harsh, the interpreter's soft and heavily accented – 'you are free to leave the palace, and I can take you to meet my father.'

Dulcie's eyes widened, and her cheeks turned pink with excitement as she struggled to sit up and swung her feet off the couch. 'Really? I'm going to meet the sultan?' She looked over her shoulder. 'Do you hear that, Kerenza? I am going to meet the sultan. He's emperor of all Morocco, you know,' she added importantly. 'There used to be four, all ruling different bits. But now he's the only one.'

'Indeed?' Kerenza murmured politely. Had it ever occurred to Dulcie to wonder how many men, women, and children might have been killed or maimed during the sultan's battle for supremacy? Feeling the prince's black gaze on her, she moistened her lips, hating what she was being forced to do, yet aware there was no alternative. 'That's a wonderful honour, Dulcie.'

Dulcie's smile faltered as she glanced down. 'But perhaps it might be better to wait until after the baby is born. It cannot be long now.'

As the Jew translated, the prince's dark eyes flicked to Kerenza's and, unable to stop herself, desperate that nothing should prevent them leaving as planned, she made a tiny negative movement.

'No,' the prince broke in, before the interpreter had finished. Then he switched to his own language. 'I do not wish to wait. You have proved you are fertile. That is of great importance in my country. We go today.' He gave a brisk nod, then

338

spoke some more.

'Your condition makes it impossible for you to ride,' the interpreter translated. 'So his highness, Mulai Aruj, has arranged for you to sail to Rabat aboard the ship *Kestrel.* Your sister will be on hand to attend to your needs, and the journey will be more comfortable for you.'

So that was Nick's plan. It was brilliant – if it worked. Kerenza could feel her heart pounding in her breast, its rhythm fast and loud in her ears as she saw suspicion cloud her sister's features.

'What about you?' Dulcie demanded of the prince. 'You are coming with me?'

'But of course,' the interpreter said, as Mulai Aruj lifted Dulcie's soft plump fingers to his lips. 'His Highness says it grieves him that you have been apart for so long. When you reach Rabat, he wishes to spend time with you for there is much to discuss.'

'Oh yes. There is indeed. When we'll be married, and where we shall live.' Dulcie laid her cheek against the prince's hand.

Kerenza looked away, unable to watch. The prince's caress and loving smiles were a lie, a Judas kiss, so he could be rid of a young woman whose life he had ruined. Dulcie's dream would soon become a nightmare. And what of her own life? Slowly, warily, she had begun to hope once again, to believe that she and Nick might have a future together. But now–

The prince snapped his fingers and the slave girl stepped forward, placed the bulky bundle on the couch and helped Dulcie to her feet.

'What's this?' Dulcie asked, as the slave picked

up a white robe and started to help her into it.

'It is a *ha'ik*,' the interpreter said. 'To cover you while you walk to the harbour.'

'But it's so hot. Why do I–?'

'Believe me, Dulcie, it's better if we are not recognized,' Kerenza said quickly, as she donned the voluminous garment and adjusted her headscarf. She would never forget the hisses and stares she had endured the day of her arrival. 'If we are dressed like Muslim women we will not be insulted, or even noticed.'

'But why should I hide?' Dulcie began.

'Dulcie,' Kerenza interrupted gently, 'it has nothing to do with hiding. The rules of behaviour are different here. The prince will expect you to set an example.' She noticed the interpreter murmuring into the prince's ear, caught the prince's dark gaze, glimpsed speculation, and looked swiftly away as fury surged through her.

Clicking her tongue, Dulcie heaved a sigh. 'Oh well, if I must.' She stopped resisting and allowed the slave to shroud her in white folds.

A few moments later, another slave emerged from Dulcie's quarters with a large bundle. With the prince leading the way, his interpreter at his shoulder, the sisters following with the two slaves behind them, the party set off through the courts and passages of the palace. Kerenza sensed their departure was being watched. Though all she glimpsed was an occasional veiled face swiftly withdrawn behind a pillar or a colourful robe disappearing through an arch.

'Did you do any gardening?' she asked, saying the first thing she could think of to distract

Dulcie's attention.

'Of course not.' Dulcie snapped, shocked and disapproving. 'Really, Kerenza, what a stupid question. There are slaves for that sort of thing. Why would I want to get my hands dirty?'

At the main entrance to the castle grounds, the prince spoke briefly to the slaves, who glanced at each other, and quickly nodded. Then, smiling at Dulcie, he spoke again. The interpreter explained that His Highness had instructed the slaves to accompany the sisters down to the beach. As soon as he had completed some last-minute business he would join them. His bags were even now being packed.

Kerenza's heart lurched into her throat as Dulcie hunched her shoulders in a manner all too familiar. It signalled mutiny.

Once more the prince lifted Dulcie's hand to his lips, kissing each finger, then covering them with both his. His harsh voice grew softer, huskier. Listening to the soothing sound, watching him bend over Dulcie's hand and fix her with his limpid dark-lashed gaze, Kerenza understood how her lonely, inexperienced sister had been beguiled. The man was a skilled seducer, practised and predatory. *Poor, poor Dulcie.*

'You must know that I cannot walk through the streets with you,' the Jew translated. 'My rank forbids it. But I will join you within the hour. Now you must go. Already I am counting the moments until we are together again.' Releasing her hand, the prince waved her away, smiling. 'Go!'

Kerenza drew Dulcie's arm through hers and coaxed her away. 'Come, Dulcie. It's not good for

341

you to be standing about. As soon as we are on board I'll ask the steward to prepare cool drinks for you. And the prince,' she added quickly.

Dulcie hung heavily on her arm as they walked down the narrow sloping streets towards the Water Gate, the two slaves following behind.

The wind funnelled up through the street, swirling and flapping their *ha'iks*. Kerenza's eyes stung and her chemise clung uncomfortably to her damp skin.

'This is awful,' Dulcie whined. 'I shouldn't have to walk. Aruj should have ordered a litter for me.'

'I think that might have been difficult because of the slope. It's this wind that's so uncomfortable,' Kerenza sympathized. 'You'll feel much better once we're on the ship. I found the movement of the waves helped me sleep.'

'I hope I won't be sick,' Dulcie said.

As they passed through the Water Gate and started down the long ramp, Kerenza's stomach cramped with apprehension as she saw the state of the sea. The wind had pushed up a heavy swell that thundered against the remains of the mole on the northern side of the bay. To the south and west, waves broke and foamed up the beach before being sucked back to rear, curl and crash again.

Kestrel had left her anchorage. Headsail and jib set, her fore and mainsails reefed down, she cruised slowly about 200 yards out. The wind was angled onshore. And Kerenza knew it would require remarkable skill to steer the packet close enough to pick up the cutter while keeping well clear of the mole. She guessed Maggot was at the wheel, assisted by Able Seaman Collins.

Searching anxiously among fishing boats for the cutter, she released a tremulous sigh of relief as she saw it nosing in through the surf. Then she glimpsed Nick at the water's edge. Just as she spotted him he turned and waved, beckoning her down.

'We're nearly there,' she encouraged. 'It's not far now.'

Suddenly Dulcie stopped, tugging Kerenza's arm. 'Look how rough the water is.'

'It's nothing to worry about,' Kerenza reassured. 'The cutter's crew is used to far worse than this. To them it's no more than a ripple. They'll have us on board the packet before we know it.'

'No,' Dulcie pulled against Kerenza. 'It doesn't look safe.'

Hearing intense whispering behind them, Kerenza glanced round. The two female slaves had stopped a few feet further back. The one carrying the bundle threw it down. Then they both turned and ran back up the ramp.

Chapter Twenty

'Where are they going?' Dulcie demanded. 'How dare they. They can't just run off.'

But Kerenza had stopped listening, her attention caught by Nick's voice. She could hear him shouting, but the noise of wind and surf made it impossible to discern the words. His waving arm urged them to hurry. As the cutter surfed in, two seamen jumped out, working swiftly with the others who used their oars to turn the boat so it was facing seaward again.

'Come on, Dulcie,' Kerenza tried to draw her sister forward. 'They are waiting for us.'

Dulcie shook herself loose. 'Well, they'll just have to carry on waiting. We can't leave without Aruj. And I'm sure that once he sees how rough it is he'll say we shouldn't go at all. And I'll have walked all this way for nothing. I don't know what you were thinking of, Kerenza.'

Kerenza's heart hammered against her ribs. To get Dulcie into the boat, she had first to get her to the bottom of the ramp. She moistened her lips. 'I expect the prince is on his way. Look, while we wait, why don't we–'

A shot rang out. Kerenza gasped as chips of stone flew off the top of the wall a couple of feet behind Dulcie's head.

'What was that?' Dulcie said sharply. 'It sounded like–'

'Quickly,' Kerenza grabbed her sister. 'We can't stay here. It's not safe. We have to get down on to the beach.'

The crack of a second shot was followed by another *ping* as more chips flew from the wall.

Dulcie's shriek was lost amid a volley of gunfire. Kerenza's heart threatened to burst through her ribs. *Who? Why?* Then she realized that though the first two shots had come from somewhere above them, the rattling fusillade had come from a different direction, from below – *from the beach.* Please God let it be from *Kestrel's* cutter. Peering

344

anxiously over the wall, she saw two seamen kneeling on the sand and shingle, guns at their shoulders aiming toward the castle, as Nick raced up the beach towards the ramp. *Nick had armed the crew. Had he suspected this might happen?*

Instinctively ducking so she would offer a smaller target, Kerenza supported her whimpering sister down the slope. Another shot cracked. Dulcie jerked, screamed and fell. The sudden dragging weight pulled Kerenza to her knees and she toppled over, landing heavily on her right shoulder and bumping her head on the stone ramp. Everything went dark for an instant and her ears rang. She longed to just curl up and let whatever was going to happen take its course. But she couldn't.

'Dulcie?' she croaked, scrambling dizzily to her knees and crawling towards the crumpled groaning figure. The sound of running feet brought her head up. 'Oh, thank God,' she gasped, as Nick and two more seamen pounded up the slope. 'She's hurt, but I don't know where or how badly.'

'We'll worry about that once we get her on board the ship.' As the two seamen hefted Dulcie's semiconscious body between them and hurried back down the ramp, she felt herself lifted to her feet.

'Were you hit?' His voice sounded rough, strained.

She shook her head and wished she hadn't, clutching at him while the world spun and black dots hovered at the edges of her vision. 'N-no, just a bit shaken. I'm all right.'

'Of course you are,' he said drily.

Hearing the underlying tenderness, she was

345

torn between hysterical laughter and aching despair. She had to be all right, for Dulcie's sake, and her father's. Nick's arm encircled her waist and she felt as if she was melting. As he took her weight, she yearned to lean into him, hide her face against his chest, and let go of all the responsibilities she had never sought in the first place.

He urged her forward. 'Let's get out of here.'

'W-who – and why?' Kerenza stuttered through teeth chattering from shock. She could hardly believe what had happened. 'I thought – surely there was an agreement?'

'A nest of snakes, more like. Treacherous bastards,' Nick spat. 'Sorry,' he muttered, 'I shouldn't have–'

'But who would shoot at us?' Kerenza broke into his apology. She was not offended. Though she would not have used such words herself, she agreed with his sentiments.

'Take your choice. It could have been the governor's men, the chieftain's, the prince's, perhaps even the sultan's Bukharis if his spies have told him what's been going on.' Nick's jaw was tight, his eyes murderous. And despite the oppressive heat, Kerenza's skin tightened in a shiver.

'But why? We're leaving.'

'The only reason 1 can think of is that your sister's pregnancy is not only a personal embarrassment to the prince, it's also a possible threat to the sultan. Yes, she's leaving. But she's still carrying the prince's child. If your father decided to lodge a formal complaint through the British Government, it could cause all kinds of political problems.'

Clinging to Nick, for her legs felt like jelly, Kerenza tried to walk faster. He was right. They had to get away as quickly as possible. Hopefully the marksmen believed they had succeeded. But what if they realized Dulcie hadn't been killed? What might they try next? Kerenza's skin crawled and her muscles tensed in dread and anticipation of further shots. But none came.

Lifted into the cutter, she clambered shakily between the oarsmen to reach her sister who was huddled in the bow, her eyes closed, the dark red stain below her left shoulder shockingly vivid against the pristine whiteness of her *ha'ik*. Kerenza clung to the gunwale as the cutter reared, breasting the rollers as they curled and broke, then plunged into the trough behind. The men strained at their oars. Then the boat was through the surf and racing towards the packet.

Drawing the scarf away from her sister's ashen, pain-furrowed face, Kerenza took her hand. Dulcie's fingers tightened on hers and she tried to speak.

'We're nearly there,' Kerenza soothed. 'Then I can make you properly comfortable.'

'Aruj?' Dulcie managed weakly.

Kerenza drew a deep breath. The only comfort she could offer her sister was to keep on lying. 'He'll be here soon.'

Carried below by Broad and Toy, Dulcie was laid gently on the lower bunk in the cabin previously occupied by the Woodrows. Reassuring Kerenza that her father, though groggy, was otherwise in good health and asking for his dinner, Broad brought Kerenza's box from the

347

trunk in her cabin, then hurried away to fetch hot water.

Kerenza stripped off her scarf and *ha'ik*. Then she took out her scissors and extended the tear made by the ball through Dulcie's blood-soaked garments. She gritted her teeth and with trembling hands carefully peeled back the layers of sodden cloth to expose the wound.

Dulcie moaned, moving restlessly. 'K'renza?' her voice was cracked and weak. 'It hurts.'

A furrow had been gouged through the soft flesh above Dulcie's right breast and across the front of her shoulder. But as Kerenza examined the wound she released her breath in a ragged sigh of relief.

'Indeed, I'm sure it must do. The gash is deep. But at least the ball didn't lodge.' Fresh blood oozed from the raw edges and welled from the furrow, dribbling over Dulcie's white skin. 'As soon as I've bathed it and put a bandage on, I'll ask Broad to bring a cup of tea. Then I'll see if I can find something that will ease the pain. You've had a nasty shock.'

There was a brief knock and, as Kerenza glanced over her shoulder, the door opened and Broad, his face carefully averted, held out a steaming jug.

'How's she doing, miss? Mr Penrose want to know if 'tis serious.'

Wiping her hands on the ruined *ha'ik*, Kerenza took the hot water. 'N-not as bad as it might have been, but–'

Suddenly, Dulcie gave a loud cry that ended with a hiss as she sucked air in through her clenched teeth.

Whirling round, Kerenza saw Dulcie was curled on her side, her knees drawn up. Her arms cradled her belly and her face contorted in a rictus of agony. 'It *hurts.*'

Kerenza stared at her sister. She knew at once. But she didn't want to believe. *Not now, not on top of everything else.* What had started it: the fall? The shock of being shot at? The physical damage caused by the injury? *What did it matter?* She clapped her free hand to her mouth, to smother the scream she could feel swelling in her chest.

Dulcie panted, her voice climbing in terror. 'The pain– I can't– Kerenza, do something. Make it stop!'

Kerenza cleared her throat, trying to quell her own panic as she turned to the steward, keeping her voice low. 'I think the baby's coming.'

'Bleddy hell,' Broad muttered. 'What can I do, miss?'

'She needs a doctor.'

'I'll tell Mr Penrose directly. But with the wind against us it might take a day or more to reach Gibraltar,' Broad shook his head. 'Be all right, will you, miss? Only there isn't no one–' He broke off with a helpless shrug.

There was no one else. She would have to manage. Kerenza struggled for control, tried to think. 'M-more hot water. And ask Maggot for some of that *kif* potion he made for Lady Russell.'

'Two shakes, miss.' The steward disappeared, closing the door.

Another loud, panicky cry drew Kerenza towards the bunk. 'Where's Aruj? Has he come yet?'

'Not yet,' Kerenza poured water into the basin and started tearing the *ha'ik* into strips. 'I'm going to put some honey on your shoulder. It will–' She stopped as Dulcie jerked, her eyes wide, the contraction so severe she didn't even have the breath to scream.

A wave of panic swept through Kerenza leaving her drenched in perspiration. It was all happening too fast. Something was wrong. *Everything was wrong.* She took her sister's hand. Dulcie gripped it tightly, panting as the pain receded.

'Where is he? He should be here by now. What's keeping him?' she moaned, as Kerenza wrung out a cloth and gently bathed the wound.

'He did say he had important business to take care of.' Kerenza's voice shook. She shouldn't have to do this. She wasn't a midwife. Nor was she a practised liar. Except that wasn't true. She had lied to Nick about her reasons for leaving her family. And she had lied to herself about not loving him. But Dulcie was her sister and had gone into labour. She couldn't leave her. So she would have to go on lying about the prince. 'I think your baby is on its way.'

'No!' Dulcie wailed. 'It can't be. I have to meet the sultan. Do something, Kerenza.'

What was she supposed to do? How could she stop nature? There was a knock on the door.

'Aruj?' Dulcie gasped. Kerenza turned away from the desperate hope on her sister's face. Scrambling to her feet she lurched across the tilting cabin to open it. Broad handed her a wooden bucket containing another jug of steaming water.

'So it won't fall over,' he said. 'Anyhow, I thought you'll prob'ly be needing the bucket.' He handed her a cup. 'I've told the cap'n – Mr Penrose. He's making for Gib. And this here's Mr Maggot's brew.' He winced, backing away as Dulcie's voice climbed in another scream. 'Dear life, in some bad way, she is.'

From then on things got worse. Dulcie spat out the first mouthful, shuddering and shrieking that Kerenza was trying to poison her. Setting the cup down and wedging it so it wouldn't tip as the ship rose and plunged, Kerenza concentrated instead on trying to bandage the wound with a honey-smeared pad to aid healing and minimize the risk of infection. But Dulcie's crying and thrashing about made it very difficult.

Two more wrenching contractions had her begging for relief and she allowed Kerenza to support her head while she gulped down half a cupful of the dark liquid. But even as Kerenza released a breath of relief, Dulcie vomited it up again all over Kerenza's muslin gown.

'Where is Aruj?' she sobbed. 'Has he come yet?'

Kerenza had to bite her tongue to stop herself shouting out the truth: that he hadn't come, wasn't coming, and never intended to come. But though telling Dulcie the truth might relieve a little of her own strain, what would it do to her sister? Wasn't she suffering enough? What kind of person would deliberately inflict even more pain?

'Even if he has,' she managed though teeth clenched to stop them chattering from nerves and stress, 'this is no place for a man.'

Later – it might have been one hour, it might

351

have been three, Kerenza had no way of knowing – Dulcie clutched her hand with cold slippery fingers.

'I can't go on with this.' Her voice was hoarse. Cracked lips peeled back from her teeth as another pain overwhelmed her. Too weak and exhausted to scream she could only groan, low and deep like an animal. The contractions were close now, and each one left her shaking violently. Her skin glistened, dark shadows encircled her eyes, and blood smeared her fissured lips. Then she curled her body and her face contorted with effort.

Kerenza barely had time to lay the wadded *ha'ik* beneath her. 'Come on, Dulcie,' she urged. 'Push. The baby's nearly here.'

A few minutes later a dusky, slippery little body slid into Kerenza's waiting hands. As she laid the baby on a clean piece of the torn *ha'ik*, tears cascaded down her cheeks. The contrast between this child's arrival in the world – *unwanted, an inconvenience* to its father – and the little girl born to Judith Russell and her husband was unbearably poignant.

Swallowing hard, she wiped her eyes with the back of her hand. Then tying the cord in two places she cut it. Little legs kicked and fists waved as the baby gave a lusty wail. Folding the cloth around the small body, she lifted the bundle and bent over her semi-conscious sister.

'Dulcie? You have a beautiful son.'

Dulcie turned her sweat-damp head on the pillow as Kerenza placed the baby against her side. She glanced at him. 'You hurt me,' she accused. Then she looked up, pleading, desperate.

'Aruj?' She tensed, shuddering as another contraction seized her.

'Later,' Kerenza soothed. 'We're not quite finished yet.'

'No more,' Dulcie sobbed. 'I can't–' She strained again, shaking with effort. But nothing happened.

Remembering what she had read in the book, one of the few sentences that offered practical advice, Kerenza placed her hand gently on her sister's lower abdomen. The flesh was spongy and flaccid beneath her palm. Then she felt the muscle beneath begin to harden as the next contraction began, and gently pressed down with the heel of her hand. Dulcie gasped her eyes suddenly wide as the afterbirth slid out.

'There, it's all over–' Kerenza started to reassure, but the words died on her tongue as it was followed by a sudden gush of blood. For an instant she simply stared, frozen in horror and disbelief. Then she dived forward, grabbing handfuls of cloth, trying to staunch the flow. *Was it her fault? Had she caused it? Should she not have tried to help?* 'It's all right, Dulcie,' she babbled, her mouth and throat as dry as ashes. 'It'll be all right.' *How could she stop it? What should she do?*

'K'renza?' Dulcie whispered, reaching out, then letting her hand fall back on to the rough dark blanket.

'Just a minute.' Dropping the dripping wad of cloth into the bucket, Kerenza seized another handful, overwhelmed by dread as it swiftly turned crimson. *Too much blood.*

'Now!' Dulcie's voice cracked with effort, and the baby continued to cry in tiny shuddering wails.

Kerenza's heart was beating so fast she felt as if a bird was trapped in her chest, frantic, terrified, and desperate to escape. She didn't want to listen. She couldn't cope with any more.

'Please,' Dulcie whispered.

Kerenza flinched. It was the first time in her life she had ever heard Dulcie say that word. Wiping her wet red hands on a remnant of cloth she knelt beside the bunk.

'Hold my hand,' Dulcie whispered.

As her sister's fingers closed on hers, Kerenza's vision blurred and she felt hot tears spill down her face as she thought of all the wasted years, the unhappiness they had both suffered.

'He's not coming, is he.' It wasn't a question.

Kerenza's chest jerked as she swallowed a sob. What good would the truth do now? 'I–'

Dulcie wasn't listening. 'Too tired. The baby – don't let – you must – he's yours...' Her voice faltered and her tongue moved slowly over her cracked lips.

No, Kerenza howled in her head. She didn't want this responsibility. She didn't want all the problems it would bring. *She didn't want to lose Nick.*

'Promise me.' Dulcie's heavy-lidded gaze was fever bright.

Kerenza looked down at the jet-black hair, skin the colour of milky coffee, and the tiny face, eyes tight shut, mouth open as he cried. She had helped him into the world. He was her sister's

354

child, her own flesh and blood. *If not her, then who? The baby was innocent, as much a victim of circumstance as she was. If she refused, how would she live with herself?*

'Promise.' Dulcie's eyelids drooped. But her grip remained steadfast, as if all her strength was concentrated in that one hand.

Blinded by tears that came straight from her heart, Kerenza let go of the dreams she had clung to through all that had happened since she boarded *Kestrel* in Falmouth harbour. 'I promise.'

Dulcie's grip slackened and her eyes closed. After a few moments she gave a gentle sigh.

'Dulcie?' Kerenza whispered, not wanting to believe what every instinct and the subtle change in her sister's stillness were telling her.

Releasing her sister's hand she picked up the baby. Holding him close, she rocked to and fro in an agony too deep even for tears as she grieved for their past and her future.

After a while she roused herself, and after washing and swaddling the baby in lengths cut from her *ha'ik* she laid him on the top bunk. Then she gently straightened her sister's limbs, pulled the torn shift and caftan down, and covered her with the blanket. *Another birth another death.*

She had almost finished cleaning up the mess when a knock on the door made her jump. 'Yes?' she called, tired to the depths of her soul. She looked round expecting the steward, but Nick stood in the doorway.

'I wondered – I heard the child cry – but when you didn't come out – is everything all right?'

Turning away, Kerenza covered her face with

both hands. She heard his footfall, felt his hands on her shoulders.

'Kerenza?' His tone was wary, anxious. Then she felt his grip tighten, heard his intake of breath as he looked past her to the blanket-shrouded figure on the bottom bunk. 'She's *dead?*'

Unable to speak, Kerenza simply nodded. She felt herself turned, felt his arms encircle her, gently, tenderly. She held herself rigid, longing to relax into his embrace, not daring to. Accepting comfort now would make coping without it even harder.

'I don't know what to say,' he sounded helpless. 'But one thing I am sure of, you'll have done your very best for her.' Anger hardened his voice. 'Not that she deserved it. You should never have had to go through all this. The way your family – it was wicked. And it wasn't only them, was it? The grief I've caused you will haunt me to my dying day.'

'Please.' Kerenza broke free, clinging to the bunk with one hand while she wiped her face with the other. 'Please don't say any more. It's too– I can't–'

'Forgive me. I shouldn't have – it's just – you see, I thought I knew you.' His tone was wry, self-mocking. 'But I was wrong, I didn't, not properly, not until this past four weeks. When I think of all that's happened on the voyage and how you've dealt with everything that's been thrown at you – Mrs Woodrow's spite, Captain Penrose's death, your father's behaviour, helping Lady Russell give birth, and then this – Kerenza Vyvyan, you put me – all of us – to shame.'

'*Please,*' she begged, as grief clogged her throat. He didn't know it, but every word of admiration drove another nail into her heart. She didn't deserve them. She had done what was necessary because there had been no one else to do it. She had given her word to Dulcie because there was no one else Dulcie could ask. And that promise was breaking her heart.

'Oh God, I'm sorry, I didn't mean to upset you. Is the child all right?'

She struggled for control. 'A healthy little boy.' Looking at the bundle in the top bunk she sucked in a tremulous breath. 'Now I have to tell my father.'

'Not about the baby. He already knows.'

'He does? But – how?'

'I told him.' As shock, relief, and gratitude brought her head up again, he lifted one shoulder. 'Your sister's screaming – it was obvious there was far more going on than treatment of a flesh wound. Besides, it wasn't your responsibility.'

She moistened her lips. 'Neither was it yours.'

'Perhaps not. But when your father receives bad news he blames whoever delivers it. I won't have him blaming you. You don't deserve it. And you've already been through enough – too much.'

Kerenza bent her head, fighting more tears. He had done that for her. *How could she bear it?*

'How did he take the news?'

'Not well, though he was more shaken than angry. He was relieved your sister had not been forcibly – but he was horrified that she could have welcomed – or allowed herself to–' With an

357

embarrassed cough Nick flapped one hand. 'He's in my day cabin. Toy's with him, letting him talk. Look, leave all this now. You've done everything you can for the time being. Let me escort you to the saloon. You ought to eat something. It's been hours since–'

'I couldn't eat.' Kerenza plucked at the skirt of her vomit-stained and blood-smeared dress and shook her head. 'And I'm not fit to be seen.'

'You're brave and lovely,' he said softly.

So he should not see her wretched tears, she turned to the bunk and lifted the baby whose mournful cry wrenched her heart.

'What's wrong with him?'

The unease in Nick's voice helped Kerenza regain control of her emotions. 'He's hungry, poor little mite. Do you think Broad would mind if I asked for half a cup of goat's milk diluted with a little boiling water?'

'You could ask Broad for the moon he'd try to get it for you,' Nick said drily. He stood back for her to precede him out of the cabin.

In the passage she sucked in a deep breath that tasted cool and wonderfully fresh. She hadn't realized how thick, tainted and cloying the air in the cabin had become. Would she ever get the stench of blood out of her nostrils? She hesitated. 'I need a clean handkerchief, to use as a – to feed the baby.'

'In your trunk? I'll fetch it. You go and sit down.'

Too tired to protest, she went into the saloon and slid into the seat nearest the door just as Broad came out of the galley.

'I thought I heard–' He glanced at the baby. 'All right is it? Poor little mite.' Sighing, he shook his head. 'How's Miss Vyvyan? Had some time of it, she did.'

Kerenza swallowed. 'Sh-she didn't – it was too–' Her voice broke and she bent over the baby. For as long as she could remember her life had been shaped by Dulcie's selfishness and her mother's resentment. Living at her grandmother's, loved and valued, had been a revelation. Then she had met Nick. After the terrible misunderstanding that had parted them and almost destroyed her, the voyage had forced them once more into each other's company. Slowly, tentatively, they had both reached out across the gulf of hurt and anger, recognizing qualities in each other they would never have discovered had it not been for the hardships and crises forced upon them by events. But now once again *Dulcie's* choices, *Dulcie's* actions, were shaping her life.

'Dear life, I'm some sorry, miss.' The steward's voice echoed his shock. 'What's going to happen to the little 'un?'

She heard Nick's approaching footsteps. Once she spoke the words out loud it would be real. There would be no going back. She swallowed again, lifted her chin. *She had no choice.* 'I shall raise him in my sister's place.'

'Broad,' Nick said from the doorway behind her, 'Miss Vyvyan needs half a cup of goat's milk topped up with boiling water for the baby.'

'Right you are, sir.' As the steward disappeared, Nick dropped the freshly laundered square of cambric on the table, pulled out the chair and sat facing her.

'Is that really what you want?' he asked quietly. 'And I don't mean the bloody goat's milk. I'm talking about' – he nodded towards the swaddled bundle nestled against her breast.

Kerenza looked down at the baby who was just a blur, not daring to blink in case falling tears betrayed her. Anguish closed her throat and she had to clear it before she could speak. She couldn't lie to him. It wasn't what she *wanted*. It was what she had to do. His implied admiration and respect touched her deeply. But what she longed for, *craved*, was his love. And he had not even hinted at such a possibility. Certainly he would not want her now. So she must let him walk away with a clear conscience. It would be her farewell gift. She forced herself to glance up.

'I gave Dulcie my promise.' But she couldn't hold his gaze and bent her head once more over the baby.

There was a pause before he spoke. 'I see.'

Broad returned with the milk and water and set it down in the angle between the fiddle rails where the tilt of the ship held it steady.

Taking the cambric square, Kerenza folded it into a cone, dipped the point in the cup and tested the temperature on the inside of her wrist. Then she dripped the liquid into the baby's mouth, an involuntary smile tilting her trembling lips at the sucking sounds he made.

Nick stood up, tucked the chair beneath the table, and moved away to speak quietly to the steward. Then as Broad returned to the galley, Nick hesitated beside her.

'I will tell your father about – what's happened.'

'Thank you,' she whispered without raising her head.

'When you've finished, Broad will bring you some hot food. You may not feel like eating, but you must try. For the child's sake.'

Recoiling inwardly from the anger that edged his tone, Kerenza focused her whole attention on feeding the baby who was far too absorbed to notice the occasional teardrop falling on to his downy cheek.

Half an hour later the cup was almost empty. Holding the baby against her shoulder, Kerenza gently rubbed and patted his back. His forehead was warm and she could feel his quick light breaths against her neck.

'All done is he?' Broad asked from the doorway. And as she nodded, he disappeared, returning a few moments later with a steaming bowl of lamb stew and a spoon. 'Here you are, miss. You get that down. Do you good, it will.'

Kerenza gazed at the food. She felt more queasy than hungry. But that was probably because it was more than eight hours since her last meal. Her stomach gurgled and Broad pulled out the chair, then held out his arms.

'Give him here, miss. I'll hold him for you. 'Tis all right, I know what I'm doing,' he grinned. 'Had two strapping boys of my own, I did. Both gone now, God rest 'em. One was took with the croup when he was no more'n a toddler. T'other one, Eddie, was lost when the *Mary-Jane* went down with all hands. Nineteen, he was. Broke his mother's heart it did. She wasn't never the same after that. Two years later she was gone.'

'Oh, Mr Broad, I'm so sorry.' Kerenza was appalled. She'd had no idea.

'Well, 'twas a long time ago, miss. But you don't forget. C'mon, give him here.'

'Thank you.' She transferred the baby and Broad sat down.

'Right, now' – he indicated the bowl with a nod – 'don't let it go cold.'

You don't forget. Kerenza looked at the stew, and recalled in vivid detail Zohra's house and the first meal she had shared with Nick, strange delicious food they had eaten with their fingers. *She would never do that again. But nothing and no one could take away her memories. Those were hers for as long as she lived.*

She picked up the spoon. The first mouthful was hard to swallow, but the second seemed to trigger her hunger. By the time she had eaten half what was in the bowl she felt far less jangled, though suddenly very tired. Which wasn't really surprising considering all that had happened since leaving Zohra's that morning.

Putting down the spoon she sat back. 'Thank you, Mr Broad, that was very tasty.'

'Glad you enjoyed it, miss. Feel all the better for it, you will.'

Hearing footsteps on the companionway, she pushed herself to her feet, surprised at the effort it took. 'I think I'll go to my cabin.'

'Good idea, miss. You go on ahead, I'll bring the babby.'

'Yes. Thank you.' She swayed, and grabbed the door surround to steady herself. There was a strange buzzing in her ears, like a swarm of bees. Her legs were tingling and the floor felt soft, as if she were walking on cushions. Ahead of her a tall figure filled the passage. The darkness that had been hovering at the edge of her vision closed in. *Nick.* She started to reach out, heard a warning shout, and tipped forward into oblivion.

Chapter Twenty One

The blackness lightened, but she hadn't the strength to open her eyes. Panic stirred. But a distant voice, low-pitched and familiar, murmured reassurance and the brief anxiety released its grip. An arm slid under her shoulders, supporting her head. A cup was pressed gently against her lips and she tasted cool honey-sweetened liquid. It coated her dry throat, eased her thirst, and she kept on swallowing. Then the arm withdrew, she sank into the pillow and drifted away once more into welcoming darkness.

The next time she floated to the surface her eyes opened easily and she saw pale light above the gap in the door. Turning on to her back she stretched, feeling more rested than she had for weeks. Yet the fact that it was still daylight meant she could not have slept for very long. The meal had obviously been just what she needed. In fact, she was still surprisingly hungry. *The baby.* Throwing back the blanket she stood up and peered into the top bunk. Neatly folded, her apple-green muslin lay towards the foot of the bunk. She snatched it up. It smelled of soap and fresh air. *Dulcie had been sick on it.* The stain had gone. The gown was clean, if a little creased.

Where was the baby? Even as panic fizzed along her veins, common sense reasoned that someone else would be looking after him while she slept. He was probably with Broad, or Toy, or maybe even her father. *Her father.* She clung to the wooden support of the upper bunk. She must go to her father. Her skin tightened in a shiver and glancing down she realized she was clad only in her shift. She couldn't remember undressing. She couldn't even remember coming to her cabin. She rubbed her face. Her head felt full of clouds.

She stumbled across to the nightstand. The water in the jug was lukewarm. *Who had brought that in?* A wash refreshed her but did nothing to allay her confusion. Opening her trunk she pulled out a clean shift and stockings then put on the green muslin. After brushing and coiling her hair, she buttoned her short wool jacket. Then she opened the cabin door.

As she hesitated, she saw Toy emerge from the captain's day cabin. Closing the door behind him, he hurried towards her. He was smiling. Yet though she sensed he intended to reassure, she felt suddenly nervous.

'Feeling better are you, miss?'

'Yes, thank you. Much better.'

'Mr Penrose'll be glad to hear that. In the day cabin he is. Your father's with him. I 'spect you'd like to see them first. Then you'll be ready for a cup of something and a bite to eat.'

'Yes, thank you. Oh, and will you bring some milk for the baby? Mr Broad will tell you–'

'Don't you worry 'bout that, miss. 'Tis all took care of.' Toy hurried past her, towards the saloon and the galley.

Kerenza's heartbeat quickened as she approached the day cabin. She could hear Nick speaking, but he had pitched his voice too low for her to hear the actual words. Would her father hold her responsible for Dulcie's death? She had done her best, done what she believed was the right thing, but ... *when had that ever been enough*. How had he reacted to the baby? Of course he would have been shocked, and grief-stricken. But would his anger at Dulcie be tempered by her death, and by the realization that this baby boy was his grandson? *The only grandchild he would ever have.*

Even though Nick was now beyond her reach, he was the only man she had ever – would ever – love. To marry anyone else, have children with anyone else – she couldn't. Drawing a deep breath, she knocked on the door.

Nick opened it. He scanned her face, frowning slightly, his expression unreadable. Beneath his scrutiny she felt her face grow hot. As she dropped her gaze he stood back. 'Come in.'

Her father sat on the far bench seat facing her, his forearms resting on the table, linked fingers tightly clasped. Deep grooves bracketed his nose and mouth. The flesh beneath his red-rimmed eyes was bagged and puffy. He had aged a great deal in the past two weeks. Behind her, Kerenza heard the door close, then felt Nick's palm warm

365

beneath her elbow as he urged her gently forward. His touch was both comfort and torture.

'Papa.' She tried to smile. He nodded.

'Kerenza.'

She glanced from her father to Nick. 'Where' – she swallowed –'where's the baby?'

'He's safe and well,' Nick replied. 'Please, sit down.'

She sat on the bench seat opposite her father. Then as Nick gestured for her to move further in, and eased down beside her, effectively blocking her exit, her heart started to thump heavily. *What was going on?*

'It must be time for his feed. I really ought to–'

'Kerenza,' Nick interrupted gently, and her first reaction was astonishment that he should address her with such familiarity in front of her father. Her surprise deepened with the realization that her father, usually so strict in such matters, did not even appear to have noticed. 'The baby is no longer on board. He was taken ashore at Gibraltar. And' – he swallowed audibly – 'and so was Dulcie.'

Kerenza stared at him in bewilderment. 'I don't understand. They can't have. You're not making any sense. We haven't reached Gibraltar yet.'

As her father sat back with a slow sigh, Nick rested his own clasped hands on the table. 'How long do you think you've slept?'

'I don't know,' she shrugged, confused and defensive. 'But it can't have been long because it's still light.'

'Kerenza.' The tenderness in his voice unsettled her even more. He shouldn't be talking to her like

366

this. *It was too painful.* Besides, her father would get angry and blame her, and it wasn't her fault.

'Kerenza? Are you listening? You have been asleep for two days. We left Gibraltar twenty-four hours ago.'

Two days? 'No, that's not possible. I don't believe–' *He wouldn't lie.* She heard herself swallow. 'But I couldn't have – not for that long. Not unless–' As she realized she turned to Nick, appalled. Shock reduced her voice to a whisper. 'You drugged me.'

'Don't blame him,' William Vyvyan intervened, before Nick could respond. 'It was my idea. Best for everyone.' He stopped, his mouth trembling, and gestured to Nick. 'You tell her. But I want it clearly understood, the decision was mine.'

'Acting on your father's instructions, as soon as we reached Gibraltar, Maggot took the baby to Lady Russell. Within an hour she had found a wet-nurse for him: the sister of one of her household staff. The woman is in her late twenties and married to a fisherman. She's strong and healthy, an experienced mother with three other children, the youngest four months old. Lady Russell has promised to arrange for the baby's adoption. He will go to a local family where he will be safe and loved, and no one will ever know his background. Your father thought it was the wisest and kindest thing to do.' After a moment's hesitation he added, 'Not just for the baby, but for everyone concerned.'

Kerenza sat very straight, her hands gripped tightly in her lap. His slight emphasis on the word everyone drew her glance sideways. She didn't

367

know what to think or how she felt. Who was *everyone?* It might have been best for her father. He would be spared further shame and none of their acquaintance would ever learn of Dulcie's love-child. But what about her?

She had been the person most closely involved. She had delivered the baby. She had promised Dulcie she would raise him, then watched her sister die. It had cost her dearly to sacrifice her own dreams to the needs of a helpless baby who had no one else to care for him. She had gone to sleep believing her future planned. Not the future she had hoped for, but one in which she would have done her very best to give the baby a good start in life. Now suddenly everything had changed. Decisions had been made and carried out without her knowledge. And the baby was already living with someone else.

As all this raced through her head her emotions seesawed between loss and shame-tinged relief, but she said nothing. She dared not, for she might betray herself. Perhaps for the baby's sake it was indeed all for the best. But where did it leave her? She felt disoriented and totally bereft.

Her father cleared his throat, his gaze darting to Nick then back to her. 'Kerenza, while she was alive Dulcie made your life a misery. I should have stopped it, but to my shame I did nothing. Now she's dead. And I grieve for her and for your mother. But what Dulcie asked of you was grossly unfair. I could not allow her to continue blighting your life.'

Kerenza reached impulsively across the table. 'Papa–'

'No, my dear.' He pushed himself wearily to his feet. 'For once in my life I have done the right thing. Though I hope one day to be worthy of your forgiveness, you must allow me to suffer a little longer. I deserve it. And now if you'll excuse me, I shall go to my cabin. I'm ... very tired.'

Nick stood up. But as Kerenza started to follow, he laid one hand on her shoulder, his voice quiet but intense. 'Please stay. There are things that – I need to – please?'

Kerenza looked quickly at her father.

'I forfeited any right to your obedience a long time ago, Kerenza,' William Vyvyan said. 'But for what it's worth, my advice is that you listen to what Mr Penrose has to say. He and I have talked a great deal this past two days. Though I think it more truthful to say that he talked and I listened. Perhaps if I had done so sooner– The point is I have found him to be a man of uncommon good sense.'

Stunned, Kerenza sank back on to the padded seat. Her father *listened*? How had Nick achieved such a thing? What had he found to talk about with her father? Dulcie, presumably. But clearly their conversations had made a deep impression. She had never known her father admit to being wrong. As for asking her forgiveness, she was still finding it hard to believe he had actually done so. But with her mother and sister dead, there were only the two of them now.

As the door closed, Kerenza gazed down at her hands. She could feel her heart thumping painfully against her ribs. Its quickened rhythm drowned the sounds of the ship.

After shutting the door on William's departing figure, Nick leaned against it, looking across the cabin at Kerenza. Her back was straight and stiff with tension. But her bent head reminded him of a flower too heavy for its stem. Between her coiled hair and the black velvet collar of her jacket her pale neck looked so vulnerable. Yet she had shown more courage, more stamina, than he would have imagined possible.

He recalled William Vyvyan's shock at being told a few necessary home truths about his attitudes and behaviour towards his younger daughter.

At first the older man had reacted with fury at being addressed in such a manner. But as, one after another, the accusations hit home: facts he could not deny or excuse, his anger and bluster were silenced by appalled realization.

When William Vyvyan had finally accepted responsibility for his own part in his younger daughter's unhappiness, Nick had changed the subject, making it clear that while he would appreciate William's approval, he did not consider it necessary. Nor would he allow *anything* to stand in his way. William's response had been shamed silence and the tentative offer of his hand. Nick had clasped it.

He cleared his throat. 'When I saw you with Lady Russell's baby, and then with your sister's child, it was very clear to me that – that when the time comes you will be a good and loving mother.' Kerenza turned her head slowly to look at him, her expression wary almost fearful. He gathered his courage. He couldn't stop now. He

370

had to know.

'The thing is, I mean, what I'm afraid of–' He stopped.

'Afraid?' Kerenza blurted. '*You?*'

Her incredulity made him smile, and that eased a little of his tension. 'Oh yes,' he nodded wryly. 'I *am* afraid, Kerenza. I'd sooner face a French privateer than–' He broke off.

'Afraid of what?'

Pushing himself away from the door, he crossed the cabin in two strides and sat down opposite her. Resting his elbows on the table, he pressed his steepled fingers against his mouth. 'That you would prefer a husband who comes home to you each evening.' He watched her eyes widen, and plunged on.

'Since I was a child my ambition has been to own and command a packet ship.'

'I know,' she said softly. 'You told me.'

'And over the past twenty years, through school, apprenticeship, and working my way up to getting my mate's ticket, I've had little time or interest for anything else. But what I've come to realize is that without you–' He took a deep breath then, laying his hands flat on the table, looked across at her again. 'At first I wanted to do it to make Sam proud of me: Sam and my mother. But now – now I want to do it for you. Without you beside me it won't mean– You're a remarkable girl, Kerenza. I – I don't deserve you, I know that. But if you'll have me I'll do my best to make you happy.'

Hope turned to horror as he saw her eyes fill. Two huge tears trembled on her lashes, spilled

371

over, and left shining silver tracks down her cheeks. Then with a relief that made his insides quiver like jelly, he realized she was smiling.

'Do you love me, Nick?' she asked softly.

He blinked, astonished and bemused by the question. 'Of course I love you. Surely you know that?'

'No. How could I know it? You hide your emotions too well.' Her smile softened the reproach.

He lifted one shoulder shyly. 'I loved you before we – before I – only I didn't know it then. I didn't trust what I felt. It had all happened so fast. I couldn't believe – but to hurt you the way I did was unforgivable. I swear to God, Kerenza.'

Reaching across the table she laid her fingers gently on his mouth, silencing him. 'That's in the past. What matters is now, and the future.'

'C-could you love me? Even after–'

'I do love you, Nick. The night we met at the Antrims' party–' He watched her face turn deep rose, but her gaze remained steady on his. 'I fell in love with you then. And I never stopped loving you.'

He gazed at her, finding it hard to believe what she was saying. 'Not even when–?'

'Not even then.' Her mouth quirked wryly. 'Oh I tried to. I tried very hard.' She shrugged. 'But I couldn't. And when my father told me we were sailing aboard *Kestrel*–' Her gaze dropped for a moment and she shook her head. 'I didn't know how I would bear it.' She looked up again, her eyes glistening. 'But if I hadn't come we wouldn't be together like this now.'

Seizing her hand he clasped it between both of

his, pressing his lips to her knuckles. 'Will you marry me, Kerenza?' Watching her closely, he saw joy flare in her eyes and felt his heart swell with pride, relief and a happiness that matched her own. Then a faint shadow crossed her face.

'I will, Nick. But–'

As the tip of her pink tongue darted out to moisten her lips, his muscles tightened in apprehension.

'But?'

'Nick, I don't want us to live apart, me back in Flushing or Falmouth, while you are away at sea.' She hesitated, and her colour deepened. 'If you can't come home each night, then I want to sail with you. I know it's dangerous, but I would rather be here at your side than back home in Cornwall waiting for news.'

'But the war.'

'Dearest Nick.' She laid her soft palm against the side of his face. 'I would rather die with you than live without you.'

Standing, he leaned across the table and, cupping her face in his hands, covered her mouth with his own in a kiss that let go of the past and cemented their future. When eventually he raised his head, her eyes were closed, her lips warm and moist, her cheeks rosy. She had never looked more desirable. A knock on the door made him curse under his breath as he forced himself to release her.

Her eyes opened and she smiled.

'All right?' he murmured. And when she nodded, he called, 'Yes?'

The door opened and Toy entered carrying a

373

tray. 'I've brung some tea and some bread and butter for Miss Vyvyan,' he announced. Setting the tray down, he frowned at Kerenza. 'You need your food, miss. Got to keep your strength up.'

'Thank you, Mr Toy. That's very thoughtful of you.'

Catching her eye, Nick saw her bite her lip in an effort to keep a straight face. He saw the servant's pleasure at the warmth in her voice. Some sailors believed that a woman aboard a ship was unlucky. As far as *Kestrel* and her crew were concerned, Kerenza Vyvyan's presence had proved to be a blessing.

'Toy?'

'Sir?'

'Ask the bosun to send the carpenter down, will you?'

'Aye, sir.' He closed the door.

'Would you like me to leave?' Kerenza offered.

Nick shook his head. 'No. In fact I'd like your opinion.'

'On what?' Dark shadows beneath her eyes betrayed all she had suffered during recent months, but there was glowing colour in her cheeks and her gaze sparkled. *God, he loved her.*

'If the post office and the rest of the share-holders agree to me remaining in command of *Kestrel*, I want some alterations made in here before we leave Falmouth on our next trip.'

'What kind of alterations?' Her expression was bright with interest.

He indicated the curtain. 'That cot is barely big enough for one. And I have no desire to begin our married life sleeping alone, do you?'

374

Her blush deepened but she met his gaze squarely as she shook her head. He bent down towards her. But just as his lips brushed hers, feet clattered on the companionway and knuckles rapped on the door.

Kerenza giggled and despite a frustration he guessed would cause him considerable discomfort during the next few weeks, Nick welcomed the sound. No one deserved happiness and laughter more than she did. Rolling his eyes, he moved away from her and the table, and called the carpenter to come in.

'I wish it might not have been like this,' Aurelia Danby sighed, as she inspected her granddaughter.

'I know, Nana,' Kerenza pressed her hands to her midriff. She felt excited rather than nervous. 'But it suits us, truly. A big wedding would have been impossible while the family is in mourning.'

'Wait a year?' Nick had barked. 'Just to satisfy our families' desire for a big show? Is that what you want? Because if it is—'

She watched his fingers curl into his palms as he forced the words out.

'If it is, then of course we'll wait.'

Knowing what it had cost him to make that offer, she held in her laughter and, taking his hand, pressed it to her cheek. 'No, Nick. It's not. I want a quiet ceremony. And I'd like it as soon as possible, so I can sail with you when *Kestrel* leaves.'

Grasping her shoulders, he had kissed her hard. 'God, what did I do to deserve you?' Then raising his head he had held her away, frowning as he searched her eyes. 'You are sure, Kerenza? My sisters' weddings were big affairs with crowds of guests–'

'And I hope they were a joy for everyone involved,' she had interrupted. 'But I am not your sisters. I'm me. And what they had is not what I want. Nick, it's our wedding. My father has given his consent, you have bought the special licence, so surely when and where we marry is no one's business but ours? A quiet ceremony at Nana's house, followed by a small wedding breakfast will be perfect. Then if we attend Maud Tregenna's ball in the evening, anyone who wants to celebrate with us may do so there.'

'I love you,' he had whispered.

Kerenza smiled at the memory. 'Besides, Nana, there wouldn't have been time to arrange a big occasion even if I had wanted one, which I don't.'

Regal in dove-grey silk trimmed with lace Aurelia sighed. 'It's just – I'm so proud of you.' She dabbed her eyes with a wisp of cambric then tucked it out of sight and tilted her chin. 'Are you ready?'

With a last look in the mirror to check her high-waisted gown of lilac silk, Kerenza touched her mother's pearls, then turned. 'Yes, Nana. I'm ready.'

As she entered the drawing-room where the parson was waiting together with Nick's mother, her father, and Maggot, her eyes met Nick's and her heart swelled. Tall and handsome in his best uniform, he looked up. His frown cleared and he smiled. He held out his hand and as she reached his side, she took it.

Chapter Twenty Two

Maude Tregenna's expression reflected her inner battle between delighted welcome and commiseration. 'My dear Kerenza, and Nicholas. No, I must call you Captain and Mrs Penrose now. I'm so glad you've come. These past weeks must have been truly dreadful for you, Kerenza. To lose your mother and your sister – but I'll say no more. Tonight your friends will want to wish you both every happiness.'

'You're very kind,' Kerenza smiled, glancing at her husband of six hours. A delicious thrill shivered through her.

'Indeed, ma'am.' Nick bent over his hostess's hand.

'I understand you sail again tomorrow, Captain?'

'We do, ma'am.'

As Nick's hand gently squeezed her elbow, Kerenza felt her heart leap. It had been wonderful to see her grandmother again. And everyone in the village had been very sympathetic about her mother and sister. Inevitably, news of her wedding to Nick had leaked out, as had the information that she would be sailing with him. That had certainly set tongues wagging.

'Are you quite sure, my dear?' Aurelia had asked, gripping both Kerenza's hands, and looking into her eyes.

'About marrying Nick, or about sailing with him?' Kerenza had smiled.

'Both.'

'Nana, I've never been more certain of anything in my life.'

'Then you have my blessing.' Releasing her granddaughter, Aurelia Danby had become brisk and business-like. 'Now, we must make a list of what you will need to take with you.'

Looking at Maude, Kerenza bit her lip. 'Mrs Tregenna, about my grandmother–'

'Don't you worry,' Maude patted her hand. 'She knows you're in good hands. And there's always so much going on in the village during the summer. I'll make sure she doesn't have time to fret. Perhaps we'll be able to persuade your father to come across sometimes. Though it may be a little while before he feels up to that. Anyway, in you go. Two ships came in today so we have even more reason to be happy tonight.'

They moved towards the crowded ballroom where the strains of a country dance mingled with the babble of laughter and conversation. Kerenza inhaled the mingled scents of the floral arrangements, a variety of perfumes, and an underlying savoury aroma of the hot and cold dishes being prepared for supper.

She tugged Nick's arm and, as he bent towards her, whispered in his ear. 'I know we had to come for Nana's sake, but I won't be sorry when it's time to leave. I'm not used to crowds any more.'

'We don't have to stay,' Nick said at once, drawing her hand through his arm as they made their way around the edge of the throng, nod-

378

ding, smiling, and thanking people for their good wishes. 'We could slip away now if you like.'

'Nick, we can't.' As he groaned softly, she added, 'Look, you go and speak to your packet colleagues while I talk to people who sent letters of condolence. That way we'll both see everyone we need to in half the time.'

He raised her hand to his lips. 'Beauty *and* good sense, and so much more.' He looked into her eyes. 'My wife.'

As Kerenza moved away she felt as if she was floating, buoyed up by joy. Suffering had left its mark. But if that offered the only route to where she was now, she would take it again.

'Well, well, *Mrs* Penrose. I understand congratulations are in order.'

Kerenza stood perfectly still for an instant. When she turned she had her anger tightly under control and her expression was coolly polite as she acknowledged him with the briefest of nods.

'Lieutenant Ashworth.' She would have turned away but he stepped forward, lowering his voice.

'You could have done much better, you know.'

'With you?' She held his gaze. 'I think not. Why would I wish to pursue acquaintance with someone who styles himself an officer and a gentleman yet is so obviously neither?'

Hot colour flooded his face. 'I don't know what you're talking about.'

'Then you should seek help for your memory.' She turned away.

'How dare you,' he muttered through clenched teeth. 'You have no right.' He flinched as Kerenza swung round.

'No *right?*' She spoke very quietly, her white-hot fury all the more powerful for being controlled and focused. 'Perhaps spreading lies about people, about me, is your idea of amusement, Lieutenant Ashworth. Whatever your reason for such behaviour, you disgrace your uniform and shame your family.'

'*Shame?*' His voice cracked on a spite-filled laugh. 'You have the gall to accuse *me?* When it's common knowledge that *your* family is–'

Kerenza saw his gaze shift over her shoulder. The scarlet flush drained from his face leaving a blotchy pallor. Before she could look round Nick strode past her, a smile on his lips, glittering rage in his eyes, as he gripped his cousin's arm between elbow and shoulder. Corded sinews in Nick's wrist and Jeremy's involuntary gasp betrayed vice-like pressure.

'Jeremy,' he said pleasantly, so those nearby smiled at the sight of the two handsome young men, one dark the other fair. 'I'd like a brief word, if you would be so kind.' He glanced back at Kerenza. 'Just wait there. I won't be long.'

Kerenza watched Nick thrust his helpless cousin towards the double doors and out of sight. True to his word, Nick returned a few moments later. Only this time he was alone. He paused, smiling, as he responded to some remark made by an elderly couple. Then his gaze sought hers, and Kerenza's heart leapt at the love she read there.

'Do you want to wait for supper?' he asked softly.

She shook her head. 'No. I have no wish to see, let alone speak to your cousin again this evening.'

380

'He won't trouble you again. Not tonight, not ever.' He flexed his right hand.

Taking it in hers, Kerenza looked at the split skin around the knuckles and rapidly forming bruise. She searched his face. 'Nick? What did you do to him?'

'Less than he deserved.' He grinned suddenly. 'But he won't want to be seen in public for a few days.'

Kerenza shook her head in a mock scold, knowing her eyes betrayed her laughter and adoration.

He bent his head so his lips brushed her ear. 'Please can we go? I've shared you all day. Now I want you to myself.'

As he drew back she glimpsed a flicker of uncertainty and smiled up at him. 'You've been reading my thoughts.'

The following morning, as the sun rose out of the sea and tinted the pearly sky pale primrose, the packet ship *Kestrel* left Falmouth harbour. Captain Nick Penrose stood with his arm around his wife's shoulders. Able Seaman Collins was at the wheel, Bosun Laity watched the crew hurrying about their duties. Maggot was below helping Broad settle the passengers.

After a brief glance back over the port quarter towards the village, Kerenza smiled up at the man who was hers, body and soul. Together they turned to look forward, towards the open sea, Jamaica, and the future.

The publishers hope that this book has given you enjoyable reading. Large Print Books are especially designed to be as easy to see and hold as possible. If you wish a complete list of our books please ask at your local library or write directly to:

Magna Large Print Books
Magna House, Long Preston,
Skipton, North Yorkshire.
BD23 4ND

This Large Print Book for the partially
sighted, who cannot read normal print, is
published under the auspices of

THE ULVERSCROFT FOUNDATION